Praise for *The Librarian Spy*

"This story blew me away. Readers will be on the edge of their seats as they are transported to 1940s Portugal and France with Madeline Martin's vivid and inspiring characters. *The Librarian Spy* is a brilliant tale of resistance, courage and ultimately hope."

—Kelly Rimmer, *New York Times* bestselling author of *The Warsaw Orphan*

"In Madeline Martin's stirring new novel, readers will be whisked into her brilliantly depicted portrayal of 1940s Lisbon, Portugal, and Lyon, France. Martin captures the essence of the French resistance in war-riddled France as we race with hearts in our throats through Elaine's harrowing tale, juxtaposed with Ava's thrilling and engrossing passages illustrated with sensory delights. Both heroines push the boundaries of their worlds, risking much in their shared missions for survival and hope. Not to be missed, *The Librarian Spy* is an inspiring novel that highlights the women who dared to resist in the face of adversity."

—Eliza Knight, *USA TODAY* bestselling author of *The Mayfair Bookshop*

"Once again, Madeline Martin shows her gift for winning readers' hearts through the struggles of two very different but courageous women operating in lesser known theatres of resistance and intelligence activity in World War II: Lyon, France, and Lisbon, Portugal. *The Librarian Spy* is compelling historical fiction, vividly brought to life through Martin's extensive research and accomplished storytelling. Don't miss it!"

—Christine Wells, author of *Sisters of the Resistance*

Also by Madeline Martin

The Last Bookshop in London

LIBRARIAN
SPY

A Novel of
WORLD WAR II

MADELINE MARTIN

HANOVER
SQUARE
PRESS

HANOVER
SQUARE
PRESS™

ISBN-13: 978-1-335-42748-9

The Librarian Spy

Copyright © 2022 by Madeline Martin

Hanover Square Press
22 Adelaide St. West, 41st Floor
Toronto, Ontario M5H 4E3, Canada
HanoverSqPress.com
BookClubbish.com

Printed in U.S.A.

To John—thank you for getting me through a roller-coaster year with your unending love and support and for experiencing part of my research with me on the trip to Lisbon that will stay with me always.

LIBRARIAN
SPY

ONE

Ava

April 1943
Washington, DC

There was nothing Ava Harper loved more than the smell of old books. The musty scent of aging paper and stale ink took one on a journey through candlelit rooms of manors set amid verdant hills or ancient castles with turrets that stretched up to the vast, unknown heavens. These were tomes once cradled in the spread palms of forefathers, pored over by scholars, devoured by students with a rapacious appetite for learning. In those fragrant, yellowed pages were stories of the past and eternal knowledge.

It was a fortunate thing indeed she was offered a job in the Rare Book Room at the Library of Congress where the archaic aroma of history was forever present.

She strode through the middle of three arches to where the neat rows of tables ran parallel to one another and carefully gathered a stack of rare books in her arms. They were different sizes and weights, their covers worn and pages uneven at the edges, and yet somehow the pile seemed to fit together like the perfect puzzle. Regardless of the patron who left them after having requested far more than was necessary for an afternoon's perusal.

Their eyes were bigger than their brains. It was what her brother, Daniel, had once proclaimed after Ava groused about the common phenomena—one she herself had been guilty of—when he was home on leave.

Ever since, the phrase ran through her thoughts on each encounter of an abandoned collection. Not that it was the fault of the patron. The philosophical greats of old wouldn't be able to glean that much information in an afternoon. But she liked the expression regardless and how it always made her picture Daniel's laughing gaze as he said it.

They'd both inherited their mother's moss green eyes, though Ava's never managed to achieve that same sparkle of mirth so characteristic of her older brother.

A glance at her watch confirmed it was almost noon. A knot tightened in her stomach as she recalled her brief chat with Mr. MacLeish earlier that day. A meeting with the Librarian of Congress was no regular occurrence, especially when it was followed by the scrawl of an address on a slip of paper and the promise of a new opportunity that would suit her.

Whatever it was, she doubted it would fit her better than her position in the Rare Book Room. She absorbed lessons from these ancient texts, which she squeezed out at whim to aid patrons unearth sought-after information. What could possibly appeal to her more?

Ava approached the last table at the right and gently closed *La Maison Reglée*, the worn leather cover smooth as butter beneath her fingertips. The seventeenth century book was one of the many gastronomic texts donated with the Katherine Golden Bitting collection. She had been a marvel of a woman who utilized her knowledge in her roles at the Department of Agriculture and the American Canners Association.

Every book had a story and Ava was their keeper. To leave her place there would be like abandoning children.

Robert floated in on his pretentious cloud and surveyed the room with a critical eye. She clicked off the table light the patron left on lest she be subjected to the sardonic flattening of her coworker's lips.

He held out his hand for *La Maison Reglée*, a look of irritation flickering over his face.

"I'll put it away." Ava hugged it to her chest. After all, he didn't even read French. He couldn't appreciate it as she did.

She returned the tome to its collection, the family reunited once more, and left the opulence of the library. The crisp spring DC air embraced her as she caught the streetcar toward the address printed in the Librarian of Congress's own hand.

Ava arrived at 2430 E Street, NW ten minutes before her appointment, which turned out to be beneficial considering the hoops she had to jump through to enter. A stern man, whose expression did not alter through their exchange, confronted her at a guardhouse upon entry. Apparently, he had no more understanding of the meeting than she.

Once finally allowed in, she followed a path toward a large white-columned building.

Ava snapped the lid on her overactive imagination lest it get the better of her—which it often did—and forced herself onward. After being led through an open entryway and down a hall, she was left to sit in an office possessing no more than a desk and two hardbacked wooden chairs. They made the seats in the Rare Book Room seem comfortable by comparison. Clearly it was a place made only for interviews.

But for what?

Ava glanced at her watch. Whoever she was supposed to meet was ten minutes late. A pang of regret resonated through her at having left her book sitting on her dresser at home.

She had only recently started Daphne du Maurier's *Rebecca* and was immediately drawn in to the thrill of a young woman swept into an unexpected romance. Ava's bookmark rested temptingly upon the newly married couple's entrance to Manderley, the estate in Cornwall.

The door to the office flew open and a man whisked in wearing a gray, efficient Victory suit—single breasted with narrow lapels and absent any cuffs or pocket flaps—fashioned with as little fabric as was possible. He settled behind the desk. "I'm Charles Edmunds, secretary to General William Donovan. You're Ava Harper?"

The only name familiar of the three was her own. "I am."

He opened a file, sifted through a few papers, and handed her a stack. "Sign these."

"What are they?" She skimmed over the pages and was met with legal jargon.

"Confidentiality agreements."

"I won't sign anything I haven't read fully." She lifted the pile.

The text was drier than the content of some of the more lackluster rare books at the Library of Congress. Regardless, she scoured every word while Mr. Edmunds glared irritably at her, as if he could will her to sign with his eyes. He couldn't, of course. She waited ten minutes for his arrival; he could wait while she saw what she was getting herself into.

Everything indicated she would not share what was discussed in the room about her potential job opportunity. It was nothing all too damning and so she signed, much to the great, exhaling impatience of Mr. Edmunds.

"You speak German and French." He peered at her over a pair of black-rimmed glasses, his brown eyes probing.

"My father was something of a linguist. I couldn't help but pick them up." A visceral ache stabbed at her chest as a memory surfaced from years ago—her father switching to German in his excitement for an upcoming trip with her mother for their twenty-year anniversary. *That* trip. The one from which her parents had never returned.

"And you've worked with photographing microfilm." Mr. Edmunds lifted his brows.

A frown of uncertainty tugged at her lips. When she first started at the Library of Congress, her duties had been more in the area of archival than a typical librarian role as she microfilmed a series of old newspapers that time was slowly eroding. "I have, yes."

"Your government needs you," he stated in a matter-of-fact manner that brooked no argument. "You are invited to join the Office of Strategic Services—the OSS—under the information gathering program called the Interdepartmental Committee for the Acquisition of Foreign Publications."

Her mind spun around to make sense of what he'd just said, but her lips flew open to offer her knee-jerk opinion. "That's quite the mouthful."

"IDC for short," he replied without hesitation or humor. "It's a covert operation obtaining information from newspapers and texts in neutral territories to help us gather intel on the Nazis."

"Would I require training?" she asked, unsure how knowing German equipped her to spy on them.

"You have all the training you need as I understand it." He began to reassemble the file in front of him. "You would go to Lisbon."

"In Portugal?"

He paused. "It is the only Lisbon of which I am aware, yes."

No doubt she would have to get there by plane. A shiver threatened to squeeze down her spine, but she repressed it. "Why am I being recommended for this?"

"Your ability to speak French and German." Mr. Edmunds held up his forefinger. "You know how to use microfilm." He ticked off another finger. "Fred Kilgour recommends your keen intellect." There went another finger.

That was a name she recognized.

She aided Fred the prior year when he was microfilming foreign publications for the Harvard University Library. After the months she'd spent doing as much for the Library of Congress, the process had been easy to share, and he had been a quick learner.

"And you're pretty." Mr. Edmunds sat back in his chair, the final point made.

The compliment was as unwarranted in such a setting as it was unwelcome. "What does my appearance have to do with any of this?"

He lifted a shoulder. "Beauties like yourself can get what they want when they want it. Except when you scowl like that." He nodded his chin up. "You should smile more, Dollface."

That was about enough.

"I did not graduate top of my class from Pratt and obtain a much sought-after position at the Library of Congress to be called 'Dollface.'" She pushed up to standing.

"And you've got steel in that spine, Miss Harper." Mr. Edmunds ticked the last finger.

She opened her mouth to retort, but he continued. "We need this information so we best know how to fight the Krauts. The sooner we have these details, the sooner this war can be over."

She remained where she stood to listen a little longer. No doubt he knew she would.

"You have a brother," he went on. "Daniel Harper, staff sergeant of C Company in Second Battalion, 506th Parachute Infantry Regiment, in the 101st Airborne Division."

The Airborne Division. Her brother had run toward the fear of airplanes despite her swearing off them.

"That's correct," she said tightly. Daniel would never have been in the Army were it not for her. He would be an engineer, the way he'd always wanted.

Mr. Edmunds took off his glasses and met her gaze with his small, naked eyes. "Don't you want him to come home sooner?"

It was a dirty question meant to slice deep.

And it worked.

The longer the war continued, the greater Daniel's risk of being killed or wounded.

She'd done everything she could to offer aid. When the ration was only voluntary, she had complied long before it became law. She gave blood every few months, as soon as she was cleared to do so again. Rather than dance and drink at the Elk Club like her roommates, Ava spent all her spare time in the Production Corps with the Red Cross, repairing uniforms, rolling bandages, and doing whatever was asked of her to help their men abroad.

She even wore red lipstick on a regular basis, springing for the costly tube of Elizabeth Arden's *Victory Red*, the civilian counterpart to the *Montezuma Red* servicewomen were issued. Ruby lips were a derisive biting of the thumb at Hitler's war on made-up women. And she would do anything to bite her thumb at that tyrant.

Likely Mr. Edmunds was aware of all this.

"You will be doing genuine work in Lisbon that can help bring your brother and all our boys home." Mr. Edmunds got to his feet and held out his hand, a salesman with a silver tongue, ready to seal the deal. "Are you in?"

Ava looked at his hand. His fingers were stubby and thick, his nails short and well-manicured.

"I would have to go on an airplane, I'm assuming."

"You wouldn't have to jump out." He winked.

Her greatest fear realized.

But Daniel had done far more for her.

It was a single plane ride to get to Lisbon. One measly take-off and landing with a lot of airtime in between. The bottoms of her feet tingled, and a nauseous swirl dipped in her belly.

This was by far the least she could do to help him as well as every other US service member. Not just the men, but also the women whose roles were often equally as dangerous.

She lifted her chin, leveling her own stare right back. "Don't ever call me 'Dollface' again."

"You got it, Miss Harper," he replied.

She extended her hand toward him and clasped his with a firm grip, the way her father had taught her. "I'm in."

He grinned. "Welcome aboard."

A week later, a black Buick came to collect Ava at 8:00 a.m. sharp from the apartment she shared with two others in Naylor Gardens. The women had thrown something of a goodbye party for her despite how little they knew one another, using the last of their sugar rations to bake her a cake with sunshine yellow rosettes clustered at the center. It was a kind gesture.

She was grateful to know they wouldn't be entirely out of sorts by her abrupt departure. In a city where housing was scarce, they already had someone lined up to take her room the next day—another government girl in the quintessential white rayon shirt with a pressed convertible collar.

Leaving the Library of Congress had been far less easy. Ava had cared for those books like they were an extension of herself, coddling and tending to them, ensuring they were loved and cherished. She'd grown accustomed to the beauty of the library, to the feast of learning at her fingertips daily. In the three short years she had been there, she had become a fount of information, ready to help anyone find anything.

She'd always been proud of how necessary she felt.

Now, she would be venturing into unknown territory, her knowledge limited to a weeklong stint of frenzied research. At least with what she had managed to obtain about Lisbon, she discovered the importance of packing several hats, which she would have easily left behind otherwise. Being seen in public in Portugal without one would label her as a prostitute.

While she was at it, she used the last of her number 17 ration stamps for a new pair of pumps. With only four color options, she chose black over brown, town brown or army russet. She wore those shoes now with a simple green A-line wraparound skirt and a white-and-green rayon blouse.

With the busywork over, all that remained was the arduous

drive to the airport. A hive of bees seemed to buzz around in Ava's empty stomach. She'd been far too nervous to bother eating anything that morning.

"Would you like to see the Mall before you go?" The driver met her gaze in the mirror. "The cherry blossoms just bloomed, and we have time."

The beauty of those trees became diminished to the nation after the horrific attack on Pearl Harbor. Four had been cut down by vandals, and many demanded that Japan's gesture of goodwill nearly thirty years prior should all be destroyed.

In the excitement of preparing to depart for her new role, Ava had not realized the cherry trees had blossomed. Ordinarily, it was her favorite time in DC even though the accompanying festival had ground to a halt in light of conservation efforts for the war.

"I would," she replied, grateful for his consideration, and a few minutes more reprieve from her dreaded flight. "Thank you."

The driver turned left and snaked along at the 35 miles per hour enforced speed limit; Victory Speed to conserve gas. At last, the Mall came into view. It didn't inspire awe as it once did, its pristine appearance marred by rows of temporary housing units and offices for government girls with antiaircraft guns sprinkled around the monuments.

But the cherry trees were laden with pink petals so heavy that they sifted away to float in the air and dance across the water of the Tidal Basin like thick, soft snowflakes. How Ava loved to stroll down the path beneath those trees, letting the flowers whisper across her cheeks as they tumbled gracefully downward on an unseen breeze.

It was precisely the distraction she had needed to pull her thoughts from the upcoming plane ride and the trepidation of facing a place she knew so little of. Truly, she wasn't sure which was worse.

At least, not until she joined the line on the runway to board and her nerves vibrated to an insistent hum.

Flying on the plane was far, far worse.

TWO

Hélène

Words had power.

Hélène Bélanger's gaze lingered on the paper plastered to the wall, clean and white against the old stonework, its message in stark, black letters.

À bas les Boches.

Down with the Germans.

The recently applied poster hadn't yet been pulled down by the Nazi forces who had occupied the Free Zone of France six months prior. She shouldn't even be looking at the note, but could not tear her gaze away. Not when it made her heart pound harder with the need to do something.

The tract would likely be torn off soon and a new one would be put up in its place; a show of defiance against their oppressors.

The Resistance—brave men and women who rose against the German occupiers—made their presence known throughout Lyon, bold and without fear.

A finger of icy air slid down the collar of Hélène's coat and a shiver rattled through her. The chill of the overcast April evening would have scarcely been felt in years before, but the limited food within the city whittled away at her body, leaving sharp bones protruding from what had once been supple curves. The Nazis did not suffer such deprivation. On the contrary, they dined lavishly on food stolen from the mouths of hungry families and consumed endless amounts of wine looted from French cellars. All for their rapacious pleasure.

She turned away from the wall and strode briskly down Rue Sala, the wooden soles of her shoes clacking against the cobblestones. The mostly empty streets and the heavy gray clouds overhead did not help the sense of dread knotting her stomach.

Her shopping basket held only a few knobby Jerusalem artichokes rolling about the braided wicker bottom. The yellow-flowered plants were once vegetation used for livestock, yet now the tubers of those weeds kept the people of France alive, replacing fats and meats that were almost impossible to find anymore.

She'd hoped to acquire some bread but arrived too late. All the stale goods had been sold with only the fresh loaves available on the back wall that could not be purchased until the following day. How she longed for the times when she could buy a loaf still hot from the oven. But that was before the ration laws demanded bakers sell bread no less than twenty-four hours old. Not only did the hardened loaf cut into precise slices for easier ration measurement, but it also kept the French from devouring their food too swiftly. Or so the officials said.

Not that any of that mattered. For the first time in years, Hélène's empty stomach did not cramp with hunger. This time, her insides twisted and clenched with anxiety for who awaited her at the small apartment on Rue du Plat.

Or rather who did *not* await her.

Joseph.

Two days and one night had passed since their argument, the

worst one yet. Words had power, and she'd turned the full brunt of them against her husband in her anger.

He was a man who fought and sacrificed in the Great War, who turned to pacifism after what he'd seen amid the Battle of Verdun, whose brilliant mind for chemistry caught her attention when she'd been a girl fresh out of secretary school.

Now she kept her gaze averted from a smear of pale, chalky blue against the wall near their apartment. It had once been a *V—victoire*, an additional mark of French opposition to the Nazis and a promise that eventually the Resistance would have their victory. That *V* hastily marked across the ragged stone had been put there by her own hand and had been the catalyst for the fight. Her fingers still recalled the dry grip of the brittle blue chalk she often kept in her purse.

The act was trite, but all she could allow herself when Joseph guarded her every move.

He had caught her midway through, his usually serene expression darkened with ire. The disagreement began as soon as they returned to their apartment, and it was then she had used the harshest of words upon her own husband.

The argument erupted in a blinding flare of their combined frustrations. He had scolded her for not being a proper Vichy wife—the type of Frenchwoman who was a mother and a housewife, obeying the orders of her husband—the type of woman she had never been. The type of woman he had never expected her to be. What's more, Vichy was the regime that worked with the Nazis who she longed to oppose. The vile suggestion had been more than she could bear. In her rage, she called his refusal to join the Resistance cowardice.

He had not been home since.

Except Joseph was not a petty man. Of the two of them, she was the one who leaned heavily on her temper, who was too impulsive. Whatever kept him from returning home was not simply malcontent.

Each attempt to see Etienne, his closest friend, had been in vain as her visits to his flat went unanswered. She considered going to the police, but knew they worked closely with the Gestapo, men who were cold and cruel and likely to be of little help.

If Joseph was not back by dawn the following day, however, desperation would draw her to the police, no matter the risk.

The massive wooden doors of her apartment building came into view, and she pushed inside to the courtyard. All was quiet within.

A quick stop by their letterbox revealed it to be empty and devoid of any clues as to Joseph's whereabouts. The sense of unease in her gut tightened further still as she tried to suppress the hope that he would be home.

She trudged up the stairs to the fourth floor and to the narrow apartment that Joseph's parents left him when his mother passed away several years before the war. Though Hélène and Joseph were in Paris at the time, he kept his childhood home with the intent to use it for holidays. They did so several times. One summer in particular, they explored the winding streets during the day and stayed out late in the evening, drinking wine along the Rhône as the warm July air cooled. Lucky for them, the apartment was a place of refuge when the Germans marched into Paris. With so many fleeing to Lyon in those days, such accommodations would have been impossible to find otherwise.

Joseph hadn't wanted to flee the City of Light when they were all warned to go, loathe to abandon his students and his work. But he had left everything in Paris for her, to keep her safe. That had been three years ago, back when their marriage had been happy.

She unlocked the door and pushed inside to reveal a dark, empty entryway.

"Joseph?"

Though she expected no answer, a sense of despair washed over her when none came. He really was gone.

But where? And when would he finally return?

★ ★ ★

The sky darkened as the imposed curfew neared. Each second dragged into a minute in her interminable wait for Joseph to come home. Hélène was preparing to retire early, yielding to the exhaustion of a heavy heart and an empty belly when a soft knock sounded at the front door.

Surely Joseph wouldn't knock. Unless, of course, he didn't have his key.

She ran to the entryway with such haste, the floorboards barely creaked underfoot. But it was not her husband who stood on the other side of the door. A woman with blond hair similar to her own regarded Hélène warily with wide dark eyes.

The blood in Hélène's veins turned to ice at the appearance of a stranger. She nearly slammed the door when the woman put her hand to the glossy wooden surface to keep it from closing.

"Pierre." She whispered so quietly, Hélène could hardly make out the name.

"Is he here?" the woman continued in her almost silent tone. "Please, I must see him." The glance she cast behind held an edge of paranoia.

Exactly the kind of thing a neighbor like Madame Arnaud was liable to notice.

Hélène waved the woman in to prevent her from speaking further. While Hélène knew no one named Pierre, the woman was obviously in danger.

Which meant Hélène was now also in danger.

But somehow, she could not turn away the woman. Not when Joseph had so mysteriously gone missing. Not when a niggling at the back of Hélène's brain suggested this might all be related.

The stranger hesitated a moment before stepping over the threshold. Her brown coat was dappled with raindrops from the evening drizzle, and the hem of a dark maroon dress fell past her knees. While her garments appeared to be clean and in good condition, her black shoes were scuffed beyond repair.

Only when the door clicked closed did the stranger speak again. "Please, I must see Pierre. I know I should not have come here, but I did not have any other choice."

Hélène shook her head. "I know no Pierre, but perhaps I can help. What's happened?"

The woman's eyes went wider still at Hélène's admission, and she backed up toward the door.

"Is it the police?" Hélène pressed in a low voice. "The Gestapo?"

Her own heart pounded at the risk she was taking. This woman could be a collaborator like Madame Arnaud across the hall, who monitored everyone like a beady-eyed predator and always commented about Hélène having no children. But then, few possessed the fecundity of Madame Arnaud with her eight sons. A proper Vichy wife to be sure.

If the stranger was indeed a collaborator, Hélène would surely be turned in for having asked about danger from the Gestapo.

The woman's desperate gaze scanned the apartment behind Hélène, like she was seeking something urgent. "I need papers."

Hélène frowned. "I don't have any papers here."

"An identity card, a new one. I was told Pierre…" Tears swam in the woman's eyes and her face crumpled. "I escaped the roundup several months ago on Rue Sainte-Catherine and have been in hiding since, but every place I go is found out. I need new papers. Ones that don't have this."

Hands shaking, she presented her identity card, declaring her to be Claudine Goldstein with a red stamp at the top. *JUIF.* Jew.

Hélène knew immediately of the roundup to which Claudine referred. Every Tuesday, beleaguered Jews lined up for food and medical attention, the oppression of their people reducing them to practically beg for their survival. It was on that day when the Union Générale des Israélites de France was allowed to offer them kindness and compassion that the Gestapo chose to attack, arresting everyone within the organization as well as those who had shown up for aid. Her heart burned with the injustice then, and the fire renewed itself now with a white-hot intensity.

Questions fired through Hélène's mind, all ones she knew the woman would not answer: Where had she been hiding? Where was she going now?

"Forgive me, but I do not know a Pierre," Hélène replied through the heavy, painful sensation pulling at her chest.

Despondency fell over Claudine's face, smoothing her features with a resigned apathy. "I cannot run any longer. If I do not have papers, I will be sent away like all the others." She blinked, and a tear trailed silently down her cheek.

She wasn't incorrect, and the fire burning within Hélène roared to life.

"Take mine." Hélène grabbed her handbag and withdrew her neatly folded papers from its depths. Not only did she include her identity card, but also her food and clothing rations. After all, they were tied to her name. Without her identity card, everything else was useless to Hélène. And perhaps that bit of sustenance and new garments might in some way help Claudine in her escape.

The woman's mouth fell open. "Yours? But how—"

"We look similar, and we are the same height," Hélène said, pushing the folded bunch into Claudine's hand.

Still the woman refused to curl her fingers around the precious papers. "What will you do?"

Hélène ignored the question, not wishing to think of the consequences. "I am not at risk as you are."

And Claudine was very much at risk. Far too many Jews had been packed into trains and never seen again—families, innocent children, it was more than Hélène could bear and why she fought her husband so vigorously for the chance to join the Resistance. Now she was in a position where she could actually help, and she would not turn away from the opportunity.

"Please." Hélène held the papers against Claudine's palm until the woman's fingers reluctantly closed around them.

"The curfew will begin soon," Hélène said. "Stay here until morning."

But Claudine shook her head. "I cannot put you at further risk, not after…" Her voice caught, and she lifted the identity card and ration coupons. "This."

Hélène wanted to argue, but Claudine was already moving toward the door, whispering her thanks in a profuse rush of gratitude.

But Hélène could not accept her thanks. It was the least any French citizen could do for the Jews who the Nazis so openly and maliciously persecuted. The memory of Lucie rose in her thoughts.

The only woman Hélène had befriended in Lyon, when they waited in a bread line one rainy afternoon. Lucie had an umbrella and offered to share. While the weather had been gray and cold, Lucie's sunny disposition more than made up for it. Like Hélène, Lucie did not have children either. Rather than allow others' opinions of her to annoy her as they did Hélène, Lucie waived their censure off with cheerful indifference.

She always saw the light in the world, no matter how dark it became.

It was her brilliance that helped Hélène through so many of those hard days when hunger began to set in, when curfew restrictions edged into their daily comfort and when one couldn't leave their house without a large wallet full of ration coupons and an identity card.

That was, until Lucie and her husband disappeared in the night, their apartment ransacked and cleared of its valuables. Hélène had been helpless to do anything to aid her friend despite the countless attempts to find her whereabouts. It was around the same time Joseph refused to allow her to engage in any Resistant activity, which rendered her impotent. The outrage had remained with her, simmering.

At least now, Hélène had done something.

She closed the door behind Claudine, and once more Hélène was swallowed up by the apartment's empty silence.

The repercussions of her decision woke her in the early hours of dawn while the rest of Lyon was still asleep. The curfew had come and gone and still Joseph had not returned.

Only now, she could not go to the police to inquire as to his whereabouts. No one would speak to her without first seeing her identity card, and if she reported the papers as lost, they would be on the lookout for a thief. If Claudine was caught with what would then be assumed stolen papers...

No, going to the police was no longer an option.

A glance in the kitchen confirmed only a heel of bread remained, along with the few Jerusalem artichokes Hélène had managed to find the day before. Such limited stores would not be sufficient to get by.

Her stomach, deprived of even a meager supper the night before, gave a low growl of hunger. The food would not last the day, let alone long enough for her to come up with a viable solution.

She would have to go to Etienne once more and see if this time he might be home, for there was no one else she knew well enough to trust for help. Their current world was a lonely one, where people had to be careful what they said, what they did, and with whom they were acquainted. Theirs was a world of enemies, where the occupiers wielded submachine guns and fear while the French had only their empty shopping baskets and the power of forbidden words.

Realizing it would be better to wait until the streets were cluttered with people to avoid arousing suspicion, Hélène boiled the Jerusalem artichokes and ate them with the small heel of

bread. Once the sun began to rise, she drew her shopping basket from the shelf along with her handbag, as she would any
ordinary day, and left the apartment. She was seldom stopped
for her papers and likely would not be troubled that day either.
She needed only to act normal.

However, acting normal with one's heart pounding was a
very difficult feat. Initially she walked too fast, the clack of her
shoes obvious even to her own ears. She slowed her pace and
kept her gaze forward, intent on her purpose in the hopes that
she would not be stopped.

She was close to Etienne's apartment in Croix-Rousse where
the streets pitched upward on an incline so steep, that she had to
slow down to keep her breath from coming out in great huffs.
A fresh smattering of papers lined one wall declaring *Viva de
Gaulle!* Long live de Gaulle, the man who encouraged them all
to resist the oppression of the Germans.

A Nazi officer rounded the corner, several feet from Hélène.
The rising morning sun reflected off his highly polished black
boots and winked at a medal pinned to his chest. His gaze sharpened as he caught sight of the tracts.

With a click of each booted heel on the cobblestones, he strode
to the wall and yanked down one of the papers. The illegal note
tore off in uneven strips, so only the top came free, and the message clung stubbornly, fully intact. He pulled again, this time
succeeding in tearing the words so only a partial "le" remained.

He spun around, his jaw locked. "You. Stop." A white-haired
man at his right did as he was bade.

"Papers," the officer ordered.

The man fished in his jacket pocket, his movements hindered
by the arthritic curl of his fingers as he attempted to withdraw
his identity card.

Hélène could be next. If she were caught without her papers,
she would have to admit they were lost. She turned the next cor-

ner to avoid the irate officer lest she be looked to next. Her heart thudded in her chest with such rapidity that she found breathing suddenly difficult. But she forced herself to keep walking, her steps measured to match those around her.

"Halt." The voice rang out from behind her.

She continued at her smooth stride.

"Madam," the guard said in a harsh voice. "Halt."

The area was unfortunately absent of women, leaving her his only victim. Three men on the other side of the street looked at her from where they stood, mute with the relief not to be the Nazi's target. In another time, they would have been at her aid, armed with French gallantry and good intentions.

Hélène turned to face the officer. He thrust his hand out, palm up. "Papers."

She tried to swallow but found her throat too dry. Her handbag felt unnaturally light where it hung on her shoulder, the tangible weight of the papers she'd given away poignantly absent.

"Of course." She kept her reply casual as she rummaged through her purse. Sweat prickled at her palms despite the damp, cold day.

The officer flexed his hand. "Now."

"*Pardon.*" She continued to rifle through nonexistent items at the bottom of her empty handbag. "I cannot seem to find them."

Many of the Germans who paraded through Lyon did not speak much French. She hoped this was the case now. An inability to communicate might be her saving grace.

The gray of the officer's eyes was like cold metal. "You do not have them?" he asked in perfect French.

Her stomach dropped. "I thought I did." She lifted her shoulders in a delicate shrug and tried a pretty smile.

His expression did not soften. "You do not have your papers?"

Rather than acknowledge she did not, she turned her attention to her handbag once more and began to rummage. His hand shot out and caught her arm in a steely grip that pinched her skin.

She cried out in surprise. Her gaze flicked to the three men on the other side of the street in time to see them scuttle away, leaving no witnesses.

Cowards.

"If you do not have your papers, you are under arrest," the German said in his immaculate French.

"Elaine," a voice called out.

Hélène and the officer both looked to the breathless man jogging toward them, holding an identity card aloft.

Etienne.

"Elaine," he chided. "You have left this at home yet again." To the Nazi, he gave an easy, apologetic smile. "Women are more concerned about how they look when they leave the house than they are about having all their necessary papers."

The Nazi officer gave him an irritated glower and held out his free hand for the papers Etienne extended toward him.

Hélène inwardly cringed, waiting to see what the officer would do to her when he realized it was not her identity card he had been given. The Nazi flicked the cover open one-handed, revealing an identity card for a woman named Elaine Rousseau whose picture was indeed Hélène.

She fought to keep her face impassive.

How did Etienne have such a thing in his possession?

All at once, the officer released her, folded the identity card closed with an audible snap and thrust it back toward Etienne. "Look after your errant wife better. She was almost arrested for her folly."

"*Oui, monsieur.*" Etienne accepted the papers with a nod and put his arm around Hélène. She slowly released the breath she had been holding, grateful for Etienne's strength. His hold steadied her as her knees seemed to wobble with how close she had come to being caught, to them realizing her papers were gone. To them looking for Claudine.

The officer turned on his heel and marched back around the

corner the way he had come, shouting orders at someone to tear the remainder of the Resistance tracts from the wall.

Etienne spat on the ground where the Nazi had stood and turned to Hélène. "Did he hurt you?"

The place on her arm still burned from where the man had mercilessly restrained her, but she had not been arrested. Claudine would not be found out. That was all that mattered. Hélène shook her head. "I'm fine."

"Where are your papers?" Etienne asked.

"Where did you get that?" She indicated the small book between his fingers.

"We cannot talk here." He led her up to his fifth-floor apartment, one smaller than her own.

It was not customary for a bachelor to entertain and so she had not been inside his home before. She stood awkwardly now in the middle of the common living space as she took in the sparsely furnished room. The open area housed not only a tired green couch that sagged at its center, but also a circular kitchen table beside a narrow oven. Another door was visible to the right, which was most likely his bedchamber. No curtains hung from the windows, and no art lined the stained walls. The shutters were mostly closed, casting the room in shadows.

There was a lingering odor of cigarettes and chicory coffee hanging in the stagnant air.

He folded one of the shutters back, their subtle clacks as loud as gunshots as he let in a stream of light to cut through the darkness. "Here, sit."

In a single motion, he swept his arm over the table, clearing away crumbs and an open newspaper that crumpled to the ground. She resisted the urge to retrieve the fallen print and properly fold it to set aside. Instead, she lowered herself to the hard wooden chair, grateful for its sturdiness as she recovered from the fear of what could have happened had Etienne not arrived when he did.

She would have been caught. Claudine as well. And Joseph…?

"Do you know where my husband is?" she asked, pressing her hands together to still their shaking.

Etienne went to the stovetop and poured out two cups of steaming light brown liquid made of roasted barley and chicory. While the brew didn't possess the fortifying effects of a strong cup of coffee, it would be welcome against her dry throat. He handed her a mug, which she wrapped her icy fingers around.

"Where are your papers?" He held out a box of saccharine tablets, the inadequate replacement for sugar these days.

She declined.

Shrugging, he dropped one into his cup with a plunk that sounded overloud in the quiet stretching between them. With a nonchalant air, he sat back in his chair, his brows lifted in expectation of an answer.

She blew at a tendril of steam curling up from her coffee and took a careful sip, uncertain how to respond.

Etienne and Joseph were as close as brothers with Etienne two years younger, having lied about his age in order to be accepted into the military during the Great War. And yet she still could not help but wonder if he could indeed be trusted.

Reaching into his jacket pocket, he withdrew the identity card and opened it on the table, revealing her picture and the name Elaine Rousseau. "We both have secrets." His blunt pointer finger rested on the document and slid it toward her.

"I gave my identity card away." She straightened and looked him in the eye. "To a woman who needed it more than I."

"Claudine," he surmised and then pursed his lips, as if wishing he could take back having said her name.

Hélène took a sip of her chicory coffee to cover her surprise. "Is she a friend of yours?"

"She is a woman in need. That is all you should know." He withdrew a rolled cigarette from a case and lit it. The odor of burning grass filled the space between them, the acrid smoke stinging her eyes and nose.

Its pungency was one she ought to be used to, as the Frenchmen resorted to smoking anything they could dry and wrap in a bit of paper when tobacco was so scarce.

"Who is Pierre?"

Etienne's face remained blank, but Hélène wasn't fooled. "Who is he?" She set her cup down but did not unwrap her hands from its welcome heat. "I want to know what is happening. I want to know who Pierre is and what he has to do with my husband's disappearance. I want to know where Joseph is." Her voice shook as she failed to quell the rise of her emotions.

Her husband's closest friend looked down at the table, mute as his right foot began to bounce with anxious energy, his foul cigarette burning to brittle ash between his fingers.

"You cannot go back to being Hélène," he said finally.

"I know that," she said in a measured tone that did little to conceal her irritation. "Where did you get this?" She picked up the false identity papers. "From Pierre?" The precious pages trembled in her grasp.

Etienne's dark brows furrowed. "You will have to leave your home if your name does not match its location," he prevaricated.

His leg continued to jog, and his mug on the table rattled with the disturbance.

She released the papers and her drink as she clapped her hand over the cup in front of him, so it went silent. "What is happening? Where is my husband?" Her gaze bore into his bloodshot eyes, and she noticed a bruise under the shadow of his unshaved jaw. There was a slight cut over one eyebrow as well. "Etienne."

His leg stopped jostling. "Joseph has been arrested." Etienne swallowed. "For political reasons."

"Political reasons?" Her world spun around her. Joseph had been arrested. And she no longer even had her identity card to go to the police and do what she could to demand his release.

"Is he…" She could hardly form the words. They felt too hypocritical after all the months of arguing. After everything he demanded of her and everything he forbade her from doing.

After she had called him a coward for turning his back on his country.

"Is he with the Resistance?" she asked. "Is he Pierre?"

Etienne took a drag off his cigarette. The tip glowed red and as he breathed out a gust of acrid smoke, his nod was almost imperceptible.

In that moment, Hélène's world flipped on its axis. All the times Joseph had claimed the Resistance did nothing, all the ways he had restricted her. And *he* had been working with them the entire time. The warning prickle of impending tears burned in her eyes, but she clenched her hands until the sensation passed.

Dealing with her emotions would come later. Now was for questions.

Her gaze fell on the identity card as she considered the picture. The dress was dark, its color obscured by the black-and-white print. But she recognized the scalloped edges of the V-shaped neckline so popular then. The garment was a deep, luxurious green and still hung in her wardrobe back home. When she'd worn it last, Joseph had told her she looked beautiful and had insisted on taking her picture.

It was silly to stand there in her apartment for a photograph with only the blank wall behind her, which was why her lips were lightly lifted at the corners in an unsure smile. Now she understood. Joseph hadn't taken the photo for a memory; he'd done it to make a false identity card. She only needed Etienne to confirm her suspicions.

Picking up the identity card, she held it toward him. "Did Joseph make this?"

"In case something happened." Etienne sighed in capitulation. "To protect you. I couldn't bring it to you until the Bosche released me."

Her gaze shot back to Etienne's bruised jaw. To the cut on his brow. He had been beaten. They would do the same to Joseph.

Pain tightened in her chest for her husband whose years as a battle-ready soldier ended long before they had met.

He had been injured by shrapnel in Verdun. He'd talked about it with her only once before, how the bomb had killed most of the men around him with the exception of himself and Etienne. Joseph had been struck in the leg. Evidence of the trauma was still visible where the skin gnarled beside his knee and curled around the back of his calf, leaving him with a slight limp.

Etienne had walked away from that battle unscathed, but then he had always been lucky. Even now, he sat before her while Joseph remained imprisoned.

"Why did they release you, but not him?" she demanded.

A fatigued look deepened the creases of his brow, and his stare drifted despondently into the void. "I am lucky." His tone was flat as he stubbed out his cigarette.

"When will he be released?"

Etienne shook his head as his attention refocused on her. "We do not imagine he will be held much longer."

"We," she repeated. "The Resistance."

He nodded.

There was a confidence to his words that eased some of the tension from her shoulders. There were people looking out for Joseph. And perhaps she could help.

"I want to join the Resistance," she said.

"No."

She stared hard at Etienne, refusing to back down, tired of always being told no by Joseph. All these months of being so eager to throw herself into the effort against their occupiers and all these months he had proclaimed the Resistance to be useless. Instead, he had insisted she remain home, to wait in interminable queues and perform feats of impossibility in the kitchen with their mean food rations.

The inability to do her part against the Nazis now felt like a betrayal. Like she was not good enough to join the men and women in their brave fight.

She would not be told no now, not when her efforts might aid Joseph to freedom sooner.

"I cannot go back to my own name," she said. "You have also mentioned I cannot remain in my home."

Etienne's dark eyes narrowed.

"I want to be part of the Resistance," she said again. "I want to help Joseph."

A muscle worked in his jaw. "Joseph doesn't want you involved."

"I'm well aware," she said through gritted teeth.

"It is dangerous work." Etienne rose from the small table, bumping it in his haste. Without looking at her, he turned to the sink to rinse his cup.

"I don't care," Hélène countered. "I'll do anything to end this occupation, to free our soldiers and my own husband. To stop the degradation of our country and the disgusting treatment against the Jews."

An unexpected smile lifted the corners of his mouth. "Joseph said you'd say that." Still, he tilted his head. "He will never forgive me."

"I don't care about that either."

At that, Etienne gave a mischievous laugh. "My friend was right in all his fears about you, madame. How fortunate for you that I've always been one who seeks forgiveness rather than permission."

She gaped at him. "Do you mean…?"

Etienne extended a hand to her and folded his long, warm fingers against hers. "Elaine Rousseau, welcome to the Resistance."

THREE

Ava

There were many ways in which one could read. Either tucked into the corner of the sofa with a strong cup of coffee or lying in bed with the book hovering above one's face—though admittedly this is not done without peril. But there were also unconventional methods, like while cooking dinner or crossing the street—sometimes even while brushing one's teeth if the story was truly that engrossing.

Apparently, sequestered in the window seat aboard a metal tube barreling far too fast tens of thousands of miles above the earth was yet another way. Thank the stars for Daphne du Maurier and her gripping tale that helped Ava forget about being on an airplane.

At least for the most part.

When the plane was gliding through the sky like a bird in flight on a clear day, it was easy to lose herself in the book spread between her fingers. However, at the slightest jolt and rattle of turbulence, fear caught her in a powerful and vicious hold, reminding her how precariously her life was held aloft by only a few inches of metal. In those terrifying moments, she couldn't help but imagine her mother and father as their plane spiraled to the earth on that fateful trip home from France. What they might have experienced, what they might have thought in those last, harrowing seconds of their lives.

Much to the disappointment of the man beside her, Ava kept the window shade snapped tightly shut. If the worst happened and the ground began rushing toward them, she did not want to bear witness to that awful event.

When they finally landed and she uncurled her death grip from the arms of her seat, it was all she could do to keep from kneeling and kissing the earth in gratitude. Knowing her new boss awaited her was a strong incentive to remain upright despite the quiver in her bones after enduring so many spikes of adrenaline throughout the journey. Instead, she ensured the felt pompadour hat with its spray of small white flowers was properly pinned over her rolled-back hair.

The air was warmer than that in Washington, DC, and the odor of jet fuel blotted out any scents of the city she might otherwise pick up. She made her way toward a cluster of people along with the other passengers of her flight.

A man with more salt than pepper in his hair held a sign with "A. Harper" written across it in a hasty, no-nonsense script. His heavy-lidded eyes were bloodshot and spoke of too many hours at work, as did the rumpled jacket of his dove-gray, three-piece suit.

"*Bom dia.*" She set her heavy suitcases down and smiled as she presented him with her first attempt at Portuguese in Lisbon.

He stared at her as if she'd grown a second head. Surely she hadn't misspoken. How hard was it to mess up bidding someone good day?

After a moment, he scoffed and shook his head. "I wasn't allowed to bring my secretary. Why is Harper allowed to bring you?"

She lifted her brows, sure she had heard him incorrectly. But no, he was still staring at her, indignant.

"I am Harper." Jabbing a finger toward his sign, she said, "*Ava* Harper."

He blinked.

She should have suppressed her sigh of irritation, but she was too tired and her nerves too frayed. The exhale blew from her mouth without restraint. "You are Mr. Sims, I presume?"

"I am." He collected himself as she'd hoped he would, keeping their introductory meeting from growing too awkward. "I was expecting a man."

Perhaps that explained why he hadn't bothered to take her luggage. Not that she would let this fluster her as she bent to lift her suitcases in either hand. It was not the first time she was relocating to a new place with her life in only two suitcases. But she wasn't a little girl anymore. She had control over what she did and who she was.

Recalling his manners, Mr. Sims reached for her bags. "Let me take that for you." He grunted at the weight as she let him pull the handles from her grip, his face flushing with the effort. "What do you have in here? Bricks?"

"Books," she answered truthfully. "Only a few." There could have been far more, but most had been packed into several boxes and generously stored in the Library of Congress to await her return.

He huffed his disapproval the entire way to a glossy black Renault where he readily deposited the suitcases in the back seat and opened the door for her.

That first drive through Lisbon would be one she would always remember as they unceremoniously sped by statues and the artistically cobbled limestone sidewalks. Too swift to discern any of the lovely detail. There were sharp turns and extreme inclines throughout their journey that took them up and down many of the famed "seven hills" of Lisbon.

It was at the base of a particularly steep slope that they stopped on a street named Rua Santana à Lapa before a large white building. A line of people stretched across the front of the high fence and snaked around the corner. Not only men and women, but children as well.

"This is the American embassy, where we do most of our work." Sims stopped the car and got out, leaving Ava's suitcases in the rear seat.

"Who are all these people?" she asked.

"Refugees seeking visas to America," he answered in a matter-of-fact tone.

As she approached the line, dozens of eyes focused on her, sharp with anticipation, many of their faces incredibly thin.

She recalled the stories she'd read in newspapers in America about how the Nazis were determined to kill all Jews in Europe, how people in several countries were pushed into certain areas of the city where they were left to starvation and disease.

"There's so many," she murmured.

"Getting here early won't mean you avoid them." Mr. Sims nudged apart the line, leading her from the crowd and through a gate. "They're here at all hours."

No doubt they were attempting to flee Europe and get to America where they knew they would be safe. "That's so terribly sad."

Mr. Sims gave a hum of acknowledgment. "That's why we have the US Legation and Consulate General to handle all that. And why you don't need to worry your pretty little head about it."

Ava bit back her sharp reply lest she come across as pugnacious on her first day. It was strange how women could now attend most colleges and embark on jobs once reserved only for men. Yet in some ways, males were determined to hold "the fairer sex" in the limited and confining roles belonging to the last century.

A woman whose sandy curls were pulled back into a roll pinned with a blue flower smiled broadly as they entered. "You must be our new IDC agent. I'm Peggy, the secretary for the ambassador. You just let me know if you need anything at all, *Miss* Harper."

Peggy's left brow quirked upright as she stressed the "Miss" in her statement and slid a triumphant smirk toward Mr. Sims.

Ava nodded, relieved to have at least one person in her corner.

The US Embassy was surprisingly like any other office space Ava had seen. Desks were laid out in a grid-like pattern and framed art adorned the otherwise bland, neutral-colored walls.

A tall man in a navy suit stopped midstride, his arm and leg going forward with an exaggerated momentum-pulled motion as he stared at her. "Who's the dish?" He flashed a smile that revealed a chipped canine. Given his slightly crooked nose and stockier build, he seemed like the sort to have barreled his way through college as a linebacker on the football team.

Based on his baby face, that might have been only a year ago.

"You mean Petri dish?" she amended with what she hoped was a good-natured chuckle. "I only just flew in and am looking forward to cleaning up later."

"I bet your arms are tired." He grinned expectantly.

Peggy pushed at him. "Aw, c'mon and leave her be. The poor girl is probably going on about twenty hours without sleep, am I right?"

It was closer to twenty-four, but who was counting at this point?

Ava gave Peggy a grateful smile.

"That's what I thought. I can't believe you were even brought in." Peggy folded her arms and directed her razor-sharp focus toward Mr. Sims.

"I wanted to," Ava admitted. "I confess I'm a little unsure what I'm even supposed to do."

They laughed, a joke everyone knew the punch line to but her.

She lightly joined in with a chuckle, so she didn't appear as left out as she suddenly felt.

"None of us had an idea what we were doing when we got here," the linebacker said. "I'll help you get the swing of things. I'm Michael Driscoll, by the way."

Mr. Sims turned and disappeared into an office with his name on the closing door.

"Nice to meet you, Mr. Driscoll." Ava's smile stretched across her dry lips. She learned a long time ago that she said the wrong things at the wrong times, only thinking of the right reply several hours later. Usually around three in the morning when there was nothing but the isolating darkness of her room to appreciate her belated wit.

"You can call me Mike." He put an arm around her shoulders. The cheap scent of rayon informed her of the fabric of his suit despite its immaculately tailored appearance. "Stick with me and I'll show you the ropes, kid."

She was likely two or three years older than him, certainly no kid in his book. "I'm certain you can do that without your arm around my shoulders." She eased out from beneath his hold with a smile to make her words less sharp.

He swiftly withdrew from her, his hands held up in proof of his innocence. "We've heard everything about you." He wagged a finger at her. "You're smart, dig into research like a bloodhound, and know your way around microfilm."

It was a reminder of her former self from DC, one who didn't have to pretend to find humor in jokes she didn't understand, who knew what went where and why. She nodded, proud of her accomplishments.

"Tell you what," Mike said. "Gather up all the daily publications and newspapers tomorrow morning and come back here. I'll show you how to get them all back to DC for filing."

"Now that I can do." While she spoke with confidence, she felt only the quivers of trepidation. She had no idea what she was looking for or where she might find it. But after his compliment, she didn't dare inquire lest she sound stupid.

He offered her a mock salute with two fingers and an amiable wink before sauntering to one of the back rooms.

Peggy gave a good-natured shake of her head. "He's a piece of work, that one." She held up a set of keys. "Your bags are still in the car. C'mon, I'll drive you to your flat. We got you a little place just off Rossio Square, all to yourself and everything."

Ava hesitated before following Peggy. "Are you sure there's nothing I should be doing here?"

"You need to get settled," Peggy said over her shoulder. The flare of her yellow skirt was far more generous than was allowed in DC. Apparently, the cloth ration was not in effect in Lisbon.

They approached the door to leave when Ava put a hand on Peggy's arm. "Don't you need a hat?"

Peggy tilted her head. "Why would I need a hat?"

Heat effused Ava's cheeks. "Won't you...be...taken for...a...?"

Peggy lifted her brows for Ava to continue.

"Prostitute," Ava whispered in a rushed breath, glancing around after to ensure no one heard.

To her great surprise, Peggy burst out laughing. "I'm guessing you read that OSS manual on Lisbon?"

Ava straightened her spine an inch taller. "Of course I did."

"A lot's changed since they wrote that straitlaced piece." Still chuckling to herself, Peggy waved for Ava to follow. "C'mon, let's get you to your new place so you can get settled."

The ride to Rossio Square only took a few minutes—likely too far to walk, but almost too short to drive. Peggy drove slower, allowing Ava to take in the ornamented sidewalks throughout Lisbon with detailed chunks of limestone and basalt laid out in an ancient art form called *calçada*, a practice dating back to Mesopotamia. Some spreads were in specific patterns and others merely a smattering of stones fitted together like perfectly made puzzle pieces. But the one Ava had most anticipated from her research was that of Rossio Square.

She pulled in a quiet breath as the black volcanic stone and white calcified rock formation came into view, its wavelike pattern shifting against the eyes depending on how one looked at it.

"Rossio Square." Peggy gestured to the stretch of ornate stonework and the statue of King Pedro VI of Portugal atop a towering column at its center. "I don't know what they call that patterned walkway, but it's lovely, isn't it?"

"Mar Lago," Ava replied. "The wide sea."

"That's fitting." Peggy pursed her lips, thoughtful. "But be warned, when those cobblestones get wet, they're slippery as a spy. How do you know that anyway? About the *Mar Lago* stuff?"

"I'm a librarian," Ava answered proudly. "I love to learn."

"You're perfect for this job. Don't ever let Mr. Sims tell you different."

Peggy pulled the car past the square. As she did so, Ava's attention was drawn from the *calçada* to the swarms of people. Chairs and tables spilled from the cafés into the sunlit pavement in such numbers, it was impossible to tell one establishment from the other.

In Ava's research through the OSS manual and other various books in the library, Portuguese women did not spend time in cafés. However, there were scores of women leaned casually back in the wooden and metal-framed seats, their legs absent stockings as they blew out graceful streams of cigarette smoke. Not a single one wore gloves, let alone a hat.

"The refugees have changed things a bit here." Peggy turned down a side street called Rua de Santa Justa and pulled the car to a stop. "Don't let this casual setting fool you. These people are in desperate circumstances. They don't care if they have hats on their heads or stockings on their legs. They're all biding their time, churning in the endless hell of transit visas, exit visas, whatever other kind of visas that can trip them up."

"Like those outside the embassy." Ava sobered as she recalled the crowd of people.

"Right." Peggy frowned to herself. "If they're lucky enough to get those visas, then they need tickets to boats that might never come and cause the crazy cycle to start all over again. You'll see."

She slid out from the car. Each woman took one of the suitcases, though Ava ensured she grabbed the heavier of the two, and lugged them up a flight of stairs in a town house to a door marked 101. Peggy pulled out a set of keys and opened the door.

"It's small, but it's more than most have. Housing and hotel space is tight. Lucky for you, it was available just before your arrival."

Ava walked into the narrow apartment where the living room, kitchen, and dining room were all rolled into one central location and a door to a bedroom was off to one side. Yet another door revealed her own bathroom, a luxury she'd never had.

"It's perfect." She set her suitcase down. "I'm from DC. This is practically a mansion."

"In that case, you're welcome." Peggy handed the apartment keys and a thick envelope to her. "Escudos, the local currency, and quite a bit. Get some rest, then snap up as many publications as you can tomorrow morning. There's a kiosk just down the street where you can get most of what you need. Someone will be by to pick you up around noon to take you back to the embassy."

Ava held the envelope. "Is that all I need to do? Buy a few newspapers?"

Peggy shrugged and headed for the door. "You'll be fine. You're made for this job."

The door to Ava's apartment slammed closed, and she was completely alone with two packed suitcases and soul-deep exhaustion.

In DC, Ava was made for the job in the Rare Book Room, a library where she could name the artist of each painting and sculpture, where the history of every nook and cranny was as familiar to her as her own. She knew the catalog of ancient tomes like the back of her hand as well as her fellow librarians and the etiquette surrounding the hushed splendor of the Library of Congress. Lisbon was a city she had only a week to study for, like a dilettante cramming for a final exam, where she didn't know the language and everything she'd learned about the culture was wrong.

To everyone, she was perfect for this job. Everyone, that is, except her.

★ ★ ★

She took nearly an age to fall asleep that night and struggled to rise at eight the next morning, her internal clock still set to DC time. Her suitcases were unpacked, her clothes pressed with an old iron she found in the closet, and her books were neatly shelved in the living area. With the exception of Louisa May Alcott's *Little Women*, which sat on the nightstand near the bed, where it always lay no matter where she lived.

When her mother was alive, they often read the same books together. It started with *Anne of Green Gables* when Ava was eight. She'd spoken of the story with such ebullience that her mother read it after her. The shared story made for many hours of lively conversation between them, smiling at Anne's witty commentary and lamenting over the foulness of that nasty Josie Pye. Ava and her mother always read the same books after that— at least, until her mother's death five years later.

Her mother had read *Little Women* first, as she often did when it came to books she feared might be too old for twelve-year-old Ava, and deemed it not only age-appropriate, but a masterpiece to be shared. Ava finished the story in her mother's absence and was near bursting with all the things she wished to discuss. Knowing her mother was scheduled to arrive the next morning, she left it on the nightstand so she could grab it first thing.

Except the plane carrying them back from France had been caught in a terrible storm and crashed into the sea. When Ava ran out of her room that morning, it was not her mother and father who waited for her, but her nanny, red-eyed and sobbing.

The copy of *Little Women* by Ava's bed did not mean her mother would come home, of course, but it was forever a reminder of her mother and their shared love of books that seemed to—even now—bring them together.

Somehow that small piece of her childhood, the familiarity of a beloved book, made these foreign surroundings feel more like home. She hadn't realized how much she'd craved the comfort until it settled around her like an embrace and bolstered her determination.

While she was no polyglot, she knew French and German and even a bit of Spanish. Surely she could puzzle out more Portuguese than she anticipated. And she would only be on her own until noon when she was to go to the embassy. How hard could her first day be?

Ava almost left her hat behind, but at the last minute fixed a black pillbox to her victory curls and slid into her new black pumps to match her dark A-line wraparound skirt and pink sweater. When she opened the door to her apartment, the man on the other side was just leaving his.

His hair was mussed with threads of silver at his temples and a weariness slackened the skin under his eyes. He took one look at her and his heavy brows shot up. "You are American."

Ava frowned. *Was it so obvious?*

"Do you have any American magazines?" he asked in accented English. "*Time*, perhaps?"

"Actually, I do," she answered slowly. The magazine had been purchased on impulse at the airport before her flight in a bid to settle her nerves. It hadn't worked and now lay on the table, still untouched.

"May I have it?" he asked.

It was such a bold question, without preamble or decorum, and she was so taken aback that she agreed before her thoughts could catch up. She slipped back into the apartment and re-emerged with the magazine, its cover still crisp and glossy.

She might as well have delivered the Gutenberg Bible to him for the joy lighting his face.

"Thank you." Then before anything else might be said, he opened his door and disappeared within once more.

The strange encounter concluded, Ava made her way down the stairs, escudos nestled safely in her purse. She exited the building and opted to go left where the bustle of people seemed to be flowing. Several paces later, her heel slipped on the slick limestone walkway.

She righted herself before the misstep could be noticed and put more focus into her gait. The stonework she had admired so ardently earlier swelled and dipped beneath its uneven paving from long ago, leaving the surface rolling like frozen waves and markedly treacherous for one in heels.

Rather than return to her apartment for more sensible footwear, she carefully navigated to a kiosk with several newspapers pinned to boards set before the small stand and along its base.

The *Daily Mail* occupied one section, its date two weeks behind on April 8, 1943, with a headline proclaiming, "Allies Close in as Rommel Runs."

Das Reich was at its side, mentioning nothing of the defeated German general. For that matter, nor did *Le Nouvelliste*—a French distributed paper that appeared to be from Lyon. She reached for the Lyonnaise newspaper to examine it more closely when a man's fingers brushed hers.

They both snatched back their hands and looked at one another. The man was tall, his blond hair swept effortlessly to the side, eyes as cerulean blue as a perfect spring sky. He gave her a broad smile that showed a dimple in his right cheek.

Adonis.

If she'd ever wondered how a god in true form might appear to mere mortals, now she knew. She had never been one for falling for any man on appearance alone, but that dimple could sweep even the most stoic of ladies away with romantic notions.

"Forgive me," he said with a light Bavarian accent.

"You're German." She stiffened, doused with icy reality. Suddenly her breathlessness had nothing to do with his good looks and everything to do with his nationality.

"Austrian," he corrected her.

"You're a Nazi," she exhaled, unable to stop the hiss of accusation.

Even as she did so, she acknowledged the sorrow at her immediate reaction. Once, the German language had made her recall fond memories of her father, whose grandparents had immigrated to America from Cologne before his mother and her sisters were born. It was their legacy that encouraged his studies and his passion for their heritage. It was why Ava had wished to learn the language as well. And now it had been sullied by the Nazis.

"A refugee," he corrected. "I came here five years ago to avoid *Anschluss*."

Heat seared her cheeks. She shouldn't have been so quick to judge. Reading of nothing but German aggression in the papers back home had given her a knee-jerk reaction she needed to temper.

While she couldn't remember much about refugees in Lisbon prior to 1940 from the little bit she'd managed to research, she was aware that *Anschluss* was the Nazi war effort that occupied Austrians were forced to join.

"I see," she replied shamefaced. "Please forgive me."

"The accent." He grimaced and gestured to his strong throat. "It is an understandable mistake."

She gave a nervous laugh that came out something like a giggle. She cut it short, resisting the urge to cringe.

"I am sure I can forgive you if you would join me for coffee and *pastéis de nata*." His lips widened into a full, devastating smile. "I'm Lukas."

Pastéis de nata.

She bit her lip to keep from agreeing, if nothing else than for the opportunity to sample the custard pastry she'd read about.

He held out his large hand. His sleeves were rolled up, revealing his tanned, strong forearms. She gave his warm hand a quick, firm shake, then forced her attention to the newsstand. "I'm afraid I have a few things to gather here first."

He chuckled, the sound a rich, rumbling timbre in his chest. "Everyone is so concerned with publications these days."

An awkward silence settled between them as the conversation volleyed back to her. "You should have seen how happy my neighbor was with a copy of *Time*," she offered for lack of anything more interesting to say.

Better to remain silent and be thought a fool than to speak and to remove all doubt. The quote from Abraham Lincoln rushed at her in that moment, and she wished she could snatch the words back from the air like pages caught on the wind.

Lukas's eyes narrowed. "American magazines are a rare find here in Portugal."

He said it in a way that suggested she might have done something wrong in giving it away.

"I can only imagine he was elated with such a gift." The shrewd expression eased into a smile once more. "I hope I may see you around, Miss..."

"Harper." She flicked a glance up and wished she hadn't when she saw the interest evident in his handsome gaze.

He nodded to himself, pleased as he backed away from her, still watching with an appreciation she should find offensive.

A dark-haired gentleman stood near her in a black suit with a robin's-egg blue tie, his stature diminutive by comparison and the corners of his mouth elevated in an amused smirk at the exchange.

She turned away from him and lowered her head to the publications that should have been the whole of her focus. A fool indeed.

"I don't recall that Americans are ones for fraternizing with Nazis."

She startled and found the dark-haired man beside her. British, judging by his clipped accent.

"What?"

"That man you were speaking with." He indicated the direction where Lukas had disappeared, melting into the crowd.

"He's not a Nazi." She sniffed and examined a page of the *Evening Standard* without focusing on the text. "He's Austrian."

"Let me guess..." The man put a finger to his chin, his expression deeply pensive. "He arrived here five years ago as a refugee to flee the Nazis? And whom Portugal has somehow kindly allowed to stay this long without kicking him out despite the people they arrest daily for such an offense as expired visas?"

Aware he had made his point, he lifted his dark brow.

But there was no rejoinder Ava could offer that would cool the heat of her humiliation, especially when she was so unfamiliar with Portuguese laws.

"If it makes you feel a modicum better, they do say that to all the American women." He offered her a genuinely apologetic bow. "And all the American women fall prey to them."

Ava stared hard at the various publications in front of her. Had she done so from the beginning, she would not be in this mess.

"I should like to start again." He cleared his throat. "It is a pleasure to make your acquaintance. I am James MacKinnon. You are Miss Harper, correct?"

"You heard my name mentioned to…the Austrian." She caught herself before calling him Lukas. If James was right, Lukas was doubtlessly not his name.

"While I confess I did receive confirmation of your identity from accidentally overhearing your exchange, I actually happen to know much about you."

"You do?" Ava studied his long face. He had a large nose that gave him a look of self-importance, but a spark in his eyes that suggested he didn't take himself too seriously.

"I've been eager to meet the librarian everyone has been talking about." He lifted his fedora half an inch from his head. "I look forward to seeing more of you as we run in the same circles, Miss Harper." He dropped his hat back into place and was absorbed into the crowd before she could summon a sufficient response.

As she searched through the sea of unfamiliar faces, worry nipped the pit of her stomach.

Whatever her role was in this war, she clearly had already failed the first step.

FOUR

Hélène becomes Elaine

Two weeks passed before Hélène began to think of herself as Elaine Rousseau. After a lifetime of one name, it was not easy to conform to another. However, the desire to ensure Claudine's safety and to belong to the Resistance spurred her determination.

Elaine pushed through the heavy door on Rue Saint Jean as the sun sank in the distance. The address was the last that remained on the list she had memorized. A courtyard filled with letterboxes greeted her. In the one marked with *Chaput #4*, she dropped the sealed envelope into the open slot above the locked box.

The message was the last of her cargo to be delivered. Immediately the tension at her shoulders ebbed. If she were caught now, the Nazis would have no evidence to use against her.

Familiar with the area, she followed the winding passage that connected the buildings, going through open courtyards to echoing tunnels toward the exit door on Rue des Trois Maries. Such passages existed all though Lyon though not all were as beautifully crafted as the one she currently made her way through, with its finely arched ceilings and rose-hued walls.

The traboules were used by the old silk workers over a century ago to travel quickly through the steeply slanting streets. The covered passages were still utilized by many to save time. As an added benefit, the winding paths made her steps difficult to trace should someone be following her.

But as she approached the large wooden door leading out to Rue des Trois Maries, a figure stood in the shadows as though waiting on her. She drew up short, aware it was far too late to turn back around.

"*Bonjour*, Elaine." Etienne lifted his head so she could make his features out in the dim light.

She exhaled a sigh of relief. "What news is there of Joseph?"

Etienne cast his eyes downward and shook his head. "He is still being held at Montluc Prison. None of his former contacts have been approached, which means he has not talked."

"Is he well?" She hated relying on these reports rather than going to see her husband herself. But doing so with her false papers would put him at greater risk should she be caught. "And has he received my packages?" The scraps of food she managed to send came from her own paltry rations. But, if need be, she could find more on the black market. Joseph could do nothing from his cell but wait for whatever she sent him.

Etienne nodded. "We believe he has received them all. They have been delivered, that much I do know."

The familiar knot of helpless frustration welled in her throat. "When will he be released?"

"Soon, we hope."

It was always the same answer, each time given with conviction. But as the days wore on, she found herself less willing to trust his assurances.

What if the food she sent to Joseph was being taken from him?

What if he was being beaten for information the same as Etienne?

What if they never released him?

The last thought was too stark to even consider.

There was much that needed to be said between Elaine and her husband after they had parted ways on such a bitter note. She had started several letters to him to include with her parcels, but no words seemed to adequately convey what ached in her chest when she thought of Joseph. And certainly nothing that could be read by a guard without confirming his guilt.

No, her apology would be better said in person, when she could look into his eyes and tell him not only the depth of her regret, but also her love; for to her, one could not be said without the other.

"You've done well, Elaine," Etienne said, interrupting her thoughts. "All your deliveries have been completed timely and without issue. You can be trusted."

She frowned at his words. "If I wasn't entirely trusted, why was I given messages to deliver?"

"They were traps." He winked. "They contained false information and would have revealed you if you were indeed a collaborator."

Her mouth fell open. All this time she had been thinking she was helping, putting her life on the line for those letterbox drops.

"Ours is a careful organization," he continued in a softer tone. Already he spoke quietly enough that the stone walls could not carry the echo of his deep voice, but now he was nearly inaudible. "We cannot trust anyone. Even the wives of our dearest friends."

The initial sting of distrust faded with her understanding.

Collaborators were everywhere. Like Madame Arnaud. A shiver crept down Elaine's spine.

"I will never dissapoint you," she said vehemently.

"That is what we are counting on. Tomorrow, go to 20 Rue d'Algérie where you'll find a bookshop. Repeat the address back to me."

"Twenty Rue d'Algérie," she recited. While she knew the area, it was not one she traveled to often.

"You can remember it?"

"Of course." She didn't bother to stifle her offense at the question. After all, she had spent the past two weeks memorizing addresses. Writing them down was dangerous. The instructions had been repeated to her by Etienne himself as well as many others.

If he noticed her irritation at his lack of faith, he ignored it. "A woman will meet you out front at noon. Her name is Nicole. Don't be late."

"Or early," she said, tossing his directives back at him to show she had absorbed everything he'd taught her.

His eyes crinkled with a smile. "You *are* good at this, Elaine."

If she was that good, she would have found a way to set Joseph free. But she refrained from saying as much. All she could do now was put her trust in Etienne and the Resistance to save her husband.

The bells chimed noon as Elaine approached the bookshop. As she did so, a woman with pale blond hair sauntered toward her, stylishly dressed in a white sweater and a knee-length navy skirt that matched the delicate brimless calot hat pinned primly to the crown of her head. Her red lips parted in a wide smile. "Elaine, *ma chérie*, it is so good to see you."

To Elaine's surprise, the pretty young woman embraced her and brushed a kiss on each cheek. Elaine did likewise, feigning familiarity so they appeared little more than old friends to anyone who might be observing them.

"Come join me for coffee." Nicole clasped Elaine's hand in hers. "Or at least what passes for coffee these days." Her pale blue eyes twinkled, and she pulled Elaine close, leading her to a door beside the bookshop.

Nicole did not drop Elaine's hand as they entered the courtyard and climbed a set of stairs. Instead, she gave Elaine's fingers a squeeze. "We'll teach you everything you need to ensure you stay safe, *chérie*."

"Safe is nice, but I want to be effective," Elaine countered.

Nicole grinned. "Denise is going to adore you."

She stopped before an apartment door and pulled out a key. Her efforts appeared to take an inordinate amount of time as Elaine waited, nerves taut with anxiety to meet the other women she would be working with. To discover what it was she was even going to be doing. At last, the heavy door clicked open, and Nicole led Elaine inside.

The safe houses where Elaine had stayed were often empty rooms with a simple mattress and a few blankets. But here, the foyer held a homey, lived-in feel with several shoes tilting in a messy line against the wall and a battered armoire sitting stout in the corner with a round mirror over it for checking one's hair before leaving.

Nicole kicked off her heels with a heavy clunk and dropped an inch in height before unpinning the smart hat and setting it aside, not a hair out of place. "She's here," she called out in a singsong voice and gave Elaine a wink.

Elaine deposited her shoes next to Nicole's and followed her into the main living area. The space was exactly what one would expect, with gauzy white curtains draped over the windows and a cobalt blue settee framed by two butter-yellow chairs. But in the center of the room was a large table that held a typewriter, various slips of paper, several pencils, and what appeared to be scraps of silk. Two women bending over something on the cluttered surface looked up with interest.

The dark-haired one's blithe gaze skimmed over Elaine, her demeanor entirely unwelcoming. The woman with light brown curls, however, gave a shy, gentle smile that instantly made Elaine like her.

"This is Denise." Nicole nodded first to the dark-haired woman, then to the one with curls. "And Josette."

Josette came around the table and clasped Elaine's hands in her warm fingers. "We are so glad to have you join us, Elaine. And now I am no longer the newest member."

Her cheeks flushed with color, and the kindness in her green eyes indicated her remark was not one of malice.

"You were enlisted by Gabriel?" Denise asked, using Etienne's Resistance name.

"Oui," Elaine replied as Josette released her hands.

Denise nodded slowly in what Elaine thought might be approval.

"Come now, Denise," Nicole scolded. "Do not scare her off on her first day."

Denise sniffed. "The Bosche will do that for her if her nerves are not strong enough."

"My nerves are just fine no matter what the Germans do," Elaine said before either of the other two women could try to rush to her aid. "Or I wouldn't be here."

Denise's eyes narrowed slightly, but Elaine refused to be cowed by the directness of her assessing stare and lifted her chin in challenge.

"Then why are you standing there and not over here learning this code?" Denise shifted over to make room for Elaine at her side.

As she took her place beside Denise, her code crafting education with the Resistance officially began.

The process of breaking down and reconstructing the words was not an easy one. The foundation was based on a poem written over a hundred years ago, selecting words from the stanza to create a code that was then used to configurate the message. This was further complicated by the poem itself, which changed to a new poem every week.

"Don't worry," Josette said in Elaine's ear as the confusing lesson came to an end. "I will show it to you again later."

Elaine gave her a grateful nod.

"This is our typewriter." Nicole indicated the glossy black Royal typewriter on the table with *Aristocrat* in gold letters on its shiny plate.

Elaine regarded the glass-faced keys, noting the unusual order. Most were in the same location she recognized from her years as a secretary, but the Q, W, A, Z, X, and M were in different places.

"It's British," Denise said matter-of-factly. "Many of the items we use in the Resistance are provided to us by British agents. Some of our courier work will even involve going to the outskirts of town where the Maquis will meet us with goods received from air drops."

The Maquis, named for the underbrush in which they hid, were men who were too young to fight at the start of the war, but were ordered in recent months to relocate to factories in Germany to work for the compulsory labor service. Many opposed this rule and instead chose to live in the dense forests rather than be slaves for the Nazis. These men fell back on the guerrilla warfare tactics of their Frankish ancestors, using the land to their favor. And from what she gathered from the ladies, the British agents were there to help.

The world wanted Hitler to fail, and Elaine was proud to finally be doing her part.

"We use silk for some of our messages," Josette said.

Nicole lifted a pale yellow scrap. Her nails were lacquered with the same vivid shade as her lips. Between that vibrant red and her white sweater and blue skirt, she had completed the forbidden tricolors of France. No doubt her fashion choice was intentional. And if it was, the show of French loyalty was quite clever.

She folded the square at the corners before pinching the middle to make a small flower. "These bits of silk would make such a lovely decoration for a hat or one's hair." Her hold on the silk released and the glossy fabric unfurled into a ragged square once more. "But unfortunately, they are all needed for messages. Silk rolls very thin and can be sewn discreetly into clothing if need be. It also burns fast, so it is disposed of quickly and easily after the recipient has read the message or if they suspect they might be caught."

Elaine studied the typewriter. "How does the fabric stay still when you're typing?"

Josette held up a needle and thread. "We sew it to the paper." She took the swatch from Nicole and wove several loose stitches to secure it to the page, then fed the result into the machine without issue.

Looking at the keys as she typed, Josette copied the line of jumbled letters Denise had pieced out of the poem she had been working on. The ink hit the silk, staining the delicate fabric until the entire code was complete.

When Josette was done, she removed the paper, clipped the threads and the silk floated to the table with the message boldly standing out against its smooth surface.

"I'm assuming you know how to type, or Gabriel wouldn't have sent you here." Nicole offered the chair to Elaine as Josette eased out.

"I used to be a secretary." Elaine slid into the seat, still warm from its previous occupant. Though she had been married for over five years, it had not been so long since she'd been in front of a typewriter. Joseph had not insisted she quit her job when they wed, despite the disparaging looks she often received from her coworkers for having kept on with her employment after marriage. He'd even encouraged her to seek a new secretary position when they first moved to Lyon. Though by then, no more jobs were available as refugees from other countries that were attacked before France had already arrived and assumed those roles.

"Mind the keys," Denise cautioned.

Elaine did as she was told, paying special care to the mismatched letters. It was an odd thing to have the familiarity of the cool, smooth keys under her fingertips, but not be able to fall back on her ability to blindly type. In the end, she removed her hands from the keyboard and pecked out the message as any novice would.

Nicole pulled the page free, and her gaze skimmed over Elaine's work. "Perfect."

They worked through the afternoon, her fingers finding the appropriate keys with less difficulty, when a knock at the door resonated through the apartment. Every woman stiffened and glanced at one another, as if confirming no visitors were expected. Of the four of them, it was Denise who approached the foyer, her feet silent as she moved over the old floorboards.

Before she could ask who it was, a voice on the other end said, *"Sous le pont Mirabeau…"*

Without hesitation, Denise replied, *"…coule la Seine."*
Under the Mirabeau Bridge flows the Seine.

Elaine frowned at Nicole with confusion.

"It is a code from *Le pont Mirabeau* by Guillaume Apollinaire," the other woman explained as Denise received a stack of papers from a male courier who departed as abruptly as he'd come.

Elaine nodded, remembering the poem about an artist and his love that she first heard while in *lycée* as a girl.

Denise returned with the pile of what appeared to be newsprint in her arms. "We have deliveries tomorrow." She set her load on the table, revealing numerous copies of *Combat*, one of the many clandestine newspapers distributed by the Resistance.

Elaine picked up a copy and read the first article detailing the arrests at Villeurbanne when the men called up for compulsory service did not show at the train station at their assigned times. The Gestapo sealed off that section of Lyon and rounded up over three hundred young men to transport to work camps by force.

"Combat is my preference," Denise said. "Though I know

Josette prefers *Cahiers du Témoignage Chrétien*, the newspaper for Christian Resistance supporters, and Nicole likes the journal *Femmes françaises* when she can get it. Which publication do you like best?"

Over six months had passed since Elaine last laid eyes on any clandestine newspaper, back when Joseph had suddenly demanded she stop all acts of resistance once the Germans returned to Lyon and stayed. But before then, they used to read through *Combat* together, the editorial geared toward soldiers and intellectuals; both aspects Joseph could appreciate. As could she, by association of her love for her husband.

"*Combat*," Elaine replied. A pang of longing struck her with the recollection of those mornings over chicory coffee, their heads bowed together as they discussed the articles in low voices.

How she missed those days with Joseph, when they worked as a team rather than opposing one another. Before she had known of his efforts with the Resistance instead of being told lies. "I used to read *Combat* with my husband. We would use what was in the paper to come up with tracts that we made on the Roneo."

The duplicating machine was a clunky thing, but it worked well enough to copy the pamphlet she and Joseph composed to churn out replicas for distribution.

Denise lifted a dark brow with interest. "You know how to use a Roneo?"

Elaine nodded. "It isn't all that difficult, so long as it doesn't jam."

"Which is often for me." Nicole laughed. "I think my specialty is in breaking most things mechanical."

"Which is why she's usually not allowed near the typewriter." Josette smothered a giggle. "Lucky for her, she is adept at transcribing messages into code."

"My husband showed me how to use the duplicating machine," Elaine confessed. "He has always been so patient with me. In truth, I joined the Resistance in the hopes there might be something I can do to help free him."

Nicole stopped sifting through the delicate scraps of silk. "Free him?"

"He's in Montluc Prison. Perhaps you know him—Pierre?" His code name was foreign on Elaine's tongue.

Josette brightened. "He made identity cards."

Elaine nodded, suspecting as much based off Claudine's arrival at her door. However, she had not anticipated the women would know of her husband, let alone what he had done. But this new insight into Joseph left her fascinated to learn more.

"He made mine." Josette's brow pinched. "Though I can't recall much else."

"I don't know anything about him," Nicole said. "But I'll do what I can to find out."

Elaine offered her an appreciative smile. *"Merci beaucoup."*

Nicole waved it off as if the gesture was nothing. But it was something to Elaine. It meant knowing exactly what Joseph did those days she thought he was at work, all the times of being a bored housewife, stewing with resentment as she waited at home.

And to think Elaine had once accused him of being as guilty as the Nazis for having turned a blind eye. The memory struck at a contrite chord within her. If only she had known then... If only he had trusted her enough to tell her.

The familiar ire welled up once more.

But any residual anger dissolved into an unsettling chill when Elaine caught sight of Denise, who was studying her with an expression that could only be considered somber.

FIVE

Ava

Ava set the five publications she'd procured onto Mr. Sims's desk. She personally had scoured through them to ensure the contents seemed pertinent to what might aid the American war effort.

He gave them a cursory glance and returned his attention to a file open in front of them, clearly uninterested in her findings. "Where are the rest?"

"These seemed to have helpful details," she replied. "I could only read the ones in English, German, and French."

Mr. Sims pinched the bridge of his nose in a manner that suggested she had just ruined his entire day. "You are to obtain any publication you can get your hands on."

"I was given no instructions, but will certainly acquire more next time," she said with measured deference. "I also would have appreciated being notified that some Nazis pretend to be Austrians."

His head shot up. "Why? What happened? What did you say?"

She shook her head so swiftly, she felt one of the pins holding a rolled-back curl slip. "Nothing, but you might have told me regardless."

"In that case." He put the flat of his palms on his desk. "Don't talk to Germans. They're the enemy and also involved with the PVDE from time to time." His eyes bored into hers.

She was about to ask what the PVDE was when he returned his focus to the folder and muttered, "And here I thought you were supposed to be smart."

His words were a slap that made tears sting her eyes. She looked down quickly to keep him from seeing them.

"Want me to show you where we do our photography?" Mike asked abruptly from the open doorway. No doubt he had heard. Likely everyone in the office had.

Ava nodded, her gaze still fixed on the floor. "That would be wonderful, thank you." But when she turned to go, Mr. Sims gave a short whistle.

He gathered the papers in his meaty hand. "Don't forget your generous haul."

Her face burned with humiliation.

Mike took the small stack and nudged Ava with his elbow. "You got three more than me on my first go of it."

She looked up. "Really?"

"Yeah, we weren't given much to work with when we first got here." He led her down a hall that held the pervasive aroma of stale coffee. "It was just me and ole Sims when all this started up. I think that's why he's being so hard on you. A rite of passage so to speak."

She didn't reply. If she were back in DC at that very moment, she would be getting ready for her job in the Rare Book Room. In an hour, she would have strolled beneath masterpieces that celebrated intellect, to breathe in that scent of old books that she already missed like a heartbeat.

Instead, she faced some juvenile rite of passage after being flirted with by a Nazi and called out by a man who knew more about her than she did him. Aristotle once said that patience is bitter, but its fruit is sweet.

That bitterness sat on the back of her tongue now, stubborn and long-lasting.

But hadn't the first day at the Library of Congress been difficult when she started? There was more to know than she ever thought possible to learn.

She'd taste the fruit of conquering Lisbon's unknown and was certain it would be sweet.

Mike escorted her to a large conference room with a table at its center, like a floating island with no chairs in sight and covered in lamps. Three boxy cameras sat to one side as well as several reels of film in their round metal boxes.

"You may be familiar with these." Mike winked. "I hear you worked with something like them at the Library of Congress."

The burden of her frustration eased as she went to the first camera. "I did. We had stacks of newsprint that was decaying and managed to salvage the information by putting it all on microfilm."

"Well, here we are doing it because of limited storage for mailing items back to DC to be categorized." He popped open the side of the large camera and Ava did likewise. "We tried sending the actual periodicals, books, and newsprint in boxes on ships, but the vessels were unreliable and apparently the German paraphernalia kept being seized as contraband." He chortled to himself. "Ole Sims is still fielding calls from the PVDE about why we have so many Nazi publications going to the States."

That PVDE reference again.

"What is the PVDE?" Ava added the full spool on one prong and threaded the film into the empty spool on the other side.

"The Portuguese secret police." He paused in his work, lid partially closed, and gave her a stern look. "You don't want to tangle with them. Ever."

She nodded and closed her own machine.

They both began the first of the eight cranks necessary to properly thread the film to the starting point within the camera. "We only have space for 165 pounds a month on the Pan

Am Clipper that goes out every two weeks. So..." He patted the primed camera. "Microfilm."

Ava paused to see what he would do. "Exactly what are we photographing?"

He indicated a table at the back wall laden with newspapers of every language as well as several haphazard piles of books, leaflets, and magazines, then held up what appeared to be a manual for a civilian gas mask. "This."

"All of it?" No wonder Mr. Sims had been disappointed with her measly collection.

Mike took off his jacket and slung it on the table beside him, a man prepping to get down to work. "You may want to get some coffee. We're going to be here awhile."

Her stomach gave an irritated grumble. The hollowness of her hunger was uncomfortable enough that she swore to never miss breakfast again. She took Mike's advice to at least grab a cup of coffee.

Warm mug in hand, she went to work alongside him, centering the content just so in the beams of light, focusing the camera and capturing the image with a tinny *click* that reverberated in the depths of the machine.

They worked like that for the better part of the day, taking countless pictures of anything and everything, until they both had several completed spools stacked beside them. An ache burned between Ava's shoulders from leaning her head forward to ensure the capture window contained all the necessary information, and her lower back felt as though it might snap if she had to bend over just one more time.

"I think that's good for one day." Mike folded the paper he'd been photographing. "If you don't have any dinner plans, you should come meet the rest of the team."

"There are more IDC agents than just us?"

"Not exactly." He pulled his jacket back on and carefully buttoned the front. "I mean the Brits."

★ ★ ★

They took one of the streetcars to the Chiado district where high-end specialty stores touted lady's gloves and glamorous hats. The windows displayed fashions that would never pass the ration codes in the United States and showcased more shoes than any government girl could dream of.

The scent of grilled fish flavored the air with a smoky, briny aroma that made Ava's mouth water. Coffee only fortified a person for so long and left her with a jittery nervousness sloshing around in her otherwise empty stomach.

She had always enjoyed fresh seafood and had anticipated the fare in Lisbon, pulled straight from the sparkling waters of the Tagus River and onto a grill.

"We work closely with the Brits," Mike said as they navigated their way up the sloping limestone path of Rua Garrett. "These boys are with The Association of Special Libraries and Information Bureau. Or ASLIB as I prefer to call it."

"Why do we all have such ridiculously long names?" Ava mused.

Mike cocked his head like a puppy, then shrugged. "Beats me." His attention darted forward. "Ah, there they are now."

Two men were already seated at a table outside beneath a dark green awning, with a third standing at their side. The gentleman turned as they approached, and Ava suppressed a groan.

James MacKinnon.

The busybody Brit who had chastised her earlier that day for "consorting with Nazis" was apparently one of the men she would meet with often. Marvelous.

Her stomach growled to her even as she considered begging off dinner. She could cite exhaustion from the day and fogginess from her travels, and grab some food to go on the way back to her apartment. But even as the thought came to her, the other two men turned in her direction. To bow out now would be more awkward than staying. After all, in a group of five, she would hardly even have to speak to him.

Her discomfort wasn't easy to swallow, but she allowed herself to be pulled over to the table by an overzealous Mike. "Hey, fellas. This is Miss Ava Harper." He gestured to a man with rosy cheeks and chestnut-colored hair carefully combed to one side. "That's Theo."

Theo nodded, his brown eyes keen but affable as he assessed her in the benign way one would a building.

"And that's Alfie." Mike pointed to a red-haired young man with a smattering of freckles that dotted his fair skin like stars. A flush blossomed under the constellation as he ducked his head.

"And James." The Englishman slid into the space beside her and flashed a grin. "To whom you've already had the pleasure of being introduced."

It wasn't much of a pleasure, but Ava didn't say as much aloud. He pulled the seat out for her, which she sank into with a nod of thanks. Then, to her chagrin, he occupied the chair directly beside her, near enough that she detected the light, clean scent of whatever soap he used.

"We've been anticipating your arrival," Alfie said in a soft, shy voice.

"You should have seen Sims's face when he came back from the airport after learning A. Harper was a woman." Mike slapped his knee with a laugh and pulled a chair over to add to the end of the table. "Just like Peggy said."

"Are you librarians as well?" Ava asked the other two, pointedly ignoring James.

"We are," Theo replied. "I've been with the London Library for nearly a decade now, and Alfie started this past fall. From what I hear, your research skills and ability to unearth difficult information will be integral to our success."

Ava fingered the menu, both proud and slightly vexed that she had a reputation preceding her—especially when such a thing would lead to expectation. "So long as I can figure out exactly what I'm doing."

They all laughed.

Irritation prickled at the back of her neck despite her forced smile. She'd had way too much coffee and not nearly enough food to be dealing with yet another joke whose punch line she didn't get.

Alfie regarded her with an observant sympathy and his mirth swiftly faded. "Unfortunately, your country has a habit of sending your people over quite woefully unprepared."

"I can show you around, if you like," James offered. "Where to go to find what, which contacts are necessary to obtain certain information."

Ava glanced back toward the empty counter of the restaurant. Surely the waiter should be approaching them now. When she returned her attention to the table, she found everyone watching her expectantly, waiting for her answer.

She waved her hand dismissively. "You don't need to take time from your day on my account. I'm sure you have plenty more to do than show me around Lisbon. And Mike can assist with whatever I need…?" She tried to keep the desperation from her face as she looked to her coworker.

"Actually, that would be a great help, James." Mike tugged at his tie, so it hung slack from his collar. "I've been swamped."

"Smashing." James cast a victorious grin in her direction. "We can start tomorrow morning at nine."

Before she could put up any sort of protest, the waiter miraculously appeared. James held up a finger to command his attention. "Super Bocks all the way around."

Once the man disappeared to fulfill the order, James turned to Ava. "You do like beer, don't you?"

True to his word, James was outside Ava's apartment at exactly nine in the morning the following day, making her almost regret providing him with her address the previous evening.

"We can't start a day in Lisbon without *bica* and *pastéis de nata*."
He extended his arm toward her in a gallant show of chivalry.

She didn't accept and certainly didn't need the support, having opted for a more sensible pair of shoes. "This isn't a date."

"I would never presume." James pulled his elbow back to his side with a haughty expression belied by the glint in his eye. "I was merely being a gentleman."

She adjusted her green hat with the white flowers, a careful adornment to the pale yellow shirtdress she wore. "I would be fine with tea as well, if you prefer."

He paused at the street as a trolly whooshed by, clanging its bells. "We're in Portugal, we'll do *bica*."

"Technically, tea is very Portuguese," Ava replied.

"Ah, yes, because of Princess Catherine of Braganza wedding King Charles II in the seventeenth century?" James strode onward as the traffic created a gap.

She studied him curiously. "Yes, actually."

"Don't be so surprised." He led them around a corner. "I know British history as well as any lad. And while it is kind of you to consider my tastes, I do quite well with a stiff cup of coffee in the morning. I'll also wager you've not had the chance to try the Portuguese sort yet."

Of course, he was right.

Mirrors and polished wood adorned the walls of the café they entered, and the counter sported a massive metal contraption that hissed and gurgled. A waiter approached as they slid into the chairs at a small table for two near the open entrance. The April morning was crisp with a light breeze that ruffled Ava's skirt against her knees. James spoke to the man in perfect Portuguese with a speed that left her unable to grasp even a single word from her very limited vocabulary.

It was not often she found herself in a position where she did not speak the language.

"How long did it take you to learn Portuguese?" she asked, envy as green as her felt hat seeping into her tone.

"You'll pick it up quickly enough." He crossed his left ankle over his right knee and looked out at the city slowly coming to life on the street. "I should apologize for how we met. I meant my chiding to be in jest."

"It didn't come out as one."

He gave a warm chuckle. "Clearly."

The waiter brought out a small plate of pastries with browned custard at their tops and two porcelain cups no taller than Ava's pinky.

"Stiff" was exactly the right choice of word for *bica*, which packed the entire force of a cup of coffee in a tiny mug with a bit of tan foam frothing at the top. Apparently, James required the edge taken off his drink as he added a helping of sugar so generous that it would make any ration-following American cringe.

Ava was far more impressed by the *pastéis de nata*. The delicate pastry on the bottom cradled the custard center, the tops toasted golden.

"Do you know the history of these?" James indicated the food.

Ava lifted one from the plate, surprised at the heft of such a small treat. "Monks used the egg whites to starch their laundry and had yolks aplenty left, which is perfect for custard. They were the first ones to bake *pastéis de nata* and they've been a part of Portugal ever since."

"Bravo." James lifted one and tapped his to hers in mock cheers before taking a bite.

The custard was warm and thick, the crust crisp and the entire concoction was perfectly sweet and delicious.

"If you like this, you'll have to try the baked goods the refugees sell." He laid some escudos on the table.

Ava pulled up her purse, but he shook his head. "Today is on the Crown. Has your research led you to the Livraria yet?"

"I don't know where anything is, but I'm always game for a book store." She stood from her seat and swung her bag over her shoulder, ready to embark on the guided trip through Lisbon.

"You needn't worry," he reassured her. "You'll become well

acquainted with it all soon enough. As well as the other book-shops in Portugal and the news kiosks and stationery shops." He held up a hand to the waiter in a departing farewell and led her from the café.

She joined him. "Stationery shops?"

"You'd be surprised how many gems are lurking among stacks of paper and cups full of pens." He continued looking forward as they walked, but spoke in a lower, quieter tone. "It would appear the police have caught on to your presence."

"What?" The word came out in far more of a squeak than she'd anticipated.

"Don't look," he warned.

She stopped midturn and fixed her gaze straight ahead as he did.

He winced slightly. "Maybe laugh or something of the like as though I've said something witty. To keep from being so terribly obvious."

Ava forced a laugh, grateful she had not fully turned around before his warning. She really was a terrible spy.

"If anyone asks, you are simply an American librarian." He maintained the pace he'd set before, but now the casual stroll seemed far too slow with the stares of the police burning at her back.

"But I *am* an American librarian," she hissed.

He winked. "Exactly." Indicating to a store located at the corner of a large building, he beamed. "Ah, here we are now."

Blue and white tiles adorned its walls, a tradition in Portugal known as *azulejos*. Were they not being followed by the police, Ava might have leaned closer to examine the glossy surface to see if pin-sized holes dotted the glaze suggesting the tiles were made prior to modern advancements.

She must still have paused somewhat as James's hand caught the crook of her elbow and half tugged, half nudged her into the shop. Inside, a man wearing a dark suit looked up. His stare lingered too long to be innocent before he turned to the side. Apprehension prickled over her skin.

"This way." James led her deeper into the store and her entire focus became the splendor that was the Livraria Bertrand.

Books layered wooden shelves from the ground all the way up to the striated-brick ceiling rising above them.

"We can only look for now," James cautioned. "Best to wait until we lose our new friends before engaging in any purchases."

Ava scarcely heard him. Her gaze was running over the outward facing spines, the titles all in Portuguese. Even still, her mind tried to coax out the meanings, as if she could will them into translation. Suddenly, she could read the words and realized they were in French. And then in German. Then several more she could not discern. Polish, perhaps?

In that moment, she had a profound desperation to not only be fluent in Portuguese, but also in Polish. And Russian. And Greek. And all the other languages that appeared to be represented on those crowded shelves of the Livraria.

Her fingertip settled on a copy of *La Séquestrée de Poitiers* by André Gide, one of the many authors whose works the Nazis banned from Germany. A sudden need to draw the book to her chest nearly overwhelmed her, to cradle it to her bosom protectively like a child. To keep the text from those who would let flames lick over it until the pages curled into brittle, flaking ash. She pulled its edge to bring it toward her from the stack. The books were so tightly packed together that several others on either side flexed forward as well, nearly tumbling from the shelf.

"Did you hear me?" James asked.

She just managed to catch the remaining books and ease them back into place after liberating Gide's works. "What?"

"We ought to consider an abrupt departure." He slid a discreet glance toward the man at the door.

She hugged the novel. Surely one book wouldn't compromise them.

James lifted a brow. "You look like a girl with a lost puppy you're going to ask if we might keep."

"There, you're wrong." She turned toward the front of the store. "I'm a grown woman with my own money who intends to purchase this to save it from the bowels of Nazi destruction." She marched to the register and bought the book. As she did so, the man perusing a shelf near the door caught her attention again. His hair was perfectly combed back, his perceptive gaze bright.

Awareness of his focus settled heavily over her as she was led to various shops through Lisbon despite not encountering him again. But like a painful memory, her thoughts drifted back toward the incident a thousand times over.

For the remainder of the day, she heeded James's prudent suggestions. By the time he saw her home that evening, Ava was entirely drained. She scarcely recalled what he said to her as she pushed through the building's large green door.

A dark apartment greeted her; a rare phenomenon she hadn't experienced with her roommates in DC who always managed to make it home before her. She clicked on the lights, tucked the book she'd purchased alongside her small collection from home, and collapsed into bed.

She wasn't sure how long she slept when an insistent pounding jarred her from her sleep. Dazed and bewildered, she shoved from her bed and stumbled into the living room, her steps visible by the glow of light lining her door.

Outside in the hall, Portuguese was spoken in aggressive tones, followed by a hollow thump and a man exhaling in an agonized grunt. Someone had been struck.

She clapped her hand over her mouth to keep from crying out herself and tiptoed to the peephole. Breath held, she silently slid the metal cover from the hole and leaned closer to peer through.

Men in black suits exited through the door at 102. They did not bother to look around to ensure they weren't seen; they weren't careful to be quiet. They didn't care who knew of their presence.

Between two men, hanging by his arms with his bare feet dragging behind was the neighbor who had asked Ava for the copy of *Time* magazine. His hair was mussed and his head lolled toward his left shoulder.

The men slammed his door closed behind them and carried him down the stairs, beyond the scope of her vantage point. Shaking, she released the metal disk to return over the peephole as she backed away from the door, her bare feet silent. Her knees trembled, and she leaned against the wall for its support, her hands clasped over her frantically thudding heart.

Suddenly a vague memory of her own words rushed back to her.

You should have seen how happy my neighbor was with a copy of Time.

What a fool indeed. That statement had been said without thought, without the realization of what kind of repercussions it might have. She hadn't thought Lukas was a Nazi, or that the Portuguese secret police might follow her, or that they might be in league with Lukas. But then, she hadn't thought it such an issue to give away a copy of an American magazine.

There were only two apartments on their floor of the narrow building—hers and his. The PVDE would have no difficulty discerning which belonged to the man she'd given the magazine to.

And now her foolish words meant to fill in a gap of awkward conversation had caused her neighbor to be arrested in the middle of the night. Perhaps she might be next.

The thought was enough to jolt her from her fear-induced paralysis. She slid down the wall to the floor and hugged her legs to her chest, staring at the door.

If they came for her next, she did not want to be caught unaware.

SIX

Elaine

The following day, Elaine found herself in the company of Josette, Nicole, and Denise once more—this time to deliver the clandestine newsprint. They had already stuffed the papers into benign-looking envelopes with recipients' addresses on them—without the names, of course. While it was generally best to memorize details, some bulk deliveries such as newspapers required at least the location.

Elaine took her sorted stack from the pile on the table and slipped them into the false bottom of her shopping basket, just as she had been shown.

"Josette and Nicole will go together. You come with me," Denise said.

The noonday bells chimed, their cue to leave. Elaine followed the ladies down the stairs. Josette and Nicole melted into the myriad other Frenchwomen strolling the streets of Lyon with their shopping baskets on their arms. Then it was Elaine and Denise's turn, going in the opposite direction. No one would question their baskets, as they were a common sight these days as women remained desperately hopeful they might come across a store with a new shipment of food.

Despite the distribution of ration cards, there was no guarantee those items would be available for sale. More often than not, their allotted rations were impossible to find on any given day, particularly meat. And of the goods that could be found, the prices were exorbitant by comparison to the prewar years, some even soaring as high as four times what it cost previously. The recipes Elaine had been forced to learn were dismal, ones centered around Jerusalem artichokes and rutabagas or trying to stretch a tin of sardines or a single egg as far as possible.

Meager though they may be, the very thought of those meals tugged at the empty place within her that was never filled, and her stomach gave a snarl of complaint.

With the force of her will and regular practice through the duration of the Nazi occupation, Elaine now was able to push aside her hunger. She was even able to set aside her unease at her new task and focus wholly and completely on what needed to be done.

Denise and Elaine worked carefully through Bellecour, a dangerous neighborhood in the heart of Lyon where the Nazis congregated. The Germans lingered in the streets with a comfortable leisure the French themselves could no longer enjoy, sitting in cafés and sipping from porcelain cups filled with precious coffee, milk, and sugar. They marched into the finest hotels, which they draped in swastikas, and they sullied what had once been fine food with the foulness of their gluttony and hatred. Even the beauty of the art in the museums was made ugly by their constant presence.

However, Bellecour was also the area where Elaine had lived in her time before joining the Resistance.

While curiosity and a longing for the normal lured her toward the familiar street, she refrained from temptation and let Denise deliver the newspapers instead.

Elaine had bid farewell to the little apartment over two weeks ago after having spent so many months there resenting the home. It remained locked up, her key nestled behind a loose brick in Etienne's building. Now, after sleeping in various locations and safe houses, she found herself yearning for the simple life she once shared with Joseph.

Suddenly she was glad she had allowed Denise to take the deliveries on her former street. Not only to ensure Elaine wasn't recognized, but also to spare her the pain of being so near home. How she missed the cool, smooth sheets of her own bed, the couch cushions that were worn soft with age, and the way the bathroom held a spice of Joseph's aftershave long after he'd left for the day.

Gritting her teeth, she forced herself to march down Rue Sala, keeping her gaze purposefully turned from the street placard of Rue du Plat that implored her to turn into its embrace.

Denise regarded her carefully when they met up once more to return to the apartment near the bookstore in Croix-Rousse.

"Our life is not an easy one." Denise adjusted the false bottom of her basket, securing it over the hidden area once more. "That was probably difficult for you, being so near your former home."

"I managed." The aroma of cooking food from restaurants serving the Nazis flavored the air with a savory aroma that made Elaine's mouth water.

It was impossible to smell and not recall the taste. Ham with the edges slightly crisped, the meat tinged black in spots where the heat seared a second too long.

It was impossible to recall the taste and not crave it with every ounce of her longing to sink her teeth into that tender morsel, free of gristle and stringy fat. Just lean, juicy meat.

"You did muster through," Denise replied. "That spirit is why you are a good fit for our group. Nicole is as well."

"And, of course, Josette," Elaine amended, pulling her focus from food she would never have and back to the conversation at hand.

Denise shifted her basket to her other arm and nudged Elaine to the other side of the street. "This is not a life for a woman like Josette."

No sooner had they crossed over the pavement than a group of Nazis strode by where Elaine and Denise had been. Their gray-green uniforms were immaculately pressed, belted at the waist and studded with medals, their hair cropped short beneath caps. Easy conversation flowed between them in their harsh tongue, without worry of retribution or concerns like hunger and cold.

Their carefree nature stoked the ire burning inside her, making it flare brighter. France had flopped on its side like a dog begging for its belly to be scratched, its people practically eager to conspire with the enemy for scraps of food.

The Nazis would face their day of reckoning. They had to.

Boys scuttled beneath the table the Germans had abandoned at the café, picking up the butts of their cigarettes. Their grandfathers likely waited at home for the gifts, eager to rewrap the remaining bits of tobacco. Rumor had it, Hitler detested smoking and ordered his men to forego cigarettes and alcohol, both of which the Nazis consumed in mass quantity regardless. The one order they were apparently willing to defy.

The men's plates had not yet been cleared, most with food decadently left to be thrown away. Bits of potato. Chunks of fat-riddled meat sitting in pools of gravy. Thick slabs of white, soft bread.

A sharp hunger pain stabbed through Elaine. All that was available in bakeries now was brown in color, with an unpleasant texture and a bland taste that usually left the burn of indigestion in its wake.

She should look away as they passed, to avoid tormenting herself with the unfinished feast. The Germans had swept through France like locusts and used their gluttony as another means of oppression. Letting her gaze linger on the food was one more way they won.

But no matter what Elaine told herself, she could not tear her eyes from the plates. Especially not after she caught sight of a greasy smear of butter glistening atop an airy piece of white bread, its crust flaky and half sodden with juices from the meat.

She swallowed, but her mouth continued to water as they walked away from the laden table. At her side, Denise had also gone silent, no doubt plagued with the same infernal ravenous hunger as Elaine.

One intrepid boy cast a cursory glance before swiping the buttered bit of bread. Elaine couldn't blame him. Even she was tempted. Not that it was worth the chance of being arrested or possibly shot.

This was why turning her focus on the Resistance was preferable to sitting home alone where boredom allowed the hunger to gnaw at her. With the café—and the distraction of food—behind them, Elaine could center her attention on more important matters.

Like why Denise had looked at her as she had the previous day when Elaine had mentioned Joseph. Her strange expression had been why Elaine had been eager to join her, but the familiarity of Bellecour had rattled Elaine and then there had been the food the Nazis left behind...

She leaned close to Denise as though sharing a tidbit of gossip for the benefit of anyone watching. "I want to free my husband from Montluc. Will you help me?"

Denise turned to her, slowing her pace but not stopping lest they call attention to themselves. Her expression remained as lugubrious as it had been when Elaine first mentioned Joseph's imprisonment, a somberness Elaine had not forgotten. The memory of it picked at her thoughts every time she lay in the unfamiliar bed of yet another unfamiliar safe house and waited for sleep to claim her.

In truth, it was that look that had prompted Elaine to go to Denise with this request. If anyone could estimate the likelihood of freeing Joseph, it would be Denise.

"Montluc is not a place easily broken out of." Denise glanced about as she spoke. "Do not confuse your bravado for stupidity."

Elaine stiffened at the derisive comment. "What would you do if your husband was in prison?"

"I certainly wouldn't put him further at risk by going to him with a false name and trying to break him out." She lifted a brow and gave a little shake of her head. "You will both end up shot. You are better off leaving his freedom to Gabriel, who has the devil's own luck."

Gabriel. Etienne. No matter what name he went by, she was correct. He had not only emerged from the Great War unscathed, but always managed his way out of scrapes now as well.

Elaine was not so swiftly placated. She stared deep into the other woman's dark brown eyes. "I don't think you would do that."

"No," Denise confirmed. "But I am better trained than you."

Her words stung, but sadly they held truth. Denise possessed a steeliness in her gaze, her time with the Resistance evident in the way her hands never once trembled and how easily she ignored the Nazis walking past.

They climbed a steep set of stairs and the conversation between them dropped with nothing more left to be said.

Elaine's shoulders relaxed as they turned into the Croix-Rousse area of Lyon where pockmarked walls were littered with peeling signs and alleyways held the lingering odor of rubbish. There was less fear of patrolling Germans who seldom deigned to walk through the workmen's district.

When Elaine and Denise entered the apartment, Nicole and Josette were already there, gathering envelopes for the second half of their deliveries.

"*Bonjour,*" Nicole called cheerfully. "We have this last bit and we are finished." Her gaze lingered on Elaine for only a moment when she declared, "What if Josette goes with you, Denise. And, Elaine, I'll show you around here."

"I would like to become more familiar with the area," Elaine agreed.

After they refilled their baskets, she allowed Nicole to lead her back down into the streets. The other woman wore an outfit similar to her last with a navy skirt like the day before, this one falling slightly below the knee, which she paired with a blue-and-white-striped shirt that called attention to her slim waist. With her red lips and nails, it was yet another clever application of the French tricolor. This time Elaine was certain the color choice was not by accident.

Of the four of them, Nicole always upheld a fashionable appearance. Denise was utilitarian in her attire with simple dresses and flat-soled shoes. The style was not much different from Josette's who was partial to neutral colors that kept her from standing out, her only adornment a small gold cross that lay on a glittering chain below the hollow of her throat. Elaine's own manner of dress was up to the standards of any housewife, her clothes clean and well-cared for despite the soap shortage, and her hair curled and swept back at the sides.

Nicole strode through the street with confidence, her wooden heels striking the ground with sharp clicks that made Elaine recall the song "Elle avait des semelles de bois" ("She Had Wooden Soles") that Henri Alibert put out after rubber and leather became too hard to find. The catchy tune called out the *click-clack* sound young women made as they sauntered down cobblestoned streets in their ration-altered footwear.

"You mustn't let Denise bother you." Nicole waved Elaine into an alleyway where they slipped into a covered alcove and discreetly deposited several envelopes into the wall of letterboxes. "She's like that with everyone." Her voice lowered to a whisper. "I think that's how it often is with communists."

Elaine's brows rose in surprise. Communists were some of the first groups cleared out by the Germans sent on trains and never seen or heard from again. A shiver slid down Elaine's spine. "Denise is a communist?"

Nicole nodded as if it didn't matter at all. "She's managed to evade the Nazis thus far. It is why she operates underground as we all do."

The openness with which Nicole spoke set a nervous edge to Elaine's newly sharpened skills as a Resistant, and yet such candor was also refreshing after Denise's stifling presence.

"What about you?" Elaine asked as they pushed back out onto the street.

Nicole bit the inside of her lip. "My brother and father both fought for France and were captured by the Bosche. Now they are in work camps in Germany. The sooner this war ends, the sooner they will be free."

"What of the *relève*?" Elaine recalled the many posters she had seen about a year prior, asking women to labor for the Nazis in order to release the imprisoned French soldiers. For every three women who volunteered to go to Germany, one man would be released back to France.

After Lucie disappeared, Elaine had insulated herself from the idea of ever forming another friendship, not when trusting people was so dangerous. Not when losing a dear friend hurt so terribly. As a result, Elaine knew no one in such a predicament as to need to participate in the *relève* program until now. In thinking of her own aching loss with Joseph still in prison, she could imagine the enticement would be tempting.

Nicole scoffed, the sound harsh and indelicate. "My sister joined the *relève*. The Germans promised she would be near her husband, but I doubt that vow was ever honored. Regarding the French soldiers who are returned to France, they are all old and injured. Young, healthy men will not be freed until the war is over and now she is trapped in Germany, working for the Bosche until then."

It was so very like the Nazis to use a woman's love for her family to coerce her into building the very weapons and machinery that would continue to keep them enslaved.

"Here." Nicole handed Elaine a stack of envelopes. "These are all to be delivered up there."

Elaine gazed up, up, up at the winding incline of Montée de la Grande Côte, a narrow street with narrower walkways on either side, shimmering with moisture from a recent rainstorm. The brown buildings stretched up to the sky, and stone-arched windows from an ancient time dotted their bland faces. Elaine hastily slid the pile into the secret bottom of her basket.

By late afternoon, the task was complete, and Elaine descended the steep slanting road, careful to ensure her shoes did not slip on the damp cobblestones. The sheen of sweat on her brow chilled in the cool breeze, a glorious reprieve after her exertions.

Her stomach pinched with hunger and in those moments of quiet reflection, she found her thoughts once more drifting to the plates of food left behind by the Nazis earlier that day. Denise and Josette arrived at nearly the same time as Elaine approached the bookshop. Suddenly, a Nazi officer emerged from a nearby café, his back ramrod straight with authority as he glanced about the street.

Josette gave a little squeak and tripped on the walkway. Though she staggered and her free arm flailed, she was no match for the wet surface slicking the pavement and she careened to the ground.

As her basket struck the cobblestones, its false bottom fell open and an envelope tumbled out.

The German looked toward the commotion, his gaze going sharp.

All at once, Nicole appeared in front of Josette and waved to the Nazi. *"Pardon, monsieur."*

His expression shifted from one of suspicion to one of interest as he strode confidently toward her. Nicole sashayed closer, blocking Josette and allowing the flustered woman the opportunity to reclaim the spilled envelope and snap the scared rabbit look from her face.

The German did not notice. "*Oui*, madam? What may I do for you?" he asked in broken French.

"Do you have a light?" Nicole drew a slim silver cigarette case from her handbag.

"Of course." The officer pulled a box of matches from his pocket, the contents giving a delicate rattle.

Nicole opened her case and giggled. "Do you have a cigarette as well? I appear to be out."

The charade was almost laughable if Josette's slip had not put them all in such terrible danger.

Without hesitation, the Nazi presented an orange pack of Sulimas to Nicole. He shook two sticks free, lighting first hers, then his own.

Nicole pursed her red lips and slowly blew out a billow of gray smoke. *"Merci, monsieur."* After gifting him with a winning smile, she sauntered away, leaving him staring after her.

In the time the exchange took place, Josette managed to collect herself and walked with Denise past the apartment as Elaine crossed the street, keeping her distance so as not to show they were together.

"Ah, Elaine, there you are, *ma chérie*," Nicole called out, waving her hand as though they were simply friends meeting up with one another.

She took Elaine's arm and led her in the direction Denise and Josette had gone, stopping when they rounded the corner. The street was empty, with most women having returned home after a day of waiting in queues for their rations. It would be Elaine's turn to queue for food tomorrow, a familiar task she was already dreading.

Nicole sucked in a long inhale of the cigarette, her eyes closing in pleasure. But as she exhaled a stream of smoke, she stubbed it out on the bottom of her shoe.

"Such commodities are too valuable to waste," she explained. "I send as much as I can to my brother and father in Germany. My hope is that..." Her lips pressed together as she pulled out her silver case and slid the black-tipped cigarette into the empty container before replacing it in her handbag. "I hope the things I can spare will be enough to get them through this awful war."

"I'm sure it will." Elaine knew nothing of the camps where the soldiers were imprisoned, especially when she had been left ignorant in the months Joseph forbade anything pertaining to the Resistance. But the wounded plea in Nicole's gaze compelled Elaine to offer some reassurance, even such a simple platitude.

Nicole pulled up her sleeve slightly to reveal a small mole just over the crook of her elbow. "My father has the same." She smiled fondly as she gazed at her own arm. "Do you see the heart?"

It was a bit of a stretch to make out a heart in the mole, but when the idea was put in one's mind, the shape became recognizable. Elaine nodded. "I do."

Nicole's smile broadened, and she pulled the sleeve of her sweater lower to cover it once more.

"I can't believe you are still using that tired, out-of-cigarettes trick." Denise shook her head with playful censure and joined them with a downtrodden Josette at her side.

The worried expression on Nicole's face brightened into one of confident victory, like a light switch being flipped on. "It's only tired if it stops working." She patted her purse. "I assure you, it is still quite effective." With a wink toward Elaine, she added, "It works every time."

Denise cast her eyes heavenward as they found the entrance to another doorway and traversed a series of traboules and stairs. Eventually, they returned to the courtyard of Rue d'Algérie. A quick glance in the letterbox revealed a small message addressed to Elaine. She snatched it out, her heart doing a flip. Once in the safety of the apartment, she ripped open the envelope, recognizing Etienne's slanted writing straight away. Unfortunately, the note was not about Joseph as Elaine had hoped.

You will be staying at 21 Rue Lanterne with a "cousin"—second floor, door on the left. I'll send your things.

If he was sending her things, it meant she might remain at the new location longer than a night. Etienne had generously stored Elaine's clothing at his apartment so she could travel from one safe house to another unburdened while more permanent lodging could be found. One small bag of effects and an outfit or two was less cumbersome than trying to haul all her belongings around.

The idea of not having to be on the constant move to a different apartment every evening brought more relief than she had expected. Sleeping in a new place always required a period of adjustment, to grow used to the sounds and scents around her. The perpetual rotation of new beds was enervating and left her mind fogged with exhaustion.

While the long-term place to stay was welcome, she could not help the ungrateful thought that she would have preferred for the missive to be good news about Joseph's release instead.

That evening, she trudged up two flights of stairs to her new accommodation, anticipating a stark room, scarcely furnished with a lumpy bed. As usual.

She rapped softly on the door and tried to ignore the spiced fragrance of cooking food and her growling belly.

"*Oui?*" a voice called.

"It's your cousin Elaine."

The door swung open to reveal a delicate blond woman in

a black dress with a hem that fell to her slender calves. Her lips twitched into a smile that her deep brown eyes did not reflect. "Ah, yes, Elaine. It is so good to see you, cousin. Please do come in."

It was a charade Elaine had played over many times if the safe house was occupied, maintaining a persona of friendship or relation. Though in many cases, the places she stayed were empty, the nights filled with silence and loneliness. Not that her hosts were ones for conversation, but at least having a presence there made the space feel less bleak.

Her current hostess opened the door, displaying a modestly adorned apartment that appeared home enough to make Elaine's chest ache for her own. The aroma of food was stronger inside than it had been in the hall. Sausage, perhaps?

Elaine breathed in discreetly, savoring the scent as if she could fill her belly with smell alone.

Yes, definitely sausage.

"I'm Manon," the woman said. "You will be staying with me for some time, I understand. Please, follow me to your room."

Elaine nodded in thanks and did as instructed. They walked through a living room with a blue velvet couch, heavy matching drapes that most women would have made into a coat by now, and a piano adorned with framed pictures. Manon opened a door to a single, narrow room, the fireplace hearth empty, but the bed layered with a thick, downy blanket. A box lay near the door, likely Elaine's clothing Etienne had sent earlier.

"I will have some supper for you in the kitchen once you are settled," Manon said. "I expect you are hungry."

It wasn't a question. Aside from the Germans, everyone was hungry these days. None of Elaine's previous hosts had been so considerate before, leaving her to eat whatever she managed from the black market or to acquire in the interminable queues.

"I had bread earlier," Elaine lied. The woman's limbs looked frail as bird's bones and her neck was so slender, it seemed almost incapable of holding up her head. Elaine would not take her food.

Manon folded her arms over her chest. "The pope has deemed it is no longer a sin to purchase items on the black market. He knows we are all starving." The corners of her mouth quivered, as if she were trying to offer a smile, but failed. "I have prepared for your stay."

Elaine blinked at such generosity. "I will be there momentarily, thank you."

Manon departed the room, leaving Elaine to settle.

The box did indeed contain Elaine's clothing, the items faded, worn and fewer in number than at the start of the war due to the ration. However, the experience of once more having her belongings tucked into the drawers of an armoire rather than stuffed into a sack like an old peddler was still enormously pleasant.

On her way out of the room, Elaine paused to look at the photos on the piano. A man and woman smiled back at her from most of the pictures while several others were of a baby boy with dimples in each of his cheeks and a swath of dark hair brushed over his round head. A moment passed before Elaine recognized the woman as Manon. Her body was fuller in the images, but more than anything, the difference was in the wide grin that left her eyes sparkling with joy.

In former days, Elaine would have asked after the man and the baby, especially with their absence so apparent in the quiet home. But those were conversations of the past. The less she knew of her hostess, the better.

Elaine straightened and went to the kitchen where Manon had laid out a plate for her with two fat lentil sausages, a few boiled rutabagas, and a narrow slice of bread. It was a veritable feast. Elaine ate everything but the bread—not because she was full, but to tuck away to have delivered to Joseph at the prison the following day. She wasn't sure such parcels made it to him or not, but it was still worth the effort to try.

Her husband weighed on her thoughts constantly now—the worry at how much longer he would be kept at Montluc, the anticipation of seeing him once more. Even as she climbed into the pillowy bed that night and folded the thick blanket over herself, she begrudged her own warm safety as she imagined what he must be enduring.

Denise claimed Elaine didn't have the training to manage a way to liberate Joseph. Unfortunately, she was not wrong, but surely Etienne would. Once Elaine had finished whatever task awaited her the next day, she would reach out to demand he do anything necessary to expedite Joseph's freedom. And she would be there to help.

SEVEN

The PVDE did not come for Ava, but nor did her neighbor return after his arrest. The next day stretched into one week and then another and then another still. Unfortunately, no movement ever came from the apartment across the hall.

Light caressed her shutters, squeezing in through the cracks to inform her of the coming of dawn. Before she even so much as dressed, she crept to her front door and glanced out the peephole as she did every morning and strained to listen.

Yet again, no sound came from her neighbor's apartment.

There was an aching need in her to ask after him. However, the fear of having her folly laid bare, especially to the likes of Mr. Sims, made her hold her tongue. Her boss's foul disposition had not brightened in the past weeks of their acquaintance despite her finally realizing what necessary publications were being sought after by their department to aid the war effort.

The stillness of her apartment was maddening and worried at a thread of guilt she could not cut away. For the first time since having read *Crime and Punishment*, she now had a modicum of understanding how Raskolnikov's fugue state could stem from the burden of his misdeeds, chipping away at the back of his logical mind until he was desperate to tell someone.

Anyone.

Even the likes of James.

Ava straightened away from where she leaned over the peephole. James hadn't been about since that first day, and she longed to inquire as to any suggestions he might offer in unearthing her neighbor's whereabouts. And just how culpable she was in his disappearance. However, now that she actually wanted to see James, he was nowhere to be found.

With a resigned sigh, she backed away from the door and readied herself for the day. In her time in Lisbon, she had fallen into something of a routine with her morning list of tasks and set out into the city with a messenger bag slung over her shoulder for her literary haul. The PVDE's curiosity in her faded several days after her neighbor's disappearance, having finally lost interest in her boring habits, and she did not mourn the absence of her unwanted entourage.

She approached the kiosk near her apartment first and waved at the young man behind the counter. "*Bom Dia*, Alfonso."

The newsstand owner grinned at her and asked how she was doing in Portuguese. It was with him she practiced her fledgling grasp of this new language. Her answers still came out slowly and with great concentration as happened with a new tongue, but experience taught her that once those new words began to seep into her thoughts, fluency would soon follow.

Not only did Alfonso let her cut her teeth on her rough Portuguese with him, he also saved the best papers for her. Like many in Lisbon, his memory ran far back to the Great War when Portugal had not been neutral, and the Germans were their enemy. A Royal Air Force pin glinted beneath the lapel of his jacket when he leaned forward, a show of support for the

Allies that many wore, though not all had to hide it from their patrons as he did.

There was always a multinational crowd waiting for Alfonso to pull up his shutters, not only to grab the newsprints of their enemies, but also to sweep away any reading material they did not want their adversaries to see.

Once there was a lull in his customers, Alfonso pulled a stack of papers from beneath his register. She accepted the pile and hastily pushed them into her messenger bag, but not before catching sight of the newest edition of *Das Reich* stating "The Most Dangerous Enemy" in a headline across the top with a picture of Jews peacefully holding up a Star of David and what appeared to be the list of commandments. Disgust for the Nazis curdled in her stomach.

"*Obrigada*, Alfonso." She passed over a wad of escudos, carefully precounted and folded neatly in half.

He put two fingers to his right eyebrow and offered her a mock salute as she strolled toward Rossio Square. As she walked, she jostled her messenger bag in an attempt to wriggle the pile in better. The thing was an inch too small, and nothing ever seemed to fit in correctly.

The owner of a kiosk beside the ever-popular Nicola's café was a curmudgeon who scowled at every nationality and disposition, equal to all in his displeasure for humanity. But he had a knack for somehow procuring *Der Angriff*, a licentious German publication laden with anti-Semitism that ironically and sadistically claimed to be "for the oppressed against the exploiters." Ava had stopped skimming that paper for possible war details and did not envy those whose jobs it was to scour the mendacious text for clues on Nazi war tactics.

She thanked the owner who grunted in return and strode back through the narrow doorway edged in lovely white and blue tile work that appeared to be from another century. Already café tables and chairs were pulled out into the warm sunshine where men and women lounged beneath a fine, opaque mist of cigarette smoke. Though she had only been in Lisbon for just under a month, it was easy to discern the refugees and guess what stage of their flight they were in.

The newly arrived were initially rigid, vigilant, their gazes darting this way and that. Then, caught in the pull of the waiting cyclone, they relaxed back into their seats, resigned to the interminable drag of time looming ahead of them. And then there were the agitated, lucky few whose fingers drummed with impatience, their visas in order and tickets for passage secured as they watched the calendar for the day creeping ever closer of a ship that may or may not arrive.

When she had grudgingly flown on the plane to Lisbon, she had not appreciated what a luxury it was. The prices to depart from Lisbon were so exorbitant that even some of the wealthy refugees could not afford them.

Regardless of which circle of hell they found themselves twisting through, the story of their struggles was written on every person. It was in the gauntness of their cheeks and the slender, frail appearance of their limbs. It was in how the children were too quiet, made solemn by the witness of images none should be subjected to regardless of age. It was in the clothes they wore, some too fine for the setting, others threadbare but clean, washed and worn daily without any other alternatives. And it was in the jewelry that adorned the women with ropes of necklaces dripping from their slender necks, bracelets layering their bony wrists and heavy jeweled ear bobs tugging at their lobes.

A few of those children perked up as Ava arrived, remembering her from her previous interactions with them. She pulled four books from her bag, purchased with her own money from Livraria. There was a Polish children's story with brightly colored drawings of animals in a forest, a similar one in French and two larger texts in French and German for slightly older readers.

The gifts were received with a joy that was echoed in their

mothers' watery thankful smiles that superseded all language. Though small, Ava knew the importance of those stories. They were a friend in a foreign, lonely place, a liberation of one's mind from the prison of circumstance, an escape from life's most brutal blows. Losing herself in stories had gotten Ava through leaving her world behind to live with Daniel after her parents' deaths, following Jo March's lead with the example in *Little Women* of finding solace in the written word.

Her final stop was the Livraria Bertrand where she basked in the musty scent of old books that tickled the edges of her memories of the Rare Book Room. There were always treasures to unearth within the homey Portuguese shop—German manuals, a Hungarian map, a pamphlet of some kind in Japanese, all items she quickly purchased.

Once her publications were properly acquired, she leaped aboard a tram that traveled the carved grooves in the street toward the American Embassy. The lines of refugees were always there, just as Mr. Sims had mentioned, and each time, those pleading faces struck Ava anew. The only difference between her and those queued was that she had been born an American. The visa in her desk had been a right of her birth and to the refugees in Europe, it was such a glowing privilege.

The unfairness of it dug into her every time she saw them. The worst part was, there was nothing she could do to help.

Once inside, Peggy always met her with a smile, Mr. Sims remained little more than a closed door, and Mike was always there to add a quip or two. That day, however, Peggy practically ran to her, flapping something resembling a card in the air like a strange one-winged bird. "You got mail." She thrust the envelope with a red *V* stamped on it toward Ava.

"Looks like it's from your brother." Peggy leaned closer. "I didn't want to infringe on your privacy, but Mike insisted I make sure it wasn't from a beau."

Ava only partially believed Peggy's protest but accepted the letter with thanks regardless. Peggy was the well-meaning sort who knew everything about everyone. It was expected and, in some cases, could be helpful.

"Don't you tell Mike I told you he asked." Peggy's mouth made an "O" of surprise as if she'd just realized the risk.

"I won't," Ava promised.

Peggy glanced around, then said conspiratorially, "But do you have one?"

Ava simply chuckled by way of an answer. There was absolutely no man she was writing to aside from her brother. Romance was hardly on her mind, and the last thing she wanted was Mike thinking she was available.

Messenger bag laden with fresh news at her side, Ava left Peggy and carried the envelope to the back room. Microfilm certainly played its role in the war, not only in the capture of documents to send back to DC, but also in communication between troops. Correspondence to and from soldiers were captured on microfilm for easier transport, then reprinted at the message's desired location. The paper was less than half the size of a normal page and didn't leave much room to be verbose, but the messages were printed clearly and were precious no matter their appearance.

It was the second letter she'd received from Daniel, and it filled her chest with a warm ache that was both painful and pleasant all at once. The love and gratitude she held for him, for all he'd sacrificed for her, the hurt of missing him, the fear for his safety. Such emotions were always there with her, tucked in a special place in her heart, and they rushed to the forefront with each letter, heightened and renewed.

The message within was similar to his last. Her eyes read the words, but it was Daniel's rich timbre in her ears.

To give it all in a single, censor-friendly statement: I'm well with enough food to eat. I hope you are as well. You know I don't like you

putting your neck on the line too, but I still have to say it: I'm damn
proud of you. Stay safe and keep your nose clean. I love you.

-D

She slid the paper back into the envelope with a smile. Setting it tenderly aside, she removed the bounty from that day's collection and set to work photographing each one. In the beginning, she'd tried to read what she captured on microfilm, but eventually learned their role was one of speed. Their task was not to absorb all the information themselves, but to get as much to DC as was possible where it would be analyzed by the government for potential use against the Axis.

Truth be told, it could be terribly boring. Open a newspaper, adjust the image. Click. Wind the machine to ready the next exposure. Repeat. On and on through the course of the afternoon.

She still skimmed through the documents for anything she thought might be pertinent to bring to attention for those poring through their compilations in DC. It wasn't only newspapers and periodicals, but texts and manuals and other foreign reading materials they could find, but had thus far not uncovered anything. Through it all, her thoughts continued to wander back to the refugees—not only those in line wrapping around the embassy, but those in Rossio Square—languishing in wait of escape.

Surely there was more that could be done for them.

It was that thought that finally propelled Ava toward Mr. Sims's closed door. She rapped upon the glossy surface and waited to be called in, which eventually came in a gruff, irritated tone.

All the carefully practiced, articulately prepared words fled her mind, chased away by his uninterested glower. "I'd like to do something to aid the refugees," she announced.

He didn't look up from a folder in front of him. "You are helping already. By sending information to DC. Acquiring these international publications opens the door to intel we might not receive otherwise."

"There has to be more we can do."

"The Allied forces, specifically America, are putting a lot of funding behind Lisbon for the refugees. As are local Jewish communities." His tone was flat, bored by his own speech. "The World Council of Churches, the Portuguese Red Cross, the International Red Cross, the Quakers, plus a bunch of acronyms like JDC, USC and COMASSIS and more that I don't remember." He flicked the file closed and gave a weary sigh as he dragged his gaze toward her. "Miss Harper, you're here to gather newspapers and books. Everyone doing their job makes the war end faster." He lifted his palms up to indicate that his lackluster presentation was finished.

She nodded and closed the door, chastised but undeterred, for surely there truly was more she could do.

Several days later while perusing the crowded counter space of a stationery store, she caught sight of a familiar face—one she had been anxious to see.

"James," she said as she approached.

He turned and smiled. "Miss Harper, seeing you is a delightful surprise."

"I've been hoping to run into you," she said quickly, perhaps too eager in her delivery, for his smile widened further still. Either way, she needed his assistance with figuring out what happened to the man from her building. And possibly even with helping the refugees.

"Then I'm quite glad to be found." He inclined his head with a slight bow, his manner cordial. "What can I do for you, Miss Harper?"

She glanced at the store whose shelves were crammed with merchandise, but whose aisles were empty of patrons, save one elderly man who appeared to be comparing various sheets of paper. Though she had only been in Lisbon for three weeks, she already knew every building had ears and eyes and every seemingly innocent person could very well be a spy.

"Would you mind if we spoke outside?" she asked.

"By all means." He indicated she should walk first and so she did, leading him from the small shop.

Outside, the May sky was cloudless, the sun fully ablaze. Being in the middle of the walkway with the heat glaring off the limestone gave one the sensation of being in an oven.

James squinted up before turning his attention back to her, a sheen of sweat already beginning to glisten at his brow. "Have you tried *capilè*? It's wondrously refreshing, and I happen to know a lovely place not far from here."

He offered her his arm, but she gave a slight shake of her head. His shoulder lifted in a shrug that indicated he was not offended, and together they strode down the blazing limestone-and-basalt-checked patterned walkway in search of a cool drink. Away from those who would listen in on their conversation.

"Is something wrong?" he asked when they were fully alone.

"Yes." A torrent of dreadful emotions whirled in her stomach at having to say it aloud. "I…that is…my neighbor… I…" She paused, frustrated with herself. For not being able to say what she needed to, for having to be in this situation at all, and for her own egregious folly from the start.

He drew her toward the side of the street bathed in shadows. The sun's rays immediately lost their vigor and a cool breeze swept over them. "Take your time, Ava."

She inhaled deeply. "Do you remember that Nazi from the kiosk?"

"I do."

"I mentioned my neighbor…" The burden of her guilt stacked upon her like boulders, crushing the breath from her lungs. "How he asked me for a copy of *Time* magazine that I happened to have and how enthusiastically he'd received it. The next day, the PVDE came to his apartment where they beat him and abducted him in the middle of the night." She looked away, too ashamed to see James's reaction to her harmful mistake. "It was so stupid, I know, but I... I am so awkward sometimes and there was this gap of silence in the conversation... It just popped out."

"Taking a copy of *Time* magazine from you is not illegal in Portugal," James replied in so gentle a tone, she glanced up at him.

His face was earnest, his eyes lacking the censure she so justly deserved. "In fact, there are several people who help the Allies obtain certain periodicals as trade for *Life* and *Time*. The PVDE was there for some other reason."

"Yes, I know that," Ava said. "About the people who receive those magazines in exchange for helping us, I mean. But what if my mentioning him put the focus on my neighbor and that revealed whatever it was that caused his arrest?"

"Then you are not at fault. His actions were his own."

If only it were so easy to brush aside an inflamed sense of guilt.

"Don't you think the timing is strange?" she pressed. "I mention it to the Nazi and the next night, my neighbor gets arrested?"

Two men strode toward them, heads lowered beneath their fedoras, their identities obscured. James gently put his hand to Ava's lower back and guided her forward, away from the strangers. "Come, we shouldn't linger in the street."

Ava allowed herself to be nudged onward, but she would not drop the topic so easily. "I want to find out what happened to him."

James's brows shot up. "From the PVDE?"

"Yes."

"Ah, here we are." He stopped in front of a blue-and-gold kiosk and ordered two *capilé*. The watery red drinks were served on ice with a neat lemon curl resting atop the liquid.

Ava accepted her cup with a nod of thanks and took a sip.

The drink was light and refreshing with a delicate grassy note, a hint of orange blossom, and the slightest whisper of citrus.

"Interesting, isn't it?" James asked. "It's made from maidenhair leaves."

"The fern?" Ava thoughtfully regarded her *capilé*. The glass had begun to sweat, leaving a frosting of condensation over the smooth surface.

He nodded and drank some of his, the ice cubes lightly clicking against one another as he did so. "Isn't that fascinating?"

"It is." Ava narrowed her eyes slightly. "Are you trying to distract me from what I was saying about my neighbor?"

"Absolutely." He lowered his glass. "Anything involving the PVDE is terribly dangerous. They would not take kindly to you inquiring after their business."

She gathered as much based on their brutal treatment of her neighbor when they arrested him. A shiver rippled down her spine.

"I feel responsible," she said miserably.

"You are not."

"And I wouldn't be asking about the police, only the man who disappeared."

"I can ask after the man for you, but even I won't goad the PVDE beast." He drained the last of the drink as though the matter were resolved.

"What?" She shook her head with a frown. "No, I refuse to let you take the risk for me. I merely wanted to know where to start."

"And I refuse to allow you to take such an unnecessary risk yourself." He tilted his head. "It appears we are at an impasse, Miss Harper." He studied her for a moment, his eyes neither green nor blue, but an interesting amalgamation somewhere in between. "Give me some time?"

Before she could protest, he lifted his hand to stop her and continued, "Two weeks to gently poke around and then we can reevaluate."

She drank from the glass and contemplated his offer. "Will it put you at risk?"

He shook his head.

"All right," she agreed reluctantly. "But if I was involved with his arrest and he's being held somewhere, we have to help."

"Let me see what I can find first."

In the distance, church bells tolled the hour. She would need to return to the embassy soon to begin the arduous task of taking picture after picture of various newspapers, magazines, and books.

"But nothing dangerous." She shifted the messenger bag at her side where the corners of periodicals jutted out.

He watched her struggle with a slight curve of his lips. "I swear it." He held out his hand for her empty glass. "And I think you need a larger sack."

Yet another attempt to distract her. She gave him her cup. "One more thing…"

"Only one more?" he teased with a grin.

Heat flushed over her cheeks. She *was* asking for quite a lot. "I want to do something to help the refugees. I thought you might suggest…?"

A somberness touched his eyes and his smile melted away. "Allow me a few days."

She nodded and tried to suppress the nettle of her forced dependence. In the past, she had always done the digging herself, flexing the acumen of her own ability to research. But this was a new world filled with new rules and going against any of them could tip the precarious scale of neutrality in a country that was allowing Americans to be there.

With that thought in mind, she had no choice but to bide her time and wait.

EIGHT

Elaine

The sky was overcast with a drizzle too light to require an umbrella, but substantial enough for the chilly dampness to seep into one's bones. An ominous sensation, Elaine's mother used to say with an exaggerated shiver and a laugh. But then, *Maman* was always cold.

It had been two long years since Elaine last saw her parents. They lived in Combs-la-Ville, a rural area about an hour by automobile from Paris where her father was the town's doctor. Elaine hadn't relished the quiet life there and had always been dazzled by Paris's grandeur. Its lure had been irresistible after she completed her courses at *lycée* and set off on her own. As their only child, they had not been eager to see her leave, but supported her decision out of love for her.

Based on the last letter she'd received from her parents, the petrol shortage hindered travel between towns, which meant the supplies generated in Combs-la-Ville were likely to remain there. Certainly, food was more abundant in farming communities than in the city.

Elaine could only pray their circumstances remained tolerable. Sending and receiving letters into the occupied zone had become difficult previously, and once the Germans swept through the rest of France, it became truly impossible.

Nicole greeted her outside the apartment, wearing her usual tricolor combination with a shopping basket that held several bundles of rutabagas with the leaves still dangling from their purple-and-white bulbs. Along with those, she added a wrapped loaf of bread from her basket to Elaine's. "We are picking up explosives to bring back into the city," Nicole whispered. "These will cover them to avoid any suspicion."

"Explosives?" Elaine asked in surprise, unable to keep from imagining those precarious objects bouncing about in her basket.

"There was an airdrop last night from Britain," Nicole continued softly as they strolled down the cobblestoned street. "And we're nearly out of what we need."

If one read the newspapers—both clandestine and otherwise—the Resistance running low on explosives seemed entirely possible considering how many random bombs burst through the city. The explosions wounded some Germans and killed even fewer. However, the destruction to factories and transformers was generally significant and created more than a few issues for the Nazis. As a result, Lyon's prefect was constantly extending hours of their curfew for several days as punishment, as if they were wayward children warranting parental censure.

But every occurrence of blasted concrete and twisted metal that stymied Nazi operations was a boon to the Resistance that chipped away at Germany's defenses. Eventually the Nazis would fall.

Now she was an integral part in the gathering of those explosives.

She stood a little taller.

They passed a queue of women in front of the grocer. "I

found out more about your husband as well," Nicole said once they were out of earshot.

Elaine's heart squeezed in anticipation, though she couldn't discern if the visceral reaction was one of hope or trepidation. She had left a message for Etienne with Manon asking him to meet with her later that day to insist on helping with Joseph's liberation. The days were growing insufferable with thoughts of her husband trapped in a cell. There had to be something she could do.

"What have you heard?" Elaine asked, breathless with anxiety.

Nicole glanced about as they stopped to wait for the tram that would take them to the outskirts of town. People strolled by, appearing preoccupied in their own concerns and lives, but one never knew who listened. Not only plainclothes Gestapo, but also the Milice—the French secret police—and, of course, collaborators, ready to turn in their fellow Lyonnaise for an extra loaf of bread.

A network of dark tram wires was draped overhead like a web where they bobbed and swayed in the light breeze.

"Pierre assisted with creating identity cards, as you know." Nicole spoke closely as though sharing a bit of titillating gossip. "His knowledge of chemistry was essential in creating stamps as well as removing them from the official documents."

Elaine couldn't help but smile. Yes, that sounded like Joseph.

The act of forging the slant of someone's handwriting to create a new identity card wouldn't have been enough for him. He would have persisted in his endeavors until he could not only remove ink from stamps but replicate necessary inks too.

"From what others say, your husband is very intelligent," Nicole said.

Heat spread over Elaine's cheeks. "It's one of the reasons I fell in love with him."

The tram stopped before them, and they climbed in through

the open doorway before sliding into the hardback seats amid the other passengers.

"Neither one of us was looking for a relationship." Elaine's shoulders relaxed with the relief of having a normal conversation where their words didn't have to be discreet. "I was determined to maintain my career as a secretary, and he had the importance of his research at the time. We never even went out to dinner together. We just talked so often that we both accidentally fell in love."

Nicole smiled. "That sounds unconventionally romantic."

"It does, doesn't it?" Elaine chuckled to herself as she relived those precious moments in her mind. "One day I was explaining why I never intended to marry since I was earning my own living, and that's when he asked me to be his wife. He said I could keep my job, and he would sign whatever was necessary for me to obtain a bank account that he would never interfere with. And I said yes."

Joseph's brown eyes crinkled at the corners as he smiled at her, his pleasure at her agreement to marry him apparent.

"You should take me out to dinner," she teased.

"Are you hungry?"

"Not now." Giddiness tickled through her, making her laugh as she threaded her hand into the warm crook of his elbow. "I mean the way other couples do."

"They do that to get to know one another." He bowed his head toward her, and the light spice of his aftershave left her with a heady sensation. "We already know each other." He studied her then as he did a calculation. "Yes, dinner." The suddenness of an answer fully realized. "I'll make reservations."

It was the first of many wonderful Parisian meals shared together with richly flavored sauces, tender meats, and confections that were as artistic as they were decadent. Meals Elaine could not think of now, not when the twist of hunger in her belly was so sharp.

But Joseph had kept his promise to her, never prying into her bank account. Not even after forbidding her involvement in the Resistance.

"Ah, the rain has cleared," Nicole said beside her, startling Elaine from her reverie. "The weather will be ideal for walking."

If anyone had asked, that was why they had come to the outskirts of Lyon, to take in the scenery together.

The tram slowed to a stop, and they disembarked, arm in arm as they made their way toward the forest. After so long in the bustle of the city, the silence of the woods around them was exquisite and called to attention the unfettered chirp of birds and the tranquil rustle of leaves.

"Have you seen the Maquis before?" Nicole asked.

"I've only ever heard of them." Elaine considered the foliage with a new perspective, half anticipating traps to be laid and men to be standing in the shadows with archaic weapons brandished. "Are they as wild as the Nazis claim?"

Nicole led the way in a pair of flat-soled shoes. "They live out here, but they are not as barbaric as they are made out to be." She pushed a strand of blond hair from her face, frowning. "Many are very young."

Elaine tilted her head to look up at the flecks of golden sunlight glinting through the copse of trees. It would be so easy to close her eyes and pretend like the world was right once more. That Joseph was home waiting for her, that they had enough food in their bellies, that Lucie had never been dragged away by the Nazis, and that they all lived without the constant presence of fear.

"Denise's husband is out here," Nicole said in a quiet voice despite them being alone. "It is why she does not come. She is afraid she will never leave if she sees him."

Elaine nodded in understanding. If she was in Joseph's arms with his familiar comfort embracing her, his gentle voice in her ears, the scent of his aftershave surrounding her, it would be like tearing her soul apart to walk away again.

A figure emerged from between the densely crowded trees, his movements so silent, he was more an apparition than a man. At least until they were directly in front of him. His shirt and trousers were dingy and stained with dirt, both so large, they hung from his lanky frame. The soft fuzz of dark hair showed on the crest of his chin and along his upper lip. Nicole's assessment of the Maquis being very young seemed correct.

These weren't men, but boys. Ones who ought to be planning out their education and doing foolish pranks together. But then, theirs was a world where many had to grow up before their time; where childhood was ephemeral, shadowed by the daily dangers they faced.

The boy grinned at them, oblivious to the harsh odor of his unwashed body, and handed a heavy bag to Nicole that was filled with paper-wrapped parcels. "Gifts for the Bosche." He withdrew something from his pocket. "And a little something for you as well."

Nicole gasped and took the small package from his hand. "Chocolate," she breathed. "You divine man, thank you." Without hesitation, she leaned forward and placed a kiss on his gaunt cheek, leaving a blazing imprint of her red lips.

The young *maquisard* flushed so thoroughly, the lipstick on his skin all but disappeared.

But Nicole did not appear to notice as she turned her attention to the wrapped bricks of explosives. "Come, Elaine, let's divide these between us to carry back."

They made quick work of the stack, so both of their baskets were weighty with their bounty and concealed beneath the rutabagas and bread.

Nicole nodded to Elaine as they stood once more. "This is Pierre's wife."

The boy's eyes widened from under the overgrown shag of

his dark hair. "It's a true honor to meet you. Pierre is a most impressive soldier."

Elaine smiled her thanks, unsure what to say to such a claim. Joseph an impressive soldier?

The boy backed away, his awed stare still fixed on Elaine before he disappeared into the woods as mysteriously as he'd arrived.

"Pierre also trained the Maquis." Nicole hooked the basket over her arm and picked at her thumbnail where the red varnish had chipped at the edge. "Apparently his aim is perfect, and he knows the best ways to set up explosives."

Elaine said nothing as she tried to wrap her mind around Joseph in the wilds sans his ever-present tweed jacket as he taught men how to fight. The more she learned about the hidden parts of her husband, the greater she longed to see him, to ask questions and hear him share what amazing feats he accomplished with the Resistance.

"Here." Nicole broke the bit of chocolate into two pieces and handed one to Elaine.

In the prewar years, such a morsel would scarcely constitute a bite. But now, it was a veritable sugar feast. Elaine popped the confection into her mouth, letting it rest on her tongue and luxuriously melt, sighing aloud with delight at the rare and unexpected treat.

The two women walked in silence for a spell, chocolate sticky in their mouths, sunlight dappling their path, and their baskets laden with food and explosives.

Elaine swallowed the last remnants of the gift as she considered everything she'd been told about her husband. "How have you found out so much about Pierre?"

Nicole lifted a shoulder in a delicate shrug and stepped around a patch of thick, wet mud. "I asked, as I said I would."

"Is there anything else you've discovered that you haven't told me?"

The other woman pressed her lips together and shook her head. An action done with too much haste.

"What is it?" Elaine asked tightly.

"Nothing." Nicole quickened her steps, as if she could be spared from saying more if she was fast enough.

A shadow fell over them as the sun was blotted out by thick, dark clouds. "Please, Nicole. If someone knew of your brother or father, wouldn't you want to know?"

Nicole slowed somewhat, but kept her focus directed on the unseen trail she followed. "Your husband was arrested by Kommandeur Werner," she said after a long pause.

Elaine stopped walking. She may not know as much as the other Resistants, but she knew the name. All the men under Hauptsturmführer Klaus Barbie were cruel, but Werner was exceptionally so, one who relished in the brutalization of his captives. Stories of his torment had reached even her ears and plucked at the darkest nightmares of her imagination.

If Joseph had indeed been taken by Werner, he would doubtless have been treated without mercy all this time. The chocolate in Elaine's stomach was suddenly too rich.

As pleasant as the break from the city had been, she wanted to be back in Lyon to meet with Etienne. No longer was Joseph's rescue to simply get him free of Montluc and back in her arms, but to spare his life.

The tram seemed to travel slower back to the heart of Lyon than it had out to the outskirts.

Nicole put a hand over Elaine's. "I shouldn't have told you."

"I'm glad you did." Elaine looked at her friend as the familiar scenery of Lyon rolled by at an unnervingly languid pace. "You would want to know too."

"I would," Nicole agreed. "But knowing does not always bring a sense of peace."

Her statement wasn't incorrect. The newfound detail buzzed

about in Elaine's brain like an overactive bee as her thoughts darted in all directions. She felt foolish, not only for her blind trust but her willful ignorance. She should have suspected he would not just be locked in a cell, but also subjected to torture.

They exited the tram amid a flurry of other passengers and made their way to Croix-Rousse, traveling in silence as Elaine inwardly berated herself. Perhaps it was the consuming manner of such a distraction that caused her to miss seeing the Nazi officer in the street as she turned around the corner.

An officer in the poorer area of Lyon was never a good sign. Had she noticed him, she would have found an alternate way back to the apartment. But she didn't catch sight of the man in his crisp uniform and polished boots. At least, not until Nicole hissed her name.

By then, it was too late.

"Halt," the man said in a hard voice. "Papers."

Elaine froze in surprise at the abrupt order, her thoughts flying to the pounds of explosives dangling at her side.

Nicole grasped her arm in a moment of quick thinking and jerked her backward, the force nearly wrenching her burden free from her hand. Their feet clacked over the cobblestones as they rounded the corner once more, pushed through a door, and slid into a passageway.

The light was dim as the door closed behind them, and the expanse of a traboule tunnel stretched before them.

Outside, the sharp strike of jackboots indicated the Nazi had not given up his pursuit.

Nicole eased off her wooden-soled shoes and Elaine did likewise. The stone floor underfoot was cold and damp, but it would be the only way to move quietly and hopefully without being caught.

Barefoot with her footwear dangling from one hand and the basket of explosives in the other, Nicole slipped down the passageway with Elaine following behind her. They entered a small courtyard where stairs ran upward and two paths went in opposing directions.

Nicole darted right without hesitation and descended to a lower level. The stone steps were smooth as sea glass and depressed in the center, worn down from decades of use. The women encountered another split with options to climb up to the apartments above, go down to the floor below or continue down the long, narrow hall.

A door banged open in the distance, making them both jump. Crisp footsteps came immediately after; the stark echo was as keen as a threat. Nicole led the way down the passage to where several doors lined either side with a shadowed alcove in the corner. She waved for Elaine to join her as she crouched into the darkness.

Elaine sank down beside her friend. Once she stopped, the racing of her heart caught up with her and left her discreetly dragging in a greedy inhale. The ground was like ice, and damp grit clung to the soles of her feet. She longed to brush at them but didn't dare move.

The traboule was one Elaine hadn't explored before and one clearly important to make note of for future use. It was far more prosaic in its craftsmanship than the one on Rue Saint Jean, utilitarian in its construction with an unsettling stench of stale urine she didn't care to consider at present.

The sharp footsteps continued to echo around them, closer and closer until they stopped just above where the women hid. They shrank back until the chill of the unyielding wall behind them seeped through their jackets, as if they could melt into the stone.

Only an hour before, they had walked a sun-spattered path through the forest, indulging in chocolate and a carefree discussion.

Elaine squeezed her eyes shut as the scrape of a boot heel grinding into the filthy floor screeched in the silence. Finally, after an eternally long moment, the officer strode away at a clipped pace, leaving them with only the thundering of their own racing pulses.

Only when the bang of a door slammed in the distance did the tension in Elaine's shoulders ease somewhat. Nicole rummaged around in her purse and dislodged a long strip of fabric. Without a word, she wrapped it around her head in a fashionable turban.

After tucking the loose end into the secure base, she pulled a second piece of cloth free and reached for Elaine.

"What are you doing?" Elaine said as loudly as she dared.

Nicole coiled the fabric over Elaine's hair with practiced expertise. "Making us look different." She withdrew a tube of lipstick and angled Elaine's face upward to apply the red with little more than a stub of makeup. "Now we won't be recognized."

The lipstick was thick and greasy on Elaine's lips with a strange waxy scent. Together, they hefted their laden baskets and exited the traboule from a different door than they had entered. There, they encountered a gloriously empty street.

Once more in daylight, Elaine could see Nicole was correct. Had the Nazi coincidentally wandered to the exact location they emerged, he wouldn't have found them familiar, not with Nicole's flaxen locks bound within the dark turban. She looked older, more sophisticated.

"You should wear your hair up more often." Nicole tilted her head as she considered Elaine. "And lipstick. Red lipstick."

Elaine's cheeks went hot. "I've never been the fashionable type."

"Why not?" Nicole smirked. "It's the only defense we women are allowed. Men have their guns and their medals. We have our charm and our cosmetics." She let her basket sway in her hand as she began to walk.

The rutabaga greens had long since wilted over the wicker

edge and now swept side to side with the motion, like sea grass in the lazy roll of ocean waves.

"I don't have the extensive wardrobe you do," Elaine protested, walking beside the other woman.

"Do you mean my skirts?" Nicole did a little twirl, so the navy skirt belled out around her knees, and winked. "I have one with six different hems that are easily adjusted to alter the length. So, you see, it only appears I possess more clothes."

While the trick was ingenious, Elaine could never imagine herself like Nicole, wearing her confidence like the season's most *à la mode* accessory, flirting with men for distraction, knowing the effect of her own prowess.

Elaine shook her head at such a possibility. Her own style was more classic than stylish and had suited her in country life as well as in Paris and now in Lyon. "I'm not glamorous. Not like you."

Nicole tossed her a conspiratorial smile. "I had unfortunate features as a youth, ones I grew into with the help of my sister. She was always so chic." Nicole's gaze lit with the memory of happier times. "Odile showed me how to put on my makeup, which fashions suit my figure, how to walk and what to say. Were it not for her, I don't think I ever would have had any confidence."

Elaine couldn't imagine Nicole being anything but lovely and self-assured. "Your sister must be very special to you."

The joy on Nicole's face faded. "She is. I long for her to return soon. As well as my papa and my brother." A hardness glinted in her crystal blue eyes. "Once this war is over and we've defeated the Bosche."

Etienne was in the apartment on Rue d'Algérie along with Denise and Josette when Nicole and Elaine arrived. His brows rose in question when he saw Elaine in her turban with bright red lips.

"A Nazi officer tried to chase us, but we escaped through a

traboule." Elaine resisted the urge to swipe the brilliant color from her mouth as she set her basket on the table. The absence of its weight immediately left her arm limp with exhaustion.

He frowned.

"Oh, don't fuss." Nicole waved off his reaction before he could protest. "We made some stylish alterations to ensure we wouldn't be recognized and departed from a different door. There is nothing to fear."

Etienne clenched his jaw. "I need to speak with Elaine."

She nodded, glad for the chance to finally talk to him. "In the kitchen."

He let her lead the way to the opposite side of the apartment where they would be afforded some privacy. His swift appearance to her request surprised her but left her grateful regardless. Especially after what she'd gleaned from Nicole.

She closed the door behind him. "There has to be something we can do for Joseph. This has gone on too long. I want to be involved."

Etienne stared hard at her.

"Don't tell me there isn't anything I can do." Irritation elevated her volume. "We have explosives." She forced herself to quiet her voice as she stated this important information, aware that all walls in France had ears. "We have men and women who are willing to help one another. We have everything at our fingertips, including British support. There has to be something I can do."

Etienne swallowed.

The fuse of Elaine's patience ran short, cut off by all the what-ifs crowding into her mind. What if they didn't get to him in time? What if he died before he could be freed? What if she never saw her husband again?

Her outrage exploded in the slap of her hand on the table with a force that jarred her bones and left her palm tingling.

"Say something, and don't you dare tell me to be patient again. I won't accept it. Not again."

"He was removed from prison today." Etienne scrubbed a hand over his hair, mussing what had been neatly slicked back.

Such a statement should have elicited relief, but the haunted expression in his dark eyes made wariness tighten through Elaine like a warning.

"Where did he go?"

Etienne's fingers dragged down his face, distorting his features until his hand dropped. "They said he left with baggage," he murmured.

She shook her head. "With baggage? What does that mean?"

He blinked, as if surprised to see her there. "At Montluc, if you are sent with baggage, it means you are going to a work camp. If you are sent without baggage…"

She lifted her brows for him to finish.

"Death."

The word hung in the air between them, like something alive and agitated and poisonous.

"He is at a work camp?" she repeated with relief. "That is not so bad. I can still send him food, I can—"

"Not where he is going. Elaine, this is a different kind of camp. One meant for those actively defying Germany, not for captured French soldiers."

She froze, her body numb. "What are you saying?"

"We can't help him."

Tears burned her eyes, and the turban on her head was suddenly too tight. Too heavy. She felt ridiculous in the waxy red lipstick and the fashionably wrapped cloth, a painted clown on the receiving end of the worst news of her life.

She had never even written to Joseph to tell him she was sorry, how much she loved him. Tears blurred her vision. Etienne reached for her, but she backed away from his hand.

"You told me to trust you," she said in a harsh whisper.

Hair had fallen into Etienne's face, and he raked it back with a growl of frustration. "I thought we could free him."

Several sheets of paper lay on the counter, and a single, desperate idea came to Elaine. "You need to get a letter to Joseph."

"I don't know that I—"

She spun on Etienne. "You promised you'd get him out. I don't care how you manage it, but you will get this message to him." The first drawer she yanked open did not contain a pen. Nor did the second.

One appeared before her, pinched in Etienne's tapered fingers. "Make it small," he cautioned.

With shaking hands, she tore off a corner of the paper and wrote out the only thing that mattered.

Dearest Joseph,
I'm sorry for everything I said. I love you always.
-Hélène

Those few precious words took up the entire scrap. She folded it in quarters, the edges blurring from tears. With the note held out for Etienne, her gaze locked with his. "Do not let me down."

He nodded, but even as he did so, his worried expression belied his fear that he would once again fail.

NINE

Ava

While Ava waited for James to investigate the matter with her neighbor, the nip of her unease began to grow teeth. Finally, the afternoon arrived for them to meet at Café A Brasileira in Chiado. Her nerves drove her to arrive early. Instead of merely waiting in the opulent café with its warm notes of ochre and red and gold throughout, brass fixtures polished to a reflective shine, she went to the long wooden counter and ordered coffees for them both.

In the time she'd been in Lisbon, she'd come to appreciate the petite cup of powerful coffee, taking not only one in the morning, but also in the afternoon as was an endemic habit of the locals.

The two saucers and small cups obtained, she settled into a high-backed chair facing the door and freely poured sugar into her *bica*. Even as the white grains spilled into the tan foam atop her coffee, the action felt wrong. Almost gluttonous.

But in Lisbon, there was no restriction on how much coffee she could drink or sugar she could consume. Bakery windows were filled with delectable pastries glittering with sweet granules sprinkled liberally over their surface and baked into gooey delicious custard centers.

A lean, masculine figure in the doorway caught her attention. She sat up in her seat, *bica* forgotten as James crossed the black-and-white-checked marble floor.

He took off his fedora with a pinch of his middle finger and thumb and settled it on the empty spot beside him as he slid into the chair opposite her. "His name is Diogo Silva. He runs a newspaper kiosk by Praça Luís de Camões."

Ava knew exactly the square he spoke of with its statue of Luís de Camões, Portugal's greatest poet. "So, he needed the magazine to sell then?" she asked. "For the Germans or Japanese to purchase as we do?"

James poured his usual helping of sugar into his *bica*. "I'm not certain, but his kiosk has been shuttered since he was taken."

Ava pulled in a breath. "What happened to him?"

He shook his head and held the handle loop of the tiny cup in his fingers. "I don't know, but your conversation with the Nazi had nothing to do with his disappearance."

Ava nodded and masked her uncertainty with a sip of coffee. James had put himself at risk enough for her sake. Any additional digging would need to be done on her own. At least now she had a name and a place to investigate and could hopefully Dick Tracy her way to getting more information.

Another familiar figure entered the café, one with prominent ears. Ava waved to Alfie and slid over so he might join them.

He rushed forward, his face paler than usual as he thunked into the vacated seat. "I just heard…"

"What's happened?" James asked.

Alfie put his palm to his brow, his long fingers curling like marble against his red hair. "Leslie Howard is dead."

"Leslie Howard?" Ava repeated the familiar name and the recognition quickly followed. The actor who had played Ashley Wilkes in *Gone with the Wind*. She hadn't seen the movie herself, but all of its stars had been plastered on every newspaper and magazine for months before and after the film's release.

Alfie's hand slid down his face and fell into his lap. "It happened just this morning." His chin quivered, and Ava couldn't help but notice how very young he looked in that vulnerable moment. "In the most awful way."

"Alfie," James said, his voice level and confident. Much in the way he had spoken her name to her the day they'd gone out for *capilé*, when he had promised to look into her neighbor's disappearance. "What's happened?"

"His plane," Alfie croaked.

Chills skittered across Ava's skin. "What about his plane?"

"The Germans...they shot it out of the sky." Alfie swiped at his large, brown eyes. "They attacked a civilian aircraft as it was flying over the Atlantic."

James's cheeks went red. "That's a war crime."

Ava held on to the table, both hands gripping the edge as if it might be the only thing keeping her tethered to the earth. Though her physical person was locked in place, her emotions spun her into another time when her parents had not returned from France.

That could have been her plane when she flew to Lisbon. That could be one of Daniel's at any moment.

Cold sweat prickled at her brow.

"Can you imagine?" Alfie said, his voice choked.

She could. She had. A countless number of times, transporting herself to the cloud-dotted expanse of endless blue sky when the turbulence gave way to violent, unforgiving jerks, that drop of the stomach as a rapid descent began. The screams. The terror.

"Enough." James's voice cut through her thoughts, and he gave her a concerned look.

Alfie touched her hand and she leaped.

"Forgive me, Miss Harper," he said in his gentle manner. "I didn't mean to upset you."

"Go back to the embassy," James said to his young colleague. "I'll join you soon."

Alfie nodded and cast another worried glance toward Ava. "I truly am sorry."

Any attempt to carve a smile on her wooden face to set him at ease was impossible.

"Ava," James said softly. "Are you well? Shall I call Peggy?"

The thought of Peggy seeing her thus was enough to snap Ava from her trance. She shook her head and swallowed the thick ache that swelled in the back of her throat. "Those poor people."

"Alfie shouldn't have been so detailed." James stood up and took the chair beside Ava. He rested a warm hand over hers where she still clutched the table. Her grip loosened under his touch and released the hard ledge.

"Are you sure you're well?" he asked again.

"My parents were killed in a plane crash when I was a girl." It was the first time she'd said those words aloud to anyone: killed in a plane crash. It was such a violent and terrible death, a wound in her soul that had never fully healed. "And my brother is a soldier, parachuting out of them all the time. Hearing about the attack today, thinking it could at any time be him…" Her throat tightened around the words, cutting them off.

"Ava, I'm so sorry." James didn't say it in that way most people did when they found out she was an orphan, in a detached, "sorry something bad happened to you years ago" sort of way. His eyes met hers with sincerity, and he spoke as though her parents' deaths had just occurred along with the doomed aircraft that morning.

The clatter of dishes and murmurs of conversation filled the space between them.

"Thank you," she said. "My brother took me in after. We'd

never been close as he was eight years older than me. We are now though."

"Yes, I imagine you would be."

"I am here for him," Ava said. "To do what I can to end this war. He's sacrificed so much for me. Too much." She touched her hand to her brow and found it damp with perspiration. "He always wanted to go to college, to be an engineer, but he had to take on a job to care for me. I wanted to go to college too, and when I finished high school, he told me he had enough savings for both of us to enroll."

Tears burned in her eyes. She didn't know why she was telling James all of this, or why she was even putting words to the ache inside her after all these years. However, once started, she couldn't seem to stop.

"When I left for Pratt, he joined the Army." Ava sniffed, and a handkerchief appeared in front of her. "There wasn't enough for the two of us. Only one."

She accepted it from James and wiped her nose. The cloth was warm from his pocket and held the faint familiar scent of him. "My brother is in this war because he sent me to pursue the dream we both wanted." She stared at the table, noting a small dark crack in one corner. "At that point, it was too late to undo any of it, so I continued on. Now I want to use everything I learned in college and after to help bring him home." She released a shaky exhale. "That's why I'm here."

Someone dropped a dish in the background, splintering upon impact with the marble floor. Ava glanced around the busy café whose patrons had tripled in the time since she'd arrived. The realization of having lost control of her emotions in so public a place hit her.

She lowered her face. "I'm sorry for bringing this up here. It's not the place, I know."

"I wasn't at all put out by it." James made a point of glancing at the surrounding tables and standing customers putting in their orders. "Nor was anyone else. I'm grateful you told me, in fact."

"I don't know why I did." Heat scorched her cheeks as she lifted her *bica* in the hopes its fortitude would bolster her own wits.

"Sometimes the things we hold inside of us need to be let out. No matter where you are or who you're speaking with." James smiled with a delicate understanding, then respectfully returned to his own seat and took up his cold coffee.

His finger tapped the side of the small cup, as if vacillating over something. "I have someone I'd like you to meet," he said suddenly. "What are you doing tonight?"

Her plans included a meal of grilled fish and settling down with *Wuthering Heights*. "My evening can be rearranged if I have good reason," she replied noncommittally.

"Perfect." He sat back in his chair. "I want you to come to Estoril with me for a dinner party."

Ava swallowed a mouthful of coffee and set her cup down, grateful to have been vague about her plans. "A dinner party? I haven't a thing to wear."

"Peggy can help you with that."

"I couldn't impose."

James chuckled. "I assure you, she would jump at the chance."

Ava cast him a skeptical look.

He put his arm over the back of the chair next to him. "You asked for something that might aid the refugees. The man I intend to introduce you to knows many people. And trust me, Peggy will be delighted."

"All right." Ava tilted her head, unconvinced and certainly determined not to beg if Peggy declined.

James, however, was right, Peggy did not say no. He was also correct when he said she would jump at the chance. She did so—quite literally—in a squeal of excitement that made Ava nervous at having asked.

Before Ava knew what was happening, she was hauled over to Peggy's apartment where her friend studied her with a discerning eye as she pressed a finger to her lower lip in thought. Peggy's place was small, like Ava's with far more color splashed about. Persimmon-colored roses sat in a bright green vase on the counter, a splay of aubergine pillows propped on a sunshine yellow couch that matched the drapes layered over the open windows.

"It's a shame we didn't have the opportunity to put your hair in pin curls." Peggy tsk-tsked. "But I'll see what I can do."

The next hour consisted of Ava's tresses being brushed and tugged, her face being powdered, prodded, and painted until Peggy stepped back with a smile and a proud nod.

"This really wasn't necessary," Ava objected, feeling rather silly.

"Trust me, you'll be glad once you're in Estoril. Everyone there is filthy rich, and the rules are much stricter."

"What do you mean?"

"I was nearly arrested once for wearing a two-piece bathing suit." Peggy rolled her eyes. "It was when I first arrived and had no idea policemen would be crawling all over the beach with their little rulers."

"Rulers?" The thought of policemen patrolling the beach to measure swimwear was far too ridiculous.

"Here's the kicker—I bought the suit at one of the shops in Estoril." Peggy threw her hands up in exasperation. "I had to practically threaten bodily harm for them to take it back."

"I think it's a good thing I don't have to worry about bathing suits."

Peggy chuffed a laugh. "You've got that right." She picked up a handheld mirror. "What do you think?"

The woman reflected back at Ava was elegant, older in a more sophisticated way. Her dark hair was gently rolled back from her face, her lashes darkened slightly but not to the point of being obvious, her skin smoothed by powder. In truth, she looked just like her mother.

Ava had been worried Peggy might try to turn her into something she wasn't, but instead Peggy had made her into the very person Ava had always secretly wished she could be.

"Oh, Peggy," she breathed. "Thank you."

Her friend beamed at her. "Now wait till you see the dress." She spun around so fast to retrieve the garment that her pink skirt belled out around her knees.

She was only gone for a brief moment before her footsteps echoed back down the unseen hallway. "I have to attend all sorts of events with the ambassador, so I have an extensive wardrobe. I'm glad to share some of these." Peggy emerged with a jewel green gown. "They're far too beautiful to leave hanging in a closet."

Ava pressed her lips together, careful not to muss the Victory red sheen on her mouth. "Is that silk?"

Peggy waved her hand dismissively. "It was bought before the war. As soon as you asked, I knew this was the dress for you with your dark hair and green eyes." She shifted the gown from her arms, and the length of it slid to the floor like shimmering liquid. It was beautiful, with a sash that tied in a bow at the cinched-in waist, the skirt loose and free-flowing. And it was strapless.

"I know," Peggy said when Ava's eyes caught the top of the dress. "Just put it on." She thrust it toward Ava and pointed down the hall.

Ava took the gown to Peggy's neat bedroom, as resplendent in jewel tones as the living area, and slipped the garment on. The fabric was cool as it glided over her skin, a sensation she hadn't expected to experience until after the war.

"It was bought before Japan joined the Axis," Ava reminded herself, smoothing her hand down the front as she turned to the full-length mirror. The cut was beautiful and fit her like it had been made for her, bare shoulders and all.

Peggy squealed from the doorway. "I knew it would be perfect. Here." She handed her a pair of long white gloves. "You can show off any skin you want so long as you have gloves."

Ava pulled them on, and Peggy gave a low whistle. "You are dazzling."

"Because of your exceptional skills and this gorgeous dress."

"Because you're a beautiful woman."

Ava's face went hot. Compliments always left her with an internally squirming sensation, like she needed to wriggle out of her own skin that always felt so unworthy of praise. "I don't know..."

"Well, I do." Peggy put her hands on her hips.

"I don't think I take compliments well," Ava admitted sheepishly.

"Most women don't. We always think we're not good enough." She lifted her shoulder, and the resignation behind it told Ava that even gorgeous, confident, say-whatever-came-to-mind Peggy was also plagued by the same monsters as Ava.

"Do me a favor," Peggy said. "When someone tells you that you look beautiful tonight—and they will—don't you dare bring my name up or offer any self-deprecating remarks. You look them dead in the eye and all you say is 'thank you.'"

James arrived in a sleek black car, wearing a suit fine enough to pass pre-ration standards with dark trousers creased sharply down the center, a fitted jacket and a starched white shirt. This look was complete with a black bow tie and a freshly shaved jaw that unhinged a few inches as she exited the building.

"You look stunning," he said, his eyes wide.

Her cheeks burned, and it was on the tip of her tongue to admit Peggy had polished her from a dull stone into something shiny.

Instead, she met his gaze and simply said, "Thank you."

He grinned.

"You clean up pretty well yourself," she offered truthfully.

The grin grew wider.

Ever the gentleman, he opened the passenger-side door for her, and she slid onto the smooth leather. He put the car into gear, and they took off, turning this way and that to navigate the streets of Lisbon. Soon the twists and turns of the city gave way to a long stretch of road and the ocean came into view, the moon glinting off distant waves like flecks of diamonds sparkling in the great, dark sea.

They didn't stop until they came to a brilliantly lit hotel called the Palacio, golden light spilling out from large glass doors. After leaving the car with the valet, he led her into the building with its glossy marble floors and windows that stretched up the length of the walls.

The architecture was as much a work of art as the painted canvases strategically placed throughout the building. It was beautiful and elegant, and she felt terribly exposed.

She resisted pulling at her strapless décolleté and, recalling what Peggy said about the gloves, edged them a little higher up her arms. Hopefully the police didn't have rulers for dresses, or the top of hers might result in a fine for indecency.

Music, delicate laughter, and conversation tinkled all around as finely dressed men and women chatted in the lounge area and inside the bar.

They were led to a ballroom with four large columns framing the middle of the room where the black-and-white-checkered marble tiles became a lovely pattern of circles and geometric lines. A long table was at its center, framed by chairs, its surface set with elegant gold-rimmed plates and white rose centerpieces that probably cost more than Ava made in a month.

All around them, people were engaged in light banter. Men wore dinner jackets and bow ties similar to James, while the women were like sparkling jewels amid all the black, their gowns brilliant in color, the sheen of silk as prevalent as the precious diamonds glittering on every neck, wrist and finger.

A delicate flute of bubbling champagne found its way into her hand, and the aroma of savory food wafted above the blend of costly perfumes that scented the air with flowers and musk. Ava took a sip from the slender glass and let the bubbles tickle down her throat.

Live music played at an ambient volume on one side of the room where the marble transitioned to a low-pile dark carpet and created an atmosphere that was as effervescent as the quality champagne.

It was surreal, this place where she suddenly found herself. One bathed in opulence and means, while so many in Lisbon lined up around the embassy and languished in front of cafés.

"Ah, James." A tall, slender man approached them, his thin dark brown hair swept neatly to the side, his skin tanned a healthy gold from the beach that was only a short walk from the hotel. "Who is this lovely creature at your side?" He spoke with a heavy French accent.

"This is Miss Harper." James indicated her first, then the man. "And this is Monsieur Blanchet."

The man took her hand and kissed the back. *"Enchanté."*

"Miss Harper is the woman I mentioned," James said.

"Ah, *oui*." Monsieur Blanchet nodded. *"La bibliothécaire américaine."*

The American librarian.

James casually lifted a finger at someone across the room. "Do excuse me a moment."

"By all means," Monsieur Blanchet said smoothly.

James glided off, leaving Ava with the Frenchman.

"It is a strange place, is it not?" he asked in French as he surveyed the room. "What is your opinion of all this?"

"It appears to be a glimpse of heaven amid the hell of war," Ava responded back in French.

"A glimpse?" His brows rose.

She had given offense. "*Pardon*, Monsieur Blanchet. I only mean that it is so small a place in times such as ours."

"Please," he said genially, "call me Lamant. And you are not wrong, so I am not offended. You needn't worry." He cocked his head. "This is a mirage, a shimmering promise on the horizon that disappears once you grow closer. I was curious on your opinion on the matter."

"Well, that's it exactly." Ava looked at the room again, at the hip bones jutting through silk gowns, at the strain lining men's smiles, at the heavy pours of amber liquid into the cut crystal glasses. "It doesn't seem real."

"It is not," Lamant agreed. "We all left our homes where we were starving. We are here until we no longer have the money to afford a room, biding our time for visas and passes as generations of inheritances trickle through our fingers like sand through an hourglass. We are safe, yes, but for how long?"

The rhetorical question lingered in the air between them, neither having an answer despite both wishing they did.

"James said I would like you and he was not wrong," Lamant said. "I have something I think you will find interesting. Something that may help. There are newspapers printed beneath that preposterous mustache of Hitler's. Men and women who risk their lives to publish the truth. I brought them with me from Lyon when I was smuggled out and have been wanting to ensure they fall into the right hands. James has told me you are such a person."

The grandeur of the room fell away, and she focused the whole of her attention on Lamant. There had been mention of these clandestine papers at the embassy, but she had failed to acquire any thus far. "I can promise you if I am given those newspapers, I will personally ensure they are seen to properly."

"It is as I figured." A grateful smile stretched over his thin lips. James made his way back toward them from across the room.

"I will have them delivered to your car while we dine," Lamant said. "I also have ways of acquiring more if you like. Mademoiselle Harper—" he bowed over her hand and kissed the back of her glove once more "—it was a genuine honor."

He left as James approached, a silent nod shared between them. "Forgive the interruption," James said. "I hope you found Monsieur Blanchet as interesting as anticipated."

He led her to dinner where they were served *soupe à l'oignon*, coq au vin and ended with a decadent chocolate soufflé. Ava ate until the narrow waist of her dress began to squeeze at her full stomach. When they had finished and the mix of a fine port weighed down the airy sips of her champagne, they departed the Palacio.

Ava's pulse quickened as the car was brought around, a large manila envelope evident on the passenger seat. She practically fell into the vehicle in her haste to see its contents. Conscious of the valet nearby, she left the packet in her lap, its heft seemingly significant. Or perhaps that was simply her imagination.

Once James pulled away, however, she opened the flap and drew out several pages of newsprint. They were smaller than expected, the size of a piece of office paper, with *Combat* written at the top with the familiar Cross of Lorraine emblazoned across the bold *C*. There were eight issues inside, their dates two weeks apart. The contents detailed the Nazi wrongdoings in France, mothers whose bread rations weren't enough to feed their babies and the failure of a program called *relève*, which claimed to send captured French soldiers home as it exhorted free labor from the women wanting to save their men. One newspaper from April even detailed a horrific event in which the Nazis set up a trap to capture Jews on the one day a week they were allowed the charity of food and medical assistance.

She couldn't help but recall the American newspapers with

buried articles about Hitler trying to eradicate the Jews. The mention of numbers killed had been exorbitant to the point of disbelief for those in America who were so far removed from the crises.

But Ava had always suspected there was something candid and awful in those harrowing words that others refused to believe. Reading *Combat* now made those seeds of trust sprout, the roots settling deep within her.

"This is incredible," she murmured to herself.

"I knew you would find Lamant helpful." James glanced at her as he drove.

"Very much so." She lowered the stack of precious pages. "But why give them to me when you could be using them?"

"My assignment here is a little different," he replied easily.

Before she could press him for more details, he continued, "Theo and Alfie are too busy for me to send these their way and they don't read French. I thought you could truly appreciate them."

"It is such an honor to be entrusted with these." She glanced down at the collection of clandestine newspapers in her lap.

What she now held in her hands was the real truth. This was a newspaper men and women risked their lives to write, to create, to distribute. One that could actually change the tide of war.

This was why she had agreed to come to Lisbon, to do something for America and all the rest of the world.

TEN

Elaine

The days ran together as scenery did on a swiftly moving train. In that stretch of June becoming July, Elaine had no word of Joseph, but that didn't mean he left her thoughts.

Through all the newspaper drops and message deliveries and transferring of supplies to and from the Maquis, Joseph weighed on Elaine's mind, leaden with many regrets.

The foremost of which being the realization that she had put too much faith in Etienne.

If she had known she would not see Joseph until the war ended, she would have found a way to go to him while he was in prison. Or written a note that hid his culpability but still conveyed the depth of her feelings.

Now it was too late.

On one overly bright morning where the sun splintered off the Rhône like shards of glass, Elaine arrived earlier than usual at the apartment on Rue d'Algérie. A slight creak of the wood floors from inside announced someone had entered before her.

Etienne came to the doorway of the living room as she toed

off her shoes. It was the first time they had seen one another since she'd learned that Joseph had been sent to the work camp. Silence burgeoned between them as the blade of grief cut through her.

He regarded her with a wounded, wary look. "Elaine."

"Did you find a way to send my note?" She didn't bother to hide the coolness of her tone.

"I put it through the channels I could."

"But you don't know if it was delivered."

He lowered his gaze.

Heat flashed in her cheeks, and her muscles tightened at the back of her neck. She should have known this would happen, but she had been foolish enough to cling to a thread of hope.

But, no, it was as she feared—as she ought to have expected. She walked around him to extract the typewriter from the hidden compartment in the wall and uncapped the case.

"I'll make this right, Elaine," Etienne said.

She glanced up. Now that she was closer, the exhaustion that bruised the delicate skin under his eyes was evident, as were the lines of his face, which had deepened since she last saw him. He was younger than Joseph, but now he looked older by several years.

"I know he was arrested by Werner, and I am poignantly aware of what that means." Elaine wanted to hurl the lid of the typewriter in an explosion of rage, but instead set it gently on the floor. "I wish you would have been the one to tell me."

Etienne blinked slowly, as if in pain. "I wanted to spare you such a detail."

"I want to be told everything," Elaine said through gritted teeth. "He is my husband."

Etienne nodded.

"Was he tortured?" She held her breath, dreading the answer and yet needing to hear it.

After a long moment, Etienne nodded again.

An ache knotted in the pit of Elaine's stomach with the confirmation of what she already suspected. She put a hand out to the table's surface, using its support to steady herself.

"Elaine, I'm sorry I could not—"

The door opened. *"Bonjour,"* Nicole sang out. "I found bread yesterday and a small bit of cheese." Her entrance was followed by the clunk of her shoes being kicked off.

The time of Nicole's arrival allowed Elaine to compose herself as the other woman hastened to the kitchen to deposit the food before she joined them in the living room. She smiled at Etienne. "Ah, Gabriel. I expect this means you have a fascinating new task for us."

He gave one final look at Elaine and his features smoothed, ready to do business. "I do."

Once Denise and Josette were with them, Etienne explained that they would be transporting pieces of a printing press from several locations to a warehouse on 35 Rue Viala. The weight of the items was considerable and required the utmost care as one broken piece might render the machine inoperable.

They all listened intently, Josette chewing at her nails as he spoke. Once he had finished, he took his leave and did not try to pull Elaine aside privately again, leaving them to eat the food Nicole procured in peace.

Regardless of the messenger, the mission was one Elaine found herself eager to embark upon. Their efforts would help release more newspapers and tracts, which would garner more support for the Resistance. Like the leaflets sent out in March that attracted so many recruits that the Savoy Maquis went from a group of only two hundred and fifty men to over five thousand.

The greater their numbers, the higher the likelihood of a swift victory. And the sooner Joseph would be released.

The success of the tracts with the Savoy Maquis was evidence that words did have power, even against a force such as the Nazis. And Elaine anticipated the opportunity to do her part to encourage France to rise together and fight.

★ ★ ★

Explosives did not tax Elaine's shopping basket as much as the foreign roller object that lay crookedly against the woven side. The oblong shape reminded her of a rolling pin, though thinner and far heavier. It was concealed beneath several pathetically small carrots, a bundle of rutabagas, and as much bread as she was allowed to buy for the week. Or rather, as much as she was able to find. More often than not, they couldn't receive their full allotment due to limited stock.

This was the fourth item she had relocated from one of the three garages where the burdensome pieces were stored. The Grande-Blanche hospital came into view, meaning she was finally close. She adjusted the heft of her shopping basket from one hand to the other and tried to avoid leaning too hard away from the drag of her cargo. It wouldn't do to bring attention to herself, especially so near the destination.

Denise approached from the opposite direction with a pram that sagged deep into its frame. She shoved her burden toward the sprawling white building with "35" inscribed above the entryway.

Elaine rushed ahead to open the door for Denise who expertly maneuvered the buggy into the entry, the wheels protesting the angle with a high-pitched squeal.

"Printing plates," she explained.

"Where did you get the pram?" Elaine closed the door behind them, its bang loud enough to echo in the long, empty hall.

"It's mine." Denise's knuckles were white as she steered the teetering baby carriage toward the warehouse within. "I have a daughter."

Elaine's shock must have shown on her face for Denise scoffed. "Don't look so surprised. It is why I am fighting so hard against this occupation. I do not want my Sophie to grow up in this world without enough food and even less freedom, to be told her only purpose is to be a uterus and her husband's housekeeper."

"Does she stay with you?" The question escaped Elaine before she could stop it.

"She is with my mother." Denise stopped before another closed door, which Elaine also pushed open for her.

There were so many more questions Elaine wanted to ask, prying ones about how long it had been since Denise had seen her daughter or how painful the separation must be. But they all had enough bruising on their hearts to know better than to prod at tender topics.

As Denise passed through the entryway, she paused. "My Jacob is Jewish. Pierre created all of our papers, including the one that keeps my daughter alive and safe every day." The sharpness of her stare relaxed with unspoken gratitude. "My husband and child are not the only Jews Pierre has saved in these harrowing times."

Joseph had been a hero to so many. The understanding left a pang of longing in Elaine to have him back. His loss was palpable always, an ache that could never be soothed.

Denise navigated her way through the open doorway without another word, as though the entire conversation had never happened. But to Elaine, the admission made an indelible imprint upon her that she knew would remain forever.

A man with dark hair closely cropped against his head like a soldier squatted by a pile of machinery with a rag loosely held in his hand. Elaine recognized the parts he pensively surveyed as the various items she and the other ladies had painstakingly transported.

Some had been fitted together and rose from the ground like a skeletal demon, its dark bones glossy with an iridescent sheen of oil. The man stood as they approached and strode toward them, their footsteps all echoing in the vast empty space amid the grating screech of the overtaxed pram wheels. A deafening silence fell over them as they came to a stop.

Grease stained his fingers with its dark smears, and its odor hung thick in the air.

"I'm Marcel." He extended his hand, then grimaced and wiped at it with the dirty cloth. "Thank you for your help in relocating the printing press. I'm aware it is quite the arduous job."

Elaine examined the beast he was assembling. "No more so than building it, I assume."

He gave a self-deprecating laugh. "It will probably take a month or two to complete with so many components." He hefted the plate from Denise's pram. The baby carriage jolted up several inches, coiling tight its springs after the cumbersome strain.

Elaine relieved her basket of the roller instrument and carried it to the partially built mechanism, adding the object to the errant spread of machinery. Curious, she studied the beginnings of the printing press and considered where certain parts might go.

Marcel joined her. "You have experience with a Roneo?"

"That's correct," Elaine confirmed, wondering who might have told him.

"We have one here." He motioned to a shelf with various items stacked upon its wide surface. "If you'd be willing, I'd appreciate your assistance."

If she were enlisted to operate the Roneo, she could play a vital part in recruitment of new Resistance members. She would have a role in the implementation of those words that swayed the reluctant French who were in a state of misled hope—that there would be enough food this year, or sufficient fuel this winter, that the occupiers would leave them to their own devices. The more their disillusionment was countered with truth, the more willing they would be to help.

And with her skills, she could be an important component.

Without looking at Denise to gauge her reaction, Elaine nodded. "I would be honored to."

Josette entered the room with a man on either side of her. The taller of the two had auburn hair and appeared younger than the other by at least a decade, his strides lanky by comparison.

"Here is the location," the older man said to Josette in a cordial manner that went along with his dress. He didn't opt for the loose trousers and simple, button-down shirt as the other men, but instead wore a tailored suit, his bow tie perfectly straight and his hair parted severely to one side.

Josette gave a nervous giggle. "I can't believe I got lost after having been here several times already." From her basket, she withdrew a strange piece with a screw jutting from it and set the item beside the roller.

Her nails had been chewed down past the raw, pink area of her nail bed so the skin there burned with an angry red. Before Elaine could ask after her friend, the older man extended his hand toward her. "I'm Antoine."

Absent any grease on his fingers, Elaine accepted his hand with a firm shake. His pensive gray eyes regarded her with lingering consideration. "Pierre taught me everything I know about the stamping process on false papers. It's an honor to meet you."

Another mention of her husband.

If only Elaine could have known the Joseph with whom everyone else was so well acquainted. And yet to her, she was learning he was an utter stranger.

Elaine murmured her thanks and struggled to figure out what to say next when the taller man stepped forward. "I'm Jean. I do the typography here." Though he was young, the corners of his eyes were crinkled before he smiled, suggesting the happy expression was commonplace.

Marcel regarded Elaine. "If you're ready to begin with the Roneo, Jean can show you where everything is."

She hesitated in her surprise.

They wanted her to start so soon?

"I…" She cast an apologetic glance toward Denise, who seemed not at all bothered by the turn of events. "Of course."

Denise gave her a nod and departed with Josette, the latter of whom waved briskly in Elaine's direction.

Jean led Elaine across the room to the duplicator with his long-legged stride. Time had left a fine layer of dust sifted over the machine, rendering the surface dull. Jean hefted it from the shelf and placed it on a desk piled with enough paper to make them seem like a supplier.

While Elaine and the other women used small bits for their messages, she had never seen so much in this quantity, not with the ration in place.

"Where did you get all this?" Her fingertips skimmed the precious stack.

Marcel and Jean shared an amused glance. Mirth sparked in Marcel's green eyes. "We are the Bureau de recherché géodésiques et géophysiques."

A bureau of geodesical and geophysical research? Elaine arched an eyebrow quizzically at the two men and their impish grins.

"Or so the Germans think," added Jean. "Marcel registered—"

Nicole swept into the room, heels clacking, her outfit chic in her usual white and blue motif, a matching hat tilted rakishly over one eye as the silky blond curls at the ends of her hair bounced midway down her back.

Jean's mouth dropped open.

"The last time I lugged something about this heavy, it was a sack full of guns," Nicole called out jovially as she exaggerated the strain of her bag.

"Who is that?" Jean asked under his breath.

"That is Nicole." Elaine gave a knowing look at the besotted man, then indicated the Roneo. "Do you have the transfer sheets? And the fluid? And possibly a rag to wipe it down with?"

"Hmm?" Jean dragged his gaze from Nicole and his cheeks went scarlet. "*Oui*, of course." He opened a drawer, displaying a stack of rags. From a bin sitting atop the desk, he presented the two-page master. She separated the paper form with its script penned in a neat, block letter text from its waxy back, which she carefully affixed to the rolling drum, wax-side out.

"And fluid." He grabbed a tin from the shelf, the contents inside sloshing.

She took it with thanks and poured the methanol into the tank on the left side of the machine, its scent sharp and unmistakable. While the liquid gurgled its way into the wick, she scanned the paper used to create the necessary wax sheet. It was a call to the people of Lyon to gather at Place de la Croix-Rousse in the evening of the upcoming Bastille Day on July 14 and proudly bear the tricolor in defiance of their German oppressors.

Her heart thumped harder in her chest. She was a part of this compelling message.

After swiping away a layer of dust, she adjusted the paper into the feeder tray—a feature her own rustic machine never had. "How many copies?"

"As many as it will do."

The Roneo could produce almost five hundred sheets, but the ink on the printed copy gradually degraded with each pass so the run likely would fall somewhere closer to four hundred and fifty if they were lucky.

She grasped the handle, rolling it forward in the way that was as familiar to her as the acrid aroma of the methanol. "I'm going to need more paper."

Not only was Elaine proficient at running the mimeograph machine, but her ability to repair it with ease was especially welcome. So it was that she never resumed her work with Nicole, Denise, and Josette, though the absence of their constant companionship was felt keenly as the days turned into weeks and then a month.

They saw one another on occasion with deliveries, but visits were few and woefully far between. And through it all, Etienne had no further updates on Joseph.

In that time, Elaine continued to reside with Manon. Though never unkind, the woman seemed disinclined to engage with Elaine. Shrouded in her own solitude, she moved through the house like a specter, adorned in loose black dresses that accentuated the frailness of her slender body. Still, she always had a meal prepared for Elaine. Though the contents were meager, they were decorously waiting on a white plate painted with violets and delicate sunshine yellow roses.

The printing press's assembly was underway, the skeleton fleshed out into a powerful beast—a machine worthy of discrediting Nazi propaganda.

There was a second press—the Minerva—that did not require electricity to make it run, but rather the pumping of one's foot on a pedal at its base. It was a noisy thing once in operation, the ink plate thwacking against the blank page to imprint the text. Coordinated effort was involved as well, with the operator simultaneously stomping the treadle, removing the completed paper and replacing it with a clean, unprinted one.

Marcel operated the Minerva when he wasn't puzzling through the myriad remaining pieces of the automatic press, until at last it was complete. The thing sounded like the five-ton monster it was, huffing and chuffing and slamming against the backdrop of the Minerva's own thundering performance. Its noise was why the warehouse was set so far from Lyon's heart and within the massive building.

The orchestra of newsprint went on without stop throughout the day until their composition fell into the background. Only when an issue occurred did the production cease, rendering the silence off-putting as one abruptly missed the symphony of its operation.

Elaine and the three men found a comfortable rhythm in their routines, with Jean printing out text in blocks of metal slugs that had to cool before being touched and fitted to plates for the presses. Marcel hovered over the automatic machine in these first days, monitoring each printout with critical study before nodding to himself in approval and returning the paper back to its neat stack. Antoine was Elaine's favorite to observe as he worked over thin sheets of zinc with a sharpened tool, etching out images with the precise skill of an artist.

"We should run the story," Antoine said one morning when Elaine walked in.

"Absolutely not." Marcel kept his stare fixed on the printing press, apparently not in the mood to argue.

Antoine slipped a finger beneath his bow tie as if easing the pressure building there. "But it is news that Max—Jean Moulin—is dead."

Max was a code name Elaine knew—not through personal introduction, for she would never warrant as much with a man of his caliber, but he came up often in conversations and coded messages. He was the right-hand man in Lyon for General de Gaulle, the war hero who encouraged French Resistance from London. Max had been charged with uniting their different independent factions into one.

What did his death mean for the Resistance? For their future?

"Do you see her face?" Marcel nodded to Elaine with a hard expression. "If you tell France Max is dead, our people will be stricken too, and you will lose support, not gain more."

Elaine immediately schooled her features to mask her emotions, a lesson she would not forget. Even among friends.

"It is news," Marcel agreed solemnly. "But our job is to gather new recruits, not turn them away by informing them that General de Gaulle's most trusted man was tortured to death by Hauptsturmführer Barbie." He turned his attention to Elaine and spoke with a gentler tone. "Max was not the only man maintaining the networks in Lyon. We will endure."

"I hear he did not talk despite the brutal torture he endured." Jean's voice was soft with an awed reverence.

"Still, it is not a story that needs to be published," Marcel said with finality and walked away with a stack of fresh newsprint in his arms.

"Tortured?" Elaine asked through numb lips.

Jean nodded, brooding aloud. "It is true bravery and strength alone that keeps one from talking."

Like Joseph.

Could she be so strong? No matter how hard she concentrated, it was impossible to weigh her own fortitude against such an unknown scale.

"None of us knows how we would react," Jean said, as though he too were lost in the same macabre thought. "I think we all hope to be so valiant and pray we never have to find out."

He tucked his hands into his pockets, his long form bent over, as if walking into a hearty wind, and returned to the small office they used for creating false identity cards.

"*Ma chérie,*" Nicole's voice called out. She sauntered in with Josette at her side, their ever-present shopping baskets looped in the crooks of their elbows. Rather than go to Marcel, Nicole marched over to Elaine and hugged her. "How we've missed you."

Elaine squeezed Nicole's slim frame in return, noting the prominent outline of the other woman's ribs and vertebrae as she did so. No doubt Elaine felt the same in their embrace.

It was a reminder of the pervasive hunger that gnawed at their unfulfilled bellies and fogged their minds with weariness. In any event, seeing Nicole and Josette again was still a rare and wonderful delight.

Or at least Nicole.

Josette's youthful glow had dimmed to an unhealthy pallor in the time since Elaine had seen her last; even the luster of her brown curls seemed to have dulled. "It's good to see you," she said in a shy whisper, her smile tight.

The printing press churned in the background, and though Elaine was deaf to its clatter, Josette flinched with every bang.

"I trust these brutes are treating you well," Nicole said aloud and looked pointedly at the men in a mock threat.

"She's a fast learner." Antoine lifted his head from his art and offered a kind smile at Elaine. "We're glad to have her."

"I'm thinking of teaching her how to use the Minerva." Marcel indicated to the smaller press.

"Are you?" Elaine's pulse spiked at the possibility of moving beyond the small duplicating machine and her clerical duties. Printing wasn't done by women. But then, there were few men now to choose from. Why not a woman?

"I'll need to go to Grenoble soon." Marcel removed a stack of papers from the press and relocated them to the table where several others lay. They not only printed *Combat*, which was written by their team, but also *Défence de la France* for the southern region.

"Grenoble?" Nicole interjected. "Why, I've just come from there and have your stamps."

What she held in the wicker's false bottom was a precious treasure. The stamps were priceless in a time when rubber was so difficult to obtain and so integral. As each new stamp was introduced for travel passes and identity papers and everything in between, an inside contact who worked as a secretary in Lyon's town hall provided them with information to replicate the originals.

"You can bring them over there." Elaine pointed to the room where Jean had gone and smiled to herself as Nicole click-clacked her way toward him.

Elaine turned her attention to Josette. "Are you doing well?"

The printing press banged, and Josette cringed. "Yes." The smile she plastered on her dry lips was anything other than genuine. "Of course I am."

Despite her obvious attempt to nudge away Elaine's concern,

Josette's nerves were raw, her fear so visceral Elaine caught its metallic odor over the pulpy, velvety aromas of ink and paper.

"Denise has gone to join the Maquis, so it's just Nicole and I now." Josette brought her hand to her mouth and nipped at the cropped nail bed with her front teeth, the action distracted and without thought.

Her behavior was distressing.

Elaine had never been much of a maternal woman, but found herself wanting to draw Josette into her arms and comfort her as one did a frightened child.

"And you are certain you are well?" Elaine pressed.

Josette chewed at the mutilated nail, saying nothing for the moment stretching between them. Elaine almost thought the other woman might offer a real answer in the silence, but then Josette nodded, her eyes squinting in a mock smile. "I'm fine."

She wasn't fine. Alarmingly so.

Nicole sauntered over to them, her lightened basket swinging in her hand. Elaine embraced her and whispered discreetly into her friend's ear. "Will Josette be all right?"

"I'll be sure of it." Nicole straightened with a bright smile, and the two were off to resume their work on messages for deliveries.

"What do you think of Josette?" Marcel asked after the women departed.

Knowing her reply might result in Josette being pulled from her duties, Elaine remained quiet. But no matter how hard she tried, she could not allow herself to be reassured by Nicole's glib response.

Marcel didn't press her, but narrowed his eyes slightly in thought, then shook away whatever was in his thoughts and waved for her to follow him. "Come, let me show you how to operate the printing press."

ELEVEN

Ava

Ava was not the only one thrilled with the discovery of the clandestine French newspaper. Mr. Sims's glower had lightened to a frown, and he informed her a month later that DC wanted more. She and Mike were to share the duty of photographing all the periodicals and publications, and she was to put extra effort into obtaining as many underground newspapers as was possible.

In the months that followed, she accompanied James to Estoril on enough occasions that she eventually acquired her own dinner party dresses and had Peggy teach her a few new hairstyles. Lamant met Ava often, providing her not only with French clandestine papers, but occasionally ones from Holland and Poland as well.

"There is an art to these," he explained after handing her a small stack to tuck into her handbag at a soiree at the Estoril bar one night. "It is resistance among oppression, words rivaling heavy artillery, seemingly insignificant and yet still efficacious. This is strength in its rawest form. It is beautiful."

Lamant was a rare soul who saw some element of magnificence in most things. She smiled at his assessment. "That's poetic."

"You must look beyond the page." He lifted his drink but paused before taking a sip. A sliver of lemon bobbed in the clear liquid. "To the men and women who worked so seamlessly together. Not only the author who wrote it, but the typographer who meticulously assembled it, to the person manning the complexities of the printing machines, to the courier who delivered it and the citizen who smuggled it from French soil to end up here in Portugal."

This was one of the things she enjoyed about the rare moments she spent with Lamant. Never had she considered more than the authors or the piece itself. But he was correct in his appraisal, at the string of involvement to bring these clandestine papers to her hand.

"Even you." Lamant gestured to her with his glass, his cheeks slightly reddened from spending too much time by the ocean. "Those papers would die here in Lisbon. They would become rubbish over time, tossed out with the rest of the trash. History discarded. But you are sending them on to America. You are preserving these moments in time so all will look back on them later."

With that proclamation, he put his drink to his lips and drained the contents so only the lemon twist remained. He held up his glass as a waiter passed to summon another. Again. As if catching her assessment, he winked at her. "This is better than the pills most refugees take for their nerves."

Regardless of what he said and the luxurious surroundings he enjoyed, the wear of waiting so many months began to whittle at his appearance. He remained slender despite the abundance of canapés and heaping plates of meats and pastries and delicacies from around the world. Most of which he didn't touch. Instead, his attention swung to what could be splashed into a crystal glass. And though he said it settled his nerves, the slight tremor in his hands never seemed to abate, and the lines around his mouth and on his brow appeared to be etched deeper every time they met.

A man and woman walked by the table, their conversation in German apparent. Lamant's hold on the cup tightened until his bony knuckles went white.

"Are you all right?" Ava asked when the man and woman passed.

He swallowed, appearing pale beneath his light sunburn and offered her a wan smirk. "Forgive me, German being spoken nearby never ceases to rattle me."

She nodded. While she would never understand on the level Lamant had experienced, she understood about the shift in emotion hearing German elicited. "My father was fluent in German. And French," she added with a smile. "Once hearing German reminded me of him."

"Now it is sullied," Lamant finished for her.

"Precisely."

A waiter appeared and exchanged Lamant's glass with a fresh one, offered on a glossy silver platter. Lamant took a generous sip and visibly relaxed. "I spent much of my life enjoying the works of Goethe and find I can only stomach his words in French now. It is a pity as the translation is never as true as the original."

"It doesn't surprise me that you are a man who appreciates Goethe." Ava finished the last of her wine as James caught her eye from across the room.

It was time to go. And time to tell Lamant the news she had been dreading the entire night.

"I confess, I have been trying to secure a visa for you from the American Embassy." Ava stared at her empty glass, a remaining circle of wine pooled at the bottom like a drop of blood. "But I have failed."

Lamant blinked in surprise. "I would never ask that of you."

"I know." Ava set her wineglass on the small table between their chairs. "I wanted to help regardless."

And she still did, to repay him for all he had done in procuring the foreign publications. At every turn, her requests had been denied. She had been warned by Peggy, then snubbed by the vice-consuls at the embassy who refused to hear her pleas and then refused by a contact in DC she knew through one of her former roommates.

"I didn't want you to think I hadn't tried," she said softly. "Not that it did any good."

A waiter whisked by, and her glass disappeared.

Lamant studied her for a long moment. "No act of kindness, no matter how small, is ever wasted," he said, quoting Aesop.

"My father used that quote often."

"Then he would be proud of you." Lamant settled his hand on hers, his fingers cold from cradling his drink. "You are meant to do great things."

Though his compliment warmed her, it was another brick of expectation she did not feel she could support. In her months in Lisbon, she had not helped the refugees save for a few books given to children in the mornings and while she worked hard at collecting the newspapers, she wished she could do more. Daniel was still in danger, she was unable to find her neighbor who had been arrested by the PVDE, the world was still at war, and she could not even procure one American visa.

She was letting everyone down.

The sense of her own helplessness did not diminish as the months slid into October, when the chill of autumn gilded the foliage, leaving the trees awash in a splay of burnished gold. However, it was then she received two letters. One from Daniel— short and sweet, erring on the side of censorship, safe rather than the elaborate. And one under the door of her apartment from Lamant who she had not seen in several weeks.

I have finally not only secured an American visa but am leaving on a ship tomorrow. I wish to enjoy the final night of Lisbon with the people I cherish most in this stunning city.

Sheer joy engulfed her at such a letter, exquisite and filled with light. Despite the hurdles in Lamant's path, he had managed to scale them and was on the other side at last. It was a worthy cause for celebration indeed.

That was how she and James found themselves navigating the ancient section of Lisbon known as Alfama with a moon hung high and full overhead in an inky, star-studded sky. The rest of the city was charted in a modern grid-like Pombaline pattern with widely spaced streets, but Alfama maintained its narrow winding passages with a complex maze of stairs and steep slopes, exactly as it had been in the medieval days.

That area was one of the few to have survived the fateful day in 1755 when an earthquake struck and destroyed most of the city. But the tragedy was not finished there. The shuddering earth enraged the Tagus River, which swelled into tidal waves and washed away pieces of Lisbon. As if that were not enough, the tipped candles and lanterns from the earthquake set ablaze what had not been reduced to rubble or submerged.

The devastation was momentous and resulted in tens of thousands of lost lives. Its worldwide news deeply impacted Voltaire who not only incorporated the tragedy into his tales of *Candide* but wrote an entire poem lamenting the disaster.

Even though by some miracle Alfama still stood, reinforcing brackets now thrust from the painted exteriors of the homes from those archaic days, like stitches on torn skin.

James was able to navigate the complex layout with an expertise she admired. The buildings around them rose three to five stories tall, their pastel faces dotted with shuttered windows, which residents leaned out of to chat with one another, some only an arm's length away. Aromas of home-cooked dinners filled the streets, sizzling sausages and smoky, grilled seafood.

Ava's mouth watered at the tempting scents, especially since they had been told to arrive hungry.

As they carefully made their way down a steep set of stairs toward a crumbling building, Ava caught sight of Lamant waiting for them at the bottom with a younger man who wore a genuine smile and a simple button-down shirt and slacks to James's and Lamant's tailored suits. Despite his youth, there was an exhaustion swelling the skin beneath his eyes and dulling his appearance somewhat.

Lamant introduced the man as Ethan Williams who worked with the American Jewish Joint Distribution Committee.

"JDC," Ethan abbreviated as he held out his hand.

Ava accepted it with a firm shake that earned her a nod of approval from the man.

"Ethan works closely with the refugees and can help you acquire more of the newspapers I've been supplying you with," Lamant said. "Which is why I found it imperative to introduce you prior to my departure." He put a hand on Ethan's shoulder and gave it an affectionate squeeze, as a father might do to his son. "Ethan has been crucial in gathering a majority of the material I pass your way, as well as finally getting me to America."

"It was so good of you to assist Lamant." She smiled at the older Frenchman and pushed down the emotion threatening to overwhelm her. Not only the sorrow at knowing she would soon be absent his company forever, but also the joy at his escape.

Ethan nodded. "Of course. I'm happy to help."

Lamant beamed at them all. "My favorite people are together here in this place of refuge even as my own countrymen tried to have me deported. I have been far more fortunate than most to enjoy the splendor of Portugal. It is a country of beauty and art and friendship, and I want to relish this final day with those I love."

His words were true. He *was* fortunate. Not only for the luxury his wealth had afforded him as he bided his time, but also in how he saw the world, like a wrapped confection with new delights beneath each opaque covering.

"And now we must hurry, or we will miss the next singer." Lamant ushered them toward the door.

Ava allowed him to guide her inside. "Singer?"

The inside of the building did not match its deteriorating exterior, but instead was filled with heavy wooden tables and chairs, the seats padded with a red, plush fabric. Overhead, the concave ceiling reflected the striated exposed brickwork she had grown so used to seeing over the last few months in Portugal.

"Fado," Lamant replied with reverence.

While she had not stayed out late enough to enjoy the music, she was aware of what fado was. The woeful lyrics were unique to Lisbon, people who had been subjected to hardships of poverty and loss, especially in the century following the famed earthquake while their city rebuilt, when fado first was noted to have begun.

They were immediately served glasses of green wine, the effervescent pale gold liquid made of grapes from the north of Portugal, consumed before the wine could mature so bubbles chased one another up the sides of the glass. This was followed by several plates of various grilled fish and octopus, as well as something that appeared to be a length of sausage curled in a horseshoe shape.

"Not pork." Lamant held up his forefinger the way Ava's philosophy instructor did when she studied at Pratt. "This is *alheira*." He lifted his knife and fork and sliced through the sausage. "It is spiced poultry and bread, cleverly disguised as pork. Have you heard of it?"

James looked to her as well, most likely expecting her usual detail of information. But in this case, she could not provide any.

"I have not heard of *alheira*," Ava confessed.

Lamant nodded sagely as he always did when he encountered something Ava had not uncovered on her own. "This was not the first time Portugal became crowded with Jews as our people were made to flee our homes to escape persecution. Near the end of the fifteenth century, Jews sought these same shores for refuge. However, the Portuguese king wanted to wed a Spanish princess and continued the oppression in an effort to appeal to Spain."

Ava nodded, familiar with the terrible history.

"Sausage has always been a popular dish in Portugal, which unfortunately made detecting Jews quite easy." He presented the food with a spread hand. "And so, *alheira*. It could be hung and dried in smoke rooms like sausage and eaten in public to keep from drawing attention. Genius, is it not?"

He cut a section from the middle and handed it to her. She took a bite and a burst of salt and garlic mixed with a spice that tingled with culinary heat hit her tongue.

Suddenly the lights were lowered and two men with pear-shaped guitars approached the fireplace. A woman joined them a moment later, a cobweb-thin black shawl over the shoulders of her rose-printed dress.

The entire room went silent.

The men's fingers moved over the strings of their instruments, teasing out silvery notes that danced through the room, enhanced by the broad, rounded ceiling overhead. The woman swayed to the rhythm, her eyes closed as if absorbing the delicate sound until they were one.

Her hand pressed to the center of her chest, and she began to sing, her voice husky and filled with a grief that reached deep into all the places in Ava's soul that had ever been raw. Agony and sorrow pulled at the woman's brow as she lifted her head, hand out in a beseeching manner that curled into a fist as the bright, clear notes faded into a vibrato.

As her palm went once more to her heart, she gazed around

the room with tears shimmering in her eyes as her song went on. A lover whose affections were unrequited, the pain relayed through her was as adroitly written on her face as the fingers of the guitarists played over those six strings.

On and on the woman sang until tears also stung Ava's eyes. The final notes tingled to a close, and the woman dropped her head to her chest.

The room exploded in an applause that the singer graciously received with the same heartfelt emotion with which she had sung. The lights were turned up once more and Ava blinked to remember where she was, having been so enraptured by the production that she'd forgotten all space and time. On the table before her, the green wine had grown warm and the food cold. But no one cared. They were all clapping with enthusiasm for what was the most incredible performance Ava had ever witnessed.

The singer and guitarists left the makeshift stage, nodding their thanks to patrons as they disappeared, and guests resumed eating and drinking once more. As Ava followed their departure, she caught sight of a familiar face, one that made her appetite shrivel despite the veritable feast laid out before her.

Lukas.

It had been months since she'd seen him. His presence was unmistakable—not only in his straight-backed appearance at a far table, tucked away in a corner, but also how he watched her, unblinking, with purpose. Except that she refused to back down from Lukas's blatant stare and met it with one of her own. She was no coward, and she would not show fear.

Lukas smiled at her then, his white teeth, which she had once so admired, flashing from across the room. She did not smile back.

In the end, it was he who rose from the table and slipped from the room, pausing only to give her one final look before taking his leave. Whatever unease Ava had set from her mind regarding their initial meeting took root once more.

She hid her malcontent from her companions, refusing to allow Lamant's last night in Lisbon to be tarnished. Much to her relief, he did not seem to notice, nor did Ethan. James, however, caught her eye several times, his expression concerned.

Once the food had all been eaten and the wine drunk, the evening stretched late into the night with performances that continued to amaze her. Somewhere before midnight, Lamant pushed back from the seat and declared he wanted a final shot of Ginjinha—a tart cherry liquor, he stated, that was made best by a woman he knew in Alfama—before falling into America's embrace.

As they wound their way into the heart of the medieval area, Ava lost herself in the convivial spirit, forgetting Lukas. Instead, she found herself entranced by the stars winking from above the narrow alleys, beyond the strings stretched between the buildings dotted with remnants of paper flowers from the St. Anthony's Festival several months before.

They stopped below blue-painted shutters where Lamant called to Senhora Ferreira, whom he deemed to be the kindest woman in Alfama. The older woman opened the shutters with a smile, revealing a neat apartment behind her lace curtains. She poured them all a bit of red liquor into small chocolate cups for a few escudos. Her eyes filled with tears as Lamant bid her goodbye, clearly another person whose life had been impacted by the insightful Frenchman.

As the last of the chocolate cup dissolved on Ava's tongue, about all she could manage to stuff into her overfull stomach, she shook Ethan's hand and embraced Lamant in a final farewell. "Remember to always look past the page, *ma chérie*," he said to her before kissing each cheek and leaving the scent of his spicy cologne lingering on her sweater.

The following day he would be on a ship bound for America, whose shores would offer him a safety that was only tenuous at best in Lisbon. He would escape the fear of Nazi observation and the threat of the PVDE. After nearly a year of being twisted in the broken visa system, he was going to be free.

"Did you like listening to fado?" James asked as he led their way through the starlit streets of a now quiet Alfama.

"It was moving," Ava said.

"It isn't common for most refugees to enjoy the sadness of it. Not when they have enough sorrow already."

Ava nodded in understanding. "Lamant sees things differently than others."

"Which is why I knew you two would get on well." James tossed her a grin.

Clipped footsteps sounded behind them. James put a hand to her lower back, nudging her to walk a little faster. Not that she needed the encouragement. The steps mingling with theirs in the thin, October night air held a note of authority and importance. This was no drunk staggering home from a late night of imbibing.

James turned abruptly down a narrow alley, then up a flight of stairs and through another slender alley. Lukas entered Ava's thoughts once more. How he had shown up that night, how he'd been so fixedly watching her.

Though Portugal was neutral, it did not mean an undercurrent of clandestine activity didn't happen beneath the government's nose. Nazis still found ways of making people disappear.

James pulled Ava into an alcove, so her back was against the wall, and he was covering her with his own body. They were face-to-face. Close. His features half-shadowed, his eyes dark in the late night, his jaw smooth from a recent shave.

But he wasn't studying her as she was him. His head was tilted, tense as he strained to listen.

Footsteps echoed in the distance. Whoever chased them knew Alfama as well as James.

"It's the PVDE," he whispered.

His attention shifted and suddenly he was noticing her, his eyes sweeping over her face like a caress. He lifted his hand and let his fingertips whisper over the edge of her chin.

Ava's pulse quickened and left her head spinning.

The footsteps grew louder.

"Kiss me," James said.

She gazed up at him in surprise. She hadn't kissed a man before. Her studies had occupied her life, and then the library and the war effort. Men's advances had always come on too strongly, their eagerness so plain, it left a wariness in her veins and a refusal on her tongue.

This was not how she wanted her first kiss, in an alley, evading someone chasing them down, like some ridiculous spy film.

"You've been to too many cinemas," she replied.

The clip of stiff-soled shoes came from the top of the street now.

James turned his gaze to the right, where the sound came from. "Haven't you at least read enough books to be tempted?"

She had. And he was no Darcy.

No sooner had the thought crossed her mind than he leaned closer, his eyes holding hers.

"'And the sunlight clasps the earth, and the moonbeams kiss the sea. What is all this sweet work worth if thou kiss not me?'" His fingertips brushed her face. "You aren't the only reader," he murmured.

As the footsteps neared and Ava tilted her head, her heart pounded like a drum as her eyes fell shut. She wasn't yielding her first kiss to a coworker trying to escape a bit of trouble in a foreign country. No, she was being wooed beneath a starlit sky, in the most romantic city in the world with a man who recited poetry.

He had won and she was happy to reward the victor.

His mouth lightly touched hers, just enough to hint at its warmth, the smoothness of his lips. The footsteps stopped near them, and the man grumbled about foolish youth or something along those lines before departing.

James pressed his mouth to hers once more even as the echoing click of hard soles departed from them. The taste of tart cherry liquor and excitement lingered on her tongue.

Only when silence blanketed them once more did James lean back with a lopsided grin. "I dare say you have saved us."

"Byron?" she asked in a bid to guess the author of the poem he'd delivered so beautifully.

"Percy Bysshe Shelley," he gently corrected her. "From 'Love's Philosophy.' However, if you're partial to Byron, I have somewhere I must take you one of these days."

She ought to decline but found herself intrigued. "I think I'd like that."

His grin grew a little wider. "As would I." He offered her his arm. This time, she slid her hand into the warm crook of his elbow, allowing him to lead her from Alfama and hopefully away from the watchful glare of the PVDE.

Though why the police suddenly followed them that night made no sense, not when they left her alone since that first week after her arrival. But she couldn't cast off her suspicion that it had something to do with Lukas.

TWELVE

Elaine

The task of learning to operate the printing press proved to be far more complicated than merely rolling the great flywheel of the Minerva and pumping the foot treadle.

The ink needed to be dribbled just so over the flat, circular disk that fed the rollers. Then the placement of the paper on the platen had to be perfectly aligned where it would be stamped with the plate. Once completed, the paper would then be shifted to the delivery board and replaced with a fresh page. It was all a careful dance to coordinate at once.

Elaine's movements were clumsy and slow at first, the shift awkward with paper slightly askew, the print either splotchy and dark or barely visible. But she was stubborn in her efforts, and over the course of the next several months, her body found a rhythm to the smaller of the two presses. Her feet and hands did their own sort of waltz, moving with alacrity and freeing her mind from being so diligently focused on the task.

Once she'd mastered the art of creating newsprint on the manual press, Marcel trained her on the operation of the automatic machine to tend to in his absence. The larger of the two machines, however, possessed a cold distance that never appealed to Elaine—not like the intimacy and skill of the Minerva.

It wasn't uncommon for the light of day to dim into night, long past the curfew, rendering her unable to make her way to Manon's. While arduous and taxed with work that followed her into her dreams, Elaine never begrudged the effort. She relished it, craving the need to put to paper the power of effective words and being part of something larger than herself.

Even sleeping in the small makeshift bedroom from a converted office on those long nights didn't bother her. What she found disconcerting, however, was the quiet once the machines went still and one's imagination was left to spin terrifying explanations for every pop and creak.

One night, as the cold seeped up through the concrete floors and the banging and whirring of the mountainous machine faded to a hum, indicating the final pages had been printed, silence sifted over the warehouse like freshly fallen snow. Elaine breathed a sigh of relief.

The agony of a pulsing headache lingered since that morning and still had not abated. While the sounds usually blended into the background, that day each slam of the printing plate seemed to strike against her tender skull.

Elaine turned the machine off and gathered the newsprint, careful not to hug them to the pressed front of her pale pink blouse. Ink did not come out easily, and soap was impossible to find. It was yet another one of life's former conveniences once taken for granted, never appreciating what had previously been so readily available.

After setting the newspapers on the desk, the silence pressed at her, heavy and seemingly eternal. She cleared her throat to minimize its weight. The sound echoed back at her.

The room was cavernous, its emptiness threatening to swallow her whole. A shiver rippled down her back. She strode to the door, flicked off the lights, and made her way down the corridor toward the kitchen. A cup of roasted barley and chicory always calmed her before bed.

An audible thump carried down the hall.

Elaine froze.

The building was only sighing into its old bones, no doubt. Nothing to work into a panic over.

With a shake of her head at her own foolish paranoia, she pushed into the dismal little kitchen and put a kettle onto the stove to boil the water. Something down the hall banged, the noise audible over the gush of the faucet.

Elaine squeezed her eyes shut and hissed out a breath, refusing to let her mind play vicious tricks.

Then came a sneeze in the distance.

Chills raced from her heart to her skin so the small hairs on her forearms stood on end. No natural sound of a building settling could mimic a sneeze.

Antoine and Jean left several hours before, and Marcel was in Grenoble. Fellow Resistance members sometimes took shelter with them when safe houses were unable to be located, but in such an instance, Elaine and the others were notified.

To her knowledge, no one should be there now.

She quietly slid a drawer open and pulled out a butcher knife. The weapon would be ineffective against a gun, of course, but the heft of the cool handle against her palm offered some semblance of security. However false it may be. She toed off her shoes and crept toward the door, straining to listen in the silence for evidence of where the intruder might be.

A whistle pierced the air and made her startle with such force, she nearly parted with her own skin. Heart racing and hands trembling, she wrenched the kettle from the stove with her free hand and turned off the heat from the burner. The shrill cry immediately cut short.

It was too late. Whoever was inside would know exactly

where she was. She crept out of the kitchen, her entire body tense as her brain screamed at her to run.

But where would she go? It was past curfew, and she was barefoot, her identity papers in her desk within the warehouse. Not to mention the damp chill as the October rains consumed Lyon. Outside, she would be even more vulnerable. At least in here, she knew where to hide. Or possibly sneak up on the intruder. If she could take the person by surprise, she might have a fighting chance.

She slipped down the hallway, her feet cold against the bare floor. The door to the bedroom remained closed, but a nagging suspicion told her the sound had come from there.

Adrenaline poured into her with such potency, nausea churned in her empty stomach. She forced herself onward, easing the door open so it moved soundlessly.

Weapon brandished, her heart pounding like a drum, she turned the corner.

A woman with dark hair pulled back from her face gazed up, a child cradled in her embrace. "Please." Her arms tightened around the boy. "We have nowhere else to go."

Caution prickled Elaine's awareness. The press was not easy to discover, especially in a place where so many warehouses were abandoned, their stores depleted by the occupation.

Elaine scanned the room. "Is there anyone else here with you?"

The mother shook her head. "It's only us."

Elaine lowered the blade but kept it in her hand as a precaution.

"My husband, Lewis, is in America," the woman stated, her stare fixed on the knife. "We are alone." Her voice caught.

"Why did you come here and how did you get in?"

"We escaped." She stroked a hand over her son's dark hair and spoke in a gentle tone. "I heard the Gestapo at our door saying they had reports of movement in the home after the occupants left, where an older couple were keeping us hidden. We went out the back door and walked as far as we could. But when the curfew began, I panicked and climbed over the terrace wall at the back of the building. The door there was open and no one was around. That's how we entered the warehouse..."

Elaine let out a slow exhale. Her foolish error could have been more disastrous. The noxious odor of grease and oil exacerbated her headache earlier, the fumes more than she could take with the press's repeated banging. But she never suspected anyone would break onto the terrace, not with the neighborhood being so old and practically abandoned.

But then, desperation often led to impulsive decisions.

Both women watched one another with wariness. While Elaine had been drilled to always be vigilant, there was something innate in her that told her to trust this frightened woman. Her young child pressed against her chest nestled closer against the black outdoor coat the woman still wore.

At last, Elaine tucked the knife behind her, and the tension drained—mostly—from her taut muscles. "Have you had dinner?"

The woman swallowed. "Please, if you have just something for my son."

"You may have some for yourself as well." Elaine had seen too many starving women giving all their food to their children.

Still, the woman hesitated, her eyes wide and cautious, as obviously disinclined to trust as Elaine.

"I'm Elaine." She waved for the woman to follow her.

The woman regarded her for a long moment. "I'm Sarah and this is Noah." The little boy in her arms raised his head and blinked up with eyes like his mother—hazel and heavily lashed, his appearance angelic. Dark curls fell over his serious brow, and a crease lined one flushed cheek where he'd been sleeping against his mother.

He was small and thin, making it hard to place his age. Perhaps between two and four. Children were no longer plump with youth as they'd once been, their growth stunted by a lack of proper nutrition.

Sarah grasped Noah to her as she rose. He laid his head on her shoulder, more for comfort than weariness, his gaze alert.

Elaine led them to the kitchen. "Please have a seat." She indicated the small wooden table that wobbled.

An old copy of *Le Nouvelliste*—the Nazis-approved publication for France's public—was wadded beneath the shortened leg like a bit of trapped rubbish, its text ragged and torn from the sharp peg. Many people who purchased the newspaper did so with the intent to burn it for warmth with fuel being so scarce.

Sarah sank into one of the mismatched chairs with her son. His wrinkled gray pants showed his ankles, and his navy winter coat was buttoned up to his skinny neck.

The water in the kettle was still hot, and while chicory coffee steeped, Elaine cut up the last of the bread.

"You are with the Resistance?" Sarah asked.

The knife gliding through the hard crust stopped short as Elaine stiffened.

"This is the office of the Bureau of Geophysical Research," Sarah said slowly. "Which does not require machines like the ones you possess. Copies of *Combat* and *Défence de la France* are sitting here on the counter." She paused, studying Elaine. "I'm not asking to frighten you, but to put myself at ease."

Sarah navigated her hand around her son to reach within her jacket pocket and spread an identity card on the table. The woman's black-and-white image looked up at her, the red JUIF stamp brilliant where it overlapped her shoulder.

"You are Jewish," Elaine said.

"You are Resistance?" Sarah pressed.

The two women stared at one another, a silent battle waging for trust, powered by fear and the threat of betrayal.

"Oui," Elaine replied at last as she scooped up the last pre-

cious bit of the strawberry jam. The spoon clinked against the glass jar as she scraped at what was left, the smear of translucent red flecked with minuscule seeds.

Saliva filled her mouth at the tart, sweet scent as she set what was to be her own dinner onto the table with a muffled clink of china against the wood.

Sarah's stare was part bravado, part fear. "*Oui*, we are Jewish."

Noah's eyes widened at the food in front of him, but he did not reach for any until Sarah gave him a slight nod. He immediately claimed a piece, taking a bite as big as his small mouth would allow.

Elaine poured a mug of chicory coffee for herself and Sarah. Noah devoured his slice and took a second.

"I've already eaten," Elaine lied. "Please help yourself."

Sarah inclined her head with gratitude and accepted some food from the plate, chewing slowly.

As she ate, Elaine gathered the remnants of bread on the cutting board into a neat pile and removed a tin from the shelf to carefully swipe the crumbs inside to join a collection of others. It was a habit formed at the start of the ration as suggested in one of the women's magazines. Those little bits of bread, once thrown away, could make such things as eggs and milk go further in recipes and offer an extra bulk that might make one feel satisfied after a meal.

Or as close to satisfied as anyone could be these days.

"You said your husband was in America." Elaine joined them at the table with her own mug as Noah gleefully consumed his fourth piece, sticky red jam glistening around his cherubic lips. "Why are you not with him?"

Sarah took a sip from her chicory coffee. "We were all supposed to flee Paris back when rumors indicated Hitler might attempt to pass the Maginot Line. Before we could go, my mother became ill. From what we understood, it was only the men who were in danger of the Germans, and so I insisted Lewis go on without us. We didn't know..."

They didn't know how the Bosche would strip away a Jew's freedom until they were relegated to a cramped life. Until they were sent away. Until those remaining had no choice but to hide in order to survive.

Sarah glanced reverently at her right hand. "My mother died several months later. Before the roundup in Paris. An organization helped us to Lyon, but that was as far as they could take us. It cost me my mother's ruby ring but was well worth the expense." She rubbed at the base of her finger where the jewelry had likely been. "We did not expect to be stranded here, but then the Nazis occupied the Free Zone."

She smoothed her son's hair from his face as he reached for the final piece of bread. "Those who aided us wanted to take Noah somewhere safe, saying it would be easier to protect him than it would be both of us together."

The little boy looked up at his mother with affection gleaming in his eyes.

"It is selfish to keep him with me, I know, but we suffered many losses before we finally had Noah." She studied her son as he took an unabashed bite of the food. "I've heard terrifying tales of organizations with children being captured, the little ones too noisy and chaotic to properly conceal." Pain shone in her eyes. "I also know there is a possibility that if I let him go, he might never come back to me. He is too young to remember his name as well as those of myself and my husband. I couldn't bear the thought of losing Noah."

Elaine and Joseph spent their marriage anticipating that she might eventually become pregnant. When a babe had failed to take root in her womb, neither of them had been overly distraught. Now she understood that perhaps they were fortunate to avoid having a child in a world such as theirs.

"Our family is broken apart." Sarah's voice was thick with

emotion. "I want to be with my husband, all of us reunited once more. Do you know anyone who can help us?"

Elaine shifted her focus into the dark, murky brew in her cup. It was one thing to find a place for the two, but quite another to manage a transport for them to America.

"Please," Sarah said when Elaine had been silent for too long. "I haven't been able to get word to him after his arrival in New York when he wrote to give the address he secured for us. It has been over two years since we last corresponded." A tear spilled down her cheek, but she abruptly swept it away. "I yearn for him. Every day without him cuts deeper into my soul until it feels as though my heart has been ripped out."

Elaine knew such loss. She pulled in a breath that made her lungs and chest ache.

There had been no word of Joseph since his departure for the camp. And while she tried hard not to let her despair debilitate her, he was never completely gone from her thoughts, keeping the flicker of hope alive.

It was that same hope that now glimmered in Sarah's watery eyes. In her lap, Noah shoved the last of the bread into his mouth, chewing groggily, his lids gradually falling closed.

"I will ask around tomorrow," Elaine said at last, resolved to bring the matter up with Marcel. "In the meantime, you should rest."

The floor of the narrow room used for identity cards and stamps was hard and frigid, but still more comfortable than if Elaine attempted to sleep in the drafty openness of the warehouse. At least being in the vicinity meant she would wake upon Marcel's arrival.

He gave her a quizzical look as she emerged from the small room that next morning. She ran a hand subconsciously down her short blond hair. "I need to speak with you."

"Did the bedding area flood again?"

She shook her head and Marcel's features relaxed. The building was subject to the plight of all older construction with faulty electricity, dampness and cold managing to always creep in. And, of course, the occasional flooding.

"It's far more delicate than that," she cautioned.

The concern was back on his face, and she quickly informed him of Sarah and Noah.

"Is there a contact who can help them on their journey to America?" she queried after her explanation.

He looked at her as if she just asked him to send them to the moon. "Everyone wants to go to America."

"Then surely there's a way."

He shook his head. "None that I am aware. I can put her in touch with one of the Jewish networks."

"They would just relocate her again or place her son in someone else's care."

"They can't get to America," he said with a finality Elaine refused to accept.

It was then an idea struck her, one inspired by the hidden messages sometimes included in the articles and images they printed in the clandestine newspapers. While she did not know all the operative phrasing used, either Antoine could help her, or she could use the coding method she'd implemented when she'd first joined the Resistance.

She tried again. "What if I compose an article with a code—"

"No." He turned to the newspapers that were printed late the prior night.

There wouldn't be any errors on the flimsy pages. Elaine saw to that with the same level of precision that Marcel himself applied. Her attention to detail was what made her such a good apprentice, and she knew it.

"We do coded messages all the time," she countered.

"Not to arrange for relocation to America." He continued to study the papers, flicking through the top fifty or so.

His disinclination to agree wasn't indicative of cruelty by any means. In the months Elaine worked with Marcel, he faced many hard decisions. Through it all, his choices were for what bettered the newspaper first and foremost, and the greater population after that.

She also knew him well enough to understand this was an argument she would not win. "I'll see if someone in the Maquis can help, perhaps."

He hummed with distracted agreement. "You will need to find another place for them to stay." He straightened from the stack of papers, his fingertips shaded with a dusting of ink. "They cannot remain here."

All the safe houses Elaine had spent time in rushed back to her, the desolate locations with sparse furnishings that reeked of solitude and despondency. The ones whose brusque hosts hurried her out in the morning just after curfew, before anyone else walked the streets. All those options were no place for a family. Not for a small boy with big hazel eyes filled with ready trust.

"I can ask Manon," Elaine volunteered.

Marcel lifted a brow. "Do your personalities not suit?"

Quite the opposite. They were both content to be left to their own demons in the tidy apartment. There was respect between them in that they never asked probing questions of one another, but they certainly had not bonded. That was yet another social relic of times before the occupation.

Without waiting for her reply, he marched over to the automatic press to examine the gears and switches, a father checking in on his child after a delayed absence.

"I'm content living with Manon, but I think her apartment would offer more of a home than other options," Elaine said at last.

"You'll need to ask Manon if she is willing to take the risk first." Marcel pulled a rag from the pocket of his coat and wiped off a fresh streak of oil from his hands. "We can provide the necessary papers and ration cards, but you said she has a son...?"

He looked at her pointedly as he asked the question and the realization dawned. Noah would, of course, be circumcised, which couldn't be hidden with false documents.

"As a father of a boy, I can tell you they aren't quiet either." An affectionate smile touched his mouth, the way it always did when he spoke of his family.

Imagining Noah with his pensive, mute stare being rambunctious didn't seem possible. But then, he had been tired the night before. Perhaps after some rest, he would be terrorizing the world with shouts and jumps as any other child forcefully restrained indoors.

"I'll speak to Manon and see if I can gather more supplies while I'm out." Elaine smoothed the wrinkles from her clothes, collected her handbag complete with her broad wallet of black market ration cards in her name, and hooked the shopping basket handle at her elbow. Sarah and Noah had consumed the last of the bread, and there were no other provisions. Doubtless, they would wake hungry for something in their bellies.

As she waited four hours in the queue at the grocer in the hopes of finding a tin of peas or even a little milk, apprehension at her decision twisted in her chest. She could accept the risk of helping Sarah and Noah herself, but was it fair to put Manon in danger?

THIRTEEN

Ava

Children rolled hoops outside the large white building, their laughter filling the refreshing October air. Ava smiled to herself at their unfettered joy as she approached the dining hall where the JDC distributed food for the refugees.

She had seen too many small, solemn faces emerging from the boats and trains depositing countless numbers in Lisbon. Inside, their parents leaned against the wall, their backs touching the long blue stripe that broke up the white paint to give the starkness a more welcome appearance. They were not at ease as their children were, their faces tense and anxious as they whispered to one another their fears to keep the little ones from overhearing.

A little girl waved to Ava, a picture book in her hand and a grin lighting up her entire face. The book was one of many Ava had purchased with her own money, and it filled her with a contented warmth to see it so loved.

Ethan strolled toward her, wearing a casual button-down shirt rolled up to his forearms. "Miss Harper. Thank you so much for coming."

"Ava, please," she said, having made a similar request when she met him the week before. "It's my pleasure."

"I know you want to meet the man who can find the clandestine press papers, but I still appreciate your generosity assisting me in distributing food. We never seem to have enough hands." He gave her a tired smile, and she couldn't help but wonder at how many hours he worked per day.

"I'm glad to be an extra set of hands and plan to come more often now that I have your permission," Ava said earnestly. And truly there was no other way she'd rather spend a day off from the office.

"My permission?" He chuckled. "More like my desperate plea." Waving for her to follow, he led her into a room supported by columns at its center, the wall bearing the same long blue stripe as the building's entry. Two rows of tables ran parallel to one another, each place set with a white plate, a spoon ceremoniously resting above it, and a blue-rimmed white mug. The yeasty scent of bread lingered beneath the savory aroma of a grill and roasting meat.

"I'll introduce you to Otto once everyone has eaten, if that's all right," Ethan said.

"Of course." Ava set to work, doling out *bifanas*, a simple sandwich consisting of bread and meat. Though the popular spiced pork was replaced with beef instead.

Many did not appear mired in poverty, but she had been in Lisbon long enough by now to know that did not mean they had money. Gemstones and jewelry were overly prevalent and sold so often, their weight scarcely fetched enough coin to feed a family for a few days, let alone a week.

She'd also learned many refugees would rather forego a meal than miss an afternoon at a café, where they could reunite with their countrymen and forget, for one brief moment, their circumstsances. It was a marvel what community could do in such times of strife, when all else felt lost.

Organizations like the JDC fostered that community and brought brightness back to the children's faces.

Four hours scrambled by in a rush of refilling food, clearing plates, carrying items for people when their hands were full, and finding vacated seats for fresh arrivals. This was accompanied by the cacophony of countless voices engaged in various conversations amid the backdrop of clinking dishes and flatware.

In the end, there was still food remaining with not one person left hungry. Once the remnants were secured for the meal later that night and the dishes had been removed from the long tables, Ethan led Ava outside to where a group of men lingered beneath a cloud of smoke. As she neared, an older man with silver hair withdrew a pipe from his mouth and nodded.

"This is Otto," Ethan said. "He often meets with newly arrived refugees and has been able to obtain several newspapers for you, specifically from France. I believe he has something else as well." He cast a questionable look to the older man.

Otto was thin, as most refugees were, his body carved away by the mean rations in France, his face lined from worry, but oppression had not yet dulled his deep brown eyes, which regarded her with a sharp clarity.

"I may," Otto said cryptically. "If you are free to talk."

"I'm here all day," Ava replied.

He inclined his head, then led her to a wooden table in the sunshine where he gestured to a chair for her as he sat in one himself. "You are an American librarian, yes?"

"I am. My name is Ava Harper."

His teeth clicked onto his pipe as he inhaled slightly, nodding in greeting. The scent of the tobacco was sweet, reminiscent of her father as he pored over various texts late at night with a snifter at his side and a pipe pinched in his mouth. The image flashed in her mind with a pang of heartfelt fondness.

Otto blew out a stream of smoke and cradled the polished

bowl of the pipe in his hand. "You are here to gather publications, as I am to understand it."

"That is correct." She sat forward. "I find value in clandestine presses. I've been reading several, especially *Combat*, and have found them to be most informative."

He nodded. "I am partial to *Combat* myself. It is for soldiers and intellectuals. I was a soldier in the Great War. And an intellectual…" His head tilted. "I'd like to think I am." He smiled at his humble statement and lifted his forefinger. "But what if I have something far greater than a newspaper?"

"What do you have?" She tried to keep her tone casual. There was always a game of patience when it came to obtaining important documents and texts, a sense that being overeager might push it from her grasp.

Dry leaves rustled overhead, and the breeze rippled Ava's skirt against her calves.

"It is something very special to me." Otto considered his pipe.

"I can ensure it is returned to you in the exact condition in which it was received," Ava said. "I need only to photograph it at the embassy."

He nodded and tucked his pipe in his mouth, puffing threads of smoke from between his lips as he reached into his breast pocket and withdrew an envelope. The cream-colored paper was dented and crumpled, dirt smeared in gritty streaks throughout. It was addressed to Otto Müller at a location somewhere in Marseille.

His gaze met hers, and he pulled the pipe free from his thin lips. "You know of the persecution of Jews, yes?"

"I do," Ava said in firm agreement. "One need only see the refugees emerging from the Nazi occupied countries to understand the truth of their oppression."

"Your country does not want to believe we are being singled out, that our people are being arrested." Color touched his cheeks. "That all around Europe, Jews are disappearing, being killed in large numbers." His fingertips tapped the battered envelope, and he regarded it with solemn reverence. "People like Petra."

A stab of patriotism demanded that Ava defend her own country, to protest that they did indeed believe. But, sadly, many did not. Newspaper accounts of the Jewish persecution were buried within the pages, the atrocities chalked up to "war rumors" that few believed.

A hoop rolled by, and a boy chased after it with a girl in a striped dress close on his heels; both wore wide grins as their hair blew back.

"We are safe here in Lisbon." Otto followed the children with his gaze and lifted a hand in a gesture like a shrug. "Well, relatively safe."

Ava knew what he meant. The PVDE kept its distance, placated by the monthly check-ins by the refugees. However, once visas expired, the secret police grew agitated, their demeanors less cordial and more contentious. As if the refugees wished to stay on Portuguese soil where Germans strode by with their ramrod straight backs and close-cropped hair, eyes hard with vile glares.

Then there was the danger of Germany making good on its threat to take Portugal...

"We all sacrificed much to be here," Otto went on. "Not only our belongings, but also ourselves." He puffed on his pipe, his teeth clicking against the stem. "To you, I am an old man." Smoke billowed from his lips as he spoke. "One who can produce these papers you seek for your country." He gave a light shrug. "I do not blame you—you are doing your job." He shifted in his seat to indicate the white building with his pipe. "To the JDC, I am another mouth to feed, a body who requires a bed for rest. To the other refugees, I am a lone person with no family." He settled back into his chair and stared at the fragrant smoke curling up from his pipe. "Here, I am no one."

"That isn't true." But even as Ava offered her protest, she was aware of the weight of his words on her conscience.

He frowned at her platitude.

He was not the only one to be disappointed. Ava understood what he meant far more than most might. There had been a time when she started over, marked with demeaning labels she did not want to identify her. An orphan, the child without parents to care for her. A new girl at a new school with no friends and a strange accent. A little sister who robbed her elder brother of the college education he should have had.

But now was not for her or her life story. Understanding and knowledge were wasted if one did not apply them to life.

Ava pushed the letter back toward him and settled her hands on the table, focusing on him and only him. "Tell me who you are, Otto Müller."

His chin lifted. "I am an engineer. I trained at Arts et Métiers ParisTech."

Ava recognized the name from a text she had recently photographed on French engineering. With so many factories in France, it had been her hope to identify weaknesses that might help the US grind Nazi operations in France to a halt.

A smile teased at his lips. "You know the school."

"It's renowned."

He nodded in gratitude. "I excelled there at industrial engineering. So, you see why I could not remain in Paris when the Nazis were coming."

A man of his experience would have immediately been put to work by the Germans to manufacture arms. At least, until all Jews were made to quit their jobs and relocate.

"I tried to convince my sister to join me," Otto continued. "But we lived in France since we were children, when our parents moved there for my father's job. He too was an engineer." He sighed. "France is home. I should have pushed harder for Petra and her family to leave as well." He shook his head, as if doing so would free him of regret.

"Even in Marseille I was not safe," he continued. "As the Germans swept over the border, the embassies were overrun as were the ticket offices. I cannot count the hours I spent waiting in an endless queue, sleeping where I stood, going without meals. But when you are a French Jew, and your other nationality is German…" He gave a cynical smirk. "I finally paid someone to forge an exit visa from France and a transit visa into Spain, then Portugal. They all worked, except Spain, who imprisoned me for two weeks before a friend could bribe my way to freedom. Once I arrived here, I fell yet again into an exhaustive wait. One of the lucky ones to have escaped…" He gave a sound somewhere between a choke and a laugh.

"The Nazis have taken everything from us." Grief lined his face and his shoulders sagged in defeat, his pipe held loosely and forgotten in his left hand. "Our families are gone, our homes commandeered and given to those who spoke against us, our jobs are nonexistent, our futures unknown and we have nothing but the belongings that will fit in a suitcase or upon our backs. We have succeeded in escaping them, but they have still succeeded in destroying us."

Ava shook her head. "No."

Otto's brows rose, his stare incredulous. "I was a man of great wealth and influence. I commanded respect wherever I went. Now I am nothing."

"You aren't," Ava said vehemently. "Not when you are here to tell your story. Not when there are those like Ethan who work miracles with limited resources to get you onto safe shores. Not when people like me are photographing your books, your correspondence, your papers, and your lives to share your heritage, to ensure Hitler can never make any of you into nothing. He will not succeed in destroying you."

Otto stared at her, and emotion sparked in his eyes. "It is the fear of every generation that the rising youths will destroy this world." He pushed the envelope toward her. "I believe you just may save it."

She hesitated as she reached for the letter.

"Let Petra's story live forever, for I believe she is no longer of this world." Otto swallowed, taking a moment before pulling another envelope free from his jacket, this one crisp and clean. "I will be able to obtain more newspapers than this, but here is what I have for now."

"Thank you for trusting me." Ava carefully accepted both items.

"Thank you for understanding." Otto nodded to Ava and pushed up from the table, leaving a cloud of sweet, gray smoke in his wake.

The temptation to remove Otto's letter from her purse and read its contents was almost unbearable. Whatever it contained was precious to Otto, and that made it precious to Ava. And so she sat back and bided her time until she was inside the large conference room of the embassy the following day.

In her time at the Library of Congress, she had handled many delicate items of note. There had been a medieval text on medicine and the power of stones from the thirteenth century with muted ink upon yellowed and brown-spotted vellum. There had been *The Federalist* from the eighteenth century with Eliza Hamilton's careful signature at its top from Thomas Jefferson's own private collection that he sold to the library after a fire ravaged its stock. She had even held the library's copy of the Gutenberg Bible.

It was with that same care and respect that she now extracted the letter from its envelope and laid it on the table to read.

Dearest brother—At present, I sit in Vél d'Hiv, the sports arena you once visited when you cheered on cyclists in the Olympics more than fifteen years ago. The glass ceiling has been painted blue to prevent visibility to bombers, and it leaves us all awash in a ghastly green pallor. Worse still, it draws the heat of the intense summer sun. They mean to keep us all contained within—the thousands of us whom they have captured and transported where we are penned like animals. The windows are sealed tightly shut, so there is no air entering to offer salvation and nothing foul may leave. And there is much that is foul. The lavatories are either locked or clogged, and the odor is so thick in the heat that I can scarce draw breath.

It was my intent to write only to let you know where we were, but now that I have pen to paper and nothing but an eternal wait ahead of me, I find myself compelled to share with you what exactly has transpired in these years in Paris. What brought us to where we are now...

Peggy came into the room and stopped short when she saw Ava, a lunch bag in her hand. "Oops, sorry. I didn't realize anyone was in here."

Ava waved her off. "I don't mind if you stay so long as the food doesn't go near any paper, including this."

"Thanks." Peggy sat at the opposite side of the long table and rustled in her sack. "What is that you have there?"

"A letter," Ava replied. "From a French engineer I met earlier who fled the Nazis. His sister wrote this." As she explained it, she recalled the way Otto had surmised Petra was no longer alive. "She was in the roundup at Vél d'Hiv and managed to sneak out this correspondence to him."

Peggy leaned closer. "What's it say?"

Ava regarded the paper, the slanted, messy text cast in the stark light of the microfilm set up. "Horrible things about the conditions in Paris and gratitude that her brother had gone to the Free Zone."

Ava continued to read of the injustices—the stripping of their rights to own radios, to ride bikes and cars and finally to work, all noted in the letter with painful detail. Then she came to the roundup itself:

We were not the only ones arrested in the building. Hundreds were gathered in the courtyard, each with that blazing yellow patch sewn to their clothing. Stars that were run aground, held captive by the sky they had once shone freely within. It was such a sight to

behold, my brother, such a sight that I shall never forget. Frightened parents trying to soothe frightened children, people with their
belongings tied into sheets instead of suitcases, friends crying out
for those who were being taken away. One woman jumped from the
highest floor with both her children. I will not share what I saw in
that terrible moment, but I cannot erase the horror etched on the
backs of my lids every time I close my eyes.

From the roundup, they were placed into the Vélodrome
where they remained for four days without additional food or
properly functioning lavatories and only one waterspout to share
for thousands. As they suffered through their endless wait, people began to die around her, desperate and helpless.

The close of the letter struck Ava with its bleakness and left
a knot in her chest as she read those resigned, ill-fated words.

We have been told we are to go to camps to labor for Germany.
I do not say this aloud to Sophie, nor even to David, who is trying
so very hard to be brave for us all, but I do not think we are going
to a work camp.

We have many children held here with us. Not simply youths
with strong limbs and boundless energy, though even this heat
has made their efforts wane. No, these are littles ones who still
cling to their mothers' legs and gaze about with mute fear. I do not
know how they could work any more than the people who are in
wheelchairs. Perhaps the Germans have opportunities for people
to remain seated as they work. Or perhaps children can perform
small tasks running items about. But there is a tension in my lower
stomach, the same one I had when Oma died. I do not think...

No, I cannot put such fears to paper.

I do not know where we are going, but want to tell you I love
you, my dear brother.

Ava explained the letter as she read it to Peggy, who had
stopped eating her lunch, listening with rapt attention. "That's
so terrible," Peggy said softly.

Ava swallowed at the thickness in her throat. "It's why we need to save this as well as the publications we're finding."

Peggy nodded and took a distracted bite of her sandwich before gathering up the rest of her meal and departing.

In the silence of the empty room, Ava leaned back in her chair and regarded the correspondence, the very reverence with which Otto had gazed upon it now resounding within her.

Suddenly the crush of what they were up against was too much. Rage flared in her, licking white-hot at her insides, scalding her heart. The stories could be buried in newspapers, downplayed by the government and denied by those with willing blinders over their eyes, but Ava knew the harsh truth without question.

The door opened, and Mike came in, followed by Mr. Sims and Peggy.

"Are you photographing letters now?" Mr. Sims's glare bored into her.

Ava looked to Peggy, who threw her hands up in a feeble gesture. "I told them about it. I couldn't stop thinking of that woman's story and mentioned it to them. I didn't—"

"We are only allotted a small amount of space per two weeks on that clipper," Mr. Sims bellowed. "And you're wasting it with family correspondence?" His fleshy face reddened. "Do you have any idea how hard celluloid film is to find?"

"And a German pamphlet of a fan is so much more important?" Ava shot back, referring to some of the more ridiculous things they sent to DC and refusing to be cowed by his censure.

Mr. Sims narrowed his eyes. "It could be useful in breaking down the mechanics of other items."

Ava stood up, evening out his advantage of looming over her. "This is important. People need to know about this."

"They already know. It's in the papers," he scoffed. "It's a letter and a waste of time."

Anger and irritation roiled in Ava's mind. "Mr. Sims, there's more to it than all that," she said levelly. "Today is ephemeral."

His face screwed up at her effrontery. "What the hell do you mean by that?"

She was saying the wrong thing again, muddying what she meant in her urgency to defend her stance. Drawing in a deep breath, she refocused her efforts and tried again. "I mean that this present we live in is tomorrow's history. You ask if this is important. This is the education for our future, to learn from the mistakes that have been made now and never let atrocities such as this continue or be repeated."

The room fell silent.

"She's got you there, Simsie." Mike's voice broke the spell, and Mr. Sims swiveled his glare on the younger man.

"Don't call me Simsie," he barked. "Or you'll be back on US soil before you can attempt an apology." With that, he stormed from the room.

Peggy mouthed, *I'm sorry.*

But Ava shook her head. This was an argument that needed to happen, one she had to win. Going forward, she would do everything possible to acquire more letters like this one, so the world would know exactly what the Jews of Europe were up against.

FOURTEEN

Elaine

Elaine found Manon sitting on the cushioned seat at the piano, her slender fingers resting on the keys without playing. As if the instrument no longer gave off music. Or perhaps it was the woman who'd lost the melody.

"Manon?" Elaine stepped lightly into the room to avoid startling her.

Manon removed her hands from the piano. "I did not expect you for some time."

"I need to speak with you."

Manon turned on the bench to face Elaine. Her dark eyes seemed larger than usual, her cheeks hollow beneath her sharp cheekbones. There was always a fragility about the woman, but suddenly she appeared immensely delicate, susceptible to being swept away by the slightest whisper of wind.

Perhaps the conversation should not be had after all.

"What is it?" Manon asked.

Elaine's tongue went still with indecision.

"Do you need my help?" Manon indicated she should take

a seat on the plush blue velvet settee. "Whatever it is that is on your mind that you are struggling to say, I want to know what it is." Despite her wan appearance, her voice was strong.

Elaine obediently settled on the sofa without leaning back, and the words dislodged from the stubborn place in her chest. "I've met a mother and son who are without a home at present. Yours would be more suited for them than other safe houses." Elaine gave a regretful smile. "I know that means I will give up my place here with you, but I think it better for them."

"You may stay as well," Manon offered. "The couch—"

"I couldn't add to your risk or theirs."

Manon gave a small, thoughtful smile. "It is considerate of you to put them first. They can come, of course."

"They are Jewish," Elaine said. "The boy…"

Manon nodded. "I understand."

"It will place you in more danger than previous guests."

Manon exhaled a bitter laugh. "Danger."

Her reaction took Elaine aback somewhat. "The child might be loud…"

The brief mirth slipped from Manon's face as she turned to the piano, studying the display of photographs. "It will be good to have a child here again."

The statement was made more to herself than to Elaine. Still looking at the pictures, Manon continued in a thin voice. "Did you know I had a son?"

Had.

Elaine couldn't help but glance up at the portraits where a black-and-white Manon leaned her head toward the dark-haired man, and another where a baby gazed out with large eyes and a dimpled smile. War was unkind to all, but mostly to the vulnerable.

"Is that him?" Elaine asked, breaking the weight of silence that settled between them. "Your son."

Manon lifted a small palm-sized frame from the piano. "Yes."

With slow and gentle care, she ran a finger down the image. "My husband was killed at Dunkirk shortly after I discovered I was with child."

Part of Elaine felt she was not worthy of this story, and yet another part of her wondered if the telling might be something of a balm to Manon's soul.

"When Claude was born, I devoted myself to him," Manon continued. "He was the only piece I had left of the man I loved so dearly." She went quiet for a while, but Elaine did not press her, content to let the conversation fade away if that was Manon's wish.

Manon sighed, as though it hurt to breathe, a discomfort with which Elaine had become personally acquainted.

"One day I was baking and needed a small pat of butter," Manon eventually said. "A friend in the next building and I often shared our limited goods. Claude was sleeping, so peaceful and precious that I did not want to rouse him for such a short trip. After all, I only planned to be gone for a few minutes at most. I left him."

The frame shook in her hand before she gingerly settled it in her lap. "When I went to see Georgette, she wasn't there, but the Germans were. Apparently, she was with the Resistance and had been caught. I was arrested as an accomplice."

Elaine held her breath, not wanting to learn the rest of the story, but unable to tell the other woman to stop.

"They refused to accept my innocence, no matter how I beseeched them." Manon's tone went flat, the way one did when they separated from all emotion. For survival. And it was no wonder when she continued. "Rather than helping me, they slapped the cell bars with their truncheons and ordered me to be silent. When they finally released me, my arms and hands were bloodied and bruised from beating on the doors of my prison. My voice was gone from crying to be heard. My shirt…" Her words caught. "My shirt was stiff with the wasted milk my body produced for my sweet son." She cradled the picture of Claude's happy visage. "They kept me for nine days."

Elaine drew in a sharp gasp and tried to cover it with her hand. But there was no hiding her shocked reaction to such horror.

Manon shifted her focus from her son's photograph to the blank wall in the distance. "When I returned home, I stood in front of my door for over an hour before bringing myself to enter. I already knew it was too late for him."

"I'm so sorry," Elaine whispered. She wished for a more insightful response, something that might be of better comfort. But there was no balm for a wound such as Manon's. Nothing could ever heal what had been so violently ripped away.

When Manon looked up, her eyes were no longer flat pools of black, but now flared with more spirit than Elaine had ever seen in them. "I joined the very Resistance they erroneously persecuted me for belonging to, and I do not worry about danger. I have nothing left to lose. If it were not for my faith, I would have joined my husband and son months ago." The blaze of her expression waned, as energy did when it burned bright and was gone just as quickly. "Perhaps this boy will be another chance for me. To save what I could not with my own."

She looked down at the picture once more, lost in her thoughts. Elaine rose and put a hand on Manon's bony shoulder. The other woman did not stir.

Her story stayed with Elaine for the rest of the day and would remain with her for her entire life. Now, however, she was glad she had spoken to the other woman and hoped that in helping to save Sarah and Noah, Manon might also perhaps save part of herself.

When Elaine returned to the warehouse, she found the print room in full production with preparations for the latest paper. Antoine was hunched over the desk, his focus as sharp as the point with which he sketched in his artistic hand over the metal.

Marcel fluttered over the printing presses like a mother hen, and Jean sat at the table where Elaine occasionally worked with the Roneo, little Noah in front of him.

Jean covered his eyes with his hands, then threw them back to reveal his face, his smile exaggerated like a performer at a fair. Sarah was at Noah's side, gazing down at her son as the boy stared up at Jean with wide, hazel eyes. Every time Jean uncovered his face, Noah's mouth would lift with the slightest hint of cautious joy.

The sight was bittersweet. The effects of war were everywhere in Lyon and the children were not unaffected, the wondrous shine of youth buffed away by the oppressive Nazi occupation.

"I found some bread and a tin of sardines," Elaine announced as she joined them. "As well as some Jerusalem artichokes and rutabagas."

Noah sat upright, no longer interested in Jean with the prospect of food.

Elaine handed her basket to Sarah. "I also found a safe place for you to stay. The woman is quiet, but kind, and her home is welcoming."

Sarah nodded her thanks.

"I am trying to do what I can to find a way for you to get to America," Elaine said in a low voice.

Sarah closed her eyes, her face relaxed in gratitude. Noah tugged at the rim of the shopping basket in an attempt to see what was inside, almost tipping the precious contents. With a patient laugh, Sarah swept it away from him and pulled her son into her arms, carrying him off to the kitchen.

Together, Elaine and Jean watched the two exit the warehouse, Sarah's footsteps drowned out by the cacophonous humming and banging of the automatic printing press.

"I'd like children someday," Jean said wistfully. "To get married after this war."

"With a certain blond," Elaine teased.

A flush blossomed over Jean's young face.

"I want to help Sarah and Noah," she said, her tone serious. "They need to be in America, to have their family reunited."

A doubtful look crossed Jean's face, much in the way that clouds blocked out the sun.

It was an impossible request that she was aware would take an act of God to set into motion. "Sarah hasn't seen her husband in two years."

"A lot of women haven't seen their husbands in that long." This was said with a somber sympathy reflected in Jean's bright blue eyes.

"Yes, but she actually stands a chance of getting to him and would be safer in doing so," Elaine said, surprised at how the truth of those words cut her. "Perhaps I am truly considering it because of my own husband."

The door to the warehouse squealed open, and Josette scuttled through the opening. Even from a distance, she appeared diminutive, her shoulders tucked forward as if silently willing to shrink herself into nothing.

Elaine went to her friend and fought to swallow her gasp of surprise. Josette's collarbones thrust out from her pallid skin like twigs, and the small gold crucifix seemed to droop an inch lower.

"Have you been ill?" Elaine asked, not embracing her for fear of breaking her.

A tic near Josette's right eye quivered. "No." She worked the corners of her mouth up in an unconvincing smile.

Elaine couldn't help but stare in horror. "What's happened to you?"

"I've been nervous lately." Josette's hand tightened around the basket handle, as if forcefully keeping herself from bringing her ragged nails to her lips.

"Perhaps taking some time off—"

"No." Josette protested with such vehemence, her voice cut

over the clatter of the printing press and called the attention of Jean, Marcel and even Antoine. Her gaze slid around the room, and she lowered her head with a shake of self-castigation.

"My neighbor was taken last night for harboring Jews, as well as those they were hiding," Josette said, her volume conversational again. "Every day we aren't doing something means more people are condemned to arrests and work camps."

Work camps.

The words always snagged at a wounded place in Elaine's heart and made all the worry for Joseph bubble forefront in her mind. Despite Etienne's constant promise to unearth information, no news was ever forthcoming.

Josette pulled an envelope from the false bottom of her basket, a slight tremor to her hands. "I must deliver this to Marcel, then I'm meeting Nicole back at the apartment."

Elaine nodded and took the item from her friend. "Take care of yourself. Please."

Josette's head bobbed in agreement, but the slide of her stare to the floor told Elaine the other woman wouldn't heed the warning.

"And give Nicole my love." Elaine embraced Josette gently, feeling nothing but fragile bones beneath her friend's gray coat.

Marcel approached as Josette strode away. "What do you think of her?" It was the same question he asked before.

Only this time, Elaine couldn't bring herself to remain silent. "I'm worried." She handed the item to Marcel.

"I am too." He didn't look at the envelope, but instead continued to study the door Josette had departed through.

Elaine left him to his delivery and went to the automatic printing press. The machine whirred with the flashing of papers, the spinning of gears and metal arms that reached and grabbed and shifted. Her own thoughts were precisely the same: in constant motion, flexing around worry and concern. For Josette whose composed nature was unraveling like a sweater with a loose thread. For Sarah and Noah who understood the poignancy of loss and the fear of losing more. For Manon and the pain of what she endured. For Joseph and how little information Elaine possessed of his location or health.

Perhaps being so lost in her thoughts kept her from noticing Etienne walk into the room.

"Elaine."

She startled at the voice beside her.

The tip of Etienne's nose was pink, his eyes bloodshot. "I need to speak with you."

A low rattle of fear vibrated through her.

Rather than share his news there, he led her to the back door where the prior evening, Sarah and Noah had slipped inside the warehouse. Elaine's knees went so soft, she worried she might slide to the floor before making it out onto the terrace.

Outside was a beautiful October day without a hint of a breeze to disrupt the crisp air as the sun streamed down through puffy white clouds. It was the kind of weather Elaine would have noticed and appreciated on any other day. Now, all she cared about was what Etienne had to say and what that meant for Joseph.

"Elaine." Etienne swept his battered old fedora from his head and clutched the brim with a white-knuckled grip.

"Oui?" How the word made it past her lips she'd never know.

"It's Joseph." Etienne's brows drew together with the intensity of one in deep concentration. As though he couldn't quite figure out what to say.

Elaine nodded for him to continue, not trusting her own voice.

He let out a shaky exhale. "I am so sorry to give you this news…"

Her stomach plummeted to the ground. She shook her head and backed away, not wanting to hear the rest. If she didn't hear, she couldn't know. And if she didn't know, it wouldn't be real.

There might still be a chance that Joseph lived. There might still be hope.

Etienne reached for her. He stank of stale cigarettes and desperation and regret. "Joseph is dead."

A blast of bitter wind swept through the terrace in that moment, upsetting the amber-colored leaves of the plane tree so they tumbled and scraped against one another.

Elaine clenched her hand into a fist and looked up at the long branches stretching into the sky overhead. The lush green foliage had faded to an autumnal gold. Another season passed with more to come, on and on in its endless cycle.

But Joseph would have no more seasons. He wouldn't witness the splendor of the world shifting into the myriad colors of the year, or feel its temperature rise and dip.

Just like he wouldn't be there to put his arm around her in a crowd of people to keep her from being jostled or prepare her coffee while she lazed just five minutes longer in bed.

There were so many times his stare went distant in the comfortable quiet moments between them. She swore his mind was made up of a complex series of cogs and gears that clicked through problems with a mechanical precision. Never again would she witness that familiar, scholarly gaze and wonder what world-changing dilemma he was internally solving.

He was a beacon of knowledge and in an instant, all the brilliance and intelligence was snuffed out like a flame, leaving not even a curl of smoke in its wake.

All that remained was a broken heart.

Hers.

"Elaine," Etienne said in a hoarse voice. "I'm so sorry."

In looking at him, her rage found its target. Grief carved deeply at Etienne's haggard face, his shoulders sloped with defeat, a soldier who'd lost his comrade.

But in that moment, when the pain of her own loss blistered her insides and left breathing difficult to drag through her aching chest, she could not summon sympathy for him. Not when she had trusted him to free Joseph from Montluc so long ago.

"Was my message delivered to him?" Anger edged her words like a weapon.

His expression was one of helplessness that tugged somewhere deep in the raw ache of her soul. "I have no way of knowing if he received your note. I can tell you that I called in every favor I had to make it happen."

Words had power.

She learned that from her fateful last fight with Joseph, painfully realizing that words spoken could never be taken back—words that no longer would be made right with an apology. The mistake was one she would not repeat even as the invective rose in her throat like bile.

He had failed Joseph. While Joseph was beaten by Werner, Etienne walked free. He left his best friend to die.

She almost choked as she swallowed down such bitterness. However, her refusal to lay such heavy accusations at his feet did not mean she would offer him forgiveness.

Instead, she put her back to Etienne and returned to the warehouse, her body numb and her heart on fire. Somehow, she managed to stay her tears. Deep down she was fully aware that when they did come, they would be like a dam breaking, flowing out in an uncontrollable wave that would be impossible to hold back.

Her actions were wooden for the rest of the day as she coordinated efforts to have Sarah and Noah settled at Manon's. Elaine brushed aside concerns for her well-being as she resumed her work. The men skirted around her, their concerned gazes flicking to her periodically as though they expected her to topple.

There were many moments she suspected she might as well.

No matter what task she set upon, her thoughts were of Joseph. From the times they strolled along the Rhône at night with stars dotting the sky like flecks of diamonds, to the countless mornings she kissed him goodbye as he left for work. With heavy regret, she also recalled when she had stopped that simple spousal affection after their fighting brought their marriage to its knees.

When the day began to darken into night, Marcel approached her. "Go to the back room, Elaine. Get some rest."

"I'd like to keep working," she replied numbly. "Being busy has helped."

Empathy showed in his eyes, so poignant it almost cracked the fragile shell of her composure. "If you think it will help," he said slowly, clearly not in agreement with her. "But only tonight."

Such kindness tugged at a guilty thread in her conscience for what she was about to do. She gave an obedient nod to Marcel, who pushed his arms into his jacket and picked up his hat, the top of his dark fedora pinched between his fingers, still hesitant.

"I'll be fine," she assured him.

He tossed a final, worried look her way, settled his hat on his head, and exited the room. Several long seconds later, the front door to the building slammed closed.

She was alone.

There wasn't a second to waste. She pulled out a piece of paper and immediately set to work to puzzle through the code, using the poem in circulation among Resistant that week: "Mignonne allons voir si la rose" by Pierre de Ronsard. That done, she went to the Linotype Machine Jean had been instructing her to use and painstakingly plucked at the keys, retyping an article on the bombing of nearby factories. Only this time, she slid the code into words, intentionally misspelling them.

The effort took a considerable amount of time on the strange keyboard. With lower letters on the left, capital on the right, and all the spacing and punctuation in the middle, it would likely be an age before she typed without looking or achieved a speed like Jean's.

The metal slugs with the lines of text slid down from the machine and cooled while she adjusted the printing sheet. Her pulse roared in her ears as she worked, carefully removing the previous verbiage and fitting the changed ones into the same space.

She readjusted the printing plate into the automatic press as it hummed to life and the papers spun their way through the ink. The first completed page settled onto the tray, followed swiftly by others. She picked it up and scanned the contents, confirming the final product to be exactly how she envisioned. Once the misspelled words were identified and the code broken, her message would be read as:

Jewish mother and child need transport to America.

It was stated as simply as she could word it. Members of the Resistance would know where to go to offer their aid. Marcel would, of course, be incensed by her direct disobedience, especially at the flawed words to the casual observer.

Elaine turned her thoughts to Joseph, to how many Jews he saved by changing their identity cards. And she recalled the woman she had given her own to, who now carried Joseph's surname.

In her husband's absence, Elaine continued on in the fight he had sacrificed everything for. And though she was aware he hadn't wanted her to be in the Resistance, he would have been proud of her.

That thought wrenched at her heart.

A tear plopped onto the page. The fresh ink sucked into the droplet, obliterating the careful lettering and turning her tear a murky black. It was followed by another and another still.

Elaine's legs were suddenly too weak to hold her upright. She folded to the floor beneath the weight of her profound grief, the pain exploding inside her too unbearable to endure. The walls holding back her sorrow became tenuous, and the dam collapsed as she yielded to the agony of a broken heart.

FIFTEEN

Ava arrived at the JDC center the next afternoon to return the letter to Otto.

"It was an honor to be entrusted with something this precious and powerful," she said as she handed it back.

He nodded and tucked the envelope into his tweed jacket pocket, pausing to give it a tender pat with his fingertips. "Petra's correspondence took several months to find me. I do not even know how it managed to be sent." Otto looked up at the sky, squinting as he did so. The way one did when trying to conceal the depth of their emotions. "Thank you for recording her words."

"I'm grateful for the opportunity to do so and would be glad to do more should anyone else have letters such as yours."

Otto nodded. "I can ask around." He withdrew another envelope from his pocket and handed it to her. "More newspapers from France."

She thanked him, promised to come by next week when she would be helping Ethan, then departed for the embassy.

And so it went for the next two weeks, receiving not only French newspapers, but also letters from refugees' family members and even clandestine publications from other areas of Europe.

Ava was familiar with *Combat* and *Libération*, but *Biuletyn Informacyjny* was a Polish one she hadn't seen before. The underground prints were easy to identify, not only by their smaller size, but by the single page, printed on the front and back. Even still, with a paper ration on and tight regulations in Nazi occupied areas, it was amazing the clandestine groups were able to find something to print on at all.

The creators of such publications would have to possess ingenuity and be utterly fearless. She often thought of all the people involved after her discussion on the matter with Lamant.

Time was of the essence while she settled them on the table in the embassy to photograph, but she couldn't stifle her temptation to skim the French and German content. Most especially *Combat*, whose forthright text appealed to her. There was no prevaricating or added filler to expand an article. It was concise, to the point, and immaculately edited.

Which was why it was so strange to come across not one typo, but several in a recent issue.

The piece was about a series of bombs in factories throughout Lyon impacting Nazi production, the typos dispersed from start to finish.

Like breadcrumbs.

The thought whispered at the back of Ava's mind, but she brushed it aside as whimsy and aimed the camera to capture the newspaper onto the roll of celluloid.

Mike entered the room with a stack of books. "Get a load of this. I found an entire set of German machinery guides in a stationery shop—that one in Chiado right next to the glove store." Arms full, he danced a few jitterbug steps and flashed her a wide grin.

"That's great." Ava put aside the boxy camera and approached him to examine his find. "May I?"

"I was actually going to ask you to lay your Kraut-reading peepers on this and let me know if it's as killer-diller as I'm hoping." He wiggled his head back and forth in a manner that suggested he already knew his hoard would be "killer-diller."

Ava laughed and held out her hand for the first book. "Let's see."

Mike placed the heavy text in her palm, and she drew open the cover. Drawings of machinery were labeled in intricate detail, the parts identified and explained in the sidelines with classic German precision. It was a tragedy that mechanical expertise as advanced as theirs was used for war and genocide when such knowledge could save the world rather than tear it apart.

She nodded in appreciation and took a second book. "This is incredible."

"Isn't it nuts to think it was there in a stationery shop?" Mike shook his head incredulously and peered at the newspapers lying beside Ava's camera. "Are those more secret prints from France?"

"They are," Ava replied, joining him. "And one from Poland. The engineer whose sister wrote the letter about Vél d'Hiv saved more for me."

"Nice going," Mike said with approval. "That's why you're so great at this job. You make personal connections. I can be kind of a fathead sometimes, I know." He held up a hand as if to stop her from protesting his statement, then pointed in the direction of Sims's office. "And we all know the big cheese isn't exactly a people-person. But you, you got this, kid."

It was genuine praise from someone who was deep down a good guy despite his bluster.

"I appreciate that." Ava's gaze wandered toward the edition of *Combat* she'd been photographing.

"Doesn't hurt that you're a real dish." Mike waggled his brows.

Ava rolled her eyes heavenward, and Mike gave a wink that

told her he knew how obnoxious he was before returning to his stack of German machinery texts. "I need to hop to it. If I want to get out of here on time tonight, I have to shoot these like crazy."

Whistling merrily to himself as he was wont to do, he opened one of the books and flexed the binding back, so the spine crackled as its glue splintered apart. Ava's mouth fell open at such abuse.

It wasn't his first offense. He was also guilty of tucking the corner of a page he needed as well as laying the book flat, page-side down when she'd complained about dog-earing.

"You need to be careful with those." Even as she spoke, she knew her note of caution was in vain.

He glanced emotionlessly at the book with the broken spine. "They're just books."

Ava didn't bother to suppress her grimace as she returned to her own work. After she'd finished photographing the clandestine newspapers, she helped Mike with his stack as he'd done with her before countless times. The sharing of labor had never really been discussed, and neither of them had ever asked the other for help. It was just something that came naturally to both of them and part of what made them such a good team.

It was also a good opportunity to handle books the way they should be.

But even as she went through the motions of repeated photography, the article in *Combat* with the typos clung irritably to the back of her mind like a burr.

Ava brought the edition of *Combat* home with her that night. First, she read through it again, searching the other articles to determine if they also contained typos she had initially missed.

They did not.

Then she set it aside and chastised herself for being ridiculous.

But even as she brushed her teeth that night, she still couldn't shake it from her thoughts.

She stalked out to the dining area where the publication sat on her table, took out a fresh pad of paper, and wrote down every wrong letter. There were fifty-eight staring back at her.

Fifty-eight in a print that never had even one typo was hardly a mistake. No, it was undeniably intentional.

She rearranged the letters, marking them off as she tried to create words in French, but nothing seemed to work. There were too many variations creating too many possibilities.

When the hands of her watch slipped past two in the morning, she resigned herself to give up for the night. The list of letters followed her into sleep, swirling in her brain and teasing at her subconscious. Not that it helped. In the morning she was just as stumped as before.

She woke to a foggy mind and an unresolved mystery. It would be best to put it aside, she knew, and yet could not stop herself from reconsidering those fifty-eight letters over and over in the background of her thoughts.

It was a crisp November day with a full sun overhead, and a breeze brisk enough to rouse the grogginess from her. Alfonso waved as she approached his kiosk.

They chatted briefly in Portuguese as they always did, though now he corrected her translation less and less. However, as they talked, there was a slight tension to him, an uneasiness that made him slide his gaze from hers several times.

"I have your papers for you." He bent to retrieve the stack. "There is one I think you should see. Just under the latest copy of *Das Reich*."

Ava thanked him, but he continued to stare at her. His smile was tight, and he gave her a ready nod, clearly wanting her to look at that moment.

Das Reich sat on top of the pile. She peeled it back to find a note. "The German has been asking about your schedule."

Ava folded the paper back into place as casually as she could and tried to ignore the unease prickling through her. "That does look interesting." She smiled and thanked him.

The German.

Lukas.

He gave her a worried wave and shifted his focus to another customer, a mother with a fidgeting toddler.

She glanced about but did not see the Nazi in the vicinity. Perhaps later, she could ask Alfonso for more information, if there was any more to be had. Regardless, the sensation of being watched suddenly crawled over her skin like something living.

A shudder ran down her back.

"Did someone walk over your grave?"

Ava spun around to find James standing behind her, a newspaper tucked under his arm, the word *Standard* from the *Evening Standard* just visible at the fold. It was the first time she'd seen him since the kiss, when the PVDE had followed them.

"I certainly hope not," Ava responded tersely.

He frowned. "Has something happened?"

As much as she hated to admit it, he might know what to do. She waved him to follow her. "Walk with me."

He joined her without question as she led him toward a café and slipped into a table at the far back. She laid the stack of papers on the rough white tablecloth and lifted it so he could read the note, aware that his Portuguese was strong enough to do so.

"The Austrian?" He arched a brow.

Ava nodded.

"I can join you in the mornings if you like." He set his newspaper down. "After all, I have my own publications to obtain."

"Isn't the PVDE following you?" she asked in a low whisper.

He waved his hand dismissively. "Not anymore. It was a matter that was cleared up. But I never did thank you for your assistance that night."

Ava's cheeks went hot as a flame at the memory. "That isn't necessary, and it won't be repeated."

The corners of his lips rose in a hint of a smile. "I would not presume."

"Good," she said, feeling suddenly awkward. "Because it won't."

He nodded, that grin notching higher. "Coffee?"

"Please," she said stiffly.

This time he didn't bother to conceal his chuckle as he pushed to his feet and ordered their beverages.

While he was gone, she opened her messenger bag to deposit the papers when she caught sight of *Combat* still resting within. She considered it for a moment and turned her attention back on James as he waited for their drinks.

The Allies all worked together, and though she hated to admit it, James was knowledgeable on many various topics. More so than Mike, she had discovered. And James was by far more approachable than Sims.

She pulled the single page of *Combat* from her bag and replaced it with the stack she'd obtained from Alfonso's kiosk. The top flap of her messenger bag hung crooked despite her best efforts to cram everything in properly.

James peered at the French newspaper as he returned with their small cups of *bica* and dumped a generous helping of sugar into the dark liquid. "What's this?"

"The latest edition." She turned it toward him, then hesitated. "Do you read French?"

James inclined his head. *"Mais oui."*

"Good." She leaned forward in her chair. "Do you notice anything unusual about this piece?" She indicated the article on factory bombings.

He winced. "It could use a strong edit."

She nodded. "Except that this particular newspaper is generally the most meticulous. I don't think it's an accident."

"Then it probably isn't." James pinched the small handle of his mug and sipped the drink.

Ava let her shoulders sag forward. "That's it, Watson?"

"You mean Sherlock, I presume." He gave a haughty tilt of his head. "I dare say, I think I'd make a proper Sherlock. I've the accent and everything."

"Watson was British too."

James nodded toward her. "True, but may I mention that you aren't British at all."

"Fair point." Ava poured a bit of sugar into her own cup and stirred. "So, what's your theory?"

"It's a coded message," he said quietly. "Presumably from the Resistance."

"There are fifty-eight displaced letters." Ava glanced around the small café to ensure no one was within earshot. "I've tried to rearrange them every way I could think possible."

James shook his head and lowered his voice to a whisper despite no one being nearby. "The Resistance uses a new poem every week. But I think you're looking at this wrong, as it's based on numbers." He pulled the newspaper toward him once more. "The typo is in place of another letter. Take the letter that should be there and use the number from its location in the alphabet. Once you have the numbers listed and the poem code they used, you'll have a way to deduce the message. See? The letters have their own system of decoding."

Ava didn't precisely see, but he did and that was what mattered. After all, she'd always understood literature and words far more than numbers and math. But none of his efforts would be effective without the correct poem.

"I can help, if you like," James offered. "Especially if I'm with you in the mornings." He gave her a grin that should have rankled her. But there was something hopelessly charming about the way his eyetooth was slightly crooked and the stalwart determination of his persistence.

She gave a dramatic sigh. "If you insist."

"I do," he replied without hesitation.

"Although I have no idea where to obtain the necessary poem from." She lifted a brow. "Any suggestions, Sherlock?"

He smirked. "I'd presume the very source you collected this newspaper from will have what you need."

Otto did not know which to use, but in the span it took Ava to help serve a meal—much to Ethan's appreciation—he was able to find someone who knew the precise poem used for coding the week the paper was drafted.

"Mignonne allons voir si la rose" by Pierre de Ronsard.

The following morning, Ava waved James into her building and brought him up to her small apartment where they could talk without the risk of being overheard. It wasn't until he was walking through her front door that she realized the intimacy of having him join her where she lived.

Peggy was far better at accessorizing her home than Ava. The small space appeared nearly the same now as it had when Ava first moved in, with the exception of a neat row of books on the shelf and a green sweater slung over the back of a dining room chair.

"I'm not much of a decorator." Ava self-consciously grabbed the sweater and pulled it on for lack of a place to stow it before motioning for him to join her at the table.

A notepad and pen were there waiting, perfectly parallel to one another with each number of the alphabet for the fifty-eight letters printed neatly along the top. Below that was the sixteenth-century poem.

"If you prefer to decorate with books rather than scattered jackets and shoes, I assure you, I shan't judge." He gave her an easy smile and slid into one of the chairs at the dining room table.

Ava sat next to James who leaned back to allow room for her

to watch as he unraveled the code. He smelled like soap and warm sunshine despite the chilly November day.

Head lowered, he got to work. He used the first five letters, assigning numbers to where they lay in the standard alphabet. From there, he found the corresponding word in the poem that matched that number. Those five words were written out and somehow James deduced a fresh alphabet based off that order.

Ava watched, equal parts perplexed by the complexity and awed by how quickly he worked through it. He wrote a new line beneath the block of squares he'd created for the new alphabet, his writing messy and bold.

As it turned out, James really was the better Sherlock to her Watson, which Ava attributed solely to her disinclination toward math. His strokes were confident and sure with the calculated code he'd broken down and rebuilt into a string of text. It was a long, jumbled line that he separated with a slash of the pen tip, partitioning the text into words that suddenly made sense.

Jewish mother and child need transport to America.

They stared down at the note and then looked at each other.

There were many people who did not believe in fate. Ava's father for one, claiming anyone educated should be sure enough in his footing to navigate his own life. But Ava was never one to let someone think for her and had developed her own interpretation of destiny. She wasn't a fatalist by any means, assuming her life entirely predestined, but she wasn't above appreciating a miracle when it shone upon her either.

Like the one she now experienced.

She had been introduced to this precise newspaper where the code had been placed. She happened to run into James, who knew how to crack it. The mother and child needed to go to America, which was where she was from. And the best way to do that would be to ask for the assistance of the British agents flying into France, of which she had the perfect contact in James.

And this was where fate took a back seat. This was where action came into play.

"We have to do something," Ava said.

James scrubbed a hand over his jaw. "It isn't that easy. Besides, there are plenty of organizations that can get them into a safe house."

"If that was possible, they'd likely have done it by now. They're probably in danger, James." She fidgeted in her chair, agitated at his hesitation. "You've seen the refugees here in Lisbon. You've heard their stories. Don't you dare tell me you are casting what they've said as mere war rumors." She stared at him, daring him to deny her. "You're too smart for that."

He exhaled a frustrated breath.

She pointed to the translated code. "They want to go to America. I can help them get there." Or at least she hoped she could. "Surely, there is someone in England who would know where the printing press is located. The Resistance receives goods from Britain all the time."

He jerked his head back and looked at her. "How do you know that?"

"Because I don't simply photograph the papers, I read them as well. Britain is working closely with the Resistance."

James twisted his lips to the side in thought. "You think you can coordinate access to America for them."

"Yes," Ava answered immediately. Doubt squeezed at her chest. It had not gone well when she'd tried to aid Lamant. But he was a man, not a woman and child. And after watching Peggy work magic through phone calls to DC, Ava was sure she could ask her for some advice.

She was nothing if not determined.

James drummed his fingers on the table. "How do we know

they haven't been relocated yet?" Sitting up, he gestured to the paper. "This was published almost a week ago."

"Imagine if they haven't, if we could have done something." Ava stared at him, beseeching with her eyes as much as her words. "What if in this time of vacillation and indecision, they die when they could have lived? Because of us."

James studied her, then shook his head. "If they allow women to become president in America, you should run." James smirked. "You'd win."

"So, you're saying you'll help?" Hope swelled in her chest, but she kept her little cry of delight contained until he confirmed.

"I will see what I can do." He put his hand on the table, so it hit with a soft thud. "That isn't the same as promising to help."

No, it wasn't, but it was still enough. For now, that is.

It was hope.

SIXTEEN

Elaine

The effort of putting everything at risk for the coded message had been in vain. Two weeks passed and still not one person had answered Elaine's call for aid. At least Marcel had begun speaking to her again.

They argued over the matter for some time, but after she asked how he would feel if it was his wife and child, his protests floundered. Not only did he accept that she had done the right thing, he also agreed to allow her to place new sets of code in the next issues until someone offered assistance.

Truthfully, Elaine had been heartily disappointed when no one came to her after the first few days of the newspaper's release. With taking such a risk, she'd been certain there would have been a brave soul willing to step forward.

While Elaine's own optimism was somewhat dimmed by the lack of an immediate response, she did not share her reaction with Sarah, whose hope remained firmly in place.

Not that Elaine could fault her when she herself harbored her own secret wishes for Joseph's miraculous survival. That the informant had been mistaken, that somewhere he was still alive, dreaming of her the way she dreamed of him, waiting for the day they could be reunited.

In the weeks Manon housed the mother and child, color had blossomed back into her pallid cheeks and smiles occasionally reached her eyes. Witnessing those glimpses of momentary joy was like watching the sun break through on a streak of cloudy days. True, the bedroom in the warehouse did not carry the comforts Elaine had grown used to, but the effects of Sarah and Noah on Manon were well worth the sacrifice.

Those were the times to be celebrated, the wisps of joy in an otherwise gray and painful world for Elaine.

December frosted over the chill of November, its dark days all the bleaker under the shroud of Elaine's mourning. The work kept her busy, yes, but nothing seemed to fill the chasm in her soul left by Joseph's death.

The following day would be the *Fête des Lumières*, a day to honor the Virgin Mary for having saved Lyon from the plague in the seventeenth century. Every year since, a procession was held for the virgin—dubbed the Lady of Lyon—in gratitude.

Elaine recalled one December she and Joseph vacationed in Lyon, before the Nazi occupation, when the river sparkled with thousands of lights and vendors called out to the crowds. Their kiosks were filled with cups of rich coffee and paper cones with *frites* straight from the fryer, crusted with granules of salt and steaming in the icy air when broken in half.

Across the Rhône, the houses stacked upon one another in pastel pinks and yellows and blues and at the peak's crest, the statue of the virgin stood proud and tall on the Basilica of Fourvière. Joseph had wrapped his arms around her, his warmth enfolding her, his spicy scent even more comforting. That's when the first set of fireworks shot into the night and sprinkled downward, their brilliance reflected on the choppy surface of the river. On and on they came as dozens of fireworks turned the sky to smoke and called to attention how the Lady of Lyon remained forever lit atop the basilica as she guarded them all below.

Elaine tried to hold on to the memory for as long as possible, but it swept from her thoughts, blown away like the billows of smoke from the fireworks that long ago night.

Such celebrations were a lifetime ago. Those quiet moments with Joseph seemed even further away. Elaine could not help but wonder if some felt the Lady of Lyon had abandoned their once hallowed city, leaving the Lyonnaise to be ravaged by starvation and fear amid the pall cast by the bloodred Nazi flag.

Especially with so many mourning the loss of their loved ones. As she did now with Joseph.

She had a job to do. The impending task jostled her from her reverie.

A glance at her watch confirmed it was nearly nine fifteen at night, the time *Radio Londres* broadcast from London.

The delicate watch was a Type 18 model from LIP, who had been making watches since the beginning of the nineteenth century. The band was a textured brown leather with an elegant, gold-plated rectangular face and had been a wedding present from Joseph. Until recently, she only wore it on occasion, like jewelry—depending on her outfit—otherwise it remained safely tucked away in its fine case.

Now the accessory had become a permanent fixture. Somehow just knowing Joseph thought of her when he picked it out, how gently his fingers moved over the slender strap as he helped her attach it to her wrist the first time, the way he always gave her a proud smile when she wore it—those were memories that brought her comfort.

The minute hand on the rectangular face settled on 9:15.

She leaned over her desk and fiddled with the knob to adjust the tuning as much as was possible. No matter how perfectly someone shifted the needle to the precise location, the message was still partially obscured by a sharp, warbling whine, Vichy's paltry attempt at blocking London's messages when forbidding people from listening had proved pointless.

"*Ici Londres...*" the voice began in a timbre distinct enough to be heard over the obnoxious background. "Before we begin, please listen to some personal messages."

Elaine sat up, her pen poised over a piece of paper, ready to quickly scribe the nonsensical statements to follow, communications meant for the Resistance. Some for their *Combat* group, others for those throughout France, and some meant for no one at all, simply added to throw off enemies trying to break the code.

"Jean has a long mustache."

"Cats are in a field of lavender."

"Grandma found a large carrot."

A string of similarly ridiculous proclamations followed. Marcel and Antoine were the only ones who could decode the phrases into the pertinent details needed. When the "personal messages" on *Radio Londres* ended, the usual program decrying Germany's false news followed. The information shared on that general, uncoded broadcast was integral for the articles in their underground newspapers. Not only to counter the disinformation and propaganda, but also to call more French citizens to their ranks. In recent issues, they urged Resistants to look to Corsica's example, the island that rose up with the Allies and, after twenty-five days of battle, was finally liberated.

Corsica had been a beacon breaking through turbulent seas, a beam of light that shot through the darkness to keep them all from crashing onto the rocks of despair. If Corsica could be wrested from Hitler's fist, so too could France.

However, the island's freedom had not only rallied the Resistance to redouble their efforts, so too had it incensed the Gestapo and their French counterparts, the Milice.

Antoine arrived early the next morning and was already bowed over his work with focused diligence.

"I have the newest codes from *Radio Londres*," Elaine said by way of greeting.

He gave a grunt of acknowledgment.

Elaine went to the kitchen and returned with a cup of roasted barley and chicory. "Will you look over the messages when you have a moment?"

"The likelihood of hearing back from anyone on your article is practically impossible." His nail beds were blue where his fingers pinched at the slender drawing stick. "Most especially London." He tilted his aquiline nose upward with a sniff.

"All the same…" She set the hot mug on the table beside him. Steam curled in the frigid warehouse air in a white-gray tendril.

He slid her a look that told her he knew exactly what she was doing. But he still took the drink in his hands.

She smiled and placed her carefully written notes before him.

He scanned over it as he took a careful sip from the hot mug, then sat back to regard her with fresh consideration.

Her chest went tight. "What is it?"

He gave a small, incredulous laugh. "It appears your message has been received."

Elaine sucked in a breath of surprise. *London* had her message. She had anticipated someone within France would be the likely candidate to offer aid. Never in her wildest dreams did she imagine help would come from London.

"Just because they have received your request doesn't mean they'll do anything," Antoine cautioned.

"I know," she replied, unable to stop her grin.

He resumed his work with a disbelieving grunt, but she saw the hint of a smile on his lips before he bent his head once more. No matter how many warnings he might offer, Elaine would not be discouraged.

That afternoon she and Jean worked side by side together, setting the typography for the upcoming edition of *Combat*.

"*Bonjour.*" Nicole's singsong voice tinkled over the clatter of the automatic press.

"*Bonjour*, Nicole," Jean called back with a shy wave. "You look beautiful as always."

She swept her hand through the air dismissively, but with apparent pleasure at his compliment.

Jean's face flushed.

"You should talk to her," Elaine said encouragingly in a whisper.

His head shook in vigorous refusal. With a sigh, she pushed up from the series of stacked typography slugs and approached Nicole, who was in deep conversation with Marcel. Elaine almost turned away until a familiar name caught her ears.

Josette.

"She is breaking," Marcel said. "Tearing apart at the seams. We cannot afford—"

"She's fine," Nicole insisted. "I'll care for her."

"Is she worth risking your life for?" Marcel pressed. "Risking your father's and your brother's?"

"That isn't fair."

"War is not fair."

Nicole caught sight of Elaine and called out with a wave, her expression set in forced joy, her cheeks blazing with color.

"*Ma chérie*, how are you?" Nicole asked, embracing her.

"Worried," Elaine answered honestly in a voice she knew Marcel wouldn't overhear. "About Josette. And about you helping her."

Nicole laughed off the warning. "She'll be fine."

"She's not well, Nicole."

Something flickered in her pale blue eyes, but she brushed it off as she did all concerns tossed her way, as if they were pesky gnats to be swatted. Truly no one in all of France possessed the bravado of Nicole, which made Elaine worry all the more.

"Do not be such a hen, Elaine." Her gaze was kind as she said it. "Trust me, please."

Elaine nodded slowly, but even as she did so, she could not stop her internal arguments from picking at Nicole's misplaced faith. But Nicole was a force to be reckoned with, more so than even Denise. Nicole couldn't be cautioned; she would have to see for herself.

Elaine only hoped that would happen before it was too late.

That afternoon, once the typography was set and the latest edition was automatically winding its way through the printing press, Elaine decided to take her mind off the exchange with Nicole by paying a visit to Manon. An earlier appointment with a black-market supplier left the warehouse kitchen well stocked enough to bring some extras to Sarah and Noah. With the greatest care, Elaine packed her shopping basket with a sack of lentils that might carry them through the week, two eggs, and a precious pot of strawberry jam. The latter had come at a steep price, but Elaine's memory of Noah's enjoyment of the treat had made the expense worthwhile.

Once at Manon's apartment, she knocked and called out. "*Bonjour*, cousin."

The door opened and Manon greeted her with a small, but genuine smile. She waved Elaine in swiftly. As soon as the door was shut once more, a little face peered around the doorway in the main living area.

"Is that Noah?" Elaine asked.

His face erupted in a grin, and he scurried toward her, his arms spread wide. She set the basket down carefully and caught him midrun, clutching him to her to keep them both from barreling over.

His reaction was likely due to the food she managed to bring with each of her visits, but she still relished his excitement regardless.

Perhaps if her womb had been more welcoming, she might have had a child like Noah, one with her dark eyes and Joseph's razor-sharp mind. They could have been a family, strolling alongside the Rhône together with pink-speckled praline brioche in their hands and pure happiness in their hearts.

She had lost a part of Joseph in having never had children with him. The poignancy of that realization hit her in the chest, visceral and sharp.

"Don't be sad, Elaine." Noah gazed up at her with his big, hazel eyes.

She blinked and rapidly cleared her mind of such ill-serving thoughts. "Of course I'm not sad. Today is the *Fête des Lumières*."

Sarah leaned against the doorway, watching her son with her arms folded comfortably across her light pink sweater. A look of pride lifted the corners of her lips.

Elaine pulled out the lentils from her basket. "I brought food."

"You did not have to do that," Manon chided. But even as she did so, she accepted the modest-sized sack.

"There are too many of you here now for your rations to do." Elaine eagerly withdrew two eggs, their shells still intact from her care upon the trek over.

Sarah joined them and accepted the eggs with gentle hands. "Where did you find these?"

"Someone from the black market stopped to see us first." Elaine reached into her basket a final time. "Which is how I was able to buy this." She held up the jar in presentation. Light glinted through the viscous red jam, so the contents appeared to glow.

Noah's face beamed with delight.

"Hold it with two hands." Elaine settled the jar in his palms. "And take it to the kitchen."

Noah did as she bade and walked with exaggerated precision, like an acrobat on a tightrope, his body tense with the concentration of youth's precarious coordination.

"That was kind of you to bring those items." Sarah hovered over Noah, deposited the eggs in the kitchen, then returned to speak with Elaine. "Manon never says as much, but I know we are straining her supplies. Especially with the way Noah eats."

"He's a growing boy." Elaine gathered her empty basket. "Let him eat whatever he can."

"Have you heard anything?" Sarah asked, her composure breaking slightly, revealing the strain beneath.

"London has confirmed receipt of my request." Elaine had to force herself to keep the excitement from her voice. "But it does not guarantee—"

"I know," Sarah said quickly. "But *London*." She clasped her hands over her heart, as though locking the hope inside lest it flit away. "This is greater than I ever anticipated."

"I will do my best," Elaine promised.

Sarah's eyes brimmed with tears. "Thank you."

That night, when the sun descended in the hills beyond where the old Roman ruins lay from the ancient city of Lugdunum, a miracle happened. Soft, golden candlelight filled the windows in Lyon. There were only a few brave souls determined to engage in the celebration, but the darkened streets lit with the ethereal brilliance of their bravery.

It wasn't a frenzy of celebratory fireworks or a procession winding up the steep hill to the basilica, but it was an outpouring of love for the Lady of Lyon with the little bit some had left to give.

Elaine strode home slowly that night, savoring the warmth lighting her way even as the bitter wind rolled off the Rhône. For the first time in so long, amid the muted observance of the *Fête des Lumières*, Elaine felt her grief give way to a modicum of hope.

Josette was late.

Elaine glanced discreetly at the small watch on her wrist, which revealed it was past six in the evening, long after Josette should have arrived. Secretly, Elaine hoped the young woman did not come, that Marcel managed to convince Nicole that Josette needed some time off to steady her rattled nerves.

Even as she thought it, Elaine couldn't stifle the pinch of guilt. She didn't blame Josette for the precariousness of her condition. It was likely anyone might suffer from such a breakdown. Everyone was on constant alert for a cold German stare that lingered too long, or a set of footsteps marching at their same pace behind them in a narrow alley, or an unknown face among the familiar. How could they not when the danger was so ubiquitous?

And yet the newspapers needed to be delivered at their respective locations. Elaine eyed the stack of newsprint, the ink so fresh, its powdery scent hung in the air.

"Is Josette coming?" she asked aloud.

Marcel's mouth tightened in a thin line. Even if Josette did arrive at her delegated time, he likely would not agree to accept her aid.

There was pride in the prompt release of newspapers, that their team was timely, not only their production, but also in the paper's delivery. No matter who among them might be arrested, what materials became short due to ration or otherwise. Or even whose nerves might have gotten the better of them. After having spent months being one of the many cogs in the machine of the clandestine press, Elaine had a profound need to continue the age-old tradition of printing that had peaked in Lyon during the Renaissance when the city was the main printing district in all of France.

"I'll handle the delivery for Josette," she volunteered. "I've already finished what needed to be done on the Minerva today." The stack of papers lay in a neat row on the table beside the archaic press.

Jean lifted his head from the Linotype machine, his fingers hovering over the keys as the rapid clacking of his typing went silent. "I can do it."

Marcel considered him for a moment. "I need the plate finalized within the hour so I can finish this print on the next paper before tomorrow."

Meaning it was a job only Jean could do. Elaine was still clumsy on the foreign keyboard. Certainly, far too slow to complete the piece in time for Marcel to get the printing press going.

"Don't be silly—it will take only a few minutes." Elaine stood and pulled on her coat before Jean could insist on going in her stead. "I'll be back before you are even done."

In the months they'd all gotten to know one another, the men had become extraordinarily protective of Elaine. Even more so after Joseph's death, though they'd finally stopped handling her as though she'd break like poor Josette. They always looked after her with concern—whether the possibility of arrest or suspicion from the Nazis, or like now—being loathe to send her outside amid December's brutal freeze.

She bundled the newsprint and hid the stack in her shopping basket. "I'll be back in time to check over the printing plate when I return."

"You do have the sharpest eyes," Jean said, always liberal with his approbation.

With a friendly wave over her shoulder, Elaine slipped out of the warehouse and into the shock of the winter wind. The colder it became, the harder it was to retain warmth. Bodies were too slight, fuel too scarce, and the chill too pervasive.

They all did what they could for the underground, for their persistent battle to resist their oppressors. Her part now was to deliver the papers and avoid notice from the Nazis.

An icy blast of wind made the tip of her nose burn and her eyes sting. She squinted as much as possible to minimize the discomfort while still allowing herself to see a slit of the street in front of her without crashing into a wall or falling off a curb. Easier said than done in the darkness of early winter sunsets.

The trams were down from a Resistance attack earlier that

day. There was nothing for it but to walk. She would not have the newspaper late on her account.

Hurried along by the gusts, she rushed to the drop location on the outskirts of Croix-Rousse. The courtyard of the building inside was empty and dark. But then, winter was such a bleak time. Branches were stripped of their leaves to reveal skeletal limbs beneath and the sky was cast in a flat gray that reflected on the Rhône, washing the world in a bland, colorless existence.

A dim light shone on a corridor containing the buildings' post boxes, only just illumining the dank open space cradled inside the building.

In the corner of the courtyard was a crate one might use to cart about goods or stand on to peer into a window. The wooden box seemed to have been there so long, the boards were stained dark with age and sagged in against themselves, a thick smat-tering of mud and grit coating the outside. Elaine slipped into the heavy shadow near the wall, lifted the crate to reveal the dry earth beneath and carefully set the papers within. When she withdrew her hand, her fingertips came away damp and filthy with a black and green organic substance she didn't care to place.

She rubbed her hands together to clean them as best she could. Her surroundings were desolate—the chipped walls, the alcove with only one bare bulb, the illumination almost drown out by an eclipse of moths.

Something in the distance clicked and the light went out, blanketing her in a momentarily disorienting darkness.

In that instant, she was entirely alone in the cold blackness of the world.

The enormity of her sorrow swelled inside her, absent any warmth or life. In that moment, the courtyard became a direct reflection of her own soul, bearing the agony of her pain, of her grief. She stumbled back into the street and struggled to drag in a breath of air even as it burned in her lungs. By habit more than in-tent, she lifted her watch to find it was very nearly eight at night.

Radio Londres would be airing soon after her return if she hurried back. There might be more detail given on Sarah and Noah.

The thought roused her to her senses, tugging her up from the doldrums by her bootstraps.

"Halt."

She spun around to find a German officer directly behind her.

"What are you doing here?" he demanded in French.

"I was visiting a friend," she said even as her mind tried to catch up with the lie her mouth expelled.

"A friend." His narrowed eyes glittered in the darkness like something evil and soulless. "This building has been emptied, all the occupants arrested this afternoon."

"That would explain why my friend was not home," she replied smoothly, her pulse pounding. "What have they done that everyone would be taken?"

But even as she feigned ignorance, she knew. Fear prickled at her scalp and screamed for her to run. Several months before, she might have been able to. Before Corsica won the battle for its freedom from the Nazi oppressors.

Now, the Germans shot without question, bathing the streets in blood with their determination to maintain their viselike grip on France.

The officer called to someone in German. A fresh-faced boy-soldier who barely looked old enough to shave emerged from the shadows beyond a streetlamp's perfect circle of yellow light.

"Go inside and see if any messages have been placed within." The officer spoke in French, purposefully wanting her to have understood him.

Elaine used all her willpower to school her face into a bland expression, refusing to betray the fear vibrating through her. If they found the papers, she would be dead.

They waited for a long moment as the boy did what he was told. She clenched her teeth to keep them from chattering from terror as much as from the cold. The officer appeared impervious to the weather, most likely from the heavy coat he wore and the girth of his prominent belly jutting beneath. The boy emerged several minutes later and spoke in German.

The officer glared at Elaine and dread tingled over her skin. Had they found the newspapers?

"I'm sure he's proven my innocence," she said in a brusque tone she prayed would be convincing.

The officer didn't deign to reply. Nor did he look convinced. Instead, he reached for her with an unfriendly hand, trapping her where she stood. "You are under arrest."

SEVENTEEN

Ava

Every day James met Ava downstairs to walk to the kiosk with her, and every day he had the same answer about the possibility of a rescue plan for the Jewish mother and child in Lyon: no news yet. Though Ava had been reluctant to accept his offer to join her in the mornings, she had to admit that she'd not seen the German since James began accompanying her.

Additionally, Alfonso nodded at their morning arrival in silent confirmation that everything appeared to be clear. So it was that time went by without incident and Thanksgiving came and went. The occasion was marked with a quiet affair at the embassy with far more roasted fowl, heavy gravies, potatoes, and candied yams than any of them could possibly eat. Ava had jokingly invited James, who respectfully declined.

The following week, the next issue of *Combat* fell into Ava's hands with a similar message slipped into yet another article. Which meant the plea for help still had not been answered. Its recurrence dug at her thoughts often enough that she tried finding her own avenue.

However, any attempts to acquire US assistance were met with a stern rejection from Sims and anyone else she managed to snag on the phone in DC.

November shifted into December with Christmas bringing a sad little tree in the corner of Ava's apartment, drenched in tinsel the way her mother had always done in their childhood. Beneath it lay a V Mail envelope with a letter from Daniel she saved to make the day more special. Only it brought scarce comfort as she read it, unable to stop the image of him jumping out of a plane into the unknown and sheltering in an icy trench somewhere. Such thoughts left her with tears in her eyes and a hollow ache in her chest.

James had shown up then with a roasted turkey far too large for the two of them as well as every pastry he could find, all sparkling with sugar crusts and some with brightly colored jams leaking from their flaky centers. He also brought a gift for her, a new messenger bag wide enough to hold the newspapers on her daily collection. It was fortunate she had purchased him a present as well: a copy of *A Study in Scarlet*, the first of the Sherlock Holmes books, which he received with a broad grin.

By the time New Year's arrived, there hadn't even been a discussion if they would spend it together. They simply went to the Palacio in Estoril where they sipped champagne and nibbled canapés in their finest clothes. What hadn't been expected was the kiss they shared at midnight and how James hadn't needed a single line of recited verse to coax it from her.

That kiss was never brought up again, but as Ava looked back on it, a fog of champagne and gaiety kept her from recalling exactly if he had leaned toward her...or she toward him. Regardless, neither of them mentioned it and the first week of January rolled by unceremoniously.

Ava received yet another copy of *Combat* from Otto, and this time there was no longer a coded message. The realization was met with a flutter of uncertainty. Had they given up or were they already rescued?

The two options were still puzzling her when she joined James the following morning to assume their usual rounds through Lisbon's kiosks and bookstores.

The collar of his dark wool coat was flipped up to ward off the cool January morning, which was by no means comparable to the bone-deep chill of DC. Still, the cold air at her legs under her navy skirt made her miss the availability of stockings. She also was glad she had not gone with a *refugiado* hairstyle when the weather was hot, named after the short cropped hair en vogue in Europe when refugees fled their homes. Her long hair kept her neck warm, swept back from her face in an understated victory roll by her right part.

"What if I told you I come bearing good news?" He glanced about as they walked, his gaze forever sweeping the streets, vigilant even as she relaxed in her complacency.

Ava stopped walking, her heart daring to beat a little faster in anticipation of what he might say. "I wouldn't believe you."

"Wouldn't you?" He slid a charming grin her way that made her wonder again if it really was her who had kissed him at the stroke of midnight on New Year's Eve.

"I suppose it depends on what it is," she answered cautiously, afraid to hope. Not when such a fragile thing was so easily crushed, especially when the stakes were so high.

He turned to her. "Britain is helping."

"How?" she demanded. "When?"

"They made the decision a while ago and have plans underway. I haven't been able to share the news until now." He grimaced. "My apologies."

She gasped a laughing cry of disbelief. "No apology at all necessary. This is incredible! How did you finally get an answer?"

He put his hands in his pockets. "I had to call in a few favors.

Now I'm the one in debt, but the cost is worth it. I would do it again in a minute to see them safe."

That was one of the many things she'd learned about James in all their time together. He genuinely did care about those trapped in Europe as they scrambled for safety. He never referred to them as refugees, but called them by their names, asking after their families and discussing details of their former jobs with them. In a world where they felt as though they'd shed the skins of their personality, he reminded them who they still were, that they mattered.

And while those interactions made the rounds of collecting newspapers that much longer for each table he stopped and chatted with, she didn't mind a bit. In fact, she joined him, bringing her usual assortment of books and treats for the children.

"It is I who owes you," Ava said. "I could never have done this without your help. Not only acquiring aid in transporting the mother and child here, but in figuring out the code."

"You don't owe me a thing," James protested. "I'm grateful for the outcome. However, once they arrive here in Lisbon, you'll have your own obstacle to scale in getting them to America."

She swallowed her trepidation and gave a firm nod. "I can do that."

And she would.

Somehow.

The warm, velvety aroma of coffee drifted on a chilled breeze, reminding her that their beverages were probably waiting for them at the small café on the corner of Rossio Square. They visited so often at the same time every day that the owner had taken to setting the drinks for them at their usual table.

James must have had a similar thought and indicated she lead the way.

"Have you been to Sintra yet?" he asked abruptly.

She frowned and shook her head. "I confess, I haven't even read much about it, aside from the palace being located there."

"You cannot come to Portugal and never experience Sintra." He paused by Alfonso's kiosk and exchanged a greeting with the owner.

Once Ava had the stack of newsprint tucked in her messenger bag, all of which now fit neatly with a flap that closed without issue, thanks to James, they resumed their walk toward Rossio Square.

A car approached, and they both waited for it to pass before crossing the street. "I'm attending a dinner party at Monserrate Palace in two days and would be honored if you'd consider accompanying me," James said.

The car zoomed past, the wind in its wake tugging at Ava's skirt and ruffling her hair. She swept her hand self-consciously over her victory roll. "A palace? How could I possibly say no?"

"I rather hoped that might be your answer."

They turned onto Rossio Square, and James was immediately pulled away by a nearby table of Frenchmen who greeted him with a wave.

James was correct in predicting her difficulty in securing passage for the mother and child. She knew that. But while the idea of helping Lamant all those months ago had shown her everything she'd done wrong, she had even less of a shot now.

"What do you mean you don't know their names?" Peggy inquired with a frown.

"It was from the article I mentioned before, the one in *Combat*," Ava explained.

"I wasn't aware you didn't even know their names." Peggy's right leg was crossed over her left, and now it swung back and forth as she pursed her lips in thought. "I have no idea how you can even begin the process without that information. You have to swear to their character in a moral affidavit to assure on your honor they are good people. How can you do that when you don't even know what their names are?"

While it was a good point, it didn't ease Ava's rising frustration. "Is there any way I can begin this process before their arrival?"

Peggy's leg stopped swinging, and she crossed her arms over her chest. "No."

"They at least need transit visas."

"To who would they be assigned?" Peggy queried.

Really, she should have said "to whom," but Ava refrained from pointing that out in the interest of her precarious situation.

"We work for the American Embassy," Ava protested. "Surely we have some clout."

Peggy shook her head, sending her sandy curls swinging around her face. "It's going to take a while, even if you are here pulling for them. You'll need a support affidavit to show they can afford to live without financial aid once in America plus the moral affidavits I mentioned as well as six copies of Form B of your request."

"Six?"

"It's a few pages, front and back." Peggy's red lips stretched in a line of sympathy as she nodded. "I can help you fill them out when it's time."

Ava gave her a sad, but grateful nod.

"You also may want to try to make friends with the clerks and officers downstairs in legation." Peggy shrugged. "They're overworked and on edge. I'm sure a little appreciation will go a long way."

Though they were all in the same building, Ava scarcely ever saw the other embassy employees. When she did, the men and women were rushing by with clipped steps somewhere between a walk and a run, coated in a sheen of sweat and with a furrowed brow.

"And you can ask the PVDE what you can do to prepare for their arrival." Peggy got to her feet and put a hand on Ava's shoulder. "They may be able to at least let you know what to make ready. All refugees have to go through them to remain in

Portugal. You're going to have to go to them regardless. Might as well get some info now."

It was another good suggestion, and as soon as Ava finished photographing the books and periodicals she and Mike had accumulated the last several days, she made her way to Chiado where the PVDE headquarters were located on Rua António Maria Cardoso.

Ava strode up the incline of the street and entered the large building, feeling as though she were walking into the belly of the beast.

We have not to fear anything, except fear itself. Julius Caesar's quote resounded in her thoughts, pushing her onward.

Her heels clicked over the polished floor and echoed off the cold walls. A man sitting at the desk in a black business suit looked up, his face blank with disinterest.

He was middle-aged and slightly out of shape, with a glint of silver in his dark hair. Despite the benign appearance, Ava knew better.

Anyone who had spent more than a month in Portugal knew of the secret police and their brutality. It was rumored they had been trained by the Gestapo in their torture techniques. As kind as the Portuguese people were to the refugees, the PVDE could be just as cruel. Merciless with their rules, pedantic with the details, and swift with the execution of punishment. When people entered prison, they did not always come out, and even the ones who did had terrifying tales to tell.

She suppressed a shiver and addressed the officer in Portuguese, asking if there was a way to register the mother and child now and provide their names later or if there was anything she might do to prepare for their arrival. She intentionally omitted the details of how they were coming and how she knew of them. The PVDE was supposed to remain impartial to either side in the war, maintaining Portugal's claim of neutrality. Not everyone followed rules, however, and it was not uncommon to find some siding with the Allies and still others with the Axis.

The man sighed in irritation at a question he apparently considered idiotic.

"When they come, you make sure they register here." His expression was stern. "They come every month, or we will go to them."

Ava smiled sweetly in the face of his bald threat. "I wouldn't dream of doing otherwise."

The only other place she could think to probe about for ideas or information she had somehow overlooked was the JDC. As she hopped on the tram, her mind worked through everyone she had ever met in DC and how they might offer some aid. She hadn't been one for making scores of close friends. She didn't have many acquaintances as it was. And certainly, none that were in positions to provide backing in a situation like this.

She'd learned that early on when trying to find a way for Lamant to get his transit visa to America.

The tram deposited her at her stop, and she walked the rest of the way toward the familiar white building, enjoying the heat of the sun on that crisp January day. Children chased one another about in a game of tag while their parents held cups of coffee and tea, engaged in their dismal low-toned conversations. The faces changed from time to time, but the situations were always the same. Adults waiting for the little ones to be distracted before whispering their fears to one another.

What if a visa didn't arrive in time and the PVDE came for them? What if a boat ticket couldn't be obtained and they had to start the process over again? What if the money ran out? What if Germany attacked Portugal and they had nowhere to go?

The worst of it was that there were no answers for any of those questions. There doubtless wasn't an answer for Ava either, but she wouldn't give up without getting advice from the person most likely to know all the loopholes in the crazy, shifting visa system in Portugal.

Ethan tossed the towel he'd been wiping a table with over his shoulder. "Ava, how did you know to come?"

She chuckled, good-naturedly. "Because you always need extra hands."

He shook his head without humor, and that was when she noticed his eyes were red rimmed.

"Ava…" Her name tore from him in a ragged, wounded way that sent a warning charging through her.

"What is it?"

He blinked and a tear dropped to his cheek. He swiped it away. "It's Otto."

"Otto?" Her blood went cold. "What's happened?"

"Ava…he…"

She stared at Ethan, her heart gripped with fear. "He what?"

"He took his own life."

Everything around her froze in that moment. She remained still, stunned, her mind grappling with the enormity of such news.

"Why?" she whispered as the questions rushed forward. "When? How?"

Ethan pinched his forefinger and thumb over his eyes and sniffed. "He was found this morning, an empty bottle of morphine tablets by his bed with a note."

Morphine tablets. Sadly, it had become a common way for a life to be ended, a bitter swallow followed by a blanket of dreamless sleep from which one never woke.

Otto was a man who fought for his success, for a chance at life. What could possibly make a man so determined give up after all this time?

"Why?" she asked. "Did the note say why?"

"He was denied an American visa again," Ethan said slowly. "He'd already tried twice before, waiting out the six months in between rejections to attempt it again. I think after the third time…"

"If he had told me, perhaps I could have—"

Ethan shook his head. "His parents were German. There was nothing you could have done."

Pain crumpled in Ava's chest with the truth of Ethan's words. There was truly nothing she—or anyone else—could have done for him. He had been failed by a system that was inherently broken.

"He left something for you," Ethan said gently. "A moment, please." He disappeared into his office, leaving Ava standing where she stood, her body numb.

She gazed across the room, seeing nothing. How could she when her thoughts were overflowing? She had intended to see Otto once she'd spoken with Ethan, to bask in the familiar sweet scent of his pipe and tell him about the mother and child who would soon be arriving in Lisbon. To seek his counsel.

How had she not seen the depth of his misery? How had he hidden such desperation from her?

The room blurred.

"Ava." Ethan put his warm hand on her shoulder.

She looked at him, her throat aching with an emotion that wouldn't let her speak.

He extended a packet of papers toward her. *Combat* showed at the top. She shook her head vehemently. She would not have his last act be retrieving newspapers for her. He was so much greater than that.

"It is not only these." Ethan sifted through the stack, finding first the well-worn letter from Petra, then a second envelope with Ava's name written in short, neat print across the front.

"What is that?"

Ethan handed her the small pile, the envelope thick with what felt like several sheets of paper. "I believe..." He cleared his throat. "I believe it's Otto's story and he wanted you to have it."

EIGHTEEN

Elaine

The Citroën sluiced through an onslaught of rain with Elaine tensely sitting on the hard leather rear seat with the officer and the young Nazi in the front. They spoke in German, which she could not understand, but she did recognize a single word that made her blood go cold: Montluc.

By some miracle, she managed to maintain a calm demeanor. Beneath the surface, however, she was a torrent of fear, worry, and doubt. If the Germans found the stack of newspapers under the filthy box, if those who were arrested gave away a name, if her identity card was spotted as a fake—she might never leave.

Upon her own inspection, the identification appeared to be an exact replica of the ones that were officially issued. But it had never been subjected to scrutiny before. Would the integrity of it hold up?

The car came to a stop, and she was yanked from the back seat into the deluge. Rain whipped at her from all directions, slashing into her eyes and leaving her momentarily blinded. The officer shoved her toward a small building, barking orders she didn't understand. Her handbag was snatched away, her identity card ripped out for examination. Thankfully her basket with its damning false bottom lay behind on the street where she had dropped it upon her arrest.

Even as she was whisked in the confusing whirlwind, some part of her mind remained calm enough to offer pithy protests declaring her innocence, claiming to be a mere housewife visiting a friend. Even when no one bothered to acknowledge she had spoken, she continued her objections.

They set aside her identity card with disinterest, and she breathed a discreet sigh of relief. She was shoved once more, urged through another door, out into the driving rain. A sound, like the opening note of a siren, blared from all around her with such suddenness, she flinched.

In that moment when she froze, wet and chilled and more frightened than she cared to admit, they grabbed the shoulders of her coat and half dragged her to a larger building, stopping in a small antechamber.

Her dress clung wetly to her legs, and her shoes had doubled in weight. An icy current ran through the high-walled room and left her skin needling with goose bumps. The officer passed her to a guard without any emotion, as if she were little more than a parcel being delivered.

The guard led her to a hallway filled with numerous doors on either side.

"I am innocent," she stammered.

The man ignored her pleas, continuing to push her onward with a force that made her stagger.

"Please, I—"

A smell hit her like a physical blow—unwashed bodies and the musty sweet odor of sickness. The fetid air crawled with low-toned conversations that vibrated in the echoing halls and buzzed in Elaine's brain.

A deep tremble settled in her bones, cold and fear clashing together until neither was discernible from the other.

"I am simply a housewife," she said in a voice that lacked any strength.

The guard hauled her up a flight of stairs, their footsteps reverberating from the hard walls. A cutout in the floor ran the length of the rows of doors, reflecting the level below and the one above—mirror images of one another. He led her down the aisle to a door on the right and wrenched it open.

Two frightened faces stared at her from within. Before Elaine could even register the color of their hair and eyes, she was shoved through the gaping doorway. The door slammed shut behind her with a bang that rang out through the pit of hell she had been manhandled into. A light from overhead illuminated the space, casting a sickly yellow pallor that revealed a small square of a room with a narrow window at the back and a metal flap at the bottom of the front wall beside the door.

The two strangers eyed her with apathetic curiosity.

"Why were you arrested?" the taller of the two inquired, her red hair as dull as the flatness of her hazel eyes.

Elaine folded her arms over her chest to allay the chattering shiver racking her body as her brain scrambled to process what had occurred in the last several minutes. Was this how it had been for Joseph?

Had he been as confused, as frightened, and overwhelmed by it all as she?

"They think I am with the Resistance," she said at last through her clenched teeth.

"Are you not?" asked the other. She was brunette with sunken eyes and cheekbones that jutted over the hollows of her face, giving her a skull-like appearance in the weak light.

"No, I am not." This time Elaine spoke without hesitation. She owed these women no explanation, no truth. For all she knew, they were collaborators, placed in the cell to ferret out Resistance members.

She studied the skeletal visage whose blue eyes were wide

and luminous against her gaunt features. It had likely been some time since she had consumed a decent meal.

Even those with the Resistance might sell secrets for a bit of food in a place such as this.

No, Elaine could not put herself in a position where anyone could disprove her story. It was far too great a risk.

"Are you a collaborator?" The redhead's eyes blazed.

"Collette, that is enough," the skinny brunette said to the other. "Would she be here if she was?"

"I'm a housewife," Elaine began.

The skinny woman's brittle smile cut her feeble explanation short. "We all are."

A small door at the bottom of the cell opened and a tray was roughly propelled inside, almost sloshing the watery soup over the rim of the single bowl. The bit of moldy bread rolled from the thin metal side and fell onto the floor.

It was hardly enough food for one person, let alone three women. The two eyed Elaine, but she shook her head. They clearly needed it more than she. Their hands trembled as they ate, snatching the meal back and forth rather than passing it to one another. The greedy gulps were followed by the sweep of their tongues over the bowl to lap up anything remaining. The scene was reminiscent of starving animals more so than humans.

This was what the Nazis had reduced them to, starved to the point of primitive, bestial behavior. Was this what Joseph had become?

The ache of pain simmered into rage at everything the Nazis had stolen from them. Lives, careers, loves, humanity. The French had lost everything under their brutal occupation. Elaine had lost everything too.

Not long after the foul meal, the lights clicked out, smothering them in darkness.

"It is time to sleep, housewife," the brunette said, the malice gone from her voice.

Perhaps the refusal of their scant food garnered Elaine some favor with them after all.

"Where?" Elaine whispered.

There were no beds in the concrete cell that was barely large enough to fit if one laid out completely straight. In order to rest on the ground, the three of them lay side by side, their bodies nesting together with their knees bent.

"This is a luxury compared to what the men have, housewife," Collette said in a quiet voice. "They sometimes have nine men to a cell like this one."

Elaine's thoughts reeled to imagine how nine men could even stand in a room this size, let alone lie down. "How do they sleep?"

"In shifts."

The warmth of the body behind Elaine ebbed the chill, and the jacket she was thankfully left with offered some cushion for her protruding hip bones against the unforgiving floor. But she still found no rest.

It wasn't the gnaw of hunger at her empty belly, the unnerving tickle of bugs creeping over her skin or even the incessant blaring alarm that kept her eyes from falling closed. It was the need to witness what Joseph had lived through in his time at Montluc.

Through experiencing the desolate despair in person, haunted by the sobs that echoed ominously through the open area, Elaine connected with Joseph in the only way she could. Suddenly she was grateful for those previous nights she went to bed hungry so she could save him an extra crust of bread or a cooked rutabaga or even an egg. If her gifts had ever made their way to him at Montluc.

She had to think they had. To consider otherwise was too dark a consideration and filled her with such despair, she could hardly draw breath around the squeeze of pain in her chest.

The morning did not come quickly.

At last a sharp rap of a truncheon on the metal door sent a

clang reverberating through the small space and snapped Elaine from sleep.

Bleary-eyed with exhaustion and rumpled in clothes still damp from the storm, she was forced from the cell with the other two women for morning ablutions. A large sink ran along the back wall of the prison, like a trough where livestock might be fed. It was there they received a splash of water so cold it took their breath and so short-lived, they all had water dripping from their chins. Several of the more seasoned inmates walked away with dirty faces, and cupped hands filled with water that they tipped into their eager mouths to slake their thirst.

Watching them made Elaine's parched throat burn and had her licking at the droplets lingering on her own lips.

Her two cellmates did not try to speak with her further, and she did not bother to strike up conversation. It was best not to know anyone as even acquaintances could leave one vulnerable.

An indiscernible amount of time later, the door swung open again to reveal a guard as miserable to be minding them as the prisoners were to be there. "Elaine Rousseau," he barked. "Come."

The other two women cast their gazes downward to avoid any unintentional association. Elaine didn't blame them. She had been guilty of a similar act when she met them.

Her blood prickled as she recalled Etienne's exclamation of how people sent without baggage were to be killed and the ones with baggage were relocated to a work camp. Like Joseph had been.

But really, none of them had luggage of any type. It was merely a code for living or dying.

That bone-deep tremble began again, the one that shook the core of her soul and made her grit her teeth to endure the rush of anxious energy.

"Where are you taking me?" she demanded with more bravado than she could physically muster.

The guard mutely led her outside where the rain still dripped from the thick gray clouds overhead. Her feet felt clumsy, her knees weak. The unknown stretching before her weighed with a maddening pressure that left a silent scream knotting in her chest.

Elaine was placed in the Citroën once more with another prisoner, a man whose face was mottled with bruising. His dark hair fell over his brow as his head lolled forward, and a sour, unwashed smell adulterated the enclosed space. It was then she noticed a wound on the end of his finger, angry and raw where a nail might have been. He shifted his hand, and she realized every digit appeared thus, each nail savagely removed.

Bile burned up her throat, but she swallowed it down. In its place remained something strange and metallic she had never tasted before, and yet could somehow innately recognize: terror.

She did not know how much time passed as they drove, the once familiar sights of Lyon now blurring into a dizzying rush. But she knew the building as they turned onto Avenue Berthelot—école de Santé Militaire—formerly used as a medical school for the military and reclaimed as the Gestapo headquarters.

Using every drop of strength within her, she kept her gaze from creeping toward the man's missing fingernails. Such a fate might soon be hers.

She had seen accounts in the newspaper of how the Gestapo extracted secrets from people, their cruelty unimaginable.

This was the exact path Joseph had been down, yanked into the dark unknown, led on a tether of fear and uncertainty.

Would she be strong enough to endure torture? Would she be the vital thread that snapped and sent all her fellow Resistants to a similar fate? She'd once tried to imagine what torture might feel like, but even then, she had not accounted for the poignancy of her own panic.

In her imagination, she kept her head lifted and back straight. But her knees were too weak and her stomach too bunched with dread.

She was led up the stairs with the man and made to wait in a hall alongside several other prisoners. They were all silent, heads bowed, bodies revealing various signs of trauma. Behind the closed doors came noises that filled in the gaps of the unknown in ways Elaine did not want to see realized.

Crunching and cracking, splashing and gasping, screaming and sobbing. The sounds of nightmares. Those involuntary cries wrenched from the victims were by far the worst—primal and raw and utterly helpless.

Would she be strong enough?

Elaine closed her eyes and willed her strength into place, like a wall being assembled brick by brick. But before the mortar of her newly constructed fortification could dry, her name was called once more.

She rose on legs that wobbled. However, she managed to stiffen her back with the consideration of all those who would suffer if she spoke. Jean with his ready smile, Antoine whose sage wisdom always came when needed, Marcel whose wife was due to deliver their new baby any day now. But not only them—Josette and Nicole. And Manon, Sarah and little Noah.

Those names swelled in a power greater than any brick and mortar. They had become a family to her, one she would die to protect.

The room she was led to held the tinny odor of a butcher's shop, which was made worse by the underlying aroma of urine and sweat. A man in a crisp Gestapo uniform waited for her, a silver medal with an iron cross glinting from his breast. There was an iciness to his gray eyes, which she knew immediately from accounts she had read.

Werner.

A light-headedness swept over her, and for a horrifying moment, she sensed she might faint.

"Sit." He nodded to a single wooden chair placed in the middle of the room. Moisture darkened the seat and the floor around it. Still, she sank slowly onto the hard surface and tried not to think of what the liquid dampening her clothes might be.

Joseph had likely been in this very room at one point, facing this very man.

He had been strong enough. She would be too.

Werner closed the door and approached his desk with a maddeningly casual air as he lifted a file. "Elaine Rousseau. That is you, yes?" he asked in French.

Elaine nodded. "Though I do not understand why I am being held."

"You were seen leaving a building known to be associated with the Resistance." His gaze was cold and lacking any empathy as he set the file down. "You were told this already."

He strode toward her with slow, deliberate steps that made her pulse throb faster.

"But I am not part of the Resist—"

His hand flew across her face, smacking her with enough force to jerk her head to the side. The coppery saltiness of blood tainted her mouth, and her mind swam for a moment to catch up with what had just happened.

She blinked against the disorienting pain.

"Do not lie to me," Werner said. "Who were you visiting?"

"Lisette Garnier." The name was one she pulled from the air, one not associated to anyone she knew. She prayed there was truly no one in all of France by that name.

Werner lifted the file once more and scanned the contents. "She is not on the list of those who lived there."

"She stayed with her aunt, a woman I never met." Elaine fabricated the lie with a smoothness that surprised even her. "I do not recall her name."

"Try harder." Something glinted in his predatory stare that sent chills crawling over her skin.

Nicole's advice rushed forefront to Elaine's thoughts, to use the masculine assumption of women against them.

"I am just a housewife." She let her eyes widen so he could see the depth of her fear. "Lisette and I were in *lycée* together.

She had been ill several months back, and I wanted to ensure she was recovered."

He narrowed his eyes. "Are you with the Resistance?"

"I would never," Elaine gasped in feigned offense.

At this, he remained silent for a while, as if deliberating over everything she had said. He glanced down to the silver iron cross on his chest and rubbed at a dull spot with his fingertip until it shone. "I think you are lying."

He untied a leather bundle on his desk and unrolled it to reveal a series of glinting metal objects. Her imagination staggered in wonder at each of their purposes, and she could not stop the image of the man she sat beside on the ride over. The way his fingernails were little more than open wounds.

The light-headed sensation returned.

"I can tell you how to wash without soap," she said abruptly. "How to collect enough breadcrumbs to make a proper meal that will fill you, or how to ensure your white clothes always remain so, or even how to preserve green beans to last into the next year."

"That is not the information I want."

"But that is all I can tell you," Elaine pleaded. "I know how to run a house, that is all."

A knock sounded at the door, urgent and insistent.

Werner flicked an irritated glare toward the interruption before saying something in German. The door opened and a young man entered, his cheeks flushed.

Elaine could not understand their conversation, but she did not mistake the look of regret that crossed Werner's face as he regarded her. He stalked toward her, his expression hard with malice. "Leave."

The word was so startling, she almost froze. Except she was not so foolish as to squander the opportunity. She leaped from the chair, practically tripping in her haste, and followed the other man. Downstairs, he led her to the entryway where a woman waited in a familiar navy skirt.

Nicole turned as they approached, her red lips parting in a smile. "Elaine," she cried. "I was so worried about you when you did not come for dinner." She turned her attention to the Nazi and batted her long, sable lashes. "*Merci, monsieur.* You are my personal hero."

"It was my pleasure, *mademoiselle*." The man gave her a sloppy, besotted grin.

"Let us get you home, *ma chérie*." Nicole threaded her arm through Elaine's and pulled her close where she whispered, "You may lean on me if you need to."

"I would not give them the satisfaction," Elaine replied.

They walked toward the door together. Even as they neared the exit to freedom, the action seemed surreal.

Could it have been so easy to escape? Would they be stopped and sent back, another nasty jest by the Nazis? They were, after all, known for such cruel tricks.

But no one curtailed them as they made their way through the doors. A shadow lingered by a window upstairs, watching them as they departed. Despite the involuntary ripple of unease, no one called to them. They continued in silence for several minutes, threading their way down the street before Nicole turned into a building and led Elaine into a safe house. It was one Elaine had stayed at in her early days with the Resistance, an abandoned home with no tenant.

No sooner had the door been locked safely behind them than all the strength bled from her body, draining away with the fear that had held her captive for the last night and day. She sagged into the chair's sturdy frame, her skirt still cold and damp.

Nicole busied herself in the kitchen, moving about with a comfort that spoke of familiarity.

"You should not have come for me," Elaine said when she had gathered herself enough to speak again.

"That is a terrible way to say thank you." Nicole filled a kettle with water and put it on the stove.

"Thank you," Elaine said from the very depths of her soul. "Thank you for risking yourself to save me."

"Thank you for sticking with the story of being a mere housewife," Nicole responded. "Had you not, we both would be in Werner's office now." She sat down across from Elaine and, with gentle fingers, turned Elaine's face to the side. "If you play to what they expect of you and apply a little flirtation, you can get nearly anything you want."

"I think I forgot the flirtation," Elaine murmured.

Nicole gave a soft laugh through the tears shimmering in her pale blue eyes. Elaine tried to join her, but the movement at her tender cheek made her wince.

With a tsk, Nicole handed Elaine a cold cloth and draped a clean dress over the chair. "Put this to your face to keep down the swelling. I can help you change when you are ready, if you need me to." Nicole drew in a soft breath. "Did they do anything else to you?"

The memory of those tools in the leather case rushed back to Elaine. She had been saved from such a fate, but Joseph likely had not. Tears swam hot in her eyes.

"What did they do to you?" Nicole demanded, her expression hardening.

Elaine shook her head. "Nothing like they did to Joseph."

Nicole's face softened and she pulled Elaine to her. "I know, *ma chérie*. I know."

Elaine melted into the comfort of Nicole's arms and, in the genuine affection of that embrace, allowed the torrent of her powerful emotions to spill over. When she had no more tears left to cry, she asked after the newspapers she had dropped off moments before her arrest. By a miracle, they had been salvaged, each delivered to the appropriate location without issue.

Which was why they had not been mentioned by the Gestapo. Elaine would never begrudge a filthy receptacle again.

They remained in the safe house through the next day before relocating to another and then another to ensure they were not being followed. In that time, Elaine continued to listen to *Radio Londres*, trying to make sense of the messages, unable to keep from wondering if any one might pertain to Sarah and Noah.

Almost a week later, she finally returned to the warehouse with Nicole at her side. It was strange how something that once felt so cold and utilitarian had somehow become home. She missed the room where her bedroll and box of clothes remained, as well as the small kitchen and the constant hum and bang of the automatic press. Antoine, Jean, and Marcel rushed to embrace her, the familiar velvety smell of ink on all of them, and she was grateful to be returned to her Resistance family.

"Have you heard news from *Radio Londres*?" Elaine queried as soon as the frenzy of welcome wishes died down.

While in those arduous days of waiting, thoughts of Sarah and Noah buzzed in her brain, the only reprieve she had from her tortuous imagination of Joseph and what he likely endured at the hands of Werner.

Antoine's eyes slid toward Marcel.

"I did," Marcel replied.

Elaine pulled in a breath. "And?"

He nodded slowly with quiet approval. "You did it, Elaine. They will be coordinating a pickup with the Maquis."

The victory of her impossible task surged through her. In that moment, she was grateful she had defied Marcel. It appeared he was glad as well; the buoyancy of his exuberance stripped away the years and stress on his features.

Nicole gave a whoop of excitement and beamed at Elaine.

"They're going to America?" Elaine asked.

"That we do not know," Antoine interjected.

"But you still are helping them escape France." Jean's eyes crinkled at the corners. "At the very least they will presumably be in England where they can be safe."

Safe.

Was such a thing even possible? In the days of slinking through shadows and hiding explosives and arranging words for a power-ful impact, the notion of safety felt as elusive as a full stomach.

"And now that you are back," Marcel said, reverting to his businesslike demeanor, "we have much work to do." He lifted the stack of newsprint he had recently gathered and strode across the room as Antoine returned to his desk with a wink.

Jean's gaze lingered on Nicole with an endearing bashfulness before he slipped away to the Linotype machine. As she turned to stroll away, Elaine caught her friend's hand. "He's in love with you, Nicole." She spoke softly to avoid embarrassing Jean.

Nicole's pleasant expression went blank as she considered the man. For a breath of a second, a wistful look crossed her face.

They would be a handsome couple—young and full of *joie de vivre*. A spark between them might be just the thing to dim the brilliance of danger and desolation.

But before Elaine could anticipate Nicole offering favorable en-couragement, her friend's demeanor frosted over, blue eyes going cold as a winter sky. "There is no room for love in this war."

The fierceness on her face was one Elaine had only glimpsed before, one of stark hate, of determination to make the Ger-mans pay for what they had done to France, to Nicole's family.

It was gone as soon as it had come, melting effortlessly into a brilliant smile Elaine now understood was little more than a mask. "*Au revoir, ma chérie*. Be safe."

Elaine embraced her. "And you as well."

Nicole flicked away the wishes for safety with a wave of her hand and click-clacked from the room, leaving Elaine to pon-der over what she had said.

There was no room for love in this war.

And she was not wrong.

NINETEEN

Ava

News of Otto's death followed Ava through the rest of the day, the envelope like a weight in her bag. She didn't take it directly to the embassy, but instead brought it home. There, she sank onto the chair and withdrew the thick letter with trembling hands.

> *There is no one to whom I can entrust this as I can with you, my dear Ava, for you are the only one who has taken the effort to see me.*

Its contents detailed a life of drive, of success and of incredible loss. His story was powerful in its poignancy as he recounted the horror in his sister's letter, the desolation of being in that cell in Spain when he'd been arrested with no food and a pervasive rattle of fear in the air.

Perhaps most impactful to her was his description of being in Lisbon where every day was another wall closing in on him, how the PVDE hovered over him like vultures, waiting for his papers to expire, which would have happened by the end of the week. The final rejection of his American visa, one he knew wasn't possible with his immediate German heritage, was the slip of his fingertips from the ledge of sanity.

He had nowhere else to go, nowhere to turn. No one to trust.

By the time she finished the letter, tears dotted the bottom of the page, and she was gripped with the profound understanding of her own powerlessness. Maybe she couldn't have done something to help, but he could have told her. She could have tried.

Tenderly, she wiped her eyes and folded the pages once more. She hadn't had the opportunity to save Otto, but now she had the chance to aid the mother and child who were traveling from France. No matter what it took, no matter whose office she had to set up camp in, she would not fail.

Fortunately, acquiring a place for them to stay was far easier than the issue with the visas, and by that afternoon, Ava had secured an apartment near Rossio Square. The landlady was a kind older woman whose family had opened the building to lodgers for two generations, and the current occupants were to leave in a week aboard one of the ships already waiting in the dock.

The melancholy of Otto's loss was like a fog around Ava and followed her every action. She had been tempted to cancel on James for the dinner party. He even offered when he found out about Otto, but in the end, she did not want to let James down when he was counting on her. Thus far, she had failed too many people.

Not knowing what to expect and mildly intimidated by visiting a palace, she dressed as she would for a night at the Palacio with a midnight blue gown that draped low at the back, and paired it with white gloves that stopped just above her elbows. A few pins to elegantly draw her hair off the nape of her neck and a swipe of Victory Red on her lips later, she was ready to go.

James picked her up in the late afternoon and drove toward Sintra, arriving just as the sun was going down. The sky was awash in an ombré of rainbow pastels amid the distant mountain, its peak so high, it was obscured with a veil of mist.

"There's a castle up there," he said.

She peered harder, straining to see through the thick gray clouds. "Is there?"

James's brows rose in surprise. "You didn't know?"

It had been her intent to research Sintra prior to their arrival, but she'd been so consumed with Otto's loss that it had slipped her mind.

"It's a medieval castle built by the Muslims who inhabited the land here until the thirteenth century," James explained, bypassing a rare opportunity to tease her for her lack of preparation. "Construction started around the eighth century. There was some damage after the earthquake, of course, but recently the government began efforts on repairs." He gazed up at it. "On clear days, you can see those ancient crumbling walls, but otherwise, it's hidden beneath the mist."

"There's something magical about that." Ava spoke the wistful thought aloud, then her cheeks flared with heat immediately after at having done so.

Except that James didn't laugh at her. Instead, he nodded and turned to her with a crooked half smile. "Just wait." He offered her his arm. "Shall we?"

A damp chill touched the air, but the warmth of his body against her side kept her from being cold as they strode together.

Lush foilage grew up on their side of the gravel path with glossy green leaves dotted with small white flowers. Large trees were interspersed throughout, stretching up to the layer of mist that clung to their tops like fine cobwebs, giving off the sense of being entirely one with nature.

Such places always made her recall the works of Ralph Waldo Emerson and Henry David Thoreau.

"If you've read *Childe Harold's Pilgrimage* by Lord Byron, the poem was about this very estate." James tilted his head and added, "Before the current updates by the new owner."

Ava looked at the vegetation around them through the lens of Byron's narrative, awed to be walking the same steps he once had. There was a natural look to the landscape that cast away the rigid, boxed-in appearance of the plants and lent the area a wild beauty. She could easily imagine it overrun as Byron had described as she breathed in deeply, relishing the fresh, verdant aroma of prevalent flora and rich, wet earth.

"What does it remind you of?" James asked. "Aside from Lord Byron, of course."

She looked around, flexing her mind to account for the many books she had consumed in her life. "*Robinson Crusoe* with some of the junglelike trees. And, of course, Frances Hodgson Burnett's *The Secret Garden*."

James nodded. "The latter is what I anticipated you'd say."

"And you've read it?"

"I have."

She looked at him with fresh eyes, reconsidering this man who knew Byron and spouted sonnets by moonlight and had read *The Secret Garden*.

"I believe my mother read it to me in a bid to keep me well-behaved." He put his free hand into his pocket, his gait loose and casual as he chuckled.

"Did it work?"

He shook his head. "Instead, I aspired to be like Dickon and came home so filthy from attempting to frolic about with the denizens of the forest that she swore she'd never let me read it again."

It was a strange thought to imagine James running about in the woods, trying to befriend birds and squirrels, and she couldn't help but laugh. The act felt peculiar somehow after the melancholic fog she'd been in following Otto's death.

"And how about you?" he asked.

"I read it with my mother." Ava recalled how they had discussed the story together over tea when she was a girl and how very grown-up she felt relaying her thoughts and opinions. "I enjoyed the book immensely. I thought Mary was a brat but hated that her parents had died. Even before I'd lost mine."

James pulled his arm from her hand and smacked his palm to his forehead. "What a dolt. Ava, forgive me for not—"

"No, it's fine." She gently tugged his arm back into place and tucked her hand against the warmth of the inside of his elbow. "The truth is that Mary being so awful actually did help me. After my parents died, I had to go live with Daniel, as I told you before."

Their pace slowed during the conversation, and their feet crunched over the gravel path. The sun had quickened its descent toward the earth, leaving a bluish wash over the garden around them, enough to see James's nod.

"What I didn't tell you is how terrible I was to poor Daniel." Ava winced. "All I could think of was how hurt I was, how lonely, how I had to uproot my life to accommodate his. Never once did I think about what he had sacrificed to care for me, a young man with this whole world ahead of him, saddled with a thirteen-year-old sister he didn't know."

"I really do think Daniel is a saint," James interjected.

Ava playfully elbowed him.

He grinned.

"He was though," she agreed. "One night, I was missing my mother and picked up *The Secret Garden*. In reading it, Mary was suddenly different in my mind. Not a spoiled girl, but a wounded one with a hard shell walled up around her. And I realized in my foul behavior, I was behaving exactly as she had."

"Perhaps that is the draw of books." James put his hand over hers. "To show us the way even when we think the path is too dark to see."

Ava didn't move her hand from beneath his, instead reveling in the connection of their touch as well as their minds.

A fountain came into view before an exquisite building aligned with columns and a grand, arched entrance. The windows were peaked at the top like the main door, all with such delicate carvings, it appeared to be made of fine lace, a combination of Indian influence with Moorish accents.

"It's beautiful," Ava breathed.

"You'll love the inside even more." James led her up the short flight of stairs and through the open door where the subtle notes of a piano trickled out into the night air. They found themselves in an octagonal room with hallways leading in four different directions. To the right and left were most impressive, with corridors of arabesque-engraved arches cascading down its length and what appeared to be pink marble columns running along either side.

James pointed upward. Ava dropped her head back as she gazed to the building's cupola, which was also carved with arabesque and backlit with a glow of red.

"James." A man's voice interrupted Ava's awed exploration as she turned her focus to the gentleman striding toward them.

"Walter." James shook the man's hand. "So good to see you again, old chap." He indicated Ava. "Mr. Walter Kingsbury, allow me to introduce you to Miss Ava Harper."

Walter took her hand and kissed it. "She's even more charming than you said, James."

Ava slid a look at James, who pointedly glanced up at the elaborate ceiling, obviously avoiding her judgment.

"Come, Miss Harper." Walter offered her his arm, stealing her away from James. "My lovely wife will be most eager to chat books with you."

"You have a beautiful home," Ava said, wishing she could stand for an hour in that one spot to fully take in the full opulence of the palace.

"Monserrate isn't mine." Walter chuckled. "I'm minding the property for a friend."

He led her and James into the dining room where a long table was prepared with centerpieces of exotic orchids and set with fine china rimmed in gold. Servers stood by at the ready, hands tucked behind their backs. The savory scents in the air promised a meal as decadent as the venue.

She and James were seated near the end of the table, her beside Walter's wife and him beside a stout man with a German accent. Within minutes of sitting, they were served a delicious soup with bits of sausage and vegetables, then came roasted venison drenched in a thick brown gravy, the meat so tender, it fell apart under her fork. This was followed by a delicate cream meringue that was just sweet enough to be satisfying.

Walter was correct in that Ava did enjoy conversing with his wife, who was very well-read and told about her life at the palace. The building was far too much for their family of four, so they only used a few rooms, and she shared how Walter created a place for their sons to swim by damming the large body of water outside with sand brought in to make it shallow and safe.

It was such an enchanting way of life that Ava almost missed it when James's voice shifted from a conversational tone to something low and nearly imperceptible. She used that very moment to take a sip of her wine and strain her ears to what he said. The word *wolfram* was mentioned, along with *contract* and *this week*.

It took everything in her not to stiffen. Most especially wolfram—or tungsten as it was called among the Allies. One couldn't be in Portugal without being keenly aware of its power over the Allies and the Axis.

The metal was necessary for creating bullet casings and other arms integral to the war effort. Portugal was its chief manufacturer, an asset that allowed them to maintain their neutrality.

Whatever James was saying sounded more like espionage and less like proper dinner conversation. Worse still, when the man lifted his own glass to drink, a gold swastika cufflink peeked out from beneath his black jacket sleeve.

The rich food soured in Ava's stomach.

What sort of gathering had James taken her to?

Whatever it was, it sounded as though he had just shared pertinent Allied secrets with a Nazi.

She set her wine down and turned to Mrs. Kingsbury once more, no longer hearing what the woman was saying.

"Do excuse me," James said abruptly in Ava's ear.

Before she could protest, he was already out of his chair, his cloth napkin abandoned on the cushioned seat as he headed toward the door and pushed into the corridor. The servants swept in once more, their backs ramrod straight with decorum as they cleared away the dessert plates. That was when Ava caught sight of a familiar face among them: handsome as a Greek statue with short cropped blond hair.

Her head spun.

Had Lukas been with the other servants all night? Did James know? Was that why he brought her?

"Are you well, Miss Harper?" Mrs. Kingsbury asked.

"Forgive me, I think I need to use the powder room." Ava pushed up to stand on weak legs.

"Of course. You'll find it down the hall."

Ava nodded her thanks and exited from the room, pausing outside the door to gather her errant wits. Or try to. They seemed to be scattered in every direction.

Had Lukas known she would be there? Was James in league with the Nazis?

Her thoughts whirled.

If James was feeding the Germans Allied secrets, she was obligated to share that information with the embassy. Soldiers' lives depended on it. Like Daniel's.

But if James was removed from his duty, would she still have help in saving the mother and child being transported from Lyon?

Despite it all, she didn't want to believe he might be in league with the Nazis, that he wasn't the good man she thought him to be.

Voices sounded somewhere nearby, muffled by a closed door. Without questioning what she was doing, she slid off her shoes and dashed soundlessly across the cold marble floor. She stopped before a set of double wooden doors carved with a handsome couple lounging beneath a large tree, the woman naked as was often the case with goddesses. Most likely Orion and Artemis based on the hunting motif.

"I best be getting back before my absence becomes prolonged." It was James's voice on the other side of the door.

Ava pulled in her breath and held it.

"Before you leave," another voice said. "Does Miss Harper know?"

"Of course she doesn't," James replied with a confidence that slapped Ava in the face.

Was she so gullible that she would believe anything he told her? A protest rose in her mind, but she quashed it.

She had spent so much of her life with a book in front of her face that she knew written characters better than real people. Yes, she could recite dates of events and names of philosophers and authors long since dead, but she also knew that there was a maddening naivete about her that she could not seem to overcome.

It led to careless mistakes, like trusting James.

"Be sure that it remains that way," the voice said dryly. "Having her find out could be dangerous."

Footsteps clicked over the floors, and she realized in a heart-stopping moment that the discussion was done. Frantic, she whisked back to the other side of the hall, slid her shoes on as fast as was possible, and slipped into the dining room with an air she hoped was casual.

"Did you find it?" Mrs. Kingsbury asked politely.

Ava blinked, her mind devoid of any thought other than the conversation she'd overheard. "What's that?"

Mrs. Kingsbury's pleasant smile remained on her face, but a mildly confused furrow tightened across her brow. "The powder room."

"Yes," Ava said quickly to make up for her own folly. "Yes, thank you."

She was saved from having to add anything further by James rejoining her at the table. Now would be an ideal time to offer up some witty comment that would encourage the table into a lively discussion so she could consider her next steps. Except nothing came to her.

The silence grew around Ava, pressing at her with urgency even as her pulse pounded, pounded, pounded in her ears.

"Dinner was wonderful," she said.

"It was," James agreed, his demeanor easy and relaxed.

That nonchalance dug at Ava, that he would so readily exploit her trust and then not even exhibit a shred of guilt. She didn't bother trying to speak with him for the remainder of the evening. When it was time to depart, she rose from her chair and strode ahead of him toward the exit, ready to be away from the ornate palace and all the ugliness its beauty could never compensate for.

There was a strangeness to her shoes as she walked, as though her footing was not balanced correctly. James looked down and raised a brow. "Are your shoes on the wrong feet?"

She glanced to where the rounded toes of her black heels were pointing out slightly in the opposite direction. In her haste to return to the dining room, she had indeed put her shoes on the wrong feet.

The drive back from Sintra had been stifling as Ava tried to avoid any sort of light chatter with James, a difficult feat when it had once flowed so easily between them. Before she knew he'd betrayed her.

She meant to wait until she'd spoken to Theo and Alfie, the two librarians James worked with, to see if they would still help the mother and child coming from Lyon. But as the car drew to a stop on Rua de Santa Justa in front of Ava's building, James turned to her, concern sharp in his eyes. "Did something happen at Monserrate?"

She shook her head.

"Ava, I know you," James said patiently. "Ever since I returned to the dining room, you have been acting strangely."

It became a little harder to breathe.

Dang it. He did know her, and it would be to her disadvantage now.

Suddenly the truth couldn't stay inside her anymore, not when it was clawing to be free.

"My brother is out there in the war." She glared at him. "Do you know that?"

"Of course I do." James had the temerity to appear offended.

Ava refused to allow her overinflated sense of guilt to plague her. Anger exploded inside her skull. "Yet you were talking to a Nazi at dinner. Sharing Allied secrets with him."

"I was not."

"I heard what you said to that man with the swastika cuff links." She put her hand on the door handle, ready to jerk it open and be free from the enclosed space with James. There wasn't enough room for them both inside that small cab.

"It isn't what you think, Ava."

"Were you sharing Allied secrets, James?" she demanded. "My brother is out there somewhere. Along with other brothers and fathers and husbands."

"My brother is too," he said sharply.

Ava quieted, stunned. In all their times speaking to one another, he had never mentioned having a sibling.

"It isn't something I care to discuss." James cut the engine and silence fell over them. "It's better that I don't think of him out there, worrying that he might be cold or hungry or in danger." His level gaze found hers. "I would never jeopardize his life."

She turned her attention to where her shoes peeked from beneath the glossy hem of her gown, now on the correct feet. As much as she hated to admit it, she could understand not wanting to think about one's brother in battle. If her mother had been alive and corresponded with Daniel, would Ava even have done so at all?

An ache in her chest gave her the answer she already knew. But then, if her parents hadn't died, she and Daniel would never have been close, especially with him living in DC and them being in Chicago.

"What did you tell the German?" She looked up at him once more.

James sighed. "I'd rather not say."

"Because, apparently, I'm not supposed to know?" The bitterness of her hurt found its target. "I heard that too. When you were behind the door with Artemis and Orion."

"How did you know they were Artemis and Orion?"

"The hunting bows," she said distractedly. "I heard you in there, James."

Church bells tolled in the distance.

James's lips pulled downward. "It's dangerous."

"That was said as well."

He regarded her for a long moment, as if considering whether to tell her or not. "Misinformation," he said finally.

"What?"

James ran a hand through his thick, dark hair. "I fed him misinformation. Something he thinks is true but is actually a falsehood. It was the actual purpose for my being at the dinner party. The last time I went, I was alone and thought doing so again would call attention."

She considered him, weighing the words to determine his candor and trying to quell the rise of her own anger so she could think properly.

"It's quite common," he continued. "The spread of false information. Rather than tell many, you only tell one and it is like a flame to dry tinder."

"If that's true," she said softly, "you used me as your cover."

"I personally did not mind." He offered a hesitant smile. "I hope you did not."

"I would have preferred to know beforehand." Certainly, a forewarning would have avoided the ugliness in which they were now embroiled.

If he was even telling the truth. The events all crowded together, making it impossible to decipher between what might be true and what might be a lie.

"I was not sure how you would act around everyone if you knew." His mouth thinned in a hard line. "But there's more to it than that. Ava, it is not safe to meddle with spies. If you didn't know, you wouldn't be in danger."

"Is that why Lukas was there?" An uneasiness snaked through her at the memory of having seen him.

"Who?"

"The Austrian," Ava replied wearily.

But rather than agree with her suspicion, the skin around James's eyes tightened. "He was there?"

"Yes, pretending to be one of the waiters. I didn't see him until you slipped from the room."

A muscle worked in his jaw. "You're certain?"

"Yes," Ava said with exasperation. "I wouldn't have mistaken him."

James nodded slowly. "I see."

She frowned. "Is that something I should worry about?"

"Of course not. Come, I'll walk you in." James got out of his car and saw her to the door. But despite his usually courteous manners, there was something else amiss, something that left him distracted.

And something they could likely discuss the next time they met, after she'd had a night to sift through everything he'd said and compose new questions. For the time being, exhaustion pulled at Ava, encouraged by the heavy meal resting in her stomach and the rich wine she'd consumed.

The following morning, however, it was not James who waited on the street in front of her building, but Alfie. The young man was wearing a coffee-brown coat with a matching fedora pulled over his red hair. It was such formal dress for the youth and made him look like a child dressing up in men's clothing. Especially when he offered her a shy wave.

"Good morning, Alfie." She smiled as she approached, ignoring the disconcerting nip at the back of her mind. "Is James all right?"

"Of course he is," Alfie quipped. "He's been sent away on a special task and will likely be gone for several months. I was told to see to you in his absence." He gave her a hesitant wince. "If that's well and good with you."

"Why was he sent away?" Ava asked, pressing the issue. "Did he know he would be leaving?"

"James receives different missions than we do." There was a finality to the way he said it that told her she'd get nothing more from him.

But Ava could not stop puzzling over James's sudden disappearance. Where had he gone and what was he doing that he would not return for some time?

And what—if anything—did that have to do with Lukas?

TWENTY

Getting Sarah and Noah from the city to the Maquis in the for-est would not be difficult. They had false papers that were well-made should they be stopped and would travel in the evening, making their forged identity cards harder to examine. It was the look in Sarah's eye that most concerned Elaine.

No matter how comfortable Sarah remained in Manon's house, she still had not lost the hunted shadow in her eyes. It was an expression that could not be masked—gaze lowered and shifting, perpetually seeking out possible threats around her, shoulders hunched as if wishing she could make herself and her son disappear from view. The demeanor couldn't be erased by will. It was engrained from the trauma of always being on the run, from safe houses suddenly becoming a threat, from the knowledge that anyone could be a collaborator—the old man smoking at a café on the corner with a smile or a kindly teacher who tended to young children.

The night of their departure came swiftly. Elaine waited for the liaison between the Resistance and the Maquis to join her at the warehouse where they would set off together. But when the person finally arrived, her stomach dropped.

Etienne.

Only he did not appear the same Etienne she had always known. His skin had gone sallow, paper-thin and speckled with a dusting of thick bristling whiskers over his unshaved jaw. The bruising of exhaustion under his eyes was all the more prominent, as though he had not slept in weeks.

He regarded her with a wounded expression, visibly pained.

Their last meeting had not been a good one and still edged into Elaine's thoughts from time to time, like when a sound jolted her from a deep sleep and her racing heart led to a racing mind in the predawn hours of another long night.

They nodded in greeting to one another, masking all that needed to be said with the veneer of civility.

Once outside in the frigid February air, the night sky dark as heavy velvet, Etienne was the first to speak. "You were arrested by the Gestapo."

The nightmare of facing Werner rushed back to Elaine, the fear of what agony might have been implemented by those vicious metal tools and the soul-shaking curiosity if she could maintain her silence.

She nodded and tensed, waiting for an accusation or an outburst of anger at how much she had risked.

Instead, he rubbed at the back of his neck and blinked slowly. "Thank God you are safe."

"Thanks to Nicole," she replied.

"I was the one who recommended you work for Marcel."

"You did?" Elaine glanced at him. "Why?"

"I knew you would be in the Resistance regardless." His expression was hidden in the shadow of his fedora. "I thought it might at least be safer. I promised Joseph I would always look out for you."

Suddenly it made sense that Marcel had taken Elaine on simply based on her experience with the Roneo. Many people knew how to operate the small duplicating machines. Etienne had pull within the Resistance; she was aware of that, even if she wasn't entirely sure of what he did.

"Being arrested was my fault," Elaine confessed. "I would have been fine in the warehouse, but I volunteered to drop off a delivery. That's when I was caught."

The tension in his shoulders relaxed somewhat. A comfortable silence settled between them.

"You do know that Joseph only wanted your safety," Etienne said. "It was why he urged you not to help."

A group of German officers strode by with women at their sides garbed in slinky dresses and fur stoles. The men didn't even notice Elaine and Etienne, too riveted by their garish dates. Etienne and Elaine fell quiet until they passed, the women's noxious floral perfume trailing in their wake.

"Not long after the Nazis occupied Lyon, Joseph and I had to travel to Grenoble," Etienne said in a gravelly, distant voice. "We went through the forest on the way back as we had rubber for the stamps Joseph needed for the identity cards. The Germans were searching everyone boarding the trains, and we could not afford to have them see our cargo."

As far as Elaine knew in her life before the Resistance, Joseph had always been in Lyon for his job. Since then, she learned not only of his heroic efforts, but also how very mobile he had been around France.

"When we were coming through the forest, we came upon a body," Etienne continued in his flat tone. "It was just a foot at first, lightly covered by the leaves. We could not leave it there and decided to bury it. In doing so, we discovered the corpse to be that of a young woman. Forgive me for saying such things, but she was nude and there was evidence of torture…"

Elaine winced in horror, and her mind immediately went to the chair in the middle of Werner's office. The gleam of those metal tools, the damp seat leaving a cold, wet impression on her bottom and the backs of her legs, the heart-pounding anticipation of pain...

A shiver rippled over Elaine's skin.

"Joseph saw the woman and thought of you." Etienne avoided a lamppost as they walked, keeping to the anonymity of darkness. "He knew your fierce determination to liberate France, to help others, no matter the cost. And while the toll was one he realized you would gladly pay, it was not one he could allow you to make."

The abrupt change in Joseph suddenly made sense, the way he had so vehemently insisted she abandon all the efforts of fighting Nazis and instead give herself over to being a good wife.

An ache burgeoned within her. "He could have told me," she said raggedly.

"Would you have listened?"

Elaine sniffed and gave a mirthless laugh. "No."

Etienne lifted a palm up, as though to say "and there you have it."

"Joseph loved you," Etienne said with vehemence. "I've never seen a man so besotted with his wife."

The agony in her chest splintered with the pain of her grief. She had been too stubborn in not sending a note to him while he was in prison, thinking more could be said in person. It was a regret that would haunt her for the rest of her life. For the thousandth time since she'd received word of his death, she wondered at the little pinch of folded paper that Etienne promised to try to deliver to him.

"Joseph knew you loved him too," Etienne said.

"Did he?" Elaine asked, her voice catching. "There was too much left unsaid." Her words choked off with contrition.

"Even if he never received the note, he knew."

While Elaine prayed he was correct, she could not stop the sliver of doubt in her mind.

"I should have written to him earlier." The admission pulled a deep, wounded chasm within her, one of her own making. One that she had unjustly placed on Etienne's shoulders. "I'm angry with myself. Not you. Forgive me for being so unfair to you."

"I let Joseph down," he said.

"No." Elaine shook her head. "If it had been possible to save him, you would have."

He jammed his hands into the pockets of his jacket and said nothing.

The clack of approaching shoes drew Elaine's eyes toward the shadow of a slender woman rushing toward them. A flicker of light whisked over her face from a streetlamp, revealing Nicole, her expression stricken.

"Someone has tipped off the Bosche," she said urgently. "They are on their way to Manon's home now."

The roar of a nearby engine rumbled through the air, as if confirming her words. With petrol being so rare, the only running vehicles were ones owned by the Nazis.

Elaine didn't wait to hear more. She and Etienne raced down the street, leaving Nicole.

"This way." Etienne shoved through a door into a traboule where the darkness of night went from delicate to consuming. He blindly navigated the passageways while Elaine remained at his back to ensure she did not lose him. They were spit out of another door and wound their way through the streets, the cobblestones damp and slick underfoot.

As they came upon Rue Lanterne, Denise strode from the opposite side of the street, from a café many Germans frequented. She was in wide-legged pants with a dark jacket, her hair bound back, her jaw locked with a hard expression. There had always been an edge to Denise, but now the glint in her eyes was nothing short of feral.

She passed by them without bothering to nod in their direction, strangers passing one another on the street and Elaine played along. All that mattered now was Sarah and Noah. And finding a way to keep Manon safe.

An explosion erupted from the building where Denise had

departed, a bloom of orange and red amid a belching cloud of black smoke, the sound deafening against Elaine's ears. A strong arm wrapped around her waist and pulled her into the door of Manon's apartment.

The heat of the blast had only hinted at her skin before its brilliant light disappeared in the darkness of the hall; even the thunderous bang was muted by the thick walls. Etienne grabbed her hand and led her upstairs to where she had lived for several months.

As the noise of the bomb faded away, the roar of engines took its place. The Bosche were closing in on them. Elaine knocked on the door and tried to keep the sound from being too loud or too rapid.

Manon opened it, her eyes darting about. Surely she too had heard the explosion.

Elaine pushed inside. "The Germans," she said as audibly as she dared. "We must go."

Sarah stood in the doorway leading to the living area, frozen with Noah in her arms, her eyes wide like a rabbit cornered by a predator. "Was that an explosion?"

"A diversion," Etienne confirmed. "Please, we haven't much time—this way." He indicated the door to the balcony with the courtesy of a maître d' at a fine Parisian restaurant.

No matter how out of place the gesture seemed, Sarah reacted, following him quickly and quietly.

Elaine tugged at Manon's slender arm. "You must come."

The slam of car doors came from outside, followed by the clipped sound of running feet and a woman shouting with indignation.

Denise.

Elaine gripped her friend more firmly. "We must go now."

Manon simply regarded her with large, calm brown eyes and shook her head. "There is not enough time."

"Manon—"

"I lost one child to these monsters." She withdrew in a firm jerk, fire in her eyes. "I will not lose another."

"Elaine." Etienne spoke in a sharp whisper, his hand extended to guide her to the balcony.

"Go," Manon said fiercely. "Get them to safety. I will distract the bastards."

Etienne grabbed Elaine's arm in a viselike grip and hauled her away. Abandoning Manon.

The horror of it left Elaine momentarily stunned.

"Think of Sarah and Noah," Etienne said harshly in her ear.

It was the reminder Elaine needed for her feet to start working on their own as they raced out onto the balcony. There they were able to pass easily into the next home, another safe house, but one without furnishings, appearing more like an apartment open to let than a place anyone ever stayed. Etienne guided them all through the empty space and down the back stairs that descended to an alternate exit through the rear of the building where a quiet street met them.

But there was no chance to breathe a sigh of relief. Not when rough, angry shouts punctuated the late evening. Sarah clung to Noah as he buried his face into the bulk of her coat, her mouth pressed closed with silent tears.

Elaine understood their terror. Her own skin prickled with it, and her stomach had gone tight. If Etienne was affected by the powerful fear plaguing them all, he did not reveal it as he navigated them through the back alley to the main street where they swept away in the opposite direction. A scuffle sounded in the distance, German orders, severe with accusation and malice. The response delivered was in a demure female voice, so soft and gentle, it could only be Manon.

Elaine slowed, warring with the need to go back to help the woman, but Etienne put a hand to her elbow and rushed her along. Their small party walked with hurried steps and skulked their way through a narrow alleyway to climb the steep, winding hill of Croix-Rousse when a chatter of submachine gunfire pierced the night air.

Elaine slapped her hand against her mouth to keep from crying out. Still, she continued on, trying to think only of what lay ahead of them. Imagining what transpired behind was far too painful. Any distraction at this point could be their demise.

The trams were still running, carting workers in Lyon to the outlying areas where many lived. Etienne guided them toward a stopped tram where they settled in a back row together, joining the quiet group whose bodies were weary and stomachs empty. It was an arduous journey where every jostle and jolt, every voice and stomp of a foot, made Elaine's nerves jump.

Sarah stared into the distance in a way that suggested she too had forced her mind to go blank. Her bland countenance was not unlike those around her as Noah clung to her with such dogged determination, he appeared to be sleeping as any child his age would. Etienne's elbow casually rested on the side of the window as he gazed out at the passing city, his demeanor calm enough to soothe some of Elaine's own churning anxiety.

Whatever fears left her strung taut as a bowstring abated when the tram slowed to a stop and deposited them near a small town set against the edge of the forest.

While the woods had been lovely in the daytime with the golden sunlight and serene shifting of leaves in the breeze, it was not so at night. The pitch black of a moonless night obscured the path in such darkness, one could not see their own feet. And where the ambient backdrop of the forest was once soothing, the clicks and cries and errant cracks of its denizens now left Elaine frightful of what might emerge from the clusters of trees and foliage.

A call came in a subtle hoot that would blend in with those around them and she looked about as her eyes adjusted to the darkness. Etienne.

The bushes rustled and a man appeared. Sarah sucked in a quiet inhale of surprise. But Elaine was not afraid, not when the man moved silently as the Maquis were wont to do. No Nazi with their heavy booted steps and stiff posture could glide unseen anywhere, let alone the forest where the floor was littered with brittle sticks and leaves.

"This is them?" the young *maquisard* asked.

"*Oui.*" Etienne stepped forward. "You have the instructions?"

"Of course."

Sarah was little more than a figure set against the shadows. Elaine turned to her. "You have been so very brave." She put a hand to Noah's back to keep from startling him. "And so have you, Noah."

She leaned closer and he curled his arm around her neck. Sarah joined her son's embrace with Elaine. "Thank you," she whispered.

"They may not be able to take you as far as America." It was a warning Elaine had issued many times already but could not refrain from offering yet again.

Sarah released her. "But we will be safe."

Safe. Yes. Far from France. And from Elaine. She would never see Sarah or Noah again. She might never learn of their fate or the details of their travels. The understanding left an ache in the back of her throat as they bid their final farewells.

Noah watched Elaine as they walked away, his gaze resting comfortably at Elaine's back until a coldness told her they were gone.

With the mission accomplished and their safety secured, Elaine's thoughts turned to Manon. To those terrible shouts and that burst of gunfire.

She knew what it meant without having to be told, but she dreaded the news regardless.

It was in that moment she fully understood why Joseph had tried to keep her from joining the Resistance. So many sacrifices had been made in the war against their oppressors. Too many. Each one as painful as the last.

And, sadly, there would likely be more to come.

TWENTY-ONE

Ava teetered by her apartment door, wriggling one foot into a pair of low-heeled black patent leather pumps while clipping her faux pearl earrings into place. Her smart yellow purse swung from her elbow with Daniel's latest letter buried within.

Such a thing was far too important to leave in her apartment, especially now that she was certain someone had been entering from time to time in her absence.

The very thought of an intruder stalking through her home, rifling through her things, touching her books, left a prickling sensation crawling over her skin. She hated being in the small space that once felt private and now carried a violated, exposed feeling she could not shake.

It started not long after James left with small shifts in the apartment that were easy to dismiss as her own forgetfulness. First was the copy of *Little Women*, resting on her bed when she returned home rather than her nightstand. She picked it up with confusion, certain she hadn't even opened it that day.

The next time, it was a chair not pushed against the table, the one to the far corner that she never sat in.

After that, she carefully set a cup and saucer by the edge of the kitchen table, precarious enough to fall and smash to pieces with the slightest brush. She returned home that day to find the dainty dishes placed at the middle of her table. Not only was the location incorrect, one set was missing from what was once a four-piece place setting in the cupboard.

Her home was being searched.

From that day on, she didn't keep anything of import there.

She glanced at her watch, noting it was twenty minutes to nine. That exact time always made her recall Miss Havisham's stopped clocks in *Great Expectations*, but she shoved the thought aside. She didn't have a second to spare for that now when she needed to meet Alfie and get to the train station before nine.

Pausing only to secure the door behind her, especially the recently installed bolt lock, she rushed from the building to find Alfie waiting on her, his reserved, affable smile in place.

"I'm sorry I'm running late." She walked as quickly as she dared in the heels. The soles were slippery as always over the stonework, and the heels still managed to catch between the limestone and basalt mosaics on the walkway.

"He'll understand if you're running behind," Alfie said as he joined her.

"It isn't James I'm worried about," Ava replied. "It's the mother and her child. I want to be there to welcome them when they arrive."

Four months had passed since Ava first saw the code in *Combat*. Which was never repeated once James informed her that England agreed to help bring them to Lisbon.

James had been gone for two of those, the reason unknown to Ava until she'd received notice from Alfie that James would be arriving at the train station at nine in the morning with two people she was eager to meet.

She didn't have to think hard to know exactly what he meant.

They crossed Rossio Square and headed toward the high horseshoe-shaped entrances of the train station. Crowds of people always thronged around the ornate white building with the statue of Sebastian, the lost king of Portugal, at its entrance.

Some were well-dressed volunteers and employees of refugee assistance charities, their faces weary as they clutched signs with various names scrawled upon them. Most were refugees, freshly arrived, their eyes wide with their first glimpse of Lisbon, their arms laden with sacks of belongings, battered suitcases, and children. Languages from all over Europe rose from the crowd, blending French, German, Czech, Hungarian, Polish, and many more into the cacophonous hum.

Ava and Alfie made their way through the crowd, salmon nudging upstream until finally they entered the internal archways to the spread of chipped-white limestone laid out before the arriving trains. In the crush of passengers disembarking, Ava caught sight of James, his jaw uncharacteristically shadowed with the beginning of a beard, his body braced to shield a woman who cradled a dark-haired boy to her chest from the jostling crowd.

Ava's breath hitched at the enormity of the moment. For months, she had anticipated their arrival, paying for the apartment to be kept empty for them, preparing the paperwork as much as possible that she'd need to facilitate their visas. They were faceless and nameless to her, but that did not stop the palpable pang in her chest for these people she'd come to care so deeply for.

Now she would finally meet them.

James looked toward Ava and he gave her a tired, lopsided smile that made her heart give a strange little skip. Shifting his attention back to the mother and child, he shepherded them closer. He appeared to be limping slightly as he did so. Ava craned her neck to see through the crowd. He strode forward, his footing solid, but then on his next step, yes—a limp.

He was injured. But how? When? What had happened on their journey?

As the three neared, they bore an untold story in the muddy stains discoloring their coats and clinging to their worn shoes, their faces road-weary. They had only one small suitcase between them. Ava's gaze was drawn back to James, alarmed at the amount of weight loss evident in his gaunt cheeks and slender neck since she'd last seen him.

Alfie and James shook hands in a gentlemanly greeting.

"Ava Harper?" The woman drew her attention, large hazel eyes brimming suddenly with tears. Her son burrowed deep into his mother's coat like a frightened little mouse.

Ava's throat was too tight to do anything more than nod.

"The American librarian," the woman said in French. "You are the one who helped bring us here?"

"*Oui.*" Ava swallowed. "I saw the message in *Combat*. I've been preparing for your arrival, to help..."

Tears streamed down the woman's face. "Thank you. For everything you've done. Thank you for seeing Elaine's message and to you, James, for taking us on this journey to safety."

Ava's eyes prickled with emotion, and she nodded as she attempted to wrest control of herself once more.

"Ava," James said. "This is Sarah and Noah Cohen."

"It is so wonderful to finally meet you," Ava choked out. "I'm grateful you've arrived safely."

Someone swept by Ava, their shoulder striking against her hard enough to make her stumble. Alfie reached to steady her, but James was there first, his solid hand on her shoulder as he threw a glare at the person who accidentally knocked into her.

"Are you all right?" he asked, his brow creased with concern.

"Are you?"

He gave an easy chuckle. "Of course."

"You're limping."

He grinned. "I have it on good authority that a chap with a limp is rather dashing."

Ava rolled her eyes at him, the way Peggy always did, but there was no real annoyance behind the action. "Come, let's get some food in all of you."

Together they walked from the train station out into the March sunshine.

Sarah stopped abruptly, her eyes widening at the city around her, taking everything in from the expanse of clear blue sky overhead to the reflection of sunlight on the limestone and the heavy flow of cars roaring by. A little girl strolled by with her mother, a large pastry in her hand. Noah had lifted his head and mutely followed their departure, gaze fixed on the confection.

Two German men nearby began speaking, their voices loud. Sarah hugged Noah tightly to her as her body went stiff.

"No one will hurt you here," Ava reassured her. "Portugal is neutral. The Germans have no power."

It was mostly true. While the Portuguese people were absent prejudice and gave freely, sharing their possessions and food with the refugees, there were always those whose loyalty could be bought.

Fortunately, the Allies had supporters in their corner too.

"Rossio Square is right around the corner," Ava said gently. "I've secured an apartment for you both there. You'll be close to restaurants, grocery stores, whatever you need."

"We don't have ration cards," Sarah whispered, her eyes fixed on everything around them, her body taut.

"There is no ration here." Ava set a hand on the woman's shoulder and gently led her forward. "I purchased some groceries for you, but nothing has been prepared to eat. If you like, we can order a meal here."

They turned the corner to reveal Rossio Square with its waving white and black stonework and towering statue, where café patrons pressed beyond the awnings into the luxurious spring sunshine. Empty cups sat before them, cigarettes were pinched between fingers, and meals lay on plates in various states of consumption.

"There is fish, meat, something called *alheira*, which is pork-free sausage stuffed with poultry and potatoes and breadcrumbs." Ava looked to Sarah, who watched the world around her as if she were fearful it would disappear the moment she allowed herself to believe it was real.

"Do you have a preference?" Ava asked.

Noah looked about with bright, eager eyes. *"Frites,"* he piped up.

Sarah gave a distracted nod as she anxiously scanned her surroundings. "I… I would like a cup of coffee. Real coffee." Her worried gaze found Ava's. "If it is truly safe."

Doubtless this was the first time she had been out of hiding in years. Ava tried to put herself in the other woman's position, to imagine the vulnerability of being in the open after having spent so long remaining sequestered, away from prying eyes and well-trained ears.

"It is," Ava answered earnestly.

Sarah's shoulders only slightly relaxed.

"Nicolas has an excellent array of anything you could ever want," James offered and led the way to the popular café with his gallant limp.

He and Alfie secured a square table for the five of them. It was crowded, but no one complained. A waiter came out for their orders. When it was Sarah's turn, she simply stared at the list of food.

"If you like fish, it is very good here," Ava suggested.

Sarah lifted her stunned gaze and nodded.

Noah didn't have any hesitation with what he wanted, he kicked his legs against the chair, his pants slightly too short. *"Frites, s'il vous plaît."*

Ava made a note to find some well-fitting clothes for him.

His eyes, hazel and long lashed like his mother's, lit with delight.

Ava glanced at James discreetly, studying him in the sunlight for any bruises or cuts. There were none. Only several days' growth of a dark beard and that limp whose origin story she had yet to hear. It was on the tip of her tongue to ask what had happened, what had held them up for over a month. But the tight, weary expression on James's and Sarah's faces had Ava holding back.

Whatever it was could be discussed later when she and James had a chance to speak privately.

The waiter came out with cups of *bica* and a bowl of sugar. Sarah stared at the glistening white grains as if they were made of gold. James spilled sugar into his coffee, and she followed his lead, adding only a fraction of his heaping spoonful. After a slow, careful stir, she brought the cup to her lips, breathed in the strong coffee in a long, slow inhale, then took a sip.

Her eyes closed in pleasure, and she held the coffee in her mouth for a second before finally swallowing. When she opened her eyes once more, they were clouded with tears.

Never in all of Ava's life had she enjoyed anything as much as Sarah had in savoring that cup of coffee.

Sarah caught Ava watching and color flushed in her cheeks. "Forgive me," Sarah said. "It has been years since I have had real coffee."

Ava shook her head, embarrassed to have interrupted the other woman's simple pleasure. "Please don't apologize. I want you to enjoy everything."

The waiter came then, the length of his arms stacked with plates full of food. Within the span of a minute, the bounty covered the small square table and filled the air with the scents of roasted meat, yeasty, fresh baked bread, salty fries and the rich, briny smokiness of grilled sardines.

Sarah gazed over it all, then lowered her head, covered her eyes with her hands and silently wept.

It was too much for her, Ava realized belatedly, kicking herself. She had meant to bring them as a kindness, but she had overwhelmed Sarah. Being outside where Sarah felt most vulnerable, the amount of food, access to anything they could want to eat. It was a blessing and a curse this first day in a foreign country after whatever harrowing journey they had endured.

Beneath the table, Ava reached for Sarah's hand and gently held it, offering a quiet but supportive show of understanding and patience.

Sarah gave her a grateful smile and, within a moment, wiped her eyes and enjoyed her first solid meal in Lisbon, and likely in years.

After they finished their food, Alfie took James back to the British Embassy. It had been all Ava could do to keep from staring at James as he was led away. When she did finally look up, she found him watching her with a longing that made something in her chest squeeze.

Ava brought Sarah and Noah to the apartment she'd secured for them, one also installed with a heavy bolt like she now had in her home.

"It has only one bedroom with a large bed, but it's big enough for the two of you," Ava said as she showed them around. "I bought what groceries I thought you might need."

Sarah stood in the center of the home, as if she was frightened to touch any of it, and held Noah. Her gaze settled on something in the neatly arranged groceries on the counter.

"Is that soap?" she whispered, her voice trembling.

"Yes," Ava replied.

When the other woman continued to stare at it, Ava regarded the small box. "Is it the wrong type? I can get—"

"No." Sarah sniffed. "It's perfect. Whatever it is, it's perfect. Thank you."

"Down, *Maman*." Noah wriggled in her grasp, but she kept him locked in her arms.

Ava nodded. "It is safe here, Sarah."

Slowly and silently, Sarah set him down. He tore off like a toy whose spring had been wound up and released. Sarah stepped toward him.

"It's fine, really," Ava offered by way of reassurance and held a small bin toward Noah that she'd filled with toys and French children's books. "There is nothing he can hurt himself on here. I made sure it would be safe for a child."

Sarah nodded, more to herself than to Ava before looking up. "Thank you," she said quietly. "For everything."

Ava smiled and fought the welling of emotion once again. "I'm happy to have been able to help. I'll leave you to get settled, but will be by to check on you later, if that is all right."

Once they had all they needed, Ava returned to her own rented home. The bolt was firmly in place upon her arrival, the small traps she'd laid about the apartment undisturbed. There was the paper near the sink that could easily tumble to the ground, one side marked with an imperceptible dot. The bedspread was pulled so crisply, it would reveal the slightest crinkle of an imprint. Then there was the strand of Ava's hair settled delicately over her books, so fine it would easily be overlooked by anyone but her.

All was as it should be.

It was in that moment when she allowed herself to relax in the comfort of knowing her space had remained her own, that she saw her apartment with fresh eyes, the way Sarah had seen her own temporary home.

Ava had never gone without, even with the ration in America. She had always had the luxury of seeing her home as one of freedom to come and go as she pleased rather than having it be the only location where she was safe, one she could not leave.

Never had she minded how heavy her tread was over the smooth flooring, or how loud a cough or sneeze might be.

Getting Sarah and Noah to Lisbon had not been easy. The difficulty of their trek had been written all over James's face. But now that they were here, now that she had witnessed with her own eyes the level of their awe at such basic things no human should have to endure life without, she was grateful beyond measure for their safety.

The next morning, it was not Alfie who waited by the door to her building, but James. Exactly as she'd hoped.

His fresh suit hung slightly loose on him, and he had a glossy black cane at his side.

She beamed at him, not even caring that he was aware of exactly how pleased she was to see him. Though she'd never admit it to him, she'd gone to great lengths selecting her attire that morning in anticipation. The Kelly green shirtdress highlighted her eyes, especially when paired with the black cardigan, belt, and leather shoes.

"If I'd known you'd look at me like that, I'd have come back even earlier." His jaw was smoothly shaved, revealing his prominent chin that had once been unappealing for a reason she couldn't recall.

The length of his hair was still longer than usual, his dark fedora pulled low in a bid to make his shaggy locks less apparent. He was a man of confidence, and the slight show of self-consciousness played an endearing chord in Ava's chest.

"If you could have come back a month earlier, you shouldn't have dallied." She readjusted the messenger bag slung over her shoulder.

"If only it could have been so easy." There was something behind his eyes, a glint of pain.

"What happened?" Ava asked.

"Will you take a walk with me?"

"Do you even need to ask?"

He tilted his head in acknowledgment that was somewhere between cocky and shy. As they strolled together, he leaned slightly on his cane, leading her down Rua Agusta where the shops were busiest and the arch spanned over one end in a gateway that opened to the sparkling river beyond.

"I admit it," she said in a conciliatory tone. "The cane does make you look quite distinguished."

"I won't say I told you so." He looked away with exaggerated innocence.

"Will you recover soon though?" she asked, her worry pressing through her teasing words.

"In time." He tilted his head. "I hope."

They passed the awnings of several cafés, stretching toward the street center where tables and chairs were already set over the sprawling stone mosaics in preparation for the crowds that would soon descend. The sweet aroma of freshly baked pastries hung in the air.

"Will you tell me what happened to your leg?" She asked hesitantly, aware that she was crossing a line of trust. Not between their friendship, but between the alliance of their country. Whatever happened was for British intelligence to know, not for her to probe about.

"I was shot." He glanced about. "In Toulouse. We were sneaking about in the dark, our sights set on scaling the Pyrenees Mountains when a Nazi officer saw us and fired. Lucky for us he was a terrible shot." He gave a dry laugh, the way people did when telling a story that had lost its humor. "One bullet ricocheted off a building and caught me in the calf."

"At least it was only your calf," Ava exclaimed.

"Yes and no," James hedged. "An injured leg prior to climbing the Pyrenees might have meant my death. Thankfully the bullet passed through a rather small area, and I was able to clean and bind the wound."

Ava had always loved Rua Agusta with the quaint shops selling teas and coffees as well as pastries and colorfully painted plates and kitchenware. But now, she found it impossible to glance toward the artful displays, her focus instead intent on James. "You should not have endured such a climb. You could have been killed."

"If I had not, they would have been." The earnestness in his face struck Ava.

"You lost so much weight," Ava said, unable to suppress her concern.

"There is little food to be had in France," he replied. "What meager supplies we had, I wanted to ensure Sarah and Noah could keep up their strength. They truly did so well and were so determined and brave." He paused a moment. "It is always interesting to return to Lisbon, to witness the abundance of food and clothing. Even the lights." His lips lifted in a smile. "London is always dark these days to prevent bombings. It's almost blinding at night here by comparison."

"I want to know everything." She folded her arms over her chest as they walked into the shade of a building, the wind pushing at her clothes and hair as they strode toward the water. "Why did they send you?"

"Not all favors are given for free."

Ava considered him. She would never have been allowed to take on so dangerous a task. But then, she was a woman, often underestimated in a field dominated by men. If she had been a man, would that still happen? Would accompanying Sarah and Noah have even been an option?

"It was not supposed to take as long as it did." James led her under the massive arch, built where the old royal palace formerly resided, to commemorate the reconstruction of Lisbon after that fateful earthquake.

Questions of James's involvement were swept away immediately by more important details. "What happened to delay you?" she asked.

The square was large and open, overlooking the Tagus River. What few people did linger nearby were well out of earshot. James glanced about still before continuing. "The Nazi aggression in France has grown. Despite what the Germans say in the newspapers, they see the defeat coming. Apparently, the loss of Corsica sent a shock wave through France, encouraging the Resistance in their efforts and leaving the Germans redoubling their determination to hold on to their occupation."

His eyes searched the horizon, over the choppy surface of the water before them. "They have been hunting the Resistance down without mercy, especially the Maquis who were our main contacts. There were several times we had to find our own way after bands of Maquis were eliminated. We shielded Noah from as much as we could. I believe he's young enough to recover, but I couldn't always protect Sarah from the things she saw…"

"James." Ava put her hand to his shoulder. "I'm so sorry."

He turned his haunted stare toward her. "I would do it again to ensure their safety. If left there, they would surely have been found out and sent to one of those camps."

Ava wanted to pull him toward her and hug away his hurt, but there was a part of her afraid that if she did, she would never be able to let him go.

James sighed and walked closer to the water. Foamy, white-tipped waves lapped at a set of stone stairs that descended into the tidal depths where two columns rose from the river, a place where royals once docked to visit the palace.

"The papers we'd arranged for did not come through," James continued. "We believe the men supposed to deliver them were captured, which meant they might potentially talk under torture. The lack of papers and possibility of our plans being leaked forced us to change our path, which took us over the snow-covered mountains where France and Spain meet. It took many days with little food and low temperatures. But we are here."

There was more to the story, an odyssey beneath the simple gloss, one rife with tragedy that left sadness in his sparkling gaze.

Someday she might hear additional details, but for now, the solemnity of his demeanor quieted her need for information. He had succeeded in bringing Sarah and Noah to Lisbon and had himself returned safely.

"Sarah is trying to get to her husband in America," James said. "He left before Paris fell, and they received only one letter from him with the address where he is staying. They have not been able to send him a letter since."

Ava opened her mouth to offer to post one for them when James withdrew an envelope, his lips quirking up in that familiar grin. "I presumed you would offer." He handed her the envelope, an address in New Jersey written across it.

"I'll ensure this gets to him," Ava promised. "And I'll have them in America with him in no time."

While she knew she could fulfill her vow to mail the letter, the latter part of her promise would be far trickier. But after everything Sarah and Noah had suffered through, she refused to let them down.

TWENTY-TWO

Elaine

Witnesses say Manon was like an angel preparing to ascend into heaven. Amid the crimson waves of violence the Germans swept over Lyon, their cruelty played its wicked hand that night when the Gestapo pulled her into the street on Rue Lanterne. She did not fight their painful grip, nor did she cringe when they pointed the barrels of their submachine guns upon her.

Elaine did not know what they said to her, only that as their voices roused the attention of the neighborhood, Manon closed her eyes and tilted her head back, seraphic, as if basking in the warmth of heaven's golden glow. The men released her, and she spread her arms at her sides in supplication as the bullets scored the night air and tore into her frail body.

Her loss was one of many etched upon Elaine's heart, and every night thereafter for those following four months, she prayed Manon had finally found peace at last with her husband and her son.

Denise was taken that night while fleeing from the bomb she'd planted as a distraction. There were also stories about her—how she lashed out like a *guivre* to avoid capture. But in the end, even the dragon-like creature itself could not have held out against the considerable force of the Germans sent to arrest Sarah and Noah. Denise remained at Montluc for only a short week, her rescue impossible, before she was finally sent to a prisoners' work camp, like Joseph.

There had been no news of Sarah and Noah since. Though perhaps that was a good thing. Regardless, they remained on Elaine's mind. They likely always would as their absence in her life was one her thoughts constantly prodded.

The newspaper rolled through the machine, its rhythm lulling her as stacks of fresh newsprint piled up. It was the middle of the day and yet Elaine had to fight the weight of exhaustion tugging at her eyelids. Marcel had been arrested nearly two months ago on suspicion of operating the clandestine newspaper, though they were still uncertain if he was at Montluc or the Gestapo headquarters...or somewhere else entirely. Regardless of his location, he hadn't talked, or they would all be with him.

So it was, they put in extra hours to compensate for his absence until he returned. If he would return.

Her head nodded forward, yielding to her fatigue when the machine's sudden *click-click-click* snapped her awake once more, indicating the print job was complete. Fatigued, she gathered the newspapers and set them beside the stack she had completed an hour earlier on the Minerva.

The Gestapo had been relentless in their pursuit of Resistance fighters and Maquis. The kid gloves with which the Nazis handled the French populace before were ripped off, their claws now bared and dripping with blood.

A dozen prisoners were slain in retaliation for the death of one German, and in the country, those suspected of helping the Maquis were dragged from their homes and killed. Arrests were a constant threat as the Milice and Gestapo tightened their grip on the throat of Lyon. Bread rations were cut, curfews extended to ridiculous hours, and harsh shouts rang out through the narrow stone streets.

The Nazis had hovered over Lyon since the occupation, but now their breath whispered hot and fetid at the neck of the Resistance network. Most especially the printers as the Nazis attempted to destroy all clandestine presses.

It was for that reason, Elaine and the others did not mind the extra hours Marcel's absence created. If the newspaper still went out on time, it would hopefully disprove his involvement to the Gestapo. Thus far, at the very least, there had been no news of his death. For that, they were all grateful.

And for every day the Gestapo didn't storm into the warehouse from whatever they may have forced from Marcel's lips, they were even more grateful.

The print job complete, Elaine dragged herself toward the kitchen to prepare a cup of chicory coffee to fortify herself and stifle the emptiness growling from her stomach as she waited on Nicole to come for the freshly printed papers. The darkened corridor was uncharacteristically quiet with the automatic machine having completed its task, and Elaine's entire body was immediately on alert.

Every footstep outside might be the Milice surrounding the warehouse. Every murmured voice might be the Gestapo infiltrating their perimeter. Every person who strode by might be a collaborator who noticed something unusual about the facade of their geological business.

That was daily life now—along with the gnawing ache of insatiable hunger, the threadbare blanket of comfort and safety ripped away with the Germans' barbaric tactics. Even in Elaine's exhausted state, every pop and creak of the old building as it settled deeper into its foundation made her jump. She was nearly to the kitchen, her nerves strung tight as a trip wire when the front door flew open, flooding the dark hall with light from outside.

Elaine's heart leaped and she froze where she stood, a deer before a hunter. Caught.

But the figure stumbling into the backlit doorway was no Nazi.

"Help me," Nicole gasped as she staggered under the weight of a man she had propped against her side.

Elaine ran to her friend without hesitation, first closing and securing the door behind them, then putting herself under the man's other arm. He was skeletal, but she and Nicole were scarcely better off, and they still struggled to keep him upright.

"I can walk." The man's voice carried a familiar timbre, both serious and authoritative at once.

Marcel.

With what little strength he possessed, he straightened, and the burden of his weight eased from Elaine's shoulders. They guided him into the quiet warehouse.

Antoine lifted his head, eyes going wide. But he did not hesitate. "Jean, come at once. Bring your kit."

Elaine pulled a chair toward Marcel. As he settled gingerly into the cradle of the seat, she could finally see his face for the first time. Bruising mottled his features, coloring his skin with the offended red of new marks, the purple of ones sustained days ago and even the yellow-green of those on their way to healing. A cut split his lower lip, and his hair, usually cropped close to his scalp, was at least an inch long and glistening with blood on one side.

As with the man at Montluc, Marcel's fingernails were all removed, leaving only patches of angry red.

No one shied away from gore these days when abuse was so prevalent. But then, never had Elaine witnessed someone with whom she was so familiar be injured as Marcel was now. In that battered visage, she still knew a proud father's smile, a man who loved his wife and cared for those in his employ, a hard worker who wanted only to see his country free and safe.

Jean settled before Marcel with a bag opened at his side. Though Jean's face remained calm, there was a tremble to his fingers as he dashed a bit of what he called Carrel-Dakin fluid over wounds Elaine had not initially noticed. While Jean was no doctor, he had been trained in first aid in his final year at school when the Germans came through Lyon at the start of the war.

"Werner," Marcel muttered. "I said nothing."

"We know," Elaine soothed. "And the papers have gone out these last two months."

"Two months?" His brows pushed together.

Elaine could too easily remember the awful cell in Montluc and the odor of fear and blood that permeated Werner's office. The memories visited her often at night and woke her with a chilled sweat. It was easy to see how time would blur in such a perpetual state.

"Yvette." His wife's name emerged from a deep place within his chest.

"She had the baby." A sad smile quivered at the corners of Nicole's lips. "A girl named Claire."

A tear trickled down Marcel's battered cheek. "Orphan," he muttered.

"*Oui,*" Elaine whispered around a fresh lash of pain for him. "Yvette took her to the orphanage as you directed."

Though no doubt it had devastated his wife to do so, her womb and heart both empty. But a child could be used against Marcel. He and Yvette had given up much for the Resistance, including their children, who had all been sent to an orphanage in the last brutal months. To protect them in the best way their parents knew how. An end to the war would finally reunite them, but nothing could bring back first steps and first words and all the other firsts their sacrifices cost them.

The tension drained from Marcel's shoulders as he relaxed into the seat, and everyone left Jean to tend to him in peace. Antoine had already returned to his work, his brow pinched in a forced concentration Elaine knew well, one that was meant to push away the horror of what lay before them.

Nicole followed Elaine to the stack of papers.

"Have you heard anything of Josette?" Elaine asked. The short window of time they saw one another every other week for newspaper deliveries was their only opportunity to discuss what the other knew.

Nicole's pale eyes darkened as she shook her head.

Josette's nerves had unraveled and torn away at something vital within her. Her parents, in their fear for their only child, kept her locked within their home lest the Nazis detect whatever had broken, and finished the job.

"Denise?" Nicole asked.

"Nothing new."

Nicole nodded slowly as her gaze wandered back to where Jean leaned over Marcel. A sharpness took hold of her eyes, imbued with scalding vengeance and rancor. "I wish I could kill Werner myself."

The look was visceral, an enmity simmered in Elaine's own soul like a pot ready to boil over. They all were in a state of agitation, their bodies exhausted but keenly alert, their empty stomachs filled only with acid that churned and roiled. And burning beneath it all was the raw hatred for the Nazis.

Either the Resistance would gain an advantage over their oppressors, or every one of them would die trying.

A month later, Elaine leaned over the desk, her pen poised over a notepad, body tensed like a horse at the races, waiting for the gate to spring open and reveal the stretch of track.

The opening notes of Beethoven's Fifth Symphony tinkled to life; the short-short-short-long notes were Morse code for V—symbolic of the Victory they all prayed to see realized. And now, after poignant loss and powerful suffering, that time might finally be coming to fruition.

Elaine was not alone as she leaned over the radio, ears straining to listen behind the pierce of whining and cracking static meant to jam up the message. Nothing could keep them from gathering the codes that had been rattled off in a seemingly endless stream in the last week. On June 1, there had been over two hundred messages.

Marcel had translated them with tears shimmering in his eyes. The Allies were coming.

He was beside her now along with Antoine, each with their own pad and pen to ensure nothing was missed.

"The long sobs of the violins of autumn," the broadcaster's voice said in French.

Antoine, a man never given to emotion, sucked in his breath.

"It is happening," Marcel said with reverent awe. In the month since his escape from the Nazis, his bruises had all healed and he was left with only a limp and ten patches of unnaturally smooth skin where his fingernails once grew.

Before Elaine could ask what he meant, the second message came. "Wound my heart with a monotonous languor."

Marcel looked to Antoine and nodded. "Go."

Antoine was already halfway from the chair when he received the order.

"The Allies will be here in less than twenty-four hours," Marcel said swiftly in the breath between messages.

A tingle of excitement had but a second to prickle through Elaine's veins before the next code came, its swift delivery demanding her full attention. But as she wrote down line after line of seemingly nonsensical statements, that fledgling tingle blossomed into the tangible flare of hope.

Once the stream of messages concluded, Marcel turned to Elaine, a smile spreading over his healing face. "Sarah and Noah are safe and will hopefully depart for America soon."

Elation soared through Elaine. "Is it really true?"

He grinned at her, revealing a missing lower left canine. "You did it, Elaine. You saved them, especially before these harrowing months."

These harrowing months—even such strong words were a trite description for what they had endured. Every day there were reports of Nazi aggression as they ferreted out where Jews were being hidden. The worst of which was in Izieu, not far from Lyon, when three Nazi trucks arrived at an orphanage for Jewish children, arresting all forty-four innocent souls and the seven brave adults who stayed with them. Elaine had written the story for *Combat* herself, her heart heavy, the typed words interrupted often by the moments needed to blot away her free-flowing tears. The orphans and their caretakers had been taken to Drancy, an internment camp in Paris where they were then sent to work camps.

What could children possibly do in work camps?

Elaine had immediately thought of Sarah after learning of those poor children of Izieu. If Sarah had done what many suggested and placed Noah in the care of those meant to save Jewish children, perhaps he might have suffered a similar fate.

Elaine sat back in her seat as the news report of *Radio Londres* detailed the losses Germany faced recently despite how the Nazis boasted their specious claims of victory. She remained sitting there long after the program ended, ruminating over Sarah and Noah's success.

The task of getting them to America had been deemed insurmountable, but Elaine's actions set their liberation into motion, along with the heroic efforts of countless others who managed to make the impossible become a reality.

Finally, it felt as if there was hope for them all.

The clandestine papers made no mention of the Allied invasion in their newspapers, but the arms stored in the basement were distributed through the Resistance in Lyon as well as to the Maquis. The Allies were finally coming; the war for independence had begun in earnest.

Allied bombings in the past had been unsuccessful in Lyon, like the one that had occurred in late May. While the explosive power did its worst on the Gestapo headquarters, so too had its destruction wreaked havoc on the local area, killing over seven hundred civilians and wounding hundreds more.

An advancing army crawling over France's verdant hills and cobbled streets, however, would be far more effective.

The printing press banged on through its process, but Elaine could scarcely concentrate enough to operate the old Minerva. She glanced down at her watch, the delicate arm stretching half past the hour. Nicole was late.

Anxiety brought an unwelcome sense of unease to the forefront of Elaine's mind. At any moment, she expected the door to swing open and Nicole's voice to tinkle out in her singsong welcome.

But it never came.

Nicole had never been late in the past. Not once.

A prickle of foreboding rippled over Elaine's skin.

She stared at the door, willing it to swing open. When it finally did, however, it was not Nicole who entered through the entryway, but Marcel, returning from a meeting in Paris with the other news printers. The Allied advance meant further recruitment for the Resistance would likely no longer be necessary. The war would surely be over any day now.

Elaine rushed to him, following his long strides as he crossed the room. "Nicole is late."

His gaze caught on Elaine's desk where the stack of newspapers lay bound and ready for retrieval. Frowning, he glanced down at his watch.

"She should have been here forty-five minutes ago," Elaine said solemnly. An ominous sensation fluttered in her chest. She looked to Marcel in the hopes he could quell the terrible feeling with a note of reassurance. "She has never been late before."

"Let us wait a moment more." A haggard exhaustion lined Marcel's face and darkened the tender skin under his eyes to the point they were reminiscent of those bruises he once carried from German abuse over a month before.

"What did they say about stopping production of the paper?" Elaine asked.

Marcel sank into a chair and removed his fedora, letting it plop onto the desk. His hair was cropped short once more as he preferred to wear it, enough that he was often mistaken for a soldier. Enough that no one could grab hold of his dark locks to plunge his head easily into water for *baignore*, the bathtub water torture the Nazis relished employing.

"Paris said that we should increase production rather than stop," Marcel answered woodenly.

The spark of determination in his eyes had dulled to something flat and unrecognizable. Defeat.

In that moment, Elaine could practically hear his thoughts. He wanted his role to be over, to reunite with his wife, for them to reclaim their children from their cold relegation to the orphanage, to relive those memories that once upon a time pulled his lips into an involuntary smile.

While Elaine did not have such a happy ending waiting for her at the end of her service, she understood the lure of such a desire. For if Joseph had lived, she would want the same—to be free of her part with the printing press, to sacrifice ink and paper and hot metal slugs dropping onto cooling trays for safety, comfort and love.

Now though, her efforts were a way to forget everything she no longer had. While she wanted the war to be over, she did not wish for her work to end. When it did, she would have to face the enormity of exactly how much she had lost.

"Perhaps they can send a replacement?" she offered even as her eyes wandered to the closed door that Nicole failed to emerge through. "Or I can take over."

He lifted his gaze to Elaine and nodded. "I know you can do the job, but I could never put such a burden on your shoulders."

"But I could—"

"No." There was a firmness to his response. While his body healed from the two months he'd spent imprisoned, his demeanor remained wounded. In all the time Elaine had known him, in all the arrests from which he had previously escaped, he had never shown fear until his most recent return. That nervous anxiety bled through his dealings with all of them, as Elaine and the others were scarcely allowed to leave the warehouse or to take on anything that might assume additional risk.

Like running the printing press as she had suggested.

His gaze slowly crept to the closed warehouse door and a pained look pulled at the new creases on his brow.

"Nicole is very late," Elaine whispered.

A muscle worked in his jaw, and his stare grew soft and distant. "I think we will not see her this day."

Marcel was correct. Nicole did not show. Worry finally gnawed through Elaine's discretion when Nicole did not appear the following day either.

There had been no reports of her at Montluc Prison, which meant only one thing.

"I'm going to try to find Nicole." Elaine snatched up her shopping basket and handbag before her nerves could get the better of her.

After the Allied bombing destroyed the old medical military school, the Gestapo headquarters had relocated to a building on the corner of Place Bellecour and Rue Alphonse Fochier. If Elaine rushed and caught the right trams, she could be there in half an hour.

Nicole had once risked herself to liberate Elaine from the clutches of Werner. Elaine would not abandon her friend now.

Marcel moved like a striking snake, grasping Elaine by the arm. "Are you mad?"

"I cannot sit by and do nothing." She hadn't meant it to come out as an accusation, but he jerked back as if she'd struck him.

"You don't even know if she's there," he said in a hard tone. "If you show up looking for her, they will kill you too."

There was nowhere else Elaine could think that Nicole would be. She would never disappear and leave her father and brother to fend for themselves without the supplies she so carefully gathered to send them. Nor would she abandon her position with the Resistance when she was its most ardent supporter.

Elaine shook her head. "She cannot be anywhere else. I cannot leave her. She didn't leave me."

Jean approached, no doubt drawn by the passion with which Elaine spoke. "Marcel is correct, Elaine. It is far more dangerous now than before." His usually jovial expression was muted by the solemnity of the situation, by the pain Nicole's disappearance evidently caused him. "That's why I'm coming with you."

The warehouse door opened and a young woman with short, dark hair entered. Nicole's replacement, Celine. There was an edge to her, aged eyes in a youthful face. She did not have the cheerful countenance of Nicole and took her place as courier in job alone.

The position needed to be filled, yes, but the haste with which it was done was an insult. As if they were all simply interchangeable. As if none of them mattered more than the role they filled. Not people, but nameless parts in the workings of the great Resistance machine.

That someone like Nicole could be so easily forgotten, that the organization could so readily move on…it was more than Elaine could stand. "I am going now."

Before Marcel could reach for her again, she was gone, sprinting toward the warehouse door with Jean close behind her. The world whirred by as she ran out into the heat of the June day.

Jean joined her, matching her pace and saying nothing, slowing only when they reached the Rhône. The shade from the plane trees lining the river helped cool the sweat gathered on her brow and dampening the lower back of her dress. But the rustle of the pointed leaves overhead drew her awareness, its sound ominous, tugging her onward with the same press of determination she'd felt earlier.

"What are they looking at?" Jean nodded toward a crowd leaning over the stone wall to the river below.

An icy premonition cascaded over Elaine as she walked on legs she could not feel. A man turned to the side and retched, creating a break in the crowd, a place to slide into and peer toward the glittering river below.

A nude woman floated in the water, bobbing facedown in the gentle waves. The stiffness of her body was guided toward the stone walkway by a police officer with a long metal pole. Blond hair floated around her like a pale mist and her skin was white as a marble statue, marred with patches of black bruises covering her legs and back. Hideous strips of meaty pink showed where skin was missing entirely, as if peeled away.

Bile burned up Elaine's throat.

"Don't go down there," Jean cautioned at her side.

But she was already making her way to the stairs, guided by the same macabre unseen hand that had led her on this path.

She had to know.

Rather, she already knew, but had to confirm.

The police officers yelled at her, but they were too busy with pulling the body from the water to physically stop her. So it was that she was there when they pulled the corpse from the lapping waves and rolled the woman face up onto the stone walkway.

Milky blue eyes stared up at nothing in a face so misshapen, the woman's features were indistinguishable. If the signs of torture were monstrous upon her back, they were nothing compared to what had been done to her front.

Elaine's stomach rolled with nausea. This woman could not be Nicole. Her light was too bright to be snuffed out, her guile too smooth to be snagged, her beauty too breathtaking to be made hideous, even with torture.

Yet even as Elaine tried to convince herself, she could not stop her gaze from creeping toward the woman's right arm, to the spot just above the crook of her elbow where a small heart-shaped mole showed black against her pale skin.

Nicole had been found.

TWENTY-THREE

At exactly noon every day, Mr. Smith—one of the vice-consuls from the legation office on the first floor of the embassy—came upstairs for a cup of coffee. And at exactly noon every day, Ava met him there.

First, she brought some *pastéis de nata* from the best bakery in the Belém district. Next, she offered him a few sausages and a tin of quality sardines as a quick lunch when she knew the staff downstairs seldom had time to eat. The day after, she presented him with a bottle of green wine.

He knew she was building up toward something with her sweet smiles and interest in his day-to-day life. Yet when she asked the first time if he'd received the meticulously written and rewritten six copies of Form B, he had the audacity to tell her she was a copy short.

It was now 11:58 a.m., and she was done being nice.

She stood up from her desk, slipped into her heels, and straightened her skirt. Peggy met her gaze from across the office and offered a nod of encouragement, her eyes narrowed with assertiveness.

At 11:59, Ava left her desk and slowly made her way to the break room. Sure enough, Mr. Smith was standing there in his ill-fitting gray suit with a skin tone to match. His dark mustache reminded Ava of the long brooms used by the cleaning crew, and his brow remained in a perpetually glossy state. He wore the same exhausted, defeated expression as his fellow vice-consuls, all of them worked to the point they were bereft of patience and on the teetering edge of losing their humanity.

He eyed her warily.

She gave him her most charming smile, exactly as Peggy had directed. "Did you receive my updated copies of Form B?"

"Miss Harper." He gave an exaggerated shift from one foot to the other, as if the weight of the world rested between his shoulders. "Was it entirely necessary to send over eight copies of the application for a visa?"

"Absolutely." Ava crossed her arms over her chest. "Considering I left you ten."

That had been Peggy's idea too. Their hands were cramping by the tenth form, but the flattening of Mr. Smith's lips beneath his mustache made it all worthwhile. The system was complicated and layered in bureaucratic tape, but she was learning to balance the twisted ropes, one grueling slip at a time.

And she would win.

The applications for the two US visas were exceptionally long and required exactly six copies for each person that she had painstakingly filled out. They had been completed in March when Sarah and Noah arrived in Lisbon. Though she had walked them downstairs herself, they refused to look at them and insisted the forms be set aside. In that time, they managed to lose a copy and took a month and a half to inform her one page was missing. She'd been waiting another month already on the second set of papers and refused to wait a single day more.

"They have been received," Mr. Smith replied tightly.

"I'll accompany you downstairs today while you approve them," Ava said.

"That isn't how it's done, Miss Harper." The condescension in his tone made what she had to do next all the easier.

"I'm well aware of how it's done." She unfolded her arms and straightened, fully prepared for this battle. "You delay visas so you don't have to issue them. I have seen it time and again. All the necessary paperwork has been submitted, not once, but twice—"

"Your paperwork was incomplete last time."

"It was not when I submitted it," she corrected him. "I still fail to understand how it even got lost when they were all bound in an envelope."

Mr. Smith narrowed his eyes. "Do I need to remind you of the fifth columnist?"

He did not. She was quite familiar with the phrase that referenced a Nazi sympathizer who might slip into the States as a refugee. The word was whispered in America with fear, and the newspapers mentioned it often enough that it practically became quotidian.

"This is a mother and child," Ava said with exasperation. "One whose husband is already in New Jersey now working as a doctor. Their support affidavits and moral affidavits were received and accepted well over a month ago. They should be free from this scrutiny and this prejudice."

Mike strode into the small room and stopped to listen, leaning against the door frame with his arms casually folded over his chest and a smirk on his lips.

Mr. Smith tossed him an irritable glare.

"I will stop by every hour on the hour if you do not do this now," Ava threatened. "Day after day after day." She added some extra sugar into her already saccharine smile.

"She's nothing if not persistent." Mike bit into an apple and chewed noisily as he watched Mr. Smith with a bemused grin.

Mr. Smith sighed, a heavy, defeated exhale that informed Ava she had won.

"They're approved," he ground out. "You'll receive them in a month's—"

"Today," she interrupted. "I expect to receive the visas today or we will be speaking regularly."

"Very well." Mr. Smith spoke through his teeth. "But the visas will only be good for two weeks."

That would allow for plenty of time to secure a boat to New York. "That's perfect."

"Is that all, Miss Harper?" The question was one of sarcasm rather than genuine helpfulness.

"Why, yes," she replied brightly. "Thank you for your assistance, Mr. Smith."

She hadn't even finished speaking when he stormed out of the room, muttering something about his sympathies for her future husband.

Mike grinned at her. "Well done."

Ava nodded, more pleased with herself than she cared to admit. When she walked out of the break room, Peggy was only a few steps from the doorway and gave her two thumbs-up.

"You did it," she squealed.

Yes, Ava had done it. Finally.

But what about all the other stranded refugees who did not have an American to fight the battle for them? It was no wonder their visas took months to be approved while most were forced to wait. Despite Ava's victory, it was impossible in that moment not to think of Otto. Of how desolate his future must have been with each rejection for a chance at freedom.

No matter what she managed to achieve, she would always be haunted by what she could not do for Otto.

As promised, the American visas for Sarah and Noah were sent upstairs by the afternoon along with the day's mail. Much to Ava's disappointment, there was nothing from Daniel. It had been almost a month since his last letter and though she tried to brush the worry from her mind, it niggled at her thoughts with each passing day.

At least she had the visas.

A week later, on a particularly sunny day, those visas were safely tucked in the purse squeezed beneath Sarah's arm. Ava led her and Noah into the Cais Do Sodré district of Lisbon where throngs of people stood in a chaotic squeeze that scarcely resembled lines.

It was Sarah's third attempt to obtain tickets on one of the ships and time was running out. They approached the American Export Lines office and joined the pressing crowd. Without shade, the June sun swiftly became merciless. It would be especially so to those in line in their winter coats, loathe to leave any of their belongings behind when they had so few.

The first time Sarah had been turned away from the booking office, the employees claimed they did not speak French and stated others whose visas were expiring before her own took precedence. The second time, Sarah said a man with blond hair had interrupted them, whispering something to the clerk. The woman's demeanor changed afterward and they were denied tickets. When Sarah described the man as handsome and tall with a dimple in one cheek, Ava understood with a sinking realization exactly who had interfered.

Lukas.

He was her bad penny, showing up randomly and leaving her wary of where and when he might be next.

It didn't matter if he appeared now or not. This third attempt would be the final one, and Ava would not leave without success.

Worry etched Sarah's features while Noah played distractedly with a small boat Ava had given him in an effort to quell his anxieties on being out on the open water. Only last month, the *Serpa Pinto* full of refugees from Lisbon had been taken by a U-boat, the crew and passengers all held captive. If rumors were to be believed—and many in this war were proving to be true—a baby had drowned amid the chaos.

"Everything will work out," Ava assured Sarah.

They had become close in those last months, and it had been difficult for Ava to witness the gradual transition as Sarah moved through the phases all refugees in Lisbon seemed to traverse. The wide-eyed awe of so much food, of ready, hot showers and clothes and the freedom to walk about.

But soon that awe gave way to anxiety when visas were not promptly approved. The perpetual state of fraying nerves. If freedom could not be had in that drawn-out stage, it was then replaced with despondency and hopelessness.

Like Otto.

Ava's heart flinched.

She waited in the line with Sarah and Noah long enough that their stomachs began to growl. It was around then that children strolled the length of the line, small sacks at their side, selling something called bolas. The Hungarian treats were sugar-crusted pastries with dough that was pillowy and sweet and had a creamy custard center. They were immediately popular once the refugees started selling them upon their arrival in Portugal and soon found their way into local cafés.

With strict rules in place to keep refugees from working in Portugal, there were few ways to bring in money. Suddenly the men who once supported their families had to sit back and allow the women to earn a living through tasks like cooking, laundry, and sewing.

Ava purchased four of the pastries. One for herself and Sarah, and two for Noah, whose stomach proved bottomless. In just the two months they had been in Lisbon, his cheeks had filled out with a healthy glow, and he'd shot up at least an inch.

The line condensed into a squeeze of people as they neared the entrance to the building, as if the sense of urgency for those few select tickets increased. For every person who emerged from the ticket office with a look of relief relaxing their features, it was one less spot open to another refugee who waited.

Sarah pulled her purse in front of her and secured it to her chest with the clamp of her arm. "What if they turn us away?"

"They will not," Ava said with conviction.

Truly, there was no reason they should. Ava could translate from French for them, Sarah and Noah were dressed in their cleanest, newest clothes that Ava had procured for them. And their visas would expire soon.

The latter point of fact ground away at Ava every day. The ship's passage should have been easier to obtain. After all, the JDC had provided the $375 needed for both Sarah and Noah, an exorbitant cost, generously offered by the JDC through Ethan for all the times Ava continued to assist on her days off. Not that she volunteered to curry favors, which Ethan knew, and she could not decline his offer to help Sarah and Noah. Certainly, the steep fares for passage on those ships was far more than Ava could afford to pay on her own.

That small fortune was in Sarah's guarded purse with those precious visas.

At last, they entered the building, and the heat of the sun overhead was replaced by the shade of a ceiling. While stuffy inside, at least they were freed of the merciless glare that left the tops of their heads burning like fire.

A large American flag hung on the wall inside, the small space crowded with people though only six reception areas were available for applicants to fill out yet another lengthy form. Sarah gave Ava the wallet containing the visas and bundle of American dollars for the passage, then pulled Noah into her arms.

He squirmed. "I want to play, *Maman*."

"You stay close," she cautioned as she set him down by her side. "And do not make any trouble."

Ava understood her concern. Clerks could deny passage for

any reason, whether legitimate or personal. All applicants were at their mercy. A wandering child could spell disaster for Sarah and Noah, even with Ava there to help.

When the next reception area was vacated, Ava approached the desk where a woman with wiry gray hair stared tiredly at her. Damp perspiration rings darkened the armpits of her red shirt.

"I'd like two tickets to New York, departing within the next week to ensure their visas don't expire." Ava laid out the visas for the woman to inspect.

"You'll need to fill out the application." The woman shoved two forms toward Ava, who had learned to develop an unnatural patience with such things in the last few months. One would never suspect paper was on ration with how many applications, affidavits, and forms one was required to submit.

Were the process for herself, Ava suspected her tolerance would be short-lived. However, in light of what Sarah and Noah had gone through, a cramped hand was scarcely nothing of note by which to complain.

As she carefully filled out the details, she glanced about, half expecting Lukas to show once more.

Sarah remained still as a soldier beside her with Noah's back obediently locked against his mother's leg. The little toy boat was held aloft in his hand, rolling through an invisible sea, his lips pursed as he mimicked the splash of waves in a barely audible whisper.

The clerk accepted the form and skimmed over Ava's careful print. The woman's mouth thinned. Seconds ticked by, scraping over Ava's nerves.

The clerk slid her gaze to Sarah with little Noah standing at her side, still holding his toy ship. He paused in waving it through the air and smiled at her in the sweet, pure way only a child can.

She huffed out a sigh. "I have exactly two spots available for this Wednesday on the USS *Siboney*."

That was in two days.

"We'll take them," Ava said, placing the money on the counter.

Minutes later, they left the travel office, precious tickets in place of the money secured in a pocket in Sarah's purse. After a celebratory treat of ice cream at one of the cafés near their apartment, Ava walked them to their door.

"Will you come up?" Sarah asked as she often did when they enjoyed lunch together.

"I'd love to." Ava followed her up a flight of stairs to the apartment that had become as familiar to Ava as her own.

"Let me settle this little one down for his nap," Sarah said. "Make yourself comfortable."

"But I'm not tired," Noah whined even as he rubbed an eye with a tight fist.

Though Ava had never been around children, Noah's habits were frequent enough that it was easy to discern what he needed despite his protests. Two months had been enough to know that Noah did indeed require a nap, or his sunny disposition would sour with shrieks of displeasure.

"No need to rush on my account." Ava waved Sarah off and went to the kitchen to prepare a cup of coffee for each of them.

Sarah emerged several minutes later with a smile still touching her lips. "He was asleep before I could even sing 'Fais Dodo.'"

Ava, who was aware just how much he loved the go-to-sleep song, chuckled and poured fresh coffee into two cups. In the time Sarah had gotten to know Ava, she had shared what Paris was like during the Nazi occupation. There had been days so cold that one would wake to frost on their blankets and food was so scarce that signs were posted to remind people not to eat rats. Then there were the times of hiding in crawl spaces meant for storage, not humans, and the joint-locking stillness required to remain unheard during the day. Not to mention the agony of keeping a small child quiet…

The stories were heartbreaking and gave Ava an appreciation for the comforts afforded to them in Lisbon. Sarah also spoke often of Elaine, the woman who created the coded message in *Combat*.

Sarah always smiled when she spoke of Elaine, who had put her role with the Resistance at risk to create the clever message and who sacrificed her own bed for Noah and Sarah. This was eventually followed by details of their escape and tears at the certainty that the shots fired had found their target in Manon, the woman who had opened her home and heart to them.

It was through these stories and ones Ava learned from Otto that she truly began to understand the haunted expressions on the refugees' faces, the brutal existence of being under Nazi occupation. Though she worried after her brother constantly, she was grateful for his role in this war, to save the innocent from being so viciously oppressed and murdered.

While Ava was relieved to finally secure Sarah and Noah passage on a boat to New York, they would be sorely missed. The lunches together and trips to the beach at Estoril and even to the old medieval castle hidden behind Sintra's misty veil wouldn't be the same without them. The adventures started as a way to distract Noah, but had made them all fast friends.

"I'm anxious, Ava." Sarah wrapped her hands around her mug despite the warm day.

"You needn't worry about the U-boats," Ava said, offering her the same reassurance she had repeated since they heard of the *Serpa Pinto*.

"It isn't that." Sarah's lips pursed in thought. "I have not seen Lewis in three years. He has been in America this entire time while we have been in France." She ran a hand through her dark hair. "I do not look the same as the woman who kissed him farewell. I am not the same woman inside that he fell in love with either. It is possible that after three years of being separated... we do not know each other anymore."

"Then it gives you both a chance to fall in love all over again." Ava reached across the small round table and took her friend's hand. "You have been so brave and have sacrificed so much for Noah, and yet, you have still retained your kindness. How could he not love you?"

Sarah's concern relaxed into a smile. She nodded. "All will be well." Her gaze found the stack of letters from her husband, tied with a precious crimson velvet ribbon that had been her mother's. "Now we only need the ship to arrive on time."

As of Tuesday afternoon, the USS *Siboney* had still not pulled into port. James insisted on accompanying Ava to the Cais Do Sodré district that evening to check on the ship's arrival.

He had lost his limp for the most part. The bullet wound healed completely, leaving only the slightest catch in his step.

"You're quiet," he noted gently.

"I'm worried," Ava admitted.

The sun was sliding low into the horizon amid streaks of vivid purples and golds and pinks that set the clouds on fire with the dying light. A cool breeze swept off the Tagus and fanned over their warm skin, bringing with it a briny, familiar scent.

"If they cannot board the vessel, their visas will expire," Ava said. "It took a miracle to get them visas in the first place. I will have to start the process over again."

The very idea put a knot of angry frustration at the back of her throat. Even with her connections and position at the embassy, she was still at the mercy of dilatory ships.

Tolstoy once said the two most powerful warriors were patience and time.

Earlier in Ava's life, she strove to hold such words of wisdom in her heart, to learn from them and grow. Now they battered around inside her head in mockery of her situation.

She would rather she was the one facing the delayed passenger ship than Sarah and Noah, whose hopes were hinged on their escape from Lisbon.

A warm hand slid around Ava's. Startled, she glanced down to find James's fingers enfolding hers.

"All will be well," he said confidently.

"I just keep thinking they might already be on their way to America if I'd gone with them the other two times." Ava quickened her step as the docked ships came into view. The crowd swelled with travelers, their few trunks stuffed to bulging with their belongings as arrivals and departures congealed into a writhing mass.

"If I'd been there to translate," she lamented. "If Lukas hadn't somehow interfered."

James stiffened. "He was there?"

Ava's stomach slid a little lower.

"Why didn't you tell me?"

"I didn't want to worry you. Apparently one day he came in and spoke with one of the clerks before Sarah and Noah were turned away." She shook her head. "I wasn't there."

James took a breath as if intending to say more, but Sarah and Noah emerged from the crowd of travelers. Noah beamed at them and triumphantly lifted the ice cream in hand, but Sarah's face was stricken.

Ava did not need to ask why.

"The USS *Siboney*..." Sarah's eyes filled with tears. "It has still not arrived."

Which meant there would be no way for it to sail out by Friday now. Ava would have to begin the process over again. She forced down the bitterness of her own disappointment. Instead, she focused on reassuring her friend she would find a way to get her and Noah to America.

And Ava would. With patience and time—both of which were now in short supply.

TWENTY-FOUR

The days following Nicole's death were some of the darkest Elaine had known.

Elaine did not remember how she returned to the warehouse after seeing Nicole's tortured body, only the sensation of being wrapped in blankets and how not even the warmth of their layers could allay her uncontrollable shivering. Afterward, once she finally shook free of her fugue state, she returned to work by rote, performing motions instilled by months of repetition rather than thought.

In the past, she had been able to outwork the horrors of war, but not now, not with such terrible images branded in her mind. Whispers followed her—ones of Nicole, of what she might have given up by the persuasion of such physical pain.

"She would never have talked." Elaine rounded on Antoine, her voice sounding foreign to her own ears after having not spoken for nearly a week.

"You can't know that," he said in a solemn tone, ever the realist.

"I knew Nicole," Elaine countered. "She would never have given the Gestapo any information about us."

"Even still," Marcel interjected, his tone paternal, "I think it best we find a different place for you to sleep rather than have you continue to stay here."

While the warehouse was by no means a home, it was familiar. The idea of going to another safe house with a lumpy mattress and empty walls left a hollowness ringing in Elaine's chest. But she could not deny that the suggestion was a sound one no matter how much it filled her with dread.

Elaine was out the door of the narrow, one room apartment as soon as the curfew lifted, eager to leave the cold loneliness of it behind. The stacks of newsprint from the night before were waiting for her at the warehouse, unfinished—something she might have completed had she been able to sleep in the back bedroom as before.

When she arrived, the front door was slightly ajar. She drew upright, her senses on high alert.

Most likely someone else had already arrived before her. They all worked tirelessly through the occupation and even more so now to comply with the massive uptick of requested production. Surely someone arrived tired, their exhaustion making them careless.

But to not close the door entirely...

They were all fatigued, but such a mistake was unthinkable. Reckless. Elaine pushed open the door and ensured it locked properly behind her. The light in the kitchen shone from a crack, dousing the hallway in a wash of dim gold.

She strode toward the room and shoved through the door with a mix of relief and irritation to discover which of them had been so forgetful. "You left the front door open."

No one was within, but the room had been entirely upended. The chairs were flipped, the table absent a leg, the cabinets hanging open in defeat, the drawers pulled from their alcoves. Even her precious collection of breadcrumbs from the last two weeks was scattered on the floor like pigeon feed.

She pulled back instinctively.

Before she could recover from her surprise, strong hands grabbed her shoulders. She spun around, her fist flying.

Antoine ducked just before her hand could connect with his face. She gave him an exasperated look, too frightened to talk. He shrugged apologetically, also remaining quiet, and put his hand up to indicate she ought to wait in the kitchen. That was an order she could not obey. She shook her head, refusing for either one of them to be alone. Whoever had destroyed the kitchen might still be inside.

The thought chilled her. Immediately her mind summoned the image of Nicole as it so often did, of what she must have endured in those terrible hours before her death.

A shiver ran through Elaine, and she shook her head again a final time. Surely two would stand a better chance than one on their own.

The rest of the warehouse looked similar to the disheveled kitchen, all drawers pulled out, cabinets opened. A typewriter was missing, as well as a lockbox that contained several thousand francs.

Neither spoke, but Elaine knew what Antoine thought. She could not even stop the consideration herself, though it was met with a burden of guilt as soon as it hit her mind.

Perhaps Nicole *had* confessed.

And if she had, who could blame her?

As they were examining the damage, Marcel and Jean joined them, also taking inventory. Marcel emerged from the fake identity card room several minutes later, his face ashen with the realization that his original identity card with his real name had been taken along with the missing francs.

Though Marcel's replacement would arrive in two days' time,

the attack surely felt like a noose tightening around his neck. He made a discreet call that afternoon, begging to stop production on the paper, but was once again denied.

Elaine was at his side when he set the receiver in the cradle, his face grim as he muttered to himself words he likely had not expected her to hear. "They have killed us all."

Elaine averted her gaze to keep him from realizing she'd overheard even as her pulse kicked up at his ominous words.

Regardless of the danger, the paper would print on and they would be the crew to see it done.

Two days later, a stocky man known as Albert, with thick round glasses and a shock of white hair, arrived to shadow Marcel to eventually take his place. The man had a serious demeanor and lacked any lines around his eyes that suggested he had never smiled once in his life.

Still, Elaine was grateful someone would be assuming the role for Marcel, to allow him the opportunity to live his life once more. To reunite with his wife whom he had not seen in several months.

With the exception of Albert's presence, the day was like any other with Antoine bent over a piece of art, Jean manning the Linotype machine, Elaine pumping the pedal on the old Minerva, her hands busily pulling the completed print while replacing it with a blank piece of paper on the small shelf.

A voice shouted from somewhere nearby, the word almost inaudible against the rhythmic thumping of the Minerva. "Surrender."

Elaine glanced about, her foot ceasing its task as the machine slowed. It was just enough time to see Antoine and Jean share a frightened look before the warehouse erupted into chaos.

It all happened so quickly, Elaine's confusion had not yet had a chance to bleed into fear. The door to the warehouse flew open, and a puff of red mist sprayed from Antoine. He fell backward to the ground as a pool of blood spread around his head, his pencil plinking against the hard floor at his side, his eyes staring up at nothing.

Elaine staggered back, stunned.

The Gestapo and Milice were there, led by a man whose face loomed in Elaine's nightmares, the iron cross medal gleaming at his breast.

Werner.

He stared at Marcel with his flat, metal-gray eyes. "Marcel," he said in a calm, even voice that set the hairs on Elaine's arms standing on end.

Jean put his hands up in surrender as Elaine backed away toward the rear door. Another burst of submachine gunfire sent Albert folding to the ground where he stood. He toppled to the floor, his white hair seeping to crimson.

Marcel ran from his side then, fast despite his limp as he grabbed Elaine's arm and dragged her back with him.

Energy jolted through Elaine like electricity, charged by the hail of bullets chipping at the wall and floor around them as they sprinted for the door. A sharp pain bit into the back of her calf, but it scarcely slowed her as they escaped to the back terrace.

Together they ran for the rear wall. Before Elaine could consider how to scale it, Marcel was lifting her as if she weighed nothing, pitching her over the ivy-layered ledge. The back of her leg burned, but she didn't stop to examine it as she staggered to her feet. Marcel was immediately beside her, grabbing her arm once more to pull her along.

Up ahead, Gestapo agents filled the alley.

Elaine skidded to a halt. Her gaze darted around the alley for any doorways or windows they might use for escape. And found none.

There was nothing but the lethal force behind them. And yet another in front of them.

They were trapped.

"Halt," the Gestapo shouted, the click of their guns echoing off the high stone walls on either side of them.

Beside her, Marcel withdrew a revolver from his gray trousers. Blood spattered his body and several bullet wounds showed against his jacket, wet with streams of blood.

But when he met her eyes, there was a strange sense of serenity within them. "They will not take me alive." His voice was weak, as if the thread of his life would soon be snipped short.

In that instant, myriad thoughts flitted through Elaine's mind. Joseph and life without him after the war. Nicole and what was done to her. What Marcel had been subjected to and his certainty that he could not withstand another round. Her own fear that she could not endure such torture without giving away secrets that might get others killed. And in that moment, she knew with certainty she could not be taken either.

"I also don't want that," Elaine breathed.

Marcel shook his head. "Do not ask this of me."

She straightened despite the pain in the back of her leg and a pinching sensation at her side. "Do not let them take me alive, Marcel," she hissed vehemently.

"Elaine." His face crumpled, his eyes filling with tears.

The jackboots pounded the pavement, coming closer.

His hand shook as he lifted the gun, its barrel mere inches from Elaine's torso. "May God forgive me," he whispered.

The gun went off and pain exploded in Elaine's chest with an impact that sent her flying to the ground. A weight seemed to settle against her solar plexus, pressing the air from her lungs and making her heart beat in heavy, thick pumps. In the distance came another single shot as the world went dark.

At least in their terrible world of ugliness and hate and war, she had managed to save Sarah and sweet little Noah. For they were her last thought as she slid into a velvety abyss. Without fear. Without pain. Without hope.

TWENTY-FIVE

Ava

Ava consulted Peggy for more of her tactics and found they had grit. Between Ava's persistence, plus a few miracles coming into play, she managed to secure an extension on Sarah's and Noah's visas. The envelope containing the updated visas was waiting for her when she arrived at the embassy early that morning when she should have been out gathering newspapers. It was a worthy sacrifice. While there still wasn't enough time to make the USS *Siboney*, unfortunately, she could secure new tickets.

Once more, Ava appreciated the elevated position her employment at the embassy allowed her in aiding her friends. A benefit to which other refugees did not have access.

Amid the victory of those updated visas, however, she could not help but feel a nip of disappointment after the mail had been distributed. Yet another delivery without a letter from Daniel.

A knot twisted in her stomach. One she'd felt only once before—when her parents failed to return from France.

"What are you doing here?"

Ava looked up from the stack of mail to see Mr. Sims looming over her desk. A shudder threatened to shiver down her spine, but she squelched the reaction. "I had something urgent to tend to."

His gaze fixed on the visas. The telltale flush of color spread over his neck, and he squared his shoulders. "Miss Harper, your job is not—"

The crackle of a radio filled the office.

"Listen to this." Peggy waved them over.

The announcer's voice filled the open office. "A bulletin has just been received from the London office of the Associated Press that quotes the German Trans-Ocean News Agency and asserting that the invasion of Western Europe has begun." The speaker proceeded to declare that German news stations were reporting of an Allied invasion on the shores of the Normandy peninsula.

"It's happening." There was an intuition in Peggy's tone that indicated she had known of this for some time—classified information Ava was not privy to. And now she found out at 8:00 a.m. in Lisbon with every other American who was awake at 3:00 a.m. in Washington.

Ava covered her mouth with her hand as she listened to the tinny voice coming through the speakers drone on, citing no reports had been given from Paris. This came as little surprise with Parisian broadcasts being owned and operated by Germany. They would not give the French hope. Not when they were already struggling to maintain their control after the Resistance uprisings following Corsica's liberation.

But it was not the French Ava was considering as that horrible familiar sensation chewed at her insides. Her thoughts were on Daniel.

Based on what he'd told her of his battalion, they were where the action was. He'd said it often and with great pride in his flashing green eyes.

"Is C Company there?" Ava asked.

Peggy looked away.

Ava rushed up to her desk. "You know and soon everyone else will too. It doesn't matter now if you say it or not." Her eyes caught Peggy's. "Is C Company of the Second Battalion there from the 506th Parachute Infantry Regiment? The 101st Airborne Division. Peggy," she pleaded.

Peggy stared up at her, heavily mascaraed eyes wide and un-blinking.

"Please," Ava whispered. "Is C Company there?"

Peggy nodded, and Ava clung to the desk to keep from slip-ping to the floor.

Daniel was on the beaches of Normandy. Her brother who had given up his youth to raise a kid sister he didn't even know when their parents died. Her brother who sacrificed all his dreams of college so she could be the one to attend. She was the reason he joined the military, why he never went to college with the money he worked so hard to save.

If he didn't come home, it was all her fault.

Tears pricked her eyes.

"This is a good thing, Miss Harper." Mr. Sims approached and clapped her on the shoulder.

"My brother is there," she said through numb lips.

"And you should be damn proud of what he's doing for the war effort." Mr. Sims nodded. "My son is out there too. You don't see me weeping." He strode away, muttering in words he clearly meant to be audible. "This is why women should never be allowed to be part of government operations."

He didn't understand. No one did.

Suddenly in that moment of gripping fear and uncertainty for the person she loved most in the world, she needed someone to talk to. Someone whose heart was strung upon the same fickle thread of life and death, who had stakes in this war that were as sky-high as her own.

Peggy didn't have any siblings, and her parents were both

home in Ohio, safe. Mike was still doing his rounds to collect newspapers that morning.

Even Sarah didn't know much about Daniel. Ava didn't speak of him often, not when she feared her worry would seep into the conversation and Sarah already had enough concerns crowding her overflowing plate.

James.

He knew about Daniel, and how much her brother meant to her. And his own brother was in the war as well.

"I have to go." Ava rushed to her desk and hastily snatched up the visas, shoving them in her purse as she left the room. Of anyone, James would understand.

Ava made her way to the British embassy, her thoughts reeling over Daniel. She clutched her purse as if it were a lifeline, the only thing keeping her centered in a world knocked off its axis.

Would it even be possible to find James?

She'd never been to the embassy before and had no idea if she could request him from the guard positioned out front. But as she hurried toward the high gate, a familiar face made his way toward her.

"Alfie," she cried out.

He regarded her with a wide smile. "Did you hear? We're finally going on the offensive in this war. I can't chat now though, unfortunately. I have a meeting." He looked at his watch and grimaced. "That started five minutes ago."

"Will you tell James to come find me after?"

Alfie frowned as he patted at his pockets. "After what?" He snapped open his leather briefcase and rummaged about, his cheeks flushing beneath the guard's impatient stare.

"After the meeting," Ava replied.

"Oh, he's not in the meeting with me." Alfie flashed an apologetic look to the guard and plucked out a small wallet that he flicked through. "It's only for ASLIB."

Ava froze. "Isn't James in the British Association of Special Libraries and Information Bureau with you?"

Alfie pulled a badge from his wallet and held it up triumphantly. His victory was short-lived, and he blinked rapidly as he turned to Ava, his reddened cheeks going pale. "I beg your pardon?"

"If James isn't with ASLIB, what sector is he with?" Ava asked.

Alfie swallowed audibly. "Forgive me, but I... I'm very late, you see. I... I have to go." With that, he clicked his briefcase shut, showed his badge to the guard, and scurried off.

What he divulged had clearly not been intentional.

Ava shifted her attention to the guard, her pulse thundering in her ears. "Please have James MacKinnon contact Ava Harper." By some miracle, her voice managed to remain calm. "The matter is urgent."

The wait to hear back from James was interminable. Ava paced her small apartment, worry building around her like snowballs rolling down a steep hill. First and foremost was Daniel and his safety surviving the beaches of Normandy. Then there was the need to obtain tickets for safe passage to New York for Sarah and Noah. And also, whatever it was that James did for the British government and why he had lied.

A sharp buzzer interrupted her thoughts and her heart leaped. She went outside to find James standing by the doorway, absent his formal jacket, his button-down shirt rolled halfway up his forearms. His breath panted as though he had run there. He held up his hand before she could speak. "Let us discuss this inside, and I'll answer whatever it is you want to know."

She folded her arms over her chest and locked away her barrage of questions. He would receive them in full force in only a moment's time. She shifted back a step in silent invitation for him to enter the building and followed him up to her apartment.

When he entered, he went first to the windows, which stood open, and looked back at Ava. "May I close these?"

She eyed him warily, not expecting the nature of his confessions to be so clandestine. The work she and Mike did as well as that of their British counterparts was not entirely so covert that it required that measure of tight security.

"You may." She strode toward her bedroom. "I'll close the others."

When she returned, a towel was rolled beneath the door to her apartment as well.

"What is this?" she asked. "Does this have to do with that night at Monserrate Palace?"

"Somewhat." James settled onto the small brown sofa, one elbow casually draped over the arm.

Ava sat on the chair beside the couch, her body stiff. "Who do you work for?"

"The British government," he answered in a quiet tone despite the precautions. "But I am not ASLIB."

She pulled in a breath. "I know."

"Please forgive the lie of omission." He gave her an earnest look, his eyes warm and soft in a way she used to find endearing. "I am part of a highly trained special operatives unit."

She shook her head, not understanding. "A spy?"

He nodded. "I was sent to Lisbon to gather intelligence to assist with the attack in Normandy that happened this morning." He leaned forward, resting his elbows on his knees. "My purpose here was to gather details. This was implemented long before the plan began to take shape, to see if such a thing would even be possible."

His face was open and honest as he spoke, but then if he truly was a spy who had received solid training, he could make anything convincing, couldn't he?

"Why did you mislead me?" she asked, regarding him with scrutiny in an effort to find something amiss, a tell that someone who didn't know him as well as she did might not be able to catch. Something she would certainly note. Or, at least, she hoped.

There was a long pause before he finally answered. "Because you inadvertently became involved."

"What? How?" Her hand clapped over her mouth as a name struck her. "Diogo Silva." The man who lived next door, who had been taken away by the PVDE after she spoke with Lukas.

"No," James said with conviction. "Though I did not impart the entire truth about him as I didn't want you digging around."

Ava opened her lips to argue that she would not have, and James lifted a brow. She stifled her protest. They both knew she would have continued to hunt for details if she'd caught a trace of a scent.

"He did own the kiosk, yes," James continued. "But he also worked for *Avante!*, an underground press here in Portugal that operated outside of their strict censorship. I lightly prodded about when I looked into his disappearance for you and ended up with the PVDE following me for weeks after. When I tell you the conversation you had with the man you know as Lukas did not result in Diogo Silva's fate, know that you can completely put your conscience to rest. You truly had nothing to do with his disappearance."

Ava released a long, slow exhale as the burden of the man's arrest eased from her shoulders. Until that moment, she hadn't realized the weight of guilt clinging to her since that night.

"Lukas, however..." James tilted his head. "Or Dieter Hoffman, as is his real name, is a spy for Germany. Unfortunately, he is very much part of this."

Ava fought to keep from fidgeting in her chair. The room was growing warm and stuffy with the sunlight streaming in through the glass without the cool breeze to offset the heat.

James leaned back on the sofa and rested his hands on his knees. "Do you recall that day you met him?"

Even now humiliation at her own foolishness burned hot at her cheeks. She would never forget being called out for flirting with a Nazi.

"I had an appointment with a fellow agent that morning at a café beside the kiosk," James explained. "Only you showed up before they did. I should have left you alone, but when I heard you speaking to him, I realized you were the American librarian the ASLIB chaps were going on about. I couldn't very well let you walk into a Nazi trap on your first day." He looked away. It was the first time his confidence waned. "I had no idea the path I was placing you on with that seemingly benign little chat."

The shift of his demeanor rankled Ava's inflamed unease. "What path was that?"

"Dieter thought you were my contact."

"Me?"

James's finger subconsciously tapped lightly on his knee. "I did not discourage him." His finger stopped. "In fact, I encouraged his confusion."

Ava's thoughts jumbled together over this news, at learning James had kept her in the sights of an enemy even after realizing a mistake had been made. "Was I in danger?" she asked slowly as all the puzzle pieces fit into a perfect, ugly truth in her head.

James swallowed. "Yes."

Disbelief and anger flashed like fire through her. "Why didn't you tell Mike or Mr. Sims at the embassy? Why didn't you tell me?"

"You're our allies. I couldn't allow the relationship between the Americans and the British to be fractured because I'd placed one of your own in danger." He gave a sigh that seemed to well up from his soul. "But nor could I allow the actual contact to be found out. While the Germans were watching your every move, they stopped looking for the real person feeding me information. I couldn't risk losing them."

"You were willing to sacrifice me?" The memory of that

kiss in the alleyway in Alfama shoved forefront in her thoughts. She wished she could take back every second she'd thought of that intimate moment, as well as the kiss they'd shared on New Year's Eve. What she had interpreted as romantic interest had simply been espionage at play.

The mortification was more than she could bear, her naivete yielding nothing more than foolish humiliation. Tears stung her eyes despite her resolve to keep them bottled up.

"Your brother is in this war, Ava," James said gently. "You know how important the offensive attack is. If my real contact had been discovered, the battle at Normandy may not have happened."

She picked at a loose thread on the arm of her chair; the pale sage color was slightly darker than the fabric.

Would she have allowed herself to be put in danger for the sake of the war? Would she have done it all to keep Daniel and the rest of the Allied men safe from the Axis if she'd known of their scheme?

Yes. Without a doubt.

"You could have told me." She lifted her gaze to James, unable to stop the ache in her chest at the depth of his deception.

"I could not compromise this mission." His expression remained cool as he spoke, a man set on his task. "No matter the cost."

"Then why tell me now?" she asked.

"The mission is complete," James explained. "There is nothing further to be compromised."

Yes, of course. There was no additional risk.

"Thank you for letting me know." She gave a stiff smile, wanting nothing more than for him to leave.

Those kisses they'd shared had been real to her. They had meant something. The time she spent with James had brought vibrance and color to the corner of her world that had been black-and-white for far too long.

But for him, she now realized, those interactions were the façade of a cover, a means to the end of a mission, part of his job.

Nausea churned in her belly.

"You don't need to worry about Dieter if that is your concern," he said gently. "I tried to enlist the PVDE's help to remove him as a threat when I learned how intently he was watching you, but it only turned their attention onto me for several months. The Allied launch has now marked a significant turn in the war and while Portugal claims to want neutrality, they are not so stubborn as to overlook when a side is winning. The PVDE has suddenly become most accommodating." He folded his hands in front of him. "That said, Dieter will no longer be bothering you."

Ava looked at the thread on her chair once more and pulled at it with the pinch of her forefinger and thumb. She didn't want to know if Lukas—Dieter or whoever—was dead or not. Only that he could no longer interfere with Sarah and Noah and their journey to America.

"There's another reason I'm telling you." James sat forward. "Ava, I care for—"

"Don't." The word erupted from her mouth before she could stop it, but she was glad for her quick response. She didn't want his platitudes.

"It's why I fought to rescue Sarah and Noah," James said. "My boss insisted if it was to be done, I had to go myself since the plans for today were already in motion. Ava, I did that for you."

She forced herself to look at him. "You did that for *you*—to alleviate your own guilt by giving me something I wanted in return for your deceptive betrayal."

He returned her stare and a muscle worked in his jaw. "That is only partially true."

"It's enough." The energy drained from her, sapped from the ache threatening to consume her. She didn't want to have this conversation, be subjected to his explanations anymore. Too much had already been said. "Please leave."

He hesitated. "Ava…"

She shook her head. Finally, he rose and slowly walked away from her. He paused before turning down the narrow hall leading to her front door. "Your brother will be fine, Ava," he said gently. "From everything you've told me about him, I have a strong idea of the type of soldier he is. And that man always comes home. He'll be safe."

Ava lowered her head into her hands, refusing to let her tears fall.

James's footsteps echoed down the hall and the door clicked closed behind him.

Silence bathed her, but it did not bring the relief she sought. There was an emptiness left in James's wake, raw and cavernous.

In the end, he had soothed the very concerns she sought him out for. He knew her so very, very well and apparently, she did not know him at all.

However, now was not the time for tears or embracing her hurt. Not when Sarah and Noah still needed new tickets to New York. The American Export Lines office would be swarming with refugees desperate to flee Lisbon on the off chance the Allies botched the attack and the war swung back into Nazi favor.

For Ava's part, she could not even allow herself to consider the battle in Normandy failing, not when she knew what that would mean for Daniel. And despite James's comforting words, she could not clear her heart of worry until she knew with certainty that her brother was safe.

God help them all through the hell of this war.

TWENTY-SIX

Elaine

"You are very lucky, *mademoiselle*." The doctor lifted his heavy brows, indicating the seriousness of Elaine's situation. He gestured to his open book where a black-and-white sketch revealed the innards of the human torso and tapped the point of his pen against the liver, leaving a small dot of black ink.

"This is where you were struck," he went on. "Thankfully, too low to do any real damage. The bullet missed your heart and lungs, barely skimming over your liver before going straight through. Truly a miracle."

Elaine stared at the drawing, numb.

The doctor's eyes were soft brown and kind. "You are very lucky," he said again.

It might have been funny if the laugh did not stick in her throat with a barely suppressed sob.

Yes, how lucky she was to be spared an immediate death so she could be slowly dismembered by the Gestapo, not only in body but also in soul, her secrets peeled away.

Already they had visited her in the last week, refusing to

allow her to speak to a doctor again until she gave the names and addresses of Resistance members. She said nothing as she attempted to will her bandaged injuries into mortal wounds. The nurses had not tolerated such tactics and badgered the Milice until finally the doctor was allowed to come to her bedside, to explain her injuries.

"The other bullets struck you in the calf and at the hip, just missing your bone." He shrugged with a smile. "Lucky, *non*?"

She swallowed the invective rising in her throat. It burned on its path down, like sour bile. Her focus shifted to the ache of her wounds, testing her weakness against its pain, weighing it to see how much more she might be able to withstand at the hand of her enemy.

Days before the warehouse was attacked, a woman arrested by the Gestapo had thrown herself from the top floor of the building they took her to for interrogation. She knew she would not be able to handle their torture without giving up her comrades, and so she bravely chose death.

Elaine's gaze wandered to the window where a cheerful rose garden mocked her. She had been allowed out the previous day for fresh air and sunshine. The first floor.

How lucky, came the bitter thought.

"There is more," the doctor continued.

Mutely, she turned to face him as he pulled a large brown bundle of cloth from his leather bag and set it on her bed. She frowned and looked up to him once more.

"You have friends who would see you recuperate in a more ideal location." He set his age-spotted hand over the cloth. "I admit, I am a foolish old man." He shrugged his thin shoulders again, his eyes twinkling. "I sometimes forget to lock the door. That is how it is when one gets old."

Elaine's lips parted, but he made a motion for her to hide the bundle. She swept it beneath her hospital sheets, the bulk pressed against her naked leg as she discreetly glanced about to ensure no one had seen. Nurses rushed by in the hall, focused on their tasks.

"As I said, *mademoiselle*..." The doctor snapped his leather case closed and lifted it by the handle. "You are a very lucky woman."

In this particular case, she was inclined to agree.

Once he left, she slid from her bed to the small bathroom and untied the cloth. Within, she found a pair of glasses, some sandals with soles made from the cutouts of rubber from old tires, a turban, a tube of red lipstick and the brown dress that held it all together, tied like a hobo's sack.

As she wound the turban around her blond hair and smeared the waxy red lipstick over her mouth, she could not help but recall the day she and Nicole had escaped the Nazi officer in the traboule. Suddenly the ache in her heart superseded the bullet wound only a couple centimeters below.

She would continue on with the fight with the Resistance. For Joseph. For Nicole. For Antoine and Manon and Marcel. For all those who sacrificed everything for the chance of freedom.

The hospital gown was a crumpled pile on the floor. She left it where it lay and strode from the room, looking more like a visitor than a patient. She kept her gait slow to avoid calling attention to her limp and strode from the hall leading to the rose garden outside. No one stopped her as she pushed on the door and walked into the heat of the summer sunshine.

Etienne was at her side immediately. He took her arm and guided her down a path to where a white van idled with its gasogene tank jutting awkwardly from its rear, a necessity to turn wood into fuel when only Nazis had access to petrol. Elaine immediately recognized it as the one sometimes used by Marcel to transport large deliveries for their false geological company.

"Marcel?" She quickened her pace, her pulse racing with the hope of seeing him once more. If she had been fortunate with her injury, perhaps the gun had delivered a similar blow to him as well.

But as Etienne caught up to her, he gently shook his head.

"Jean?" she asked, her voice pitching with a note of desperation.

His gaze lowered as he opened the van to reveal a young man with blond hair, someone Elaine had never seen before. Etienne helped her climb into the seat before jumping in beside her and slamming the door closed.

Marcel was dead. Sixteen bullet wounds had seen to that, the last of which being inflicted by his own hand. Finally, after three rounds of arrest, he had made sure they would never capture him again.

Jean was arrested and interrogated. But despite the torture, he did not speak against his fellow comrades. He died by firing squad, refusing the blindfold, opting instead to face the men who would end his life. Where once he had doubted his strength to remain silent, he had now proven himself more than capable, dying a hero.

The automatic printing press that Marcel had painstakingly transported across France and spent months assembling was now destroyed, but the old Minerva had been salvaged. It was on that archaic press that Elaine would eventually return to her work several weeks later in a new location. The warehouse was destroyed by a vengeful Werner, and the operation was forced to move to a narrow, insulated basement without windows and only one door.

As soon as she was able, she went to Nicole's apartment and found the address of the camp where her friend's brother and father were located, resuming the task of sending supplies. It was the least Elaine could do for Nicole and wished there could have been more.

Two months later, the Allied forces surrounded Lyon. Rather than consider a tactful strategy for exit, Klaus Barbie ordered the execution of hundreds of Montluc's inmates. Now backed with the power of the oncoming army, the Resistance rose up against their oppressors and managed to retake the prison before more French blood could be spilled. By August 25th, the tricolor flag flew over Montluc Prison once more. It was a victory Elaine had almost lost hope of ever witnessing.

There were other accounts of the Germans fleeing in those next ten days, abandoning their posts and scattering like vermin when a light was flipped on. They inflicted their extreme cruelty to the very end, even firing upon women and children scavenging after a Nazi infirmary was abandoned on Tête d'Or and left precious commodities like blankets, sugar, and soap scattered in the street. Forty-six were slain that terrible day with over one hundred left wounded.

It was that particular story Elaine was writing the first day of September when Etienne entered through the solitary door and slowly approached, his stare bright. She pushed up to her feet as he stopped before her desk, his hands folded together in front of him.

"Etienne." A million thoughts crowded her mind. But one more than all the rest. "Is it Joseph?"

It was in that knee-jerk reaction, that ready question on her lips and in her heart when she realized she had never truly abandoned the hope he might have somehow survived this terrible war.

Etienne shook his head slowly.

Elaine exhaled a pained breath, hating herself for having hoped for the impossible. After all she had lived through, she was far too much of a realist to entertain such whimsy.

"I went to see Werner," he said.

Her eyes widened. "You should never have put yourself at risk—"

"Nicole never talked." He shook his head. "It was the new girl who told, the one who took her place. It was she who shared the location of the press."

Agony and rage blossomed anew in Elaine's breast. Nicole, so brave and lovely, loyal to the bitter, terrible end.

"For Nicole." Etienne extended his fist over the desk. "And for Joseph." The item he released clattered with a metallic clunk that rattled into place. When he drew his hand away, a silver iron cross lay on the table, smeared with fresh blood.

She sucked in a breath and looked up at him to find his eyes burning into hers.

"The bastard was rushing to clean out his office, preparing to flee." Etienne spoke through gritted teeth, his expression fierce. "I could not allow him to leave—not when he hadn't paid for what he had done."

She went to him and opened her arms. They held one another as their tears fell for the loved ones they could never bring back. For the pain of so much loss.

They had finally won, but the cost had been dear indeed.

TWENTY-SEVEN

Sunlight sparkled over the Tagus with a brilliance that left Ava shielding her face with the flat of her hand. The noxious odor of smoke from the massive ship obliterated any freshness the water might have cast off. All around her, people rushed this way and that, their bulging suitcases clutched at their sides, children herded close to their parents.

Ava scanned the sea of people, seeking out Sarah and Noah.

They had been lucky to obtain tickets on the SS *Drottningholm*. Ava had been correct about the lines at the office being even longer after the Allied attack.

Fortunately, the invasion appeared to have been successful with securing Allied soldiers into the occupied territory and putting Nazis on the run. But the victory had come at a steep cost with thousands dead. Thousands she could not allow herself to think of.

"Miss Ava." A squeal of excitement pulled her attention to the right as Noah barreled toward her with Sarah following closely behind.

Ava caught him and swung him up into a big hug, cherishing the moment, for it would be the last—at least in Lisbon. He grinned at her and pointed to the towering SS *Drottningholm*. "Is that ours?"

"It is," Ava confirmed. "Are you ready?"

"Yes," he shouted, practicing the American word. He had quickly learned several phrases and was eager to learn more.

Ava laughed and set him down. He immediately dug out his toy ship and held it up, comparing it to the original. "Ship," he said slowly in English, and she nodded in approval.

"I cannot thank you enough for all you have done." Sarah swept forward to embrace her.

Ava waved off her gratitude, especially when the effort had been that of so many people, namely Elaine Rousseau. And James.

An ache filled Ava's chest, and she shoved the thought of him aside.

"It was a combined effort," Ava replied. "It is so good to know you will be reunited with Lewis soon."

"You will visit when you return to America?" Sarah gazed imploringly at her.

"I absolutely will."

The horn on the ship blared, and the crowd collectively pushed toward the open gangplanks.

"It appears the time of our departure has come." Sarah took a large breath and let it whoosh out.

"He is still going to love you," Ava said reassuringly and hugged her friend.

"Merci." Sarah beamed at her and took Noah's hand. The little boy turned and waved until the crowd swallowed them up. Though Ava knew him well enough by then to realize he was likely still waving long after.

Ava didn't leave until the large vessel glided from the dock amid a puff of thick, dark smoke. People stood at the railings above, calling out their farewells. Though Ava couldn't discern any one person there from the other, she still waved and shouted her well wishes.

And then, as soon as they had come into her life, Sarah and Noah were gone. Finally on their way to America. To safety. To be reunited as a family.

A week letter, a V Mail appeared on Ava's desk. She opened it with trembling fingers and sobbed an exhale of relief as she read the five simple words.

I'm safe. I love you.
–D

Short and sweeter than any mail she'd ever received. Daniel was safe.

After so many tense years of uncertainty and loss in her life, finally things seemed to be going right.

The foreign newspapers dwindled over the next four months as the Allied advantage became undeniable and Germany was squeezed in on all sides. It was then the notification came from Washington that the IDC's efforts of information gathering in Lisbon were no longer needed. Mike was to be transferred to Switzerland. Ava had been offered the same but declined.

While she loved gathering information and meeting people she would always remember, she wanted to settle down in DC, preparing for Daniel's inevitable return when the war ended. Something she hoped would happen sooner than later.

They had already spent far too long apart. She missed his brotherly advice that teetered on the edge of a lecture, meeting up for game night on Fridays and laughing until her face hurt, like they used to do before the war. Those days that had once been so common now felt a lifetime ago.

And, if truth be told, she was still licking her wounds over James.

She hadn't seen him since the day of his confession in her apartment. At first, she had been glad for his absence, but as the days churned into weeks she regretted the sharpness of her words.

"You have mail." Peggy slid a V Mail envelope onto Ava's desk.

Ava beamed and picked it up.

"Did you hear about Sims's boy?" Peggy asked in a hushed whisper.

Ava's own excitement dimmed at the solemn tone, and she shook her head.

The corner of Peggy's mouth turned downward. "He's gone."

Ava sucked in a shocked breath.

"So maybe keep your letter under wraps." Peggy lifted a shoulder. "Just to be kind."

"Of course." Ava slid the letter with the unmistakable *V* in red off her desk and glanced toward the closed office door where Mr. Sims's voice boomed behind it.

He was staying later at the office and scarcely took a lunch the last week. She had assumed his redoubled efforts were to wrap up loose ends before their departure. Now, she saw the assiduous efforts for the deflection they were.

She read her letter quietly, unable to help her gratitude that Daniel had remained safe. But it was Mr. Sims she thought of as she sifted through the paperwork on her desk to determine what was needed and what should be destroyed.

The last convivial lunch at the office was with Mike and the ASLIB boys to bid a final farewell. Any hopes James would be in attendance were immediately dashed at the four-person table without another chair waiting for an unassumingly debonair Englishman with the slightest hint of a limp.

She suppressed her disappointment and together with Theo and Alfie, she and Mike feasted on an assortment of Lisbon's best foods: greasy, spiced sausage and grilled fish and briny sardines on hard bits of bread. But before a round of Super Bock could be ordered, Ava took up her purse and excused herself to return to the office.

"You're going back there?" Mike asked, incredulous. "I'm done with that place."

Ava shook her head with a laugh. "I have one last drawer to clean out."

"Suit yourself." He held open an arm toward her. "Bring it here, kid."

She stepped into the hug. "You do know I'm around the same age as you."

"Yeah." He grinned. "I know."

"Viel Glück," she said, wishing him luck in Swiss. She had spent a week studying it as she vacillated over her decision before finally turning the offer down.

Mike's brow crinkled. "Huh?"

"It's Swiss," she laughed.

"Yeah, I knew that." He offered a reassuring nod and clapped her on the shoulder. "Let me know if you ever want to come join me. It'd be great to work with you again."

"I'll keep that in mind." She embraced Alfie and Theo before taking her departure, refusing to think of James as she did so.

Back at the office, she didn't last long before the heavy meal in her stomach left her eyelids feeling leaden. She pushed up from her seat and made her way to the back room where a pot of restorative coffee was always at the ready.

Her heels clicked over the glossy floor as she turned the corner and stopped short. Mr. Sims stood near the coffeepot, his large hand braced on the vanilla speckled Formica countertop, his head bowed.

This was clearly a moment of a man needing his privacy and yet Ava could not bring herself to leave.

"Mr. Sims," she said softly.

He straightened and cleared his throat, opening his mouth

to speak before closing it again only to shake his head. His gaze slid away. And then his chin trembled.

Ava said nothing but strode over to him and opened her arms. He sagged against her, his breath warm where he sniffled against her shoulder and the bulk of his large body trembled with the power of his grief. He stayed there for a long moment, clinging to her the way Noah did when he would wake from a nap after a nightmare.

There was something so humbling about witnessing such a proud man forced to bend under the weight of loss. She knew the burden well and wouldn't wish it upon anyone.

"I'm so sorry," she said gently.

"He always wanted to make me proud," Mr. Sims said raggedly.

"You've never been anything less," Ava offered in reassurance. "He knew that."

The older man straightened, his eyes bloodshot and his nose red. He pulled a handkerchief from his pocket and gave her a grateful nod. "Don't you have a desk to finish cleaning out, Harper?" His question lacked its usual sharpness. "You know you won't get paid extra."

"Yes, sir, I do." She turned, leaving him to recover in peace.

It didn't take long to sift through one final stack of papers. When she was done, she handed the box to be destroyed to Peggy.

"I'll be joining you in DC sooner than later," the secretary said. "I expect you to show me around all the good dance halls and jazz clubs."

Ava chuckled. "I'm not sure how adept I'll be at that, but I can give you a personal tour of the Library of Congress."

"I'll take it." Peggy beamed and gave her one final hug. "Have a safe flight."

Once upon a time, Ava would have shuddered at the mention of flying. Though she still didn't relish the idea, it didn't terrify her anymore. In the last year and a half, she had been trailed by the PVDE, stalked by a Nazi, and duped by a spy. Daniel had jumped out of planes on a beach in Normandy and fought for his life. Even more powerful was what she had witnessed of others in her time in Portugal.

She had seen people subjected to endless waits for visas they were never granted, suffer from delayed ships that started the abysmal process over again, and even people who were cheated out of their life savings in a desperate bid to book passage from Lisbon. Only the extremely wealthy could afford seats on the plane she would be boarding the next morning. The letters she had salvaged spoke of the Nazis' unimaginable brutality, as had the stories she'd heard. Yet so many had endured, resilient and brave as they left their lives behind to save their families. And, as she so often did, she thought of Otto whose barred entry from her homeland had been so great, he could not bring himself to continue on even one more day.

Plato said courage was knowing what not to fear. In looking back on her time in Lisbon, Ava realized now that wisdom was also knowing what to fear. In the face of what so many others had endured, flying was such a pale, petty thing.

The morning of her flight came upon her quickly. She was ready with her small apartment neatly packed into two suitcases and the copy of *Little Women* carefully tucked among her folded dresses.

She pushed out the door of her building and nearly ran headlong into a man. With a gasp she drew herself upright, having come face-to-face with James for the first time since his confession.

"Ava." His blue-green eyes locked on hers, and her heart squeezed with more feeling than she wished.

His lean frame had filled out in the months since they'd seen one another. Beneath a gray fedora, his hair was freshly trimmed, and his skin glowed with good health. He put his hand out to stop her from leaving. "Please let me speak."

Once before she'd told him to go away and had spent the time since regretting the decision. She would not make the same mistake again.

"Have you been waiting out here for me?" she asked in surprise.

He gave a sheepish smile. "I couldn't miss a final opportunity to talk."

No matter had fully she thought she quashed all sense of hope, it now flared to life, foolish and eager, revived by his mere presence. For all she knew, he was there to apologize one last time.

She tensed, bracing herself for what he intended to say.

"I have something for you." He reached into his pocket, the contents of which gave a slight rattle.

She held out her hand and was surprised to find a set of aged, yellowing dice fall into her palm, their dyed black grooves chipped in several places. They were still warm from the heat of his body.

"For luck," he said. "My father was a fighter pilot in the Great War and gave them to me to keep me safe. I know you're flying out today and I thought…"

"You thought it would give me confidence on the plane," she said with a smile at the generosity of his gift.

He nodded.

"I'm not as afraid of flying as I once was." She extended her hand to give the dice back.

"All the same, I'd like to know you're safe." He did not reach for the dice. He wasn't even looking at her hand, but at her, studying her face as if he expected to never see her again. "The thing of it is, Ava, I care greatly for you. I cared for you before, but in the absence of your company, I cannot seem to put you from my thoughts. And I do not even begrudge the space you occupy in my mind. Rather, I find it comforting in a familiar, pleasant manner. I…" He exhaled a laugh. "I'm making a bloody fool of myself."

All the willpower in the world would not quell the heat blossoming in Ava's chest. "I thought you were doing very well."

He gave a lopsided grin and put his hands in his pockets. "I'll be returning to London soon, with a proper address. Perhaps we might write, or even see one another. Alfie said the London Museum has heaps of material in French and German to sift through. Journals and letters, like the ones you were collecting. Maybe someday you might come for a week or so. Or I might—"

Ava stepped toward him, cupped his face in her hands, and kissed him. His lips were warm, his chin smooth against hers. He drew his arms around her, holding her to him as his pleasant, clean soap scent enveloped her.

A car pulled up alongside them and they drew apart abruptly, each with a shared, private grin. Ava touched her mouth where her lips still tingled from the brush of his.

Her ride to the airport was ready to whisk her away. The driver busied himself in the car a moment, clearly giving them time.

"I'd love to write to you," she said.

James withdrew a scrap of paper with an address in London printed on it in familiar messy, bold letters, then remained with her in the short time it took for her driver to fetch her things. When she rode away, James gave her one last lopsided smile that sealed itself in her mind and left not a modicum of space to even worry about the plane ride.

Life in DC was not the welcome embrace she had assumed it would be. After the easy, languid existence in Lisbon, the American capital seemed to sweep by too quickly and left Ava feeling as though she were standing still amid a torrent of activity.

Her position at the Rare Book Room had been filled, of course. Such an important job could not remain open for long. Instead, she was placed among the polyglots who categorized the countless boxes of microfilm sent by herself and the other members of the IDC. It was quite often she came across a box labeled carefully in her own looping writing and even the jagged script of Mike's quick hand.

The ration was still in place in America and took some adjusting to, especially as she'd grown to taking her coffee sweet. More than anything, though, was the great wanderlust that had been awoken in her and now would not be quieted, leaving her humming with restless energy. This was further fueled by the letters from James as he returned to London and shared pieces of his life with her.

It was through their correspondence that she learned he had spoken the truth of himself when he was with her, that his stories and his family were not simply fictional details of a spy on the job. His brother had also thankfully survived the war and they celebrated with grateful, joyous letters to one another that both their siblings had emerged from such dangers unscathed.

Eventually, 1944 gave way to 1945 when the horror of the concentration camps was discovered in April. In those shocking images of skeletal men, women and even children plastered on the front of every newspaper, she saw the fear the Lisbon refugees realized. However bad anyone thought the situation was for the Jews, the truth was far, far worse.

It had been a devastating blow to know the many hopes she heard whispered among the refugees for their families would be crushed by such a heavy reality. And it made her burn with rage for the many who had brushed aside the truth for so long, casting it benignly into the category of simple war rumors.

Hitler put a cyanide capsule in his mouth and a gun to his temple not long after. Many saw his suicide as a coward's way out. For Ava, there was some justice in knowing that Hitler had died with the same scrabbling fear as so many of his victims.

When at last the war ended on September 2, 1945, with the formal surrender of Japan, DC kicked off its war-rationed shoes and celebrated with great jubilance. Ava had not joined in the ebullient throngs crowding the streets. There was no win without loss, and the tolls exacted through those bitter years of war had been enumerable.

Instead, she took the day to honor the memories of those she had personally known as well as those she was acquainted with through what she read. Those letters and journals, written in a frantic script, stained after being shoved from view in clandestine hiding places, were all that remained of so many.

Several months later, Ava found herself on the platform at Union Station with a crowd of others, all dressed in their finest clothes. Women scraped the hollowed-out tubes for the vestiges of their lipstick, pressed their least worn dresses, and tucked ribbons and flowers in freshly curled hair.

Their men were coming home.

The doors to the train swept open and the crowd surged forward, Ava with it, drawing the lot of them toward the uniformed men with freshly shaved, eager faces. And that's when she saw Daniel for the first time in five years.

His stare found hers and gave her that familiar easy grin he'd always had.

Ava's eyes went hot with tears, but she didn't waste time wiping them away as she ran forward and threw her arms around him. He smelled foreign, like wool and burned starch with a slight undertone of mechanical oil.

"My kid sister." He drew back and took her in with such pride, it made her heart ache.

The five years of war had aged him, carving lines at the corners of his eyes and across his brow. But his gaze still held that jovial sparkle she'd always known, and his smile didn't bear the wobble of some returned men.

He was home, safe and sound.

The stretch of time between them dissolved as it always did

with close siblings, fading amid ready conversation and jaunts down memory lane. The evening found them at the dining room table of the apartment Ava had secured, the jumbled letters of the Criss Cross Words board game laid out before them.

Ava shuffled the letters in front of her, navigating the Q, U, and X around a C until the answer came to her. In a flash, she transferred the tiles onto the board.

"'Quixotic,'" Daniel read. "Are you serious? Is that a word?"

She put her hands on her hips where she sat. "Of course it is." It took her a moment to dredge up its meaning from her memory. "It's something unrealistic or impractical."

"You always were good at this game, sis." Daniel leaned back in his chair and took a pull from his beer bottle. "That's why you needed to go to college."

Ava's triumphant play was short-lived at the mention of college. He had always shrugged off not achieving his dream of getting a degree and having sent her to pursue hers instead.

"If I'd known you weren't going to college because I was, I never would have gone." She stared at him, still smarting from the decision he made.

He chuckled. "And that's why I didn't tell you."

"You can go back now that the war is over."

Silence fell between them.

"A lot of men will be going to school again," Ava said.

"It's not that." Daniel set his beer down. "I don't want to get out of the Army. I'm a Screaming Eagle through and through, sis."

Ava stared at the board, no longer seeing the letters, but instead the blank months that dragged by as she waited for him to return to DC. "But that means you'll be relocated again."

"I know," he said gently.

She looked up, hating the lump forming in her throat.

"I didn't know how to tell you, but I'm not a studious kind of guy, not like you or Dad." Daniel lifted a single shoulder in a half-hearted shrug. "I only wanted college because I thought it was what he would want for me. Until I saw you and how much you enjoyed all that studying." He put his large hands on the table. Pale nicks and scars flecked his calloused fingers. "The Army suits me, Ava." He leaned over the table, his gaze concerned as he studied her. "You're not too upset, are you?"

Ava chewed her lip and forced herself to examine the uncomfortable emotion knotting her stomach. It wasn't Daniel she was upset with, it was herself.

She shook her head slowly. "I think I'm relieved, actually."

Daniel's brows shot up. "I'll try not to take offense to that one." The flash of his familiar grin told her he really wasn't hurt by her statement. In fact, he looked relieved too.

"I have been trying to find my normalcy here," Ava said aloud as she puzzled out the details herself. "But it's not fitting because I'm not the same person I was before."

"Sounds pretty quixotic." He winked at her.

She laughed. "Yeah, it is."

"So, where are you going to go?"

Ava didn't even have to think. "To England, to see about a position at the London Library."

"I've always wanted to see London." Daniel nodded in approval. "I'll have to plan a visit."

Ava beamed at him. "I'd love that."

Daniel studied the letters in front of him and turned them toward her. "All right, Ava, what can you do with this jumble of madness?"

She studied the small blocks, then referred to the board for other words she could play off. Using the first *I* of *QUIXOTIC* and an *E* from *SEEN*, she spelled out the word *FULFILLED*.

An appropriate and perfect word to describe what they had both realized and where they were both going to be.

EPILOGUE

Elaine

The day after Etienne killed Werner, the Nazis fled. Explosions filled all of Lyon as they blew up the bridges behind them to keep the Allies from giving chase. The cowards.

General de Gaulle himself arrived two weeks later and honored Lyon by declaring it the capital of the Resistance. The day was one of great victory that seeded itself in Elaine's soul, for in that veneration was the appreciation for brutal sacrifices. For those who had been strong enough to endure torture. For those who had paid with their lives. For those whose hearts had been gouged from people they'd lost.

At last, she had heard from her parents. As she had hoped, they fared better than most through the occupation. Their time in the small rural town whose doldrum existence she had resented in her youth had been their salvation, providing them with enough produce to make it through the leaner years.

Prisoners did not return from the camps until the beginning of 1945, and when they did, France was horrified at the zombie-like people who arrived, bone-thin with large haunted eyes set in skulls with only taut skin stretched over them. The ration was still enforced, though not to the strict standards of when Lyon was under German occupation. But when the people from the camps returned, there was not a soul in France who did not offer their own share to help feed them.

Denise returned a month into the prisoners' liberation, skeletal like all the others, and missing several teeth, but with that familiar fire still bright in her gaze.

It was with their arrival that Elaine found new purpose. So vast was the number of people seeking family members, that she printed lists of survivors to reunite them with who had been lost. She relocated the heavy printing press once more, this time to a room with a wide window facing the street to let in sunshine and make her efforts known. It was from there the Minerva put forth the power of words, no longer enlisting an army to fight hate but reuniting friends and family and restoring love.

It was through those lists that she found Nicole's father, Olivier, who towered well over six feet and bore the same heart-shaped mole on his emaciated arm. He listened to the tales of Nicole's bravery with tears in his eyes and confirmed that it was through her packages that he and his son had managed to survive. Nicole's sister and brother-in-law both made it through their ordeal in Germany as well, and every night the four of them said a prayer for the empty seat at the table that lay between them.

Josette never fully recovered from her precarious state, her nature too delicate to endure the prolonged stress. Elaine had visited once under the disapproving glare of Josette's mother, who blamed Elaine and the rest of the Resistance for what happened to Josette. Though Elaine wanted to return, her mother barred any future visits.

Lucie did not come back to France. Nor did her husband, both having perished in a camp in Poland called Auschwitz. Every image of the terrible place made Elaine recall her friend who had always been so beautifully optimistic and ache for what she must have endured.

★ ★ ★

Elaine returned to her home eventually at Rue du Plat, pausing outside with poignancy at what lay on the other side. Not the layers of dust, but the memories of a life that seemed to have belonged to someone else.

When at last she entered, she found an envelope just inside the entryway, a scrape of dust in its wake from where it had been shoved beneath the door. She kept it pinched between her fingers as she slowly walked through those once-familiar rooms. To the sunny kitchen where she used to pore over issues of *Combat*, back before she'd ever known what a printing press looked like, let alone how to operate one. To the armchair in the living room where Joseph would bend over his research, his warm brown gaze distant with calculations. To the bedchamber where they had slept in one another's arms until she allowed his need to keep her safe to drive a wedge between them.

Tears burned in her eyes.

What she wouldn't give to have those days back, to set aside her anger and still allow herself to revel in their love. She entered the bathroom last where the spice of his cologne still lingered two years later.

It was then that her knees gave out and she sank to the floor in a fit of sobs for the man she loved. The man who was gone forever.

When at last her tears had dried, she remembered the letter still in her hand. She drew back the top to reveal a note inside along with an identity card for Hélène Bélanger.

A name as once familiar as the apartment in which she now lay crumpled on the floor.

With trembling hands, she unfolded the note.

I waited for several hours, but I fear you do not reside here any longer. I hope you receive this as I have no other way to locate you. I want to thank you for the time you allowed me to use your name, though truly

this note is so ineffectual to express the depth of my gratitude. You saved
my life with your sacrifice. It only seemed right to return this to you.

Elaine looked down at the identity card once more.

It had never occurred to her that she could take her name back. In the last two years, Hélène had become something of the past. A woman who selfishly made demands of what she wanted in her life, who thought she could bend circumstances to her will, who allowed her temper to squander the last precious days of her time with Joseph.

But Bélanger…yes, she would take that name once more, to have and to cherish the eternal gift bestowed upon her by the man she would always love.

A week later, when she arrived at her printing press to begin a fresh list of survivors that needed to be printed and shared, she found Etienne waiting for her with a painfully thin man at his side.

The stranger's shoulders were hunched forward, his hands clasped together in a diminutive stance, as if trying to make himself as small as possible. But he kept his head lifted, his large dark eyes watching her with interest.

It was not the first time Etienne had brought one of the camp survivors to her. He too spent most of his days tracking down family for those who had been unjustly imprisoned. Perhaps it was his time as a soldier that led him to such philanthropic pursuits, though Elaine suspected it had much to do with his personal penance when it came to Joseph and others he had not been able to save.

"It is good to see you, Etienne." She kissed his cheeks and was met with the familiar scent of cigarettes. He and the other men of France—and some women as well—were relieved to have their tobacco stocks restored.

She turned her attention to the man.

"This is Saul." Etienne set a hand gently to the man's thin

shoulder, the gesture one of affection as well as being somewhat reverent.

"*Bonjour*, Saul." She offered him a smile and kept her tone gentle. Many camp survivors still jumped at being spoken to, haunted by the nightmares of their daily life of barking orders and senseless, unwarranted punishments. "May I help you?"

"I may help you." His voice was thin and reedy, his breath whistling in his narrow chest beneath clothes that were far too large for his shrunken frame. He held out his fisted hand, which she opened her palm beneath.

"I'm sorry for its state," he said as he spread his long fingers and let a scrap of paper fall into her waiting hand. "I kept it within my shoe for months."

Elaine used two fingers to gently pry apart the paper and immediately recognized the handwriting as her own. She drew in a shaky inhale at the familiar words.

Dearest Joseph,
I'm sorry for everything I said. I love you always.
-Hélène

"He was with Joseph," Etienne said.

Elaine's throat went tight with emotion. "How?" she managed to croak.

"We were in Auschwitz together," Saul replied. "The first week I arrived, I became very ill. I survived only because of your husband. He held me upright through the work, doing my share and his so I would not be shot. I do not even know where he found the strength. Perhaps in you." He gestured to the paper. "He looked at that often, cupped in the cradle of his hand, protected in the heel of his shoe otherwise. One day, an officer caught him smuggling potato peels to give to a man in our row who could not raise himself from bed. I was with Joseph when the officer shot him. He was clutching your note when he died." Saul's voice caught and his eyes welled with tears. "I thought it only right to keep it for him, to return his most cherished possession to you."

Elaine's mouth stretched over her teeth as she tried to keep back her tears, to summon the words to thank the man for such a precious gift. All these months, she had tried to push this note from her mind, to not dwell on the fear that Joseph had died never knowing how truly sorry she was, how very much she did love him.

A sob choked from her. "I love him so much."

Tears ran down Saul's cheeks, and he opened his thin arms to her. "And he loved you." The man whose body was little more than the bones framing his skin and who had endured cruelties beyond imagination, offered Elaine solace and comfort greater than any she had received in a long time. He had known Joseph in those final months, in the final seconds.

"Thank you," she whispered with all the love in her heart. "Thank you for this gift."

Saul smiled up at her through his own tears and gently patted her face.

But he was not the only one owed her gratitude. She reached for Etienne's hand and squeezed it with all the appreciation welling within her. "You got the note to him."

"I told you I would do all I could."

Saul and Etienne were not the last of her guests that week. On a sunny Friday, after the bells tolled half past noon, a quiet rap sounded at the door. Elaine crossed the threshold to welcome another visitor in search of their loved one.

A pretty young woman stood on the other side, her dark hair pulled back into victory rolls to reveal intelligent, clear green eyes. "Are you Elaine Rousseau?" she asked with a dialect Elaine could not place.

"Bélanger," Elaine answered. "But once known as Rousseau, yes. How may I help you?"

The woman reached into a small handbag hanging from her elbow, one far too small to hold the series of ration cards still needed for daily life. From it, she withdrew a black-and-white photo. "My name is Ava Harper, and I was the one who received your secret code in *Combat* to help bring Sarah and Noah Cohen to America."

She handed the photo to Elaine, whose heart caught in her throat. Sarah stood in a yard before a modest-sized house with dark shutters against its pale exterior. At her side was a dark-haired man with broad shoulders and a euphoric grin. They both rested their hands on the shoulders of a little boy with long-lashed eyes Elaine knew to be hazel. His cheeks were plump with good health and his mouth was partially open, his hand pointing in the distance, as if he was excitedly chattering about something he saw. The way children ought to be.

Sarah and Noah had made it to America and reunited as a family. Elaine's efforts had not been in vain. Her fight had not been in vain.

Joseph may not have wanted her to engage in such dangerous work, but she knew her husband: he would have been proud.

Ava

Ava could recall perfectly the day she'd taken the picture. It had been a fine April afternoon with a gentle breeze stirring the fresh shoots of grass in the verdant yard. Sarah's neighbor had recently acquired a new puppy, a puff of white with an overeager pink tongue, and Noah could not stifle his adoration long enough to sit still for the photograph.

Whatever Sarah's fears might have been about losing Lewis's love, they were entirely unfounded. Never had Ava seen a man look at a woman with such tenderness as Lewis did with Sarah.

It was Sarah's fondness for Elaine that sent Ava to Lyon before she went on to England. To meet the woman who had risked her life creating publications to squelch the dissemination of the Nazis' spurious claims, to meet the woman who had brought the Cohens into Ava's life and helped them to freedom.

Her search for Elaine in Lyon had taken several days of going to various locations and seeking out every name Sarah had provided her with. Time was running out and Ava's flight would be soon departing, but she was grateful for her success in finally locating the woman who had done so much for others.

Elaine looked up from the photograph with tears in her dark eyes. Her cheekbones were high and sharp, her wrists slender where they thrust out from the red sweater she wore. "Are they happy?"

Ava couldn't stop her own smile. "Very much so. And they all survived the war because of you."

"Not me." Elaine shook her head, setting her thick blond hair swishing over her shoulders. "I merely put out the message."

"Yes, but it was so cleverly hidden," Ava said. "I recognized it immediately because your usual work in *Combat* was so immaculate, but no one else would realize that if they were not familiar with the newspaper."

"We always were so proud of how perfect the final product was." Elaine gave a sad smile. "I am grateful you decoded my message, that you were able to help them." A flash of pain touched her eyes. "There were so many who could not be saved."

Ava felt the weight of those emotions in her very soul and nodded in understanding. "I was in Lisbon, but I saw the refugees come through, I heard their stories. Even in a place of safety, some were still lost." The force of her grief for Otto resonated through her. It always would.

"I heard of the attack on you and your coworkers." Ava had been shocked to learn about the attack on the warehouse in a letter from James. "I am so sorry for your loss."

Elaine lifted her chin at a slightly cocky angle, as if confidence could cast aside grief. "It was a dangerous role. We knew the risks."

Ava caught sight of a large machine in the corner of the room. "Is that your press?"

"*Oui.*" Elaine looked at it over her shoulder. "Would you like to see it?"

"I would." Ava stepped closer to examine the different levers and plates and rollers. The scent of metal and grease blended with a powdery aroma of ink hanging in the air. While she could piece out what some items were, the rest was a fascinating enigma.

The written word held such importance to her through the years. Books had been solace in a world turned upside down, a connection to characters when she was utterly alone, knowledge when she needed answers and so, so much more. In the war, they had given her insight, understanding, and appreciation. And even through letters and journals, words granted immortality for those whose stories she had been honored to capture.

"It's beautiful," Ava whispered.

Elaine considered her. "Do you think so?"

"Absolutely," Ava replied without hesitation. "Without machines such as this, we would never have books." She let her fingers gently brush the lever, cool against her touch. "Words have such incredible power."

Elaine studied her, and the tension on her face melted away to reveal a youthful visage. "*Oui,* they do."

They spent the afternoon together as Elaine showed Ava how the press worked, even allowing her to create a few impressions. The ease with which Elaine operated what she called the Minerva was enviable, her slender, tapered fingers like that of an artist as she adroitly performed several tasks at once.

Church bells chimed outside, marking the hour and the time Ava had to leave to catch her plane to England. Before departing, she withdrew two items from her purse—a sealed letter from Sarah to Elaine and the other a folded picture Noah had drawn of himself holding a jar of something red.

When Elaine opened the one from Noah, she exhaled with something between a laugh and a sob. "Strawberry jam." She touched the image with a smile of affection.

"Is that what it is?" Ava asked.

"It was a treasure during the war." Elaine pressed her lips together, composing her emotions. "He loved it."

"That explains why it is his favorite even still," Ava said.

A tear ran down Elaine's face. She swept it away with trembling fingers. "You came all this way to see me?"

"Yes. To tell you how very clever and brave I find you and to share with you what an impact your risks have had." Ava had initially questioned if it was a good idea to come to Lyon, if she would even be able to find Elaine. But standing here now in front of the thin woman whose face glowed with pride, Ava knew she had made the right decision.

Elaine opened her arms and captured Ava in a fierce hug. "This is truly the greatest gift." She released her and smiled through her tears. "Thank you."

Ava disembarked from the plane in London where James would be waiting for her, the man whose set of dice even now clicked together in her pocket as anticipation for a fresh adventure blossomed in her chest.

Britain was another world to explore. One that birthed Geoffrey Chaucer, who gave the English language its literary feet, one where Shakespeare's theater had once entertained the masses with stories that would be retold for centuries to come. It was the city where Charles Dickens set so many of his books, educating people not with instruction, but by connecting the character to the reader and pulling them on a journey. It was where Thomas More framed a perfect fictional society that mirrored a monastic lifestyle in *Utopia* and where Jane Austen's characters strolled in their endeavors of marital pursuits.

The wealth of Britain's history was so rich, Ava could feast on it for decades and never be full.

She had spent her entire life reading of such experiences and was now ready to enjoy them in the flesh. Perhaps even have the opportunity for a chance at love.

Regardless, she was eager to work in the London Library, once more surrounded by tomes that spanned centuries past, doing her part to record the history so it would always live in the minds of future generations. After all, there was nothing Ava loved more than the scent of old books—except, of course, the power of the written word.

★ ★ ★ ★ ★

AUTHOR NOTE

I was inspired to write *The Librarian Spy* after reading about the librarians who were sent to neutral Lisbon during World War II to gather books and newspapers in order to glean intel on the enemy. This became especially interesting after learning they were initially thrown into their jobs with very little training and Lisbon was teeming with people from all over the world, agents and refugees alike. Espionage was rife on Lisbon's crowded coastline, where power and wealth were played like a well-guarded hand and countries operated clandestine activities on the razor's edge of neutrality beneath the noses of Portugal's secret police.

While the IDC (Interdepartmental Committee for the Acquisition of Foreign Publications) did not send any female operatives to Lisbon, I chose to create Ava Harper—a woman confident in her own element at the Library of Congress, only to arrive in a place where she had more questions than answers. I had the good fortune to know a few librarians who offered great insight with which to build Ava's character. I also was able to travel to DC to the Library of Congress, where I spent the day researching in the beautiful Reading Room and toured the premises.

Portugal was the last corner of neutral European territory from which refugees could sail to South America, Africa or North America to escape the Nazis' wrath. And while it was a place of relative safety where refugees were protected under neutrality laws, there was always a constant threat of various visas expiring, resulting in arrest by the Portuguese secret police. Additionally, there was the perpetual fear that Germany would attack Portugal and refugees would once more be under Nazi occupation. The waits these refugees endured for their various visas and boat tickets were long and terrible, even for people who had maintained their wealth, though many arrived with only the clothes they wore.

Spies swarmed in this community where publications and news from all over the world mixed among the conglomeration of foreigners. They secretly paid the locals and police to listen and report, they rubbed elbows with the wealthy in glitzy hotels to gather intel, and they dotted disinformation around to spread like wildfires to keep the enemy from suspecting their next move. All of this made for a very exciting environment.

I was fortunate enough to be able to travel to Lisbon, despite the pandemic, during 2021. I had never been to Portugal, and it was important for me to experience the culture I had learned so much about in my research. I found it to be exactly as I had read: beautiful with incredible food and people who were kind and generous. I had an amazing tour guide, Raquel Estevens, whose 101-year-old grandmother shared details about how life was when the refugees came to Lisbon. Raquel not only planned out tours specific to what I needed for my research, but was always so patient with all of my questions. I'm immensely grateful to her and her grandmother.

One man I unfortunately did not get to mention in my book, but I feel also deserves to be noted here, is Sousa Mendes, a Portuguese consul in Bordeaux, France. In June 1940, when Germany took France, people were being attacked and cities were falling under Nazi control, and people were desperate to flee, he defied strict orders to not authorize visas. As the Portuguese consulate filled with desperate people, Mendes went with his heart and conscience and vowed to sign as many visas as he could regardless of nationality or religion, and he did so without taking payment. For three days, he signed and signed and signed, his name reduced to only "Mendes," but the consulate stamp on those visas was enough to let refugees flow through the borders. Before he was forced to stop, he managed to sign at least 3,800—this number has been confirmed with certainty by the Sousa Mendes Foundation (survivors and descendants of the families he saved with those visas), though estimates of the number range between 10,000–30,000. For his defiance, he was stripped permanently of his title, shunned by António de Oliveira Salazar, the prime minister of Portugal, and never again able to secure employment. Sousa Mendes is noted to have said: "I could not have acted otherwise, and I therefore accept all that has befallen me with love."

Though I researched Lisbon during World War II extensively, please be aware that any errors are entirely my own.

Which brings me to the second narrative of *The Librarian Spy* in Lyon, France, with Elaine. While doing research, I happened to stumble upon a woman in France named Lucienne Guezennec. Plucky, brave and a woman of integrity and honor, she was a true inspiration. She gave her identity card to a Jewish woman to save her, joined the Resistance and became an apprentice at a clandestine newspaper, was the only survivor of a Nazi attack on the press, and even stood up for the women whose heads were being shaved in retaliation for collaborating with Nazis at the end of the war. I do not mirror her life, though I used her as a strong influence for Elaine's character. Antoine, Jean and Marcel are also loosely inspired by the real men who worked with Lucienne at the clandestine press: Marcel after André Bollier, Antoine after Francisque Vacher and Jean after Paul Jaillet.

Another important character on the French side of my book was Kommandeur Werner. I made him from a combination of real officers who existed in Lyon during the occupation with a primary tie to Klaus Barbie—a man so cruel, he was dubbed the Butcher of Lyon. I won't go into the unspeakable things he did to earn such a title, but I will say he did not stand trial for those heinous crimes until he was an old man. Even then, he received life in prison, where he remained only four short years before passing away. His victims never received such mercy as he was afforded. I confess, I am a reader who likes to see a villain get what they deserve and so I created Werner.

Many of the other characters were inspired from women I read about in my research, including Manon. The real woman who suffered such a heartbreaking loss of a child was not named in the research book that mentioned her, nor was her future following the loss of her child shared. I took it upon myself to place her in the Resistance to retaliate as she could against the Nazis.

I was also extraordinarily fortunate to be able to travel to Lyon while I was writing this book. Not only did I spend most of my time walking the streets and traboules to absorb the beauty and feel of the capital of the French Resistance during WWII, but I also spent an extraordinary amount of time at the Resistance museum (Centre d'histoire de la résistance et de la déportation) and the museum at Montluc Prison. Both museums were powerful showcases for what the French endured during Nazi occupation and highlighted the bravery of those who fought back. Additionally, I was fortunate to find an incredible tour guide, Jean Martinez, who is an absolute wealth of knowledge about the Resistance and France during World War II and was kind enough to answer questions for me throughout the writing of this book.

As with Lisbon, my research with Lyon and the French Resistance was extensive and any errors made are my own.

One important aspect of the book that I feel like I want to touch on in this note is the code used between Elaine and Ava through the newspapers. While coding was an important aspect of the French Resistance, I could not identify the exact code used by the Resistance and so implemented a poem code that was in operation at one point with SOE agents that I adapted slightly to fit this story.

I am immensely grateful for all the experts who helped shape this novel, from tour guides to museums to authors of nonfiction material and eyewitnesses who opened their hearts to share their stories. I hope that I have done justice to the beautiful countries I visited and the brave men and women I discovered in my research. May their memories remain with us all for generations to come.

ACKNOWLEDGMENTS

It is such an honor to have the opportunity to write another WWII historical fiction novel. I'm so immensely grateful to the amazing team at Hanover Square Press for not only giving me the chance to lose myself in research and write a slice of history again, but also being so wonderful and supportive along the way. Thank you to Peter Joseph and Grace Towery for your hard work in making my novel shine. Thank you to Eden Church and Leah Morse and Kathleen Carter for your stellar publicity work in helping launch this book out into the world. It is such a pleasure to work with every one of you.

Thank you so much also to my agent, Kevan Lyon, for being with me every step of the way on this book and for your exceptional advice and counsel.

Much of my knowledge of this time period would not have happened without the expertise of professionals. Thank you to Jean Martinez for all the knowledge you shared on the tour through Lyon about the brave feats of the French Resistance and detailing how life was during Nazi occupation. Thank you to Raquel Estevens for sharing the beauty of Lisbon with me and for all your digging into extra facts that helped flesh out my book. Thank you to Judy Gann and Margaret Murray-Evans for letting me pick your brains for details on the librarian mindset. Thank you to the authors of nonfiction books, whose endless drive for the truth is integral to the creation of all my books. And an enormous thank you also to the men and women who work tirelessly to establish and maintain museums throughout the world that keep history alive and in our memories so we never forget.

In writing this book, I was surrounded by the love and support of my family and friends. Thank you to my parents for always being so proud of me and to my mother, who always reads through my books with a fine-tooth comb. Thank you to my husband, who has my back even when I don't realize I need it, and to my children, who are my biggest fans and who don't mind eating ramen from time to time when days turn too swiftly into nights. Thank you to my ultimate BFFs, Lori Ann Bailey, Eliza Knight and Brenna Ash—you ladies keep me sane and smiling. I seriously don't know what I would do without you. Thank you to Eliza Knight for being side by side with me on this journey and for all your amazing help. Thank you to my dear friend Tracy Emro for all your assistance with every book I write from creation to final read through—your suggestions and notes are always on point. Thank you to the Lyonesses, whose collective talent and guidance and support is always appreciated more than words can possibly express. And thank you to my reader group, who is always there for me with support and amazing suggestions and input.

Thank you to the librarians and booksellers who not only put my book into readers' hands but help spread the news of its existence. Additionally, thank you for all the books you've put into my hands and heart through the years. I don't know where I would be without my love of books.

To all the book bloggers, reviewers and bookstagrammers, thank you for all you do—not only for this novel, but also for the writing community in general. Your passion and love of reading and your talent in sharing help readers find new books they otherwise might not have known about.

And an enormous thank you to my readers. Thank you for the time you invest into my book, for sharing in the world I've researched and detailed in these pages, and for loving these characters that I crafted with my whole heart.